A
MIDNIGHT
ROMANCE

M.J. HUXLEY

Cover Design: Okay Creations

Copy Editing: Caroline Palmier, Love and Edits

Developmental Editor: Salma R.

Interior Formatting: Wicked Reads Services

First Edition: August 2025

 Formatted with Vellum

A Midnight Romance is for the girls who always end up falling for the villain.

AUTHOR'S NOTE

Your mental health and triggers matter.

This novel is unlike anything I've written previously. To be my true authentic self, I knew I had to write a story that combined two things I'm fascinated with—*true crime and romance*. And thus, *A Midnight Romance* was born. I hope you stay on this journey with me as we head *Into The Night* for this dark romance series.

Although each of us readers have our own levels of darkness, the themes in *A Midnight Romance* make it a dark romance. Please look at the trigger list in the paragraph below, containing topics you can expect in the book.

This story addresses topics such as:

Murder, explicit sexual content, dubcon, stalking (despite the MMC's denials), blood play, kidnapping, drugging, and off-page sexual assault and torture, some in detail, others only briefly.

PLAYLIST

"Day 'n' Night" —Kid Cudi
"So High" —Ghost Loft
"What I've Done" —LINKIN PARK
"Helena" —My Chemical Romance
"Until the Day I Die" —Story of the Year
"Hurt" —Nine Inch Nails
"Every You Every Me" —Placebo
"PARADIGM" —Avara & Deb Fan
"I Don't Wanna Be In Love" —Good Charlotte
"Chokehold" —Sleep Token
"Him & I" —G-Easy & Halsey
"Descending" —Sleep Token
"Die With A Smile" —Lady Gaga & Bruno Mars

" *Life is merely a disturbance in death. But death is the origin.*"
Edgar Allan Poe

CHAPTER ONE

RIVER

As I stare at my recent target's brain matter splattered on the wall behind him, I only have two things on my mind: *what can I do better next time* and *how quickly we can get to the next predator?*

"He sure was a talker," Sebastian comments as he unlocks the handcuffs.

"I mean, I love the commentary and all, but..." I reply as I unscrew the silencer and slide the handgun into the back of my pants. "Like, telling these guys why we're here doesn't mean we need their whole life story." And not to mention the more obvious reason—my compulsive need to kill.

"Yeah."

"And?"

"What if on the next one we brought photos?"

"Of their victims?" he asks, bending to grab the empty shell casing from the thin, lime green carpet then slips it into his kill bag.

"Yeah. We need to remind them of the people they've hurt."

The victims aren't here to speak for themselves and we created this entire operation for them, but I fear the simple reminder doesn't prove much of an impact.

"That's not a bad idea." He arches a brow in agreement. "It would make what we're doing more poetic that way."

"And you know how I feel about poetry," I say, packing up a few more items.

The works of Edgar Allan Poe helped me grieve the death of my parents. Most of his words were beyond my understanding at the time, but as I grew older I related to the obscurity of them.

"And your need for *more* control."

"That's the only way everything runs smoothly."

Sebastian turns on the sink in the corner of the motel room to wash any trace from the kill off his gloved hands. "I'm well aware. You've been that way since we were kids."

Our fathers were brothers and often held multiple contracts with the government until one went terribly wrong. Sebastian and I were only five and three when we witnessed our parents' murders while we were traveling with them. Neither of us has been the same since then, and it's probably the reason why we do this now.

"But that's what makes us a great team." I walk over to the sink to wash up after him, but not before laying a playful slap on his shoulder.

Suddenly my phone vibrates in the front pocket of my pants. I dry my gloved hands, then pull it out.

"Hi, Aunt Mae."

"Good morning, River." Her warm voice greets me. "Are you and Sebastian still out?"

I glance over at my cousin, who's standing next to the body of Gill Pembroke—a college fraternity brother who tried to rape a girl he went to school with but ended up killing her instead—already on the phone with the night crew organizing the cleanup.

"We are. Is everything okay?"

Aunt Mae clears her throat. "Everything's fine, but I wanted to remind you of the board meeting you have at TI's office."

Thompson Innovations—the company of our fathers that we took over when we were of age.

I am one man by day and another by night.

I rub my forehead, suddenly remembering that we have our bimonthly board meeting this morning. "I'll be there."

"Do you know what time the meeting is scheduled for?" she asks to confirm I'm not lying.

"Seven thirty."

"And do you know what time it is now?" she presses. "You don't want to be late again."

"I do, and like I said, I will be there."

"You better be. I'll see you both later this evening."

I quickly hang up after saying our goodbyes and turn to Sebastian, who's staring at me.

"I've got to go. I forgot about the bimonthly board meeting," I tell him.

Sebastian folds his arm across his chest. Although he may have stepped away from his role at the company to run the night crew—a group of guys who help with our nighttime activities—we both retain equal ownership. "I'm so glad I don't have to worry about that anymore."

"Yeah, you just like to collect the money," I spit playfully.

"What can I say? You make better decisions than I could ever have. Besides, this"—he gestures at the body in front of him—"has kept me more than busy."

"Fair enough."

"Need anything else before I go?" I ask, slinging my bag over my shoulder as I walk to the door of the motel room we rented for this kill.

"Do I ever?"

Sebastian has been running an efficient and effective night crew since stepping away last year. Which means, I'm left with handling the logistics and overseeing the entire operation. It works well, I must say. And with help of our FBI contact and his hacking skills, we have one hell of a team.

I shake my head at him and let out a laugh. "I'll see you back at the manor."

"Have fun with the suits," he comments.

After a quick once-over of the room, I step out in the crisp morning air. It's been raining in Seattle over the last few days so there's a mist in the air from a typical summer night storm.

I make a beeline for my car parked directly under a tree in the back of the lot. Once inside, I quickly remove my black hoodie and shirt, then reach into the back seat to grab my bag. I always carry a backup set of clothes just in case I need to look presentable.

I pull out a white button-up shirt, and after slipping it on I glance down at my black slacks. They still look good and there're no blood stains on them. After changing into a pair of black shoes, I turn on the engine and head down the windy highway into downtown. It takes a little under an hour to arrive at the Thompson Innovations headquarters, where I pull into my parking spot a few minutes before 7 a.m.

"Good morning, Mr. Thompson," Tiffany, the blonde receptionist, greets me with a smile when the elevator doors to the second floor open.

I flash her a broad grin and walk around the high counter,

stopping only a few inches from her. "What are you doing here this early?"

She bats her eyelashes a few times. "Felix told me you guys had a board meeting this morning, and I didn't want to give up the chance to see you."

Tiffany has been with the company for less than a year and has made it her mission to capture my attention each time she sees me.

"I'm flattered," I say, with a warm smile. I may not be interested in her, but I can't be disrespectful. "But go get yourself some coffee or breakfast and come back when you have to be here."

"You're the best." Tiffany bends to grab her purse from under the desk. "Can I get you anything?"

"No, I'm okay, but if you could return with donuts for everyone that would be great," I say, handing her the company card. "Just slide it under my office door when you get back."

"You got it. Thanks, Mr. Thompson." She blushes as the elevator door closes.

"She's got it bad for you," Felix comments as he walks briskly down the hall toward the lobby.

"Not interested."

Women vying for my attention is nothing new. Sure, I might be considered one of the most eligible bachelors in Seattle, but I'm not interested in anything romantic.

"Oh, the woes of being River Thompson." He smirks. "But I'm happily married so I'll never know what that feels like."

Before I can say anything back, the sound of his three-year-old daughter yelling my name interrupts our conversation.

"Wivver!" Sophie says as she bolts down the hall, behind him.

I crouch down to catch her, scooping her up into my arms. "Hey, Sophie, what are you doing here?"

"You were the one who wanted it to be today. I was supposed to be off," her father answers for her. "And my wife is away for the weekend on a girls' trip."

"We'll make this quick so Daddy can go home," I joke, turning my attention back to Sophie.

I don't want to be here as much as Felix. But if I want to keep my nightly operation running, I have to maintain my regular daily life, which means ensuring I still have a hand in the successful technology company Sebastian and my parents built. That's why I still hold my position as CEO while Felix, our COO, runs the day-to-day operations.

Felix shakes his head. "The rest of the board is waiting for you," he tells me, taking Sophie from my arms, then lowers her to the ground and takes her hand.

I follow behind them as we walk past the rows of employee offices, each with a view of the downtown. I chose this exact building because I wanted my staff to have the best workspace so they wouldn't notice my constant absence.

"Did she get the gift I sent her?" I try to lighten the mood, although I'm the one who hasn't slept all night.

He shoots me a glare from over his shoulder. "You mean the obnoxiously loud drum set?"

I knew he'd love that. "That's the one."

"Yes, we did. I love waking up to the sound of banging drums at five a.m. on a Saturday morning," he deadpans.

"It's my absolute pleasure." I give him a friendly slap on his back. "Her birthday's coming up soon, right? I'll make sure to send another thoughtful gift her way."

"How kind of you," he retorts, opening the glass doors to the conference room.

Six out of the seven suits who make up the Thompson Innovation's Executive Board are all waiting. Felix places Sophia in a rolling chair next to him.

"Good morning," I greet them. Each member appears more than a little tired and disheveled, but they all return my jovial grin with weak smiles. So I decide to tease them a little and reinforce the persona I'm putting on. "Aren't you guys supposed to be at work at eight a.m.? This isn't that much earlier."

"That's subjective," Felix comments playfully.

"Then we'll make this quick."

A collective sigh of relief floats through the room as I slide in my usual chair at the head of the table near the presentation screen. I then give a nod in Felix's direction, indicating for him to begin.

"Thompson Innovations has been working closely with the Department of Defense for years, but we haven't provided them with any new prototype in some time," he begins, handing me the briefing before taking his place at the front.

I'm scanning over the front page, absorbing this month's objectives while Felix goes through his entire presentation. This meeting was scheduled last minute, but Felix's presentation is extremely thorough—which isn't surprising. He's been loyal to our company for years and never comes unprepared.

"Go on."

Felix clears his throat. "I would like to allocate more money to Research and Development for the upcoming quarter."

"I think that sounds great. Did you already have a project in mind?"

"As a matter of fact, I do," Felix says, his voice filled with excitement. "Check this out." He beams, then removes a small cylinder no bigger than the length of the tip of my finger to my wrist from a bag on the floor.

He presents it to me, like I should know what it is. "What is this?"

"A lip gloss Taser." He hands it to me. "It's only a prototype, but I wanted to show it to you before we sent it off to the FBI for field testing."

"What does it do?" I ask, examining the product.

"It's a Taser," he tells me.

"I got that part," I say with a light chuckle. "But does it work?"

He laughs. "Fortunately—*and* unfortunately—all of our developers can attest to its efficacy."

I grimace. "Ouch."

"With your approval, we'd like to send it within the next week."

"How many of these have we manufactured so far?"

"Twenty," he tells me.

I examine the clear tube more closely. "Make that nineteen. I'm keeping this one."

"You always like to use the gadgets first, don't you," he quips.

I put the gadget into my pocket. "Perks of being the boss." I smile, which earns me a chuckle from the other board members.

As the meeting presses on, my eyes grow heavy from the events of the night. I need to head back to Thompson Manor for some sleep.

"If there's nothing else I have to leave, but you have my approval to move forward." Before I leave the room, I give the executive board one more friendly smile before turning to our CFO, Becky Hooper. "Will you send me the cost breakdown and the source of the expenses once this is all sorted?"

"Will do," she replies, taking notes down on one of our branded notepads.

"And keep me updated on the field testing," I direct toward Felix.

"Goodbye, Mr. Thompson," says a chorus behind me as I step into the hallway.

Once I'm alone and headed for the elevators, I breathe in a deep inhale—as relief washes over me. I plan to head back to Thompson Manor, catch up on a few hours of sleep, and then continue working on my next target. The hunger never dulls and it's only a matter of time before I'll need to kill again.

CHAPTER TWO

LUX

"How's your first draft coming along?" my editor asks, checking in on the progress of my current manuscript.

I slide my sunglasses down from the top of my head as the setting sun shines into my eyes the moment I step outside the self-defense studio.

"It's going." I'm a little behind on this one.

Writing fiction crime books is my passion, but the research process can be emotionally draining. Sure, they're only fiction but all fiction is based on reality in some way.

"That doesn't sound good," she comments. Ellie has been my editor for all the books I've written and we've just settled into a groove. She knows I need time between each release, but she's always good about keeping me on a timeline. "Do you need me to jump on a call with you?"

Ellie's great, but I prefer full control over the plotting part of my writing process. Because once I get an idea in my head, it's hard to change my mind.

"No, I'm good. I just got out of a self-defense class and I'll be home soon to get back to work."

"Are you sure?" Ellie asks.

"I'm fine, I promise." I slide into my car and set my workout bag on the passenger seat. "And besides, aren't you packing for Hawaii?"

"Don't remind me. My sister's wedding is supposed to be fun, but I've been so stressed about leaving for that long."

"How long are you leaving for again?"

"Per her request, everyone will be there for two weeks, but then my husband and I decided to stay an extra week and have our own little vacation."

"I'm jealous," I whine, pulling out of the parking garage and heading for home.

"But don't worry, you can still reach me if you need anything."

"No, enjoy some time off. Besides, it will give me time to focus on getting it done without having to worry about you checking in on me constantly," I playfully say.

"Fair enough." She laughs. "Well, sending you good writing vibes for flowing ideas."

"Okay, we'll talk soon. Safe travels."

Shortly after we end the call, I'm pulling my townhouse property in a quiet suburban neighborhood right outside of Seattle.

After a quick shower, I make myself something to eat, then head back upstairs to my office to get to work.

I only manage to write for an hour when I get the urge for some caffeine. I could make it at home, but my favorite coffee shop is down the street. So I slide on my shoes, grab my purse, and head to the front door. But as soon as I open it, my sister is walking up the path.

"Hi!" Stevie yells as she approaches in workout clothes.

"Are you staying over tonight?" I joke glancing at the large black bag on her shoulder.

"Nice to see you, too." She smiles and shoves passed me into my house.

I follow behind her and then shut the door behind us. So much for a caffeine fix.

"You live ten minutes away from me. We see each other all the time."

Stevie drops her bag on the floor and falls into my couch. "I'm bored. It's Friday night and I don't have to work late."

"I hate to burst your bubble, but I'm on a deadline. I was just about to run out and grab some coffee at The Overcast Cafe. You're more than welcome to tag along."

She shakes her head, arching her upper lip. "You don't need coffee. You need a large glass of wine." Then pops off the couch and skips into the kitchen.

"The red is in the fridge," I tell her, knowing that's what she's looking for.

"Eww, I forgot you like it chilled."

I hear the cupboards open then close before she reappears in the living room holding the bottle in one hand and two glasses in the other. She hands one to me, and I reluctantly take it, knowing sometimes I write better after a few glasses— if I don't fall asleep first.

"This is peer pressure."

She flashes me a smirk as she sits crossed legged onto the couch. "Not if you actually want to do it."

"Ha-ha," I say wryly, slumping onto the cushions next to her.

Stevie places the bottle on the coffee table. "So what were your plans for tonight?" she asks, and I'm already annoyed with where she's going. "Coffee and hanging out in your office all night?"

"I just told you, I'm on deadline."

"Boring," she says, rolling her eyes. "Friday nights are for going out."

"Out? Where?"

"Like, to a club?"

I almost spit out my sip when I hear her suggestion. Stevie knows that's not my scene. It's hers once in a while but we haven't gone out like that since college. "Are you serious?"

"Yeah. Why not?"

"We're too old for that. And clubs aren't safe."

"Twenty-nine isn't old." My sister rolls her eyes. "You sound like Dad. Can we pretend to be unaware and live in perpetual ignorance like other people?"

Stevie's only two years younger than me, yet the difference in our personalities is as distinct as night and day.

"You know how many predators hang around places like that. Sociopathic men waiting to take advantage of a drunk college girl? Or slip something into their drinks?"

Stevie cocks her head to the side while frustration sweeps across her face. She's annoyed but recognizes I'm right. "Fine, those things can happen. I get it. But the benefit to us is you, my skilled big sister, can identify a man with ill intentions at first glance."

"A skill, yes, but not something to be solely relied upon."

With us being raised by a single father who is also a homicide detective meant our childhood focused more on being more alert than other children our age, who lived carefree lives believing the world was a good place and imaginary monsters only lived under your bed.

Seeing that her argument for leaving the house isn't going as she planned, Stevie takes a new approach. "You live and breathe your job."

"What can I say?" I shrug, clutching my wine glass close to my chest. "Crime happens to be my entire personality."

Growing up, I watched my dad agonize over grizzly homicide scenes, and the ones that involved women or children were always the most difficult for him. Ever since, I vowed to use my natural ability to write and my curiosity about crime to write stories involving women who get revenge on their attackers. I like to think of it as my own way of serving justice.

"And dead people are mine," she retorts, flashing me a toothy smile. "I love owning a mortuary, but you don't see me trying to hide behind them in order to avoid a dating life."

I try to ignore my sister's passive aggressive comment, but it's difficult since she's, once again, spot on. "I'm not trying to avoid dating."

"I think you are."

"What about you?"

"Me? I have a Nick, remember?"

Oh yes, the college sophomore my sister met last year when she worked his grandmother's memorial service.

"And where is he tonight?" I quip.

Her eyes lower at my condescending remark. "He's at a friend's wedding. I'm sure he'll text me later tonight."

"So you want me to find someone to just hook up with?"

Stevie shakes her head. "That's not what I'm saying." She sighs. "After Mom died, Dad's job took over his entire life. I guess I just don't want us to live like that."

Stevie and I lost our mother in a car accident when we were very young. Her loss was hard on our dad, and to deal with his grief, he threw himself into his work.

"Do you think he's unhappy?" I ask.

"I don't know." she says, running a hand through her almond corkscrew curls. "He works himself into the ground.

That's all we see. Maybe it's just my own concern and I'm pushing it off on you."

"No, you're right. It's just hard to find time for anyone else when I find myself obsessed with writing these stories."

"I get it."

If I don't end this conversation soon, Stevie will drag me down a rabbit hole of philosophical discussions about why I became intensely fixated on writing thriller and her becoming a mortician to take care of people after they've passed. And will end with us talking about our father and whether we would have chosen different professions if we hadn't lost our mother so young.

I sigh, feeling my mind slowly changing. With an exaggerated eye roll, I turn to my sister. "One drink."

"Really?"

Against my better judgment, while anxiety simmers below the surface for both my deadline as well as my dislike of clubs, I give in to her. Maybe she's right—a little break might be good for me?

"I guess."

"Awesome. Then we can come back here and watch a movie until Nick calls."

"You promise?"

We do a quick pinky promise like when we were kids, then I grab the empty glasses from the coffee table.

"But wait, you don't have any clothes here?" I ask walking into the kitchen to put the glasses into the sink.

"I'll just wear something you have!" she tosses over her shoulder while sprinting up the stairs.

"Funny how nothing has changed since we were kids." I follow her upstairs and quickly find her rummaging through my closet.

"How about this?" She holds up a little black dress with sequins.

I pull out my laptop and sit on the side of my bed, knowing she'll need more time to get ready than I will. I may as well sneak in a few words. "I like it."

"Or this one?" She carries a red halter top dress from out of the closet, chuckling. "You need new clothes."

I ignore her and continue typing.

She walks over and tents the top of my laptop. "Does Dad know that you stole his logins to the police department's database?" ·

My armpits sweat knowing I'm doing something unlawful. But it's been helpful with the research process when I write. "Of course not."

She rolls her eyes.

"Blinded by the love of his innocent daughter." She heads back into the closet.

"Maybe."

"Are you going to get dressed?"

Hanging my head low, I shove my computer to the side and drag my feet until I join Stevie. "Yes."

Stevie and I spend the next half hour getting ready, then it takes her another thirty minutes to figure out where we're going. And before long, two sets of heels *click-clack* on my hardwood floors as we head into the night for what I expect to be uneventful, all while wishing I was cozy in my pajamas sitting at my desk writing.

CHAPTER THREE
RIVER

The wooden dance floor rumbles under my feet as my eyes scan the room, gazing from one sweaty body to another. Around me couples dance erotically under the influence of alcohol—or something else. The twinge of envy isn't always a shock, but it reminds me I'll never live a simple life like this.

I'm incapable of loving any other human.

And even if I was no one would ever accept my darkness.

My gaze scans the room before landing on a woman with medium brown hair dancing with another woman slightly taller. I find myself distracted by how her body sways to the electronic bass. My hungry eyes fall to her black high heels, before traveling to her leather skirt and low-cut sequined top. I clamp my eyes shut, refocusing on the task at hand tonight.

Hunting my next victim.

"What's the plan?" Sebastian asks, his voice almost lost in my earpiece because of the loud music.

My eyes snap open, but instead of refocusing, my gaze catches a bead of sweat rolling down her chest. I wonder what it would be like to glide my tongue across her skin, tasting the moistness of it. I'm not one to ever be distracted, but the manner she moves in is mesmerizing. I imagine my hands gliding up the bare skin on her arm, when my stare narrows, irked by a dark figure stepping in front of her, holding hands with a girl much younger. He obstructs my view.

Watching from a safe distance, I witness the man drop the hand of the woman he's with and move on to the brunette I've had my eyes on. A dense heat settles over me, causing the tiny hairs on my body to stand when I recognize another predator.

"Hang on," I say to Sebastian, unable to tear my focus from them.

She scoffs off whatever advances he's forcing on her. The man flips his neck around with frustration, finally giving me a clear view of his face.

Andrew Hughes.

A trust fund baby—his parents own one of the largest hotel chains in the Pacific Northwest—and my target for the night.

Andrew drugged and raped his high school girlfriend after a night of drinking. The girl went on to press charges, but they were subsequently dropped six months before they were set to go to trial.

Since we run in the same wealthy circles, the ones who believe they have unlimited power and control, a small fact about him hasn't sat well with me.

"Got him," I state with confidence. "Keep with the plan we discussed and make sure you're recording."

My work from the last few months is about to pay off.

"I have it taken care of," he assures me.

The wave of the crowd parts, opening a direct line to Andrew, the brunette, and her friend, who he still hasn't left.

Inhaling deeply, I straighten my shoulders as I make my way over to them and prepare to be River Thompson, the young billionaire tech mogul. My daily persona, the one I've carefully curated to hide behind.

"Andrew!" I shout over the music. Placing a forceful hand on his shoulder, he stiffens and turns around. At first, his face hardens with surprise and anger, but when he recognizes me his expression relaxes.

"Fuck, River, I was about to knock you out," he says, greeting me with a handshake.

"Like you could," I playfully retort.

"Maybe," he bites back, shrugging like a typical alpha male. "Glad you could make it."

He invited me to this god-forsaken club weeks ago, and of course I said yes. I've been stalking him and his fellow imperious friends for some time and this was the perfect opportunity to get him in my grasp—and hopefully my kill room.

"So, what are we doing here?" I reply, but my eyes are back on the woman with the leather skirt.

But this time, a pair of large brownish-green irises meet my stare. Her lashes flutter a few times, holding my gaze while her friend takes the opportunity to get away and slowly drags her off the floor toward the bar. She eventually disappears amidst the crowd as it fills in behind her. I'm left wondering who she is and why she captured my attention so naturally.

Andrew curiously follows my line of sight. "Fucking hot, isn't she?"

Prick.

I smile. "Hell yeah."

Andrew flicks the bottom of his nose, rimming one nostril with a finger. Looks like he's had his fair share of blow tonight. "Let's go meet the rest of the guys. We have a proposition for you," he rushes out.

I nod, following him off the vibrating floor. More women in short skirts and too much makeup grind their bodies against us as we slide past them, headed for the stairs. Andrew gestures at the bouncer near the steps to the VIP section. He responds by removing the red velvet rope and allowing the two of us to pass.

Once we're upstairs, I glance over the railing through the layer of fog combined with rising heat from the sea of people. I search for the brunette once again, but before I find her Andrew leads me into a secluded room on top of the club.

There's a middle-aged man, taller than average, leaning against the wall in the corner of the room. His pants dropped to the ground while a young woman kneels in front of him. He shoves his dick down her throat while his hand grips her head securely, not seeming to care that we walked in on them.

He gives me a quick nod with a prideful smirk, before refocusing on her.

"This is Nolen Pierce," Andrew says.

I return a slight bob of my head in his direction.

My searching gaze moves to the next piece of shit lounging on the leather couch in the back of the room.

Richard Smith. I mumble.

"Isn't that the accountant our company tried to hire back in spring before that sexual assault charge came up?" Sebastian reminds me.

Smith interviewed for a position at Thompson Innovations, but despite his impressive credentials, a few unfavorable skeletons—including the charge—crawled out of his closet during background checks and we didn't extend an offer.

"Yep," I confirm under my breath.

I have to remember to send HR something special to have dodged that bullet.

"Of course, these are the types of guys Andrew would be associated with, especially given his background with women."

Andrew gestures for me to follow him over to the couch.

"Rich, this is River Thompson—" he begins, slumping into the vacant spot beside his friend as he rests comfortably on the velvet couch.

"I know who he is." Richard's leveled tone and scowl tell me he's still bitter about not getting the job. "So, *you* want in?"

Unsure of what he's referring to, I'm sensing something more nefarious.

"Before I agree to anything, I'll require specifics," I say confidently, pretending to have some knowledge of what I've walked into.

Richard glances at Andrew. "I haven't filled him in yet, but he's solid. Don't worry," Andrew reassures him, evidence of him falling for the mask of my everyday facade.

If they only knew who I turn into behind the black sheet of night, they wouldn't be so eager to bring me into the fold.

As much as Andrew blindly trusts me, it appears Richard doesn't feel the same when he shoots me a distrusting stare as he leans in. A powerful scent of cherry cigars overpowers the musty cigarette smoke that's filled my senses since I arrived at the club.

"What can I get for you, sexy?" A cocktail server suddenly appears by my side before he can say anything.

"Whiskey neat," I tell her.

Andrew and Richard exchange another quick glance before they both refocus their attention on me.

"We have a little arrangement," Richard begins.

"I'm intrigued." I match his posture on bent knees. Anxious energy pulses through my veins, causing an itch to settle below my skin as I grow eager to find out more of what they're referring to. My back flexes when I sense someone behind me.

"River Thompson. Glad to finally meet the local billionaire

tech mogul." My name rolls off the person's tongue with confidence like they know me and I don't like it.

"Hello." I turn my body fully to greet the familiar man, then extend my arm for a firm shake.

Duncan gives my hand a quick tug then sits down on the sofa, followed by Nolen.

"Done getting your cock sucked?" I quip.

Duncan plucks a cherry from the bowl on the cocktail table and pops it into his mouth. With a broad smile, he turns to face me. "Play your cards right, tech geek, and you could, too."

"I don't need your dirty whores," I reply. I wouldn't let a woman like that anywhere near me. Who knows what else her lips have touched?

"You haven't faced enough temptation," Duncan shoots back, too sure of himself.

A drink is placed in front of me. I wipe the rim of the glass with a napkin before bringing it to my lips. I swish the warm liquid in my mouth and discreetly spit it back into the cup. I never consume alcohol when on the job. A stable mind is the best weapon.

Rich turns to Nolen. "Pretty soon, he's going to have all the pussy he wants."

All four men have surrounded the small table in this germ-filled club. I hope we can soon get down to why this evening has turned from me tracking down Andrew to now involving a group of random guys who all have a secret they are bursting at the seams to share. If I won't get in a good kill tonight, then this better be worth my while.

"So, what's this little arrangement you're talking about?" I press, getting back to business.

I'm met with silence.

Andrew bends forward, his eyes flicking around the now-empty VIP lounge. "Has a woman ever turned you down? One you *had* to have?"

No. "Sure, who hasn't?"

Andrew licks his lower lip, and a heinous expression sweeps his face. "Well, what if they couldn't say *no*?"

The tips of my ears burn at the thought of what he's implying, but I keep my expression neutral. "What do you mean?"

Rich rests his back against the couch with one arm lying across the cushion behind him. With arrogant confidence, he explains. "Women don't want ordinary guys anymore. They want rich bastards"—he sips his cocktail—"like you."

"Go on." I swallow hard, letting him continue.

"We work hard and make an honest living, yet we're still not good enough for these gold-digging women who only want our money," Rich complains, an undertone of anger to his words.

I raise a brow, still in the dark about where he's headed with this.

"We intend to avenge men by getting back at the self-serving women who've sidelined them in favor of better-looking, more successful ones."

Nolen smooths his suit. "The ones who spend their hard-earned money on buying drinks and dinners, to only get a quick peck on the cheek at the end of the night and sometimes not even a call back."

Such a stand-up guy. I wonder why anyone wouldn't want to date him?

"With my support, we have the funds to lure, capture, and keep these women," Andrew chimes in. "For a very negotiated price, any man can take advantage of our services, intending to do whatever they choose to do with them."

I've had my suspicions about Andrew awhile, and it looks like my instincts were correct again.

"For forty-eight hours, we get to share them," Nolen adds with a sick twinkle in his eye. "We're guaranteeing that hard-working men will receive what they desire after they've fully paid."

What the fuck.

"This is an entire operation," I hear Sebastian comment.

I subtly adjust my earpiece but don't respond.

Sucking in a breath, I hide my disgust, morphing back into character. "Tell me more."

Looks like I've added three more monsters to my kill list.

CHAPTER FOUR

LUX

The man had vanished into the crowd nearly ten minutes ago, but my body reacts as if he is still watching me. When our eyes locked from across the dance floor, heat crawled down my spine so suddenly it felt invasive. The connection lasted barely a second before he looked away first and then disappeared into the crowd alongside *Mr. Expensive Shoes.*

"I can't believe you dragged me out tonight," I mutter. "That guy in the loafers was such a douche. His shoes probably cost more than my car."

Stevie laughs beside me, hips swaying lazily to the music vibrating through the club. "That's expected in places like this. But we're safe. And deserve to live a little."

"I feel old," I whine. "And we aren't actually *safe.*"

"Just let go for a bit." My sister rolls her eyes. "Pretend you're not so uptight, okay?"

"Men don't come here looking for connection." I say. "They come here to hunt."

Stevie cocks her head, the amusement fading slightly from

her expression. Then, she playfully slaps my bare shoulder. "Normal people just drink and dance."

"Normal people end up on true crime documentaries." My eyes scan the length of the bar on the far corner of the club. Young people line both sides, begging to drink away their worries and sorrows. "I can't help that I'm more aware than most people. You should be like this too."

"You know, you really should have become a cop like Dad wanted." She flashes me a toothy smile. "Then your behavior would be more justified."

"Please," I scoff at her comment. "I'd have been fired on my first day."

Stevie snorts. "That's actually true."

"I don't like being told what to do."

"You got suspended in fourth grade because Mrs. White told you to stop investigating who stole the class hamster."

"Nibby deserved justice."

Stevie nearly chokes on her drink and laughs. "Lux, the hamster, escaped because no one latched the cage door."

"That's what they *wanted* us to believe."

"Oh, my God." She palms her forehead. "You were a conspiracy theorist at nine."

"I solved the mystery."

"There wasn't a mystery."

"Agree to disagree." I shrug.

Her laugh rings out above the music, and for a moment, I forget to scan the room. Forget to worry that men like the one in expensive shoes exist.

Stevie nudges my shoulder. "Remember when Dad bought you that detective kit for Christmas?"

I groan immediately. "No."

"With the little fingerprint powder?" She teases.

"Nope."

"What about the magnifying glass? I'm sure you remember that."

"Absolutely not." I look away, biting back a grin.

"You dusted every surface in the house."

A hand flies to my hip. "I was conducting an investigation."

"You accused me of stealing your notebook."

"You *did* steal my notebook."

Stevie points triumphantly. "See? Twenty years later and you're still holding a grudge."

"Because you admitted it!"

Stevie laughs so hard she has to brace herself with my arm. Watching her smile makes something warm settle in my chest. No matter how different we are, it's always been like this. Just Stevie and me against the world.

"One more drink. And then we can head back to my place to watch a movie." She throws her hands into the air in surrender. "Fair enough."

"Come on," I urge, gesturing toward a quieter area where I can think straight.

My sister follows behind me as we push through the crowds of people packed on the other side of the dance floor.

A breadth of space opens for us to walk through, almost as if the pulse of body's senses my unrest.

As we approach the bar, a bartender appears with a welcoming smile. "What can I get you ladies?"

"We'll both take vodka tonics." I blurt out before Stevie has the chance to speak. He nods and turns his back on us. My eyes focus on the bottles he's grabbing and how his hands move. Some may call it paranoia. I call it being cautious.

She leans in, covering her mouth as if anyone could hear us over the vibration from the bass. "He's cute."

"Stevie," I warn, narrowing my eyes.

She shrugs. "What?"

"Stop," I tell her. "I don't have time to entertain a love life."

"Workaholic."

Every few months, my sister lovingly reminds me of what I'm missing in my life. Like hers is any better?

"It's called having a purpose."

"I know. I have one, too." She plucks a cherry from the canister behind the bar and pops it into her mouth. "Yet, I also appreciate having my needs satisfied from time to time."

"Connecting with people is simpler for you than it is for me," I tell her with a heavy sigh. "Look. I like my quiet little life buried underneath case files and behind the comfort of my laptop."

She rolls her eyes. "I can't believe Dad still doesn't know you use his credentials."

Do I feel bad about it? Yes. But am I going to stop? No. Sometimes bending the rules is necessary, especially when it's in the name of something good. "And he's never going to find out. *Stevie*."

"Blinded by the love of his innocent daughter." She quips. "Of course. I'd never rat you out."

"Good." I smile. "Thank you."

My sister can be scatterbrained and is more impetuous than I am, but her and I never keep secrets from each other. I trust Stevie with everything. We're all each other has had.

The bartender places two drinks in front of us.

Stevie nudges my arm, gesturing at him as he moves on to the next person waiting to place a drink order.

"Okay. Fine. Let's say I talk to this blonde bartender, and he asks what I do for a living?"

"Then tell him."

"That I write stories about women seeking revenge?" I shake my head scoffing at my own idea. "My only options in life are to date someone in law enforcement," Stevie opens her mouth for a rebuttal, but I stick my finger in the air, silencing her, "or a serial killer. Those are the only two things I'm familiar with and that wouldn't find my job weird."

She flips her long, corkscrew curls. "You profile everyone. Maybe you should've joined the FBI?"

"Being a crime writer works better for me."

"I know, I know," Stevie gives up and waves me off.

"And I don't profile everyone."

She cocks her head to the side, not buying my defense. "You do. And I love telling people I'm a mortician." She laughs, crossing her arms over her chest. "It's a conversation starter."

"It's not the same. I spend all my time tucked away in my writing cave, obsessing over grisly crime scenes. Sounds sexy and alluring, doesn't it?"

"I know. It's sad," Stevie grimaces, grabbing the drink placed in front of her. "I guess I will forever be your only friend, too."

With the short black straw held between my fingers, I take a sip. "I have friends."

"Who?" Stevie's eyebrows raise. "The woman you try to avenge through your stories?"

"I give my female main characters their lives back, even if only through words."

"I get it, Lux." Stevie puts an arm around my shoulder, pulling me closer. I tuck my head under her chin. "We both found ways of dealing with growing up around death and murder, didn't we?"

I chuckle at the irony. "And that's why I write my thrillers under a pen name. So I can trauma dump freely."

Under all the good I proclaim to create with my books, the revenge plots, the feminine rage –a darkness lives inside of me enjoying the thrill of taking justice into my own hands. Like a bull bucking the earth at its feet, eager to be released from the iron cage that suppresses it.

"I know," she says.

I shove my drink to the side, growing antsy to leave. "Let's call it a night."

"A deal is a deal." Stevie does the same, still three quarters of the liquid left in the glass.

"I barely had anything to drink." I reach for Stevie's car keys since we drove together. "I'll drive us back instead of you."

"I had like two sips." She retorts, yanking her keys back from my hand.

I smile. "Fine. Have it your way."

A short time later, Stevie and I are walking up to the courtyard of my townhouse complex.

"You didn't have to walk me to my door." Our arms are linked as we stroll through the small space.

Since your garage door keypad won't be fixed until Monday, I thought parking at the bottom of the stairs and walking up with you is the safest option. This way, we can keep an eye on each other."

My mouth falls open, stunned at my sister's sudden awareness. "Look at you being responsible."

"Maybe your paranoia is rubbing off on me?" She laughs, then reaches into her purse to grab her phone. "Nick texted me."

"Your fuck buddy?" I quip, clutching my keys between my fingers. A light rain drizzles, peppering the bare skin on my arms. My eyes dart around the courtyard. The neighbors across from me are out of town and their porch light isn't on, so it's darker than usual.

She pauses before following me the rest of the way to my door. "You need one."

I shake my head, "I think I'm okay."

She flips her long hair. "Suit yourself. You'll be good on your own?"

"Of course." I wave her off as my feet hit the *welcome* mat at my front door. "You have fun. Text me when you get back to your place or his."

"He's meeting me at my place." She blows me a kiss, then hops down the steps and into her car. "Love you!"

"You too," I smile, taking one last look at the car headlights as she pulls away. Then I turn to my door and twist the key into the lock.

But the silence feels wrong now. It's too quiet. My keys tremble slightly as I slide one into the lock. But behind me, there are footsteps coming fast.

My body barely has time to react before something pricks my neck. And the last thing I hear is my keys clattering against the porch.

Then darkness swallows everything.

CHAPTER FIVE

RIVER

"They'll catch you, you asshole." This piece of shit is the man we captured at this hell hole of a cabin, and he's referring to the four men involved in a ring of the rape and torture of women.

When the head guys looped me into their little organization two nights ago at the club, I knew I had to step in. After a call with my FBI contact, we were able to quickly put the pieces together. I realized these sick fucks are trying to mimic a college ring that was busted twenty years ago.

With a balaclava comfortably covering my face and my favorite knife at his throat, I shrug and say, "Maybe they will. Maybe they won't."

"Do you know who I am?" he threatens, his limbs thrashing against the thick rope binding him to the rickety wooden chair.

Based on the information Sebastian uncovered, this guy is their scout. His job consists of finding secluded locations where they can conduct their *business*.

"I do not," I say. "However, judging by your appearance, you're probably a low-level henchman."

He grits his teeth together, the stains telling me he's been up in the mountains for some time without a toothbrush. "I run this whole fucking place."

"I'm sure you do," I tell him, clamping his shoulder. "And now you're going to tell me what I need to know."

A sinister smile creeps across his complacent face. "Fuck you."

"My friend," I start, pressing the blade harder against his skin. "This can go one of two ways. Either you tell me more information about if there are more locations you use, or my cousin Sebastian will hold you down so I can sever each of your fingers one by one."

A small drop of blood leaks onto his lip from the cut where I knocked him out earlier. His tongue darts out to lick it. "I'm not telling you shit."

"Why do they always make it difficult on themselves?" I roll my eyes. These fuckers always do. "Look, Pete. Can I call you Pete?"

"You're going to regret this."

"I doubt that," I reply, circling his chair. I move my knife down and across his chest, behind his back, before I return to the front. He winces, attempting to move away, but he's bound to the chair.

"The rest of the house is clear." Sebastian's boots slam against the hardwood floor as he enters the room. "But there are women in the basement," he adds with a sigh.

"How many?"

"I counted four."

"Are they—"

He nods, answering the question before I ask it. "I didn't check, but from the looks of it"—he sighs—"they're all dead."

The way these men trapped those women and the horrendous acts they may have endured fuels my anger—and my hunger to take out the *trash*. I grip the longer hair on the back of Pete's head and jerk it backward. "You and your friends have been busy, haven't you?"

His beady eyes meet mine. "What can I say? I love me some good pussy."

I wring my neck. "You just signed your death warrant."

A chilling scream erupts from his throat before I glide the sharp side of my knife across his throat, sending a waterfall of blood down his chest.

"Did you get any information out of him?" Sebastian asks, slipping his gun into the back of his black pants.

"Nothing we weren't already aware of," I say, looking around for a sink.

"There's one in the basement," he tells me as if he knew what I was looking for. "But be prepared. These are some sick bastards. I'll stay up here and start cleaning."

"It's what you do best," I comment.

He shoots me a look over his shoulder. "Yeah, maybe it's about time to discuss our roles in the operation."

"Maybe," I say, then give him a curt nod and leave him to it.

He may complain, but he's the best at managing the night crew.

I take a sharp right turn out of the bedroom and down the hall that leads to the basement. Once at the padlocked door, I move past piles of rubbish and discarded furniture and descend into what I can only describe as Hell.

Thick metal chains hang from holes midway up the concrete wall, while blood-soaked linens are haphazardly piled into a large basin.

A dense scent of copper and mildew infiltrates my nostrils.

My eyes scan along the cement basement where I find four beds—each one with rose-stained sheets. Four women in total, all lying on different beds with their arms chained to the iron frame above their heads.

"*Fuck,*" I say under my breath, taking in the surrounding sights.

All of the women have matted, dirty hair and are positioned on their backs. Three of them have their legs fallen open, exposing their insides. Only one is slightly covered with her knees bent to one side. I'm surprised she doesn't appear to be as dirty and beaten up as the others.

It's possible she hasn't been here as long.

I can't leave them all in this position. They don't need to be exposed like this when the police find them. So, one by one, I close their legs and pull the tattered blankets to cover them.

Once I'm done, my eyes dart over to the last woman lying in the corner near the window. Completely naked, she is exposed to the chill of the basement. As I move across the room toward her, I secure my black latex gloves by weaving my fingers together from each hand. When I reach the side of the bed, I assess every inch of her mangled body before I reach pick up her leg and move it even closer to the other.

A subtle bounce of the mattress stops my movements. At first I think I've imagined it, but when I grab the knife in my pocket, her leg twitches.

I stand still.

"Please don't hurt me," she begs with a shaky voice.

She's alive.

She has a blindfold on and I'm still wearing my mask, so I'm certain she can't see me. But I can't risk being discovered.

The police will be on their way as soon as I can get the fuck out of here and alert them. So, I quietly walk around to her side, past an open tiled shower fit into the corner of the room and toward the stairs. She flinches with each thud of my heavy boots as they hit the concrete floor. I watch the rise and fall of her chest matching the rhythm of the incessant drip of a leaky pipe on the far side of the basement.

"Please," she whimpers again. "Don't hurt me. I only want to go home."

I ignore her pleas, briskly stepping onto the first step.

"Upstairs," she says, "I heard you."

I know I should focus on getting out, but intrigued by her admission, I walk back over to the side of the bed. Tangled long brown hair frames her face, and a cut mars her bottom lip.

Curiosity gets the best of me, because I'm not sure if what she said was an accusation or an appeal to show she has knowledge about what Sebastian and I did.

"Did they get to you?" I ask. My protective instincts get the best of me while I examine her body for more injuries.

"What?" she spits out. "Do you want me all to yourself? Is that why you killed the guy upstairs?"

She thinks I'm one of them.

I slip the black mask over my face, then reach over to slowly push the blindfold up on hers. Two large hazel eyes with specks of green expose themselves to me. A smudged her mascara, leaving a line of black ink down her cheek.

Why does she look so familiar?

"Did they get to you?" I repeat.

Her frightened orbs bounce between mine for a moment before she answers in a soft voice.

"Only one."

Her answer lifts a weight of concern from me, but it suddenly returns because one is too many.

"What are you going to do to me?" She swallows hard.

I shake my head, unable to tear my eyes from hers. "Nothing."

"Are you planning to let me go?"

"No."

Her swollen bottom lip quivers. "So, you're not going to hurt me or let me go?"

I shake my head once again. "I'm not sure yet."

The previous terror in her eyes transforms into a frenzied panic. "Are you going to leave me here for when they come back?"

"No one will be returning," I tell her coldly. "The police will be here soon."

Attempting to escape, she sharply tugs on her wrists, forcing a stream of blood to trickle down her arm.

I never talk to them, because it's too dangerous. *She is a victim—part of the job*, I remind myself. But then why do I feel this palpable pull toward to her?

Fuck, I need to get out of here before I do something I'll regret. Giving her my back, I start walking toward the stairs.

"How do you know?" she rushes out, the farther away from her I get.

"I'm going to call them," I toss over my shoulder.

"Will you stay until they come?" she cries.

I pause before my boot hits the cracked tile in the shower. I was hoping to wash up the best I can before heading upstairs. "Why do you want me to stay? I could've lied to you about being one of them."

"You're not." She sniffs, answering with confidence. "You said you're not."

Slowly, I turn to confront her. "And you believe me?"

"I can sense it," she admits, her words coming out breathy. "But if you're not one of those monsters, then why are you here?"

Why the fuck does she keep talking to me?

Climbing up the creaky wooden stairs, I ignore her question once again.

"Please get me out of here." She sniffs. "I can't be here when the police come."

I'm about to tell her no when her last comment stops me in my tracks. Against my better judgment, I ask, "Why?"

"Why what?"

"Why can't you be here when the police arrive?"

"I can't tell you that."

Irritation whips at me—both from her continued communication and now her lack of transparency when *she* wants *me* to help her. But also by my inability to leave her behind. I straighten my posture and head back to the bed. The sound of my feet on the floor makes her flinch.

"You better start talking," I warn, fixing her stare with mine.

Wait. She's the woman from the club! The one Andrew was bothering when I interrupted them.

She hesitates for a moment before licking her lips. "My father works for the police department."

My fucking luck. The only woman alive is the one who's connected to law enforcement.

"Well"—I raise my eyebrows—"now there's no way I can let you go now that I know you're connected to the police."

"Please!" The woman flops aggressively. "You have to help me. Keep me blindfolded, throw me into your trunk, and drop me off at my house," she says, "I don't fucking care, but I can't stay here!"

"No."

"Please!" she screams. "Please!"

"Are you all right down there?" Sebastian's voice bellows from the top of the stairwell.

I lean in closer, bringing my face within inches of hers. "Don't you dare move."

"Help me!" she screams. "Let me out of here!"

Frustrated with her lack of compliance, I sprint over to Sebastian anyway.

"One is alive," I tell him.

His boots descend the steps. "Oh, wow. Okay."

"We're taking her with us," I say with apprehension lacing my voice.

"What?" he whispers. "Are you serious?"

"I don't want to talk about it," I dismiss him. A wave of relief washes over me as time passes and we go deeper into the nighttime hours. "Get the tarp and line the trunk with it. We'll drop her off at her house."

Sebastian's eyes are wide with confusion, but like the most loyal cousin and friend he is, he agrees. "I found these on our buddy Pete," he says, tossing me a ring full of keys.

I catch them in my palm. "Perfect."

Frustrated with myself for getting involved, I angrily make my way back and march to the side of the bed. As soon as I get rid of her I can return to my goal—bringing those sick bastards down.

"We're taking you home, but I swear to fucking god, if you try anything I will not hesitate to end you," I threaten, sliding the keys from my pocket. I only have to attempt two before I get the correct one that unlocks her chains. "I'm going to handcuff you again."

Although her eyebrows furrow, she nods in agreement. Once her arms are secured, I pull her blindfold back down, plunging her into darkness. A shiver wracks her body, so I quickly take the thin sheet from her bed and wrap her bare body with it.

"Thank you," she whispers through clattering teeth.

I lean in, my lips brushing her earlobe through the material of my mask. "Don't think I'm a good guy."

A sharp rise of her chest catches my eye. "You said you wouldn't hurt me."

"Never believe what people tell you," I reply, bending to scoop her up into my arms.

CHAPTER SIX

LUX

I peel my eyes open to find myself in my bedroom. A wave of panic washes over me as I can't recall when or how I returned to my townhouse.

The sun warms my sore cheek as I reach up to rub the back of my neck which is also tender to the touch.

What the hell happened?

Did I have a nightmare?

My heart leaps from my chest when my bed vibrates, but I breathe a sigh of relief when I see it's my phone. In a state of alarm, I frantically search the bedsheets for a few terrifying seconds until I find it resting on my nightstand, plugged into the charger. Grabbing it with desperation, I'm shocked to discover it's Monday.

"Hello?" I answer.

"Hey, I haven't spoken to you all weekend," Stevie exclaims. "I was a little worried, but then I thought that you were holed up in your office, writing."

"Yeah, that's where I was," I respond, confused.

"Sorry, I didn't stay with you Friday." After brushing the

nervous moistness from my brow, I settle back into bed. Stevie left after she walked me through the courtyard of my town-house. "I told you to go, remember?"

Suddenly, memories from this weekend roll in. We were together at the club on Friday night, but she left to hook up with that guy she's been seeing. Then I remember waking up unclothed and restrained to a bed, and I'm certain someone...

A churning in my stomach brings on a wave of nausea, so I squeeze my eyes shut at the memory before opening them again, hoping to stop the room from spinning.

Tears spill from my eyes while my throat closes, forcing me to suck in a breath. Those fucking psychos were waiting for me. But how did they...my hand flies back up to the side of my neck.

The needle.

The sharp pain.

They fucking drugged me.

"I knew you'd get it." A door slams in the background. "Hey, I have to run, but remember we're meeting at Dad's favorite restaurant at six for his birthday dinner."

With my hands still trembling from fear or maybe the lack of food I've had in days, I switch my phone to the other ear. My throat constricts as bile shoots its way up.

"Yeah, of course," I rush out, my voice strained. "I'll see you there," I add, ending the call before she responds.

Jumping off my bed, I run to the bathroom and dry heave multiple times, emptying the minimal contents of my stomach into the toilet. My muscles scream in pain from the violent thrusts forward while the soft pile rug cradles my fall as my legs buckle, sending my knees to the floor.

"Oh god," I whimper to myself, tears pouring from my eyes.

I need a fucking shower. I need him off me. I need to be clean.

With a swing of the shower door, I turn the faucet on as fast as I can manage. The sudden coolness of the water takes my breath away as soon as I step in. My skin breaks out in goose bumps, but I don't care, I need to be clean. Shivering, I stand under the spray, waiting for the temperature to change.

The water grows warmer and eventually the heat intensifies, but it's not hot enough. Wrapped in a blanket of steam, I snatch the body soap from the ledge, squeeze as much as I can fit onto the washcloth and start scrubbing my skin. Hard.

I turn the knob all the way to the other side, and continue to scrub every inch of my body, until my skin burns from the heat and repeated friction.

I'm not clean enough.

My mind flashes through blurry images of a man on top of me. The weight of his body applying a heavy pressure on my lungs, that I can barely take in a full breath. In a panic, I take two fingers and rub them between my legs. My body doesn't feel like mine anymore. Foreign under my own touch, the realization is overwhelming, and I lurch forward again dry heaving in place.

Still not good enough.

The heated shower water continues to soothe my aching muscles, providing a false sense of cleanliness before I eventually get out. Catching myself in the mirror, I'm overcome by how red my skin is. Raw and irritated, pulsing with the color of crimson, and matching the rage now brewing inside. Like a monster, it grows with every flashback that comes into focus.

But then a different type of memory forms when the guy in the balaclava shows up. Like a dark shadow, donned in a black fabric mask, leaving only his eyes visible. His steady energy was all I could hold on to, and I remember begging him to take me home. What was most striking from the horrific weekend was the intensity of his stare and the quiet firmness of his voice, and I can still picture them when I close mine. The man in the mask said he'd take me home, and it seems he kept his word.

Burying my feelings for later, I spend the next few hours pulling myself together while trying to snack on a few crackers and ginger ale. My thoughts cycle through every piece of information I can recall from the weekend.

I can't tell my sister what happened and my dad can never know—and that's why I begged the masked man in the basement to take me home. It would ruin him. The thought alone of knowing his daughter could have become his next homicide victim would drive him to insanity, and I can't allow my dad to carry such an unnecessary burden.

Silence surrounds me like an eerie fog as I pull my hair away from my face into a loose bun. When I lower my arms, the bruises on my ribcage ping with deep ache.

I'm not sure if the men who kidnapped me are local to the area or not. People are more likely to commit crimes in areas they're more familiar with, but if the police already responded to the 911 call from the cabin, the guys might be lying low for a bit to avoid coming after me if they realized I had been rescued.

Assuming the cabin where I was held is in the same county, my dad and his detectives most likely went to the scene over the weekend. Which means, the first forty-eight hours are the most critical, so he'll have to eat and run. An alarm goes off on my phone to remind me of our dinner tonight and snaps me out of my spiral.

To avoid my dad and sister seeing the cuts from the metal chains on my wrists, I slide my watch lower to cover them up. The searing pain is intense and I think of removing it because it's almost unbearable. Then, I reach for my jewelry box, searching for as many gold bracelets as possible to stack on the other wrist.

Deciding to deal with the pain, I gather the rest of my things and head toward the door.

By the time I get to the restaurant, which is only fifteen minutes from my place, I've nailed down the specific questions I want to ask my dad about the cabin crime scene. My hope is that he's able to share anything he might have found out that could lead to me understanding about what went on with me and those other women over the weekend. But the moment I step out of the car, I'm struck with the realization that I'm not waiting for details from a crime scene I'm not connected to—I'm asking them for *me*.

Behind the open driver's side door, I lower myself and throw up the small amount of food I managed to keep down today. Once my stomach settles, I linger by the car a bit longer, building confidence before stepping inside.

Third on 3rd has been my dad's favorite spot since Stevie and I were young, because of his obsession with their early bird special and coconut cream pie. My dad was never much of a cook, so we came here at least once a week. And although we don't frequent the restaurant as much nowadays, we still enjoy celebrating birthdays and special occasions here.

The fresh smell of chicken pot pie on a cool summer evening is all it takes for me to find a slice of peace in the painful world I've found myself in.

Wiping my watery eyes, overwhelmed by what has happened to me and the thought of keeping this from the two people I love the most in the world, I swallow my feelings. With a brief scan of the cozy place, I find my dad and sister at our regular table.

"Lux!" my dad greets me as I approach them.

"Happy birthday, Dad," I say as he stands to pull me in for his typical bear hug.

I usually would welcome it, but my limbs lock instinctively

into place. Panic surges through my veins and I back away from him quickly. Visions of waking up in that basement, staring at the cement ceiling while drifting in and out of consciousness. The indescribable weight held my limbs down, barely able to move.

"You all right?" My father's voice penetrates the flashbacks and I'm sucked back into reality. His eyes are narrowed, and worry transforms his features.

Swallowing hard, I take in a weighted breath and say, "Yeah, I got pretty beaten up the other day in self-defense class."

"Oh yeah?" He cocks his head to the side. "Well, good. This is the exact reason I forced you two to take them all these years. To be able to protect yourselves effectively."

"I thought you were writing all weekend?" Stevie chimes in from the other side of the table, always trying to call me out for something.

I settle in next to my dad, sitting carefully in the chair, and being cautious not to worsen my injuries. "I did, but I made time for a quick one-hour class."

Stevie's face twists with slight skepticism. She doesn't seem to believe me, and before she can grill me with questions, Dad interrupts her.

"I hate to do this, but I can't stay long." He waves over our server. "I was called out Sunday around two a.m. for a grizzly scene, and I have to get back to the station."

You can do this, Lux.

Shifting in my seat, I turn to my dad, masking the conflicting emotions bouncing around inside me. "What happened?"

Just then, the server appears at our table so we all take a quick moment to order before my dad turns back to us with a solemn expression. The restaurant is buzzing with chatter, but a dense silence rolls in, surrounding my ears alone.

Bending forward and lowering his head, my father glances around a few times before speaking. "We found the bodies of three women shackled and badly beaten in the basement of a rundown cabin up north."

The pounding in my chest pulses through my ears. "Where up north?"

"About an hour north of Seattle," he tells us, trying to use discretion with the more specific details of the case. "According to forensics, someone raped and tortured them."

Stevie gasps. "Fuck."

"We don't know a lot right now and the last thing we want to do is create a panic, so the press can't find out yet," he instructs. "My instincts are usually right on these things, but I think this is only the beginning."

I grip my fingers with my entire hand waiting for his response.

"What makes you say that?" I ask, remembering there were different men coming in and out of the basement.

"You remember that college sex ring from twenty or so years ago?" he asks.

"Yes," I breathe out. "Of course, I do."

I was barely nine at the time, but that case was hard on my dad. He worked around the clock and it consumed his life for months. That was the earliest recollection I have of understanding what his job entailed.

The first book I wrote was loosely based on that case.

"I think there are multiple perpetrators involved." He pauses, sighing. "And it might be a copycat."

Fuck.

Based on what I heard while held captive, I figured that

was the case, but to hear my dad—*the police*—verbalizing this causes my head to spin.

Writing always gave me the opportunity to right the wrongs and help others get the justice our system never gave them. But is it enough? There will always be more victims. More women dying and suffering at these hands of predators.

And now I am one of those women.

CHAPTER SEVEN
RIVER

I will be the first to admit my own flaws and hold myself accountable, but one thing I will never apologize for is my protective instincts.

And right now, they are focused on Lux Levinson.

It's been a week since I dropped her off at her townhouse and have spent each night parked across the street under an overgrown tree that gives me an unobstructed view of her home.

But unfortunately for me, watching Lux through the cameras on my phone is no longer enough to satiate my infatuation. I need to be near her, *touch* her. The desire to protect her has intensified to a level where I now find myself outside of a self-defense studio on a late afternoon, watching as she walks up the busy sidewalk toward the entrance doors.

Her matching workout clothes hug every curve of her delicious body while her luscious ponytail bounces between her shoulder blades, making my fingers itch with the urge to wrap my hand around it.

She whips her head around a few times, checking her

surroundings as if she's afraid someone might be following her. I'd much rather her stay locked in her house until Sebastian and I can eliminate the threats, but it's not like I can walk up to her and demand something like that.

She reaches for the gym's front door, and with one more glance over her shoulder, her eyes land directly on my car parked a few feet away. Although my windows are tinted to the darkest shade legally acceptable, I instinctively duck deeper into my seat and secure my aviator sunglasses to hide my face.

Our gazes meet, and for a moment makes me believe she can see me, but that would be almost impossible.

Lux slips in through the glass doors and disappears for her hour-long class.

Feeling bold and slightly desperate, I take that time to head back to her townhouse only a short distance away. I pull into the same spot under the tree and after a quick scan of the neighborhood to make sure no one's around, I step out of my car and head toward the green belt at the back of the homes. Once I reach her back gate, I flip up the latch and walk onto a small patio. Potted white roses line one side of the area while others climb a wooden trellis standing next to the sliding glass door.

She would love the gardens at Thompson Manor.

Pushing the fleeting thought away, I slide my laptop from my bag and open my company's software to jam the signal of the security sensor on the door. After successfully turning off her security system, I put my laptop back in my bag and quickly glance at the back door lock, which is a typical Mortice lever.

Being familiar with its type, I squat in front of the door and after a few quick movements, a subtle click breaks the quiet afternoon.

Carefully stepping inside, I'm met with the overpowering

smell of her. I bathe in it, welcoming the electric shot it sends through my veins.

My boots barely hit the tiled kitchen floor when suddenly the front pocket of my pants vibrates.

"Aunt Mae?" I answer as my eyes scan the small feminine space decorated with monochromatic colors.

"Hi, River. Sensei Clark is here waiting for your martial arts training."

"I'm on a stakeout right now," I tell her, heading out of the small eat-in kitchen and up the carpeted staircase that leads up to the second floor where Lux's room is. "Can you coordinate with him another time to come?"

"Sebastian said you two didn't have anything planned for today and were still waiting for Christian to get back to you with more information," Aunt Mae huffs out. "And you know if I reschedule with Clark, he's going to be annoyed."

There's no way I can get all the way back there that quickly.

I rub the back of my neck, not wanting to explain the object of my recent obsession. She won't understand, or like Sebastian would—try to talk some sense into me. "It's something I'm working on alone."

"You never work on anything alone," she comments, but there's a lightness to her voice telling me she is holding back a chuckle.

I briefly poke my head into the bathroom and Lux's office before something on the wall catches my eye. Walking toward her desk, I see a framed quote and to my surprise, it's one from my favorite poet, Edgar Allan Poe, *"I am a writer. Therefore, I am not sane."*

My new obsession, a Poe fan? I smile to myself, appreciating a small thing we have in common. And it only makes me even more intrigued by her. I stay in her office for only another second before heading to her bedroom.

"I do on occasion," I defend, but I'm barely paying attention to what Aunt Mae says when my eyes hone in on Lux's bed. The comforter is a cream color, fluffy and inviting. I envision her lying softly between the sheets like I've watched on the cameras.

"River," she scolds. "You have enough things on your schedule. You do *not* need another thing added to it."

I close the small distance to where Lux laid last night and I glide my fingers across the soft fabric, imagining what it would be like if she were laying in it now.

"Did Sebastian say something to you?" I ask absentmindedly.

"He told me you've been going over to that girl's house every night for the last week."

I sit on the edge of Lux's bed and let my eyes roam over the space. It's simply decorated with a long dresser on the adjacent wall and a matching tall one in the corner, but then I notice the closet door ajar and it catches my attention. I need to get her off the phone so I can enjoy this time in Lux's house.

"Can you reschedule my session with Sensei Clark for Friday?"

"River, don't change the subject."

I lift off the bed and walk toward the closet, pushing the door open to expose rows of shoes and racks of clothing. "Aunt Mae."

"Fine. I'll reschedule."

"Tell him I'll pay him double for him coming all the way out to the Manor."

I'm about to end the call when Mae's distant voice calls my name.

"River?"

"Yes?

"Remember not to get caught up in your impulsivity," she kindly reminds me.

I sigh and take two fingers, rubbing my temples. "I know, Aunt Mae."

"See you when you get home," she says before ending the call.

Morphing into River Thompson, the kindhearted and eccentric billionaire is something I'm good at, even with my aunt. Although she's aware of our nightly operations, no one truly knows how dark my blood runs.

Not even Sebastian.

And besides, isn't that the key to lying? Believing it enough yourself first?

Eagerly turning my attention back to the clothes hanging in front of me, I run my fingers along the fabric. This entire closet is dripping with her scent and despite my best efforts, I cannot help myself but bring one of her sweaters up to my nose. With a full breath, I take in her scent, enjoying how fucking divine it is.

Before I lose myself here for hours, I pull back and check the time on my watch. I should head out before her class is over, but I stop in my tracks when I notice black lace peeking out of one of her dresser's drawers. I turn to walk away but stop in my tracks.

Fuck it.

I grab the pair of panties and shove them into my pocket.

Then take the steps two at a time, walk through her kitchen, but stop at her refrigerator. After a quick look around, I sense my time growing short, so I leave through the back door, then quickly lock it behind me. With a quick reset of the alarm, I head back to my car.

Within no time, I park in my usual spot and wait for her to come out.

I watch her walk down the street alone, but as she passes my car, I catch a worried look on her face. That's when a man, looking no older than her, comes out of the studio and jogs up to her.

Who the fuck is that?

He rests a hand on Lux's arm and she doesn't back away. There's a familiarity between them and although their conversation seems innocent, it doesn't tamp the rising jealousy boiling inside of me.

Calm down, River. It's probably only a friend from class.

I almost convince myself this is nothing, until I catch him grinning as he nervously shoves his hands into the front pockets of his unnecessarily tight joggers. He gestures to the coffee shop and against my better judgment, I move to step out of my car when I see her gently shake her head.

Good girl.

I watch Lux get into her car, but instead of following her home like I usually would, I make a U-turn and trail him into a parking garage a few streets down.

Maybe I can have a simple talk with him. Tell him Lux is off-limits.

I park on the lower level and keep a safe distance between us as I tail him to the upper floor where he's parked. Slipping my mask over my face, I wait for him to reach his car.

Once he does, I rush toward him and with one swift motion, throw my body into his from behind, slamming him against the driver's side of his BMW.

"What the f—"

His words are cut off when I wrap my arm around his neck, crushing his windpipe.

"It'll be easier if you stop resisting," I warn him as he flails under my grip, his hands coming up to my forearms.

He reluctantly eases, and I take the opportunity to shift him so he's facing me.

"Who are you?"

"Your worst nightmare if you ever speak to Lux again."

"Lux?" he grits out, his face turning new shades of scarlet as I tighten my hold.

"The woman you asked out."

When he doesn't respond, I press my forearm deeper against his throat until he nods his head in understanding. I keep my arm tightly against his windpipe a few seconds longer, his face turning a deep shade of red, before I finally let him go.

Gasping, he crumbles to his knees, trying to catch his breath.

I slightly bend down until I'm sure he can hear me. "And I'd suggest you find a new class to attend."

I don't have to wait for his answer to know my message was received loud and clear.

CHAPTER EIGHT

RIVER

"That's interesting." I nod, taking all the information in from my secure landline.

My mind works overtime learning as much as I can about Lux. There's a force motivating her to keep going and I'm determined to figure out what it is.

"I'm sending over all the documents. You should have them any minute now," Christian, my FBI contact, tells me. His hacking skills, combined with TI technology, has been instrumental with each one of our missions. His father used to work with mine and Sebastian's parents while they collaborated on government contracts overseas. "I almost lost my shit when I saw her dad is the homicide lieutenant."

"Yeah, I'm still in shock," I say, pulling up our secure email server. As I tuck my phone between my ear and shoulder, I scroll through the first few pages. "Thank you, Christian."

"You know you can always count on me."

"You're the best," I mumble, scanning through the documents.

"So, outside of this woman, what are we working on next?" he asks.

In his own rogue nature, his participation in what we do is limited, but I believe it's driven by the guilt he still holds from his father's participation in the job that cost my parents their life. But whether he is willing to admit it, his own cravings for the hunt hasn't manifested into something big enough for him to get his hands dirty, yet.

"You know Andrew Hughes, the hotel heir, we've been watching?"

Papers rustle in the background. "Yeah?"

"Well, he's part of an operation a little bigger than I thought," I tell him, shoving Lux's information into the top drawer of my desk. I'll get back to her later.

"Go on."

"There's a group of men who appear to be mimicking the college sex ring from two decades ago." I slump into my chair, glancing out over the ocean through the panoramic windows in my office. The night sky is black and welcoming, which means I have an hour left until midnight—the time I come alive. The urge to escape the manor and head into the city streets intensifies by this time. If I'm not on the hunt, I'm usually chasing the next one. And with uncovering Andrew's sex operation, I'm foaming at the mouth to get my hands on him.

"I'll need their names," he states, preparing to dive into what he does best.

"Andrew Hughes, Nolen Pierce, and Richard Smith," I name them off, aware that Christian will unearth everything we need to know about them to help us expect their next move the moment we end our call. "Oh, and Duncan Jones."

He blows out an audible breath, the sound of his rapid

typing filtering through the phone. "That's a random bunch of guys."

My eyebrows raise with the same thought I had when Hughes introduced them to me last weekend. "Right?"

"I'll see what I can find," he tells me, and if I had to place a bet, I'd say he's about to pull an all-nighter.

"River?" Aunt Mae calls on the intercom through the entire house. She's lived with Sebastian and I since we were kids. Then when we built the manor, it only made sense for her to come with us then too. Now she manages the manor and our daily calendars, including my obligations with Thompson Innovation.

"Wonderful. Talk soon." I end the call before answering Mae. "Yes?"

"Ben is about to head home for the night. He wants to review the meals for next week with you," she informs me.

"I'll be right there." Getting out of my seat, I walk over to the wall where computer screens cover every inch of it. Typically it usually only displays the other rooms in the house and the outside of my twenty-three-acre compound, I focus on the few new feeds I've become captivated by and realize she's not asleep yet.

I was unaware of Lux's nocturnal habits before I began watching her a week ago, but I'm positive now she sleeps all day and stays awake at night. A behavior I've been familiar with for most of my life.

At first, she tries to fall asleep, but ends up tossing and turning for hours, until she gives up.

I examine every inch of her body as she lies on her side with one leg under the blankets, the other resting on top. Her shorts ride high, exposing a smooth, toned thigh. Blinking a few times, I pull myself away as to not get trapped staring at her from my office all night.

Walking through the house on the main level, I head right into the kitchen to find Mae, Ben, and Sebastian gathered around the large island, looking at printouts of meal options.

"River," Ben greets. "I won't take too much of your time." Ben has worked here for years and has learned my taste in food, but still insists on me approving the menu.

"How are the wife and kids?" I ask, rounding the island.

"Great as always." He smiles.

"These look good," I tell him, glancing over the options laid out on the granite countertop.

Ben turns to Mae and they exchange a look, before she faces Sebastian. "Is there anything you'd like to change, dear?"

"Nah, you know I'm easy, Aunt Mae," he replies, his attention fixated on the phone clutched in his hands.

"Fabulous. Everything is already cleaned up, I'm going to head home for the night." Ben gathers his laptop and notebook before turning to exit the kitchen.

"Thanks, Ben," I call out.

Mae wraps an arm around me as Sebastian lowers his phone and hooks an arm around her. "Okay, I'm going to bed. I will see you two in the morning."

I lean in to kiss her cheek. "Sleep well."

Sebastian gives her a tight squeeze before she slips from our embrace, but before she turns in for the night, she focuses her attention on me. "Oh, and River, the board confirmed for the next bimonthly meeting."

"Yes, I saw you add it to my calendar."

"Don't forget to—"

"Promise, I won't," I toss back as she waves us off and heads toward the south wing, her personal space on the property.

Once Sebastian and I are alone, he tucks his phone into the front pocket of his pants. He glances up at me with a questioning look on his face, and I have a feeling I know what he's about to ask me. But I won't admit it. Some aspects of my life I'm not willing to discuss.

"What is it?"

"Where are you going tonight?" he asks with an accusatory tone. Sebastian's the only person who knows me almost as well as I know myself, and sometimes that can be a bad thing.

"What's that supposed to mean?" I challenge, narrowing my gaze.

"I'm not stupid," he quips. "You can't keep anything from me."

I scoff at him off, and start to walk away, hoping to create distance from his probing.

"River."

"I don't want to hear it, Sebastian," I grit out, losing my patience with his persistence. By the time I make it back to my office, my cousin is hot on my heels.

"You've been to her house every night this week. She'll figure out you've been watching her."

"Don't you think I know that?" I sneer, shoving my hands into the front pocket of my pants, keeping my focus trained on her on the screens in my office. *She's still not asleep.*

Sebastian comes to stand at my side. "We dropped her off and now it's time to return to business."

"She isn't sleeping," I tell him.

He rolls his eyes, huffing with frustration. "I told you we shouldn't have installed those cameras in her house. You're becoming obsessed."

"I only want to make sure she's fine," I say, staring as she flips around and stares at the ceiling above with an arm tucked behind her neck. I can tell she isn't scared because she's attempting to return to her daily activities. I glance over at him and give him a pointed look. "And I am not *obsessed.*"

Sebastian cocks his head. "Sure, keep telling yourself that."

I ignore him, turning my attention back on the screen as he takes a seat at my workstation.

Lux holds herself with a confidence I haven't seen in previous people we've helped and I'd be lying to myself if I said I wasn't attracted to her.

"We've been doing this for years. You and I have helped and rescued a lot of women, none of whom have shown up at their house every night to guard them." He pauses. "Let alone install cameras inside their homes to watch them like a creep."

I whip around and find him leaning back on my chair, with his shoes resting on the glass top. "First, get your fucking boots off my desk," I warn, the sight of dirt from the bottom of his shoes near my keyboard irks me. He immediately brings them to the floor with a huffed laugh, his hands raised in mock surrender. "And like I've told you a million times already, there's something different about her."

"What do you mean?" he asks, resting his elbows over my desk, his hands clasped under his chin.

Breaking my gaze away from the screens, I stalk over to him and grab the dull yellow folder from I tucked it earlier, dropping it in front of him. "Here."

"What's this?" he asks, flipping it open to the first page, which has a copy of her driver's license. "Other than the fact that she's pretty, I don't see your point."

Leaning over him, I grab my phone and swipe up to the notes I collected at 2 a.m. the other night while sitting in my car, parked outside her townhouse. "She's a crime author who writes under a pen name."

"And?"

"Her dad is a homicide lieutenant," I add, waiting for him to connect the dots.

Sebastian suddenly sits up straight when it finally registers. "Is that why she didn't want to be there when the cops showed up?"

"That's my guess." I lean a hip against my desk and continue. "And get this, the books she writes are inspired by some of the biggest homicide cases in the Pacific Northwest." I press my palm against the stack of documents in front of us. "I spoke with Christian earlier and he sent me everything he has on her."

"Now, *I'm* intrigued," he says, bringing two fingers to his chin. "Do you think she's somehow connected to the ring, and that's why they took her? Like, they know who her dad is?"

"I'm not sure yet what their exact motive was, or if they knew her father is part of law enforcement."

"Or she was a random woman?" Sebastian folds his arms across his chest.

"Could be," I agree. "Christian is working on discovering more about Hughes, so hopefully we can determine a better motive than their desire to get back at women in general."

"I also think *you* wanted more information about the woman from the cabin, as well."

"Lux," I correct him using her name.

The corner of his mouth quirks. "Yeah."

I sigh. "Fine. You're right. I also wanted it for myself. Happy now?"

"Not until you say it."

I roll my eyes, annoyed that he's putting me on the spot like a young kid with a crush. "I think she's attractive, but there's more to her story. I know it."

"And I bet you're going to make it your mission to find out?"

I push off the glass edge and toward the door of my office. "The rest of the men are still out there. If they discover she's still alive, they could capture her again." I'm surprised by my need to protect her. Have I somehow made it my responsibility? What makes her so different? "It's about keeping her safe."

Sebastian rises to his feet. I'm prepared for him to continue to push back, but he doesn't. He might be concerned, but he lets it go. "You're right." His eyes flick to the camera displaying Lux's bedroom. "And we've only sunk our teeth into how to bring these guys down."

"Exactly," I agree.

This project will be the biggest and most complex one we've ever undertaken. Lone wolves are never a match for my team, but taking on a group of sick fucks will be a challenge.

Sebastian rubs the back of his neck, absorbing the information I've just told him. "When will Christian have another update?"

"He said in a few days," I gesture for him to follow me out the door.

"Going to her house?" He already knows the answer.

"Yes."

Once we're out of my office, I turn to set the security system attached to it.

"Still don't trust me with your office?"

"I trust you with everything," I reply. "But I don't allow anyone in here without me. You know that."

Sebastian has his own study, almost identical to mine, in the West Wing of the house. He wants access to this one because it belongs to me. *Sibling rivalry as we did grow up like brothers.*

He huffs. "I don't need your space, anyway."

"Sure," I say with a quick shake of my head before stepping into the elevator that leads to the underground garage. "I'll be back in the morning."

He waves me off as the metal doors close.

Anxious to keep watch over her, I entertain thoughts of possibly teasing her with my presence on the way to her house.

CHAPTER NINE

LUX

It's been exactly seven days since I escaped the hell that whoever those men were put me through.

Falling back into my typical routine has become more of a burden than I could have imagined, and the turmoil within me is becoming harder to contain. I've always had a clear purpose, and with losing that I find my anger conflicted between the assault and the control I once thought I had.

A desire for vengeance pumps through my veins while a restless need for answers about who those men were, and why they targeted me breeds an anxious and unsettled feeling preventing me from focusing on anything else.

It's almost 11 p.m. and my desk is covered with files I find impossible to peel my eyes from. If my dad found out I'm using his logins to get information, he'd lose his mind.

But I can't stop.

The events of that night started rolling in like waves one after another, and from there some of the pieces began to fall into place. While coming in and out of consciousness, I was able to recognize the man with the bad comb-over even though he masked his face. His voice is very distinct as well, remembering the slight drawl at the end of his sentences. I knew I recognized him from the club that night when he obnoxiously approached Stevie and me.

With his expensive shoes and dressed like he's beyond his years, it was Andrew Hughes, the hotel heir. Once I found his picture in the database, I've spent the last week researching everything about this man in a failed attempt to make myself feel better. Like it would somehow help to know who did it or why.

A startling vibration shakes me from a trance. I grab my phone from the top of my desk and open it to find a text message from an unknown number.

> UNKNOWN
> Why aren't you sleeping?

My blood instantly runs cold.

No...

My eyes dart around my office as if he can see me. Fear seizes hold of me, rendering me frozen, locking my limbs in place. Not knowing what to do or how to respond, I remain still. Is it Andrew? Does he know I'm still alive? If he took me from my house before, he knows where I live and can come for me again.

Before I can spiral more, another text comes through.

> UNKNOWN
> When I dropped you off last week, I told you to put this behind you.

Wait. It can't be...

Realization dawns on me.

The guy in the mask who brought me home that night.

Why is he contacting me? What should I do?

Since that night, I've found myself thinking about him. This man could have killed me but he chose not to. I should block his number or ignore him, but against my better judgment, I pick up the phone with trembling fingers, my heart pounding against my ribcage and I type out a response.

ME

I don't like being told what to do.

UNKNOWN

Or you're not as smart as you think you are.

ME

Excuse me? How did you get my number, anyway?

UNKNOWN

I have my ways.

What does that even mean?

ME

Is that all you're going to say?

UNKNOWN

You need rest. You've been through a lot.

ME

How do you know I'm not asleep yet?

UNKNOWN

I can see you're not.

Fear grips my insides, capturing my breath.

ME

What's that supposed to mean?

UNKNOWN

Do you really want to find out how I'm certain you're not asleep beside the fact that you're texting me back?

Panicked and unsure what to do or how to respond because he might be someone more dangerous than I want to believe. I rise to my feet, sending the chair rolling backward and move from my office to the bedroom, pacing and contemplating calling the police—*but I can't.* With a deep breath, I gather the courage to sweep the rest of the top level, before heading downstairs.

ME

Yes.

It's silent for a beat, each nerve ending in my body heightening with every passing second, waiting for a reply.

UNKNOWN

I'm outside.

ME

I'm calling the police.

Why are you telling him that? My mind admonishes me. Before I can complete my next thought, he already sends another message.

UNKNOWN

No, you're not.

ME

Yes, I am.

UNKNOWN

If you were, you would have done it already.

He knows I'm not going to call the police. I can't bring my

dad into this, because what happened to me would destroy him and it bathes me in shame—*and anger.*

A million questions assault my mind, and before I can think better of it, I yank my front door open and march toward the black car I've noticed following me around over the last week.

I need answers and he may have them.

The only thing keeping me from buckling with terror is the adrenaline pumping through me, pushing me in his direction.

"Keep your shit together, Lux," I whisper. "If he didn't hurt you before, he's not going to now."

The dim lights in the courtyard illuminate the bushes in front of the doorsteps of my neighbors. At right before midnight, the moon is full and nestled in the black sky above me.

I sweep every angle of the open space while a brisk wind dances across my bare shoulders, causing a shiver. With my phone held firmly in my grasp, I almost make it to the parked car when a sudden shadow steps in front of me. Startled, I jump back, my back slamming against the trunk of a tree.

"Why did you come out here?" The masked stranger's tone is ominous, but his mild annoyance is hard to miss.

I freeze, unsure whether to run back inside or stand my ground.

"Lux." My name rolls off his lips like an aged whiskey, sending a shiver down my spine. I wave it off to fear, but realize I never told him my name.

"How do you know my name?"

"You need to be more careful until this is all over." He takes a step closer to me.

So I was right about the fact that he knows more about the men who captured me.

"What do you mean until this is all over?"

"You need to go back inside." His tone is sharp.

"Not until you give me answers."

"It's nothing to concern yourself over."

Exasperation bubbles from within. "That's not your decision to make."

He looks away, his eyes trained elsewhere. "Trust me, the less you know the better."

I swallow hard. He won't give up anything. "Can you at least explain why you're outside my house in the middle of the night, then?"

He saunters forward, eating up the space separating us. The beating in my chest quickens. "I need to make sure you stay safe."

Oh.

His words blanket the cool night air leaving me in shock. This masked stranger has not only rescued me from the worst night of my life but has taken it upon himself to ensure my safety.

None of my criminology or psychology classes in college prepared me for someone like him or how to deal with him making my stomach do things it shouldn't in a situation like this. They didn't exactly cover *questionable men who might have an interest in a woman's safety* in my school textbooks.

"I'm fine."

He clicks his tongue as if chiding me. "You walked outside in the middle of night after an unknown number messaged you." He leans down, his breath fanning across my skin. "Your decision-making abilities are questionable, so pardon me for not taking your word for it."

He's right, and it pisses me off. This isn't like me, but who is he to lecture me?

"I knew it was you."

"And you're not afraid of me?"

I'm terrified, but I'm not about to let him know that.

"No," I say with an unstable confidence.

A rumble bellows from his chest as he lets out a sinful chuckle while his fingertips glide up the bare skin of my arm. "You should be."

Afraid to move, my arms remain stiff at my sides. "And why is that? You said you're here to make sure I'm safe." I part my lips, sucking in a breath of courage. "If you wanted to hurt me, you would have already."

He's silent for a beat. His enigmatic nature confuses me, but then he speaks.

"What do you want?" he asks with slight frustration, crossing his arm across his chest. The rapid change in his demeanor is unsettling—*yet infatuating.*

"Answers," I plead, shocked by hearing the raw honesty in my voice.

"I can't give you answers." Through the tiny holes in his mask, I can see his eyes narrowing. "Now go inside, Lux."

A false sense of control pings my insides. It brings to the surface the turmoil and desperation I've lived with every minute of every day in the last week.

"How do you know so much about me while I know nothing about you?" I challenge, but my voice is frail and trembling, barely carrying my defiance.

"You don't need to know who I am."

"I *love* how this entire conversation has been you telling me what I should and shouldn't know," I retort.

"Get inside. Don't make me repeat myself again."

"At least tell me your name." A last ditch effort for something I can hold on to. Some sort of win for myself.

Before I can register what's happening, he throws me over

his shoulder and carries me back into my house. My feet barely touch the hardwood floors before he's gone, the front door slamming shut behind him.

I regain my balance just as my phone buzzes again in my hand. With a nervous glance down—it's a new notification from him.

UNKNOWN

My name is River.

UNKNOWN

Lock your doors and go to sleep.

River.

Still dazed from his touch, I bring my hand up to type in the code.

My phone buzzes with another text.

UNKNOWN

Good girl.

Ignoring the heat his praise sends down my spine, I leave my phone downstairs before I do something stupid—like continue texting him—and trudge up the stairs to my bedroom, ready to finally get the sleep I've lacked recently. But as I pass my office, I change my mind and step inside.

My eyes bounce from one box of case files to another, all scattered on the floor. I look to the whiteboard hanging on the wall in the far side of the room. It holds every planned-out detail for my next story. On the opposite wall, a corkboard covered from top to bottom with printed copies of Google searches and plotting notes.

Dragging my feet across the carpet, I reach up and pull down each piece of paper, then watch as they drift to the floor.

Making my way over to the whiteboard next, I take both

palms and wipe off every word, leaving the board completely blank.

I have no idea where to go next, which is a first for me, but I know this is my story and I am determined to avenge it.

CHAPTER TEN

RIVER

It's been a quiet couple of days at Thompson Manor while I wait for updates from Christian and for a possible call from Andrew. I'm confident Christian will get back to me as soon as he's uncovered anything.

At the club almost two weeks ago, Andrew mentioned he'd be in touch with further details on what the next steps are with my involvement in their group, but I still haven't heard anything. I hate to be at his mercy and wait—it's a *power move* by him to remind me of who's in control.

A spiteful laugh echoes inside my car as I drive down the dark highway and into the city.

You have no idea what you're in for, Andrew.

It's also only been a few days since I let Lux know I've been watching her. Sure, it pissed me off that she willingly walked out of her house and into possible danger. But she did it because she believes I won't hurt her and it heats my insides with pride.

The city lights illuminate the dark night as I pass downtown Seattle on my way to Lux's suburban townhouse on the edge of the city. The late hour reveals my favorite time of the night leaving the roads deserted as the clock in my car approaches midnight.

As I turn down the shadowy road I grow more anxious to see her. I park my car in its usual spot nestled under a large tree a short distance away from her row of townhomes. After a quick scroll through the screens, I find her tucked into the corner of her couch with a blanket wrapped around her body. She seems unfocused without a book or laptop to occupy her time. I'm surprised by the sadness that moves through me as she appears to be so lonely. Something about her sitting by herself in the middle of what appears to be an empty house leaves me unsettled.

ME

Are you alright?

She leans over to the coffee table and grabs her phone. A subtle smile pulls at her lips.

LUX
You're back.

ME

I am.

LUX
Why do you think I'm not alright?

ME

You went through a traumatic experience. It would be expected to struggle.

LUX
Yes I am struggling, if you want to know.

The camera shows her run a hand through her tousled hair. My eyes follow the movement of her fingers as they move through the strands. I imagine burying my nose into the top of her head, breathing in the scent of her lavender shampoo.

I want to offer her something.

ME

I have something for you.

LUX

Information you're willing to share?

ME

Meet me on your doorstep.

LUX

I thought I wasn't supposed to open the door
for strangers anymore.

I shake my head at her comment appreciating the feisti-ness of her personality. I put my phone in my back pocket and slide my balaclava over my face. Strutting up to her front door, I bend to leave the weapon on her *Welcome* mat.

ME

It's on your doorstep.

I quietly step behind the large bushes that give me a clear view and watch as she cautiously opens her front door. My eyes immediately dart to her pajama shorts riding high and showing off her toned legs.

"River?" Lux whispers into the night as she glances down to find the gift I left for her. I've heard my name said by different people throughout my life, but hearing it fall from her lips is a sound I never knew I needed.

I probably shouldn't follow through with the thought that crosses my mind, but I do anyway. Because when it comes to Lux, I'm pushing my typical boundaries.

With a deep inhale, I step out of the shadows and say, "It's a lip gloss Taser. Be careful."

When her eyes meet mine. A surprised look sweeps across her face, so I pause my steps and maintain distance for a moment. But then, a quick rise and fall of her chest shows me she's relieved, although the stiffness in her posture means she's still cautious.

"A *lip gloss* Taser?" she repeats with her brows furrowed, crouching down to pick it up.

I take a few steps in her direction, but she doesn't back away or startle at my proximity. The unexpected display of trust has me wanting to test how close I'm able to get, but I decide not to push her.

"Aim the cap at your target, then pop it off, and it will shoot in the direction you're pointing it."

Lux curiously twists the clear cylinder in her hands. "Thank you?"

"Keep it with you," I instruct, then point at the bottom. "Make sure the safety is on, in case it gets triggered by an accident."

"Can I use it on you?" she asks playfully.

A chuckle rumbles through me. "Not if you value your life."

A subtle smirk pulls at the corner of her lips, sending my mind into a tailspin. Being in her presence brings a lightness to my chest which is a foreign yet pleasant feeling.

She's silent for a moment, the chirping of crickets filling the night air. "So..." she starts, sliding the lip gloss into a pocket, "masked and dressed in all black, you lurk in the shadows, and not to mention own gadgets like this?"

"Yeah?" I ask, not sure where she's going with this.

"Are you some sort of Batman?"

I can't help but let out a small laugh. "Batman? Didn't I already tell you my name?"

"You could be lying."

"I wouldn't lie to you," I reply, closing more of the distance between us. Even if I shouldn't.

She doesn't withdraw. We're both silent for a beat as her eyes bore into mine, trying to read me. It's the only part of my face she can see, and for a fleeting moment I get the desire to take it off, but it dissipates just as fast. I know better than to trust.

"You remind me of a raven," I blurt. A thought I've been thinking for some time.

"The bird?"

"They're inquisitive and read other birds well," I say.

She smiles and plays it off, but since I've seen the Poe quote on her desk, I know she's aware of exactly what I'm referring to.

"I'm familiar. And thank you for the compliment."

We sit in silence for a moment before I decide to speak. "I'm going to head out. Make sure you keep that safety on," I remind her gesturing toward the lip gloss Taser.

"Are you going to get back to your car now?"

"Yes."

"Oh."

"Do you not want me to?"

"Since you come and go from outside my house as you wish, I'm sure you can make your own decision," she says.

"Or you can invite me in to watch you." I'm testing her feistiness.

She clicks her tongue with a playful annoyance. "Not a chance."

I laugh. And it's a full belly laugh, one that makes me heart skip a beat.

"So, what do you do during the day when you're not sitting outside my house anyway?"

I smile behind the fabric, warmed by her genuine curiosity and how she's trying to keep our conversation going. "I run a tech company."

"Interesting. That explains the gadgets."

"Yes."

Lux leans her back against the wall next to her front door, folding her arms across her chest. "What type of technology? Like hacking?"

"Not really. More like inventions. My research and development team creates advanced technology and weaponry for the government," I tell her, feeling comfortable not giving to many specifics.

"What's it called?"

I palm the side of her house with an outstretched arm leaning in closer to her and shake my head. "Nice try, but no."

"Fine." She looks away hiding a frown.

Lowering my head to capture her beautiful brown eyes, I pick up the sadness I saw on the camera a sort time ago. "How are you holding up?"

"As to be expected. I'm angry and lost." She runs a shaky hand through her long tousled hair giving me a whiff of lavender. The scent is dizzying. "And the only other person who understands what happened or has any answers for me refuses to share any information."

She's implying me and my lack of transparency. I wish she'd understand it's for the best.

"I know you want more, but I'm doing what I believe is best."

"But do you see how frustrating that is? You're keeping me in the dark."

I exhale in frustration with myself and try to look away, but the doorstep light shines on her face and I catch dark circles under her eyes. "You need to try to sleep."

"I..." Her eyes swell with tears.

"Trust me, I am handling it."

"What's in this for you, River?" she challenges. "Why are you going after this random group of men, anyway?"

Another question I can't answer.

"I can't—"

"You can't tell me," she interjects. "I get it."

A single tear rolls down her cheek. With the back of my finger I wipe it off, but she jerks away. "I'm sorry."

"Yeah." Lux quickly turns her back to me and heads into her house.

I'm left staring at the empty spot on the wall, contemplating my choices from the last week and the one's I'm about to make. I can't bring myself to give her space and I haven't figured out why.

CHAPTER ELEVEN
LUX

My gaze blurs as I struggle to keep my eyes open while staring at the empty screen of my computer. Despite the deadline with my editor looming over me, I'm struggling to get the words out. I can't focus on anything else but what happened last night.

I've spent all day in my office, meticulously documenting every detail I recalled from that weekend since writing wasn't happening. Some memories have been clear, while others haven't. I usually do best by relying on my senses, but they are failing me now. The parts that come in murky are the memories I need to retrieve the most. And as soon as I get frustrated with myself, a dark image of River flashes in my mind. I haven't seen his face, but his presence and his need to keep me safe are enough to create a little flutter in my stomach.

Frustrated, I run a hand through my hair, but then I catch sight of my phone on the floor, charging.

What if I texted him? Why do I want to?

He's the only other person who knows what happened to me and he's the only one I've spoken to about it. But the waiting is making me anxious. I can't focus on writing, or getting back to my regular life, because the unsettledness of what I went through has formed an itch that's embedded itself into my nerves. Unable to satisfy it for the sheer ignorance of having no clue how to move forward. The desperate need for closure or *vengeance* is pointing me in River's direction.

I glance around the four walls in my office as my breathing picks up. Like they're closing in on me, I panic and rise from my chair. With a quick glance out the window, I see the sun is setting over the horizon, and I realize I'm destined to spend another night chasing sleep, so I may as well get a coffee and some fresh air.

I swiftly slip on my shoes, grab my purse, and head out the door. Typically, I'd walk to my favorite local coffee shop, because it's only a short distance down the street, but after everything that's happened recently, driving seems like a safer option. I've been going there for coffee since I moved into my townhouse a couple years ago. It's the perfect spot for those long days of writing on a deadline.

When I walk in, the fresh aroma of coffee grounds hits me and gives me a temporary boost of energy while providing a desperate hit of relaxation, too. I take my place in line behind a taller gentleman.

While I wait for my turn, I take in the surroundings—instinctively analyzing the place and the people inside. I take note of the amount of customers, what each of them are doing, and if anyone looks out of place. Growing up with a police officer as a dad, I've learned these behaviors but I'm even more diligent now.

"I guess they're out of vanilla scones," The man in a navy suit in front of me says. At first, I think he's muttering to himself but when I glance toward at him, he's looking straight at me.

I flash him a quick smile before turning my gaze away, making it clear that I'm not interested in small talk with a stranger.

"In case that's what you planned to order," he adds, gliding a hand through his greasy hair.

His sudden interest and demeanor raises the hairs on my arms and my stomach churns, putting me on alert.

There's something off about him, but I don't want to draw his attention, so I simply say, "I wasn't, but thanks."

"Of course," he replies with a leery smile.

Once he's done placing his order, I do the same before standing to the side and keeping my distance from him. But instead of getting the message, he moves to stand next to me, and I catch the faintest breeze of his scent.

Cherry cigar.

The smell triggers fear and familiarity, but it could simply be a coincidence. Cherry is a common tobacco flavor, so I'm probably being paranoid because of what I went through.

While we each wait for our orders, I can sense him watching me intently, and it sends chills up my spine.

Do I know him? Was he one of the men that took me? Does he recognize me?

He might not have been the one who raped me, but the strong cherry stench clung to him. One that almost made me gag when the other had finished and he leaned in and whispered in my ear, *"I'm next, so keep the pretty little pussy wet for me, darlin'."*

My heart rate skyrockets forcing me to take a breath. But I force myself to shake the thought away.

He couldn't. I was blindfolded and naked while being held chained to that bed.

"Rich!" the barista shouts as he walks up to her.

My eyes widen at the name.

*Rich...*Andrew said his name in the basement, but only out of anger since the guy with the cherry scent ejaculated all over my chest when he wasn't supposed to. No one was allowed to have me except Andrew. I vaguely remember hearing conversation about how he didn't want them to know what I look like or have me. Do the men take turns or something?

Could this be one of the men there that night?

Wetness gathers on my forehead and I swipe it away nervously while my mind grapples with the possibility.

He takes the paper cup from barista's hand and gives her a warm smile, as if they know each other.

"How's your dad?" he asks the young employee.

She continues working, but answers. "He's good. You know him, always working hard."

His shoulders straighten while his eyes shoot me a look before he responds. "That he does. Tell him I'll see him next tax season."

Tax season?

She chuckles. "I will."

"Have a good day, darlin'." He suspiciously looks over at me one more time before leaving the coffee shop.

No...it is him.

I know it.

Fuck.

I knew I should've stayed home. Why did I leave....

Swallowing hard, I attempt to keep the panic induced bile from rising up from the back of my throat.

When I see the barista coming to the counter with my drink, I rush over and interrupt her before she calls out my name.

"That's mine!"

Her expression brightens as she hands it to me. "Oh, perfect!"

I'm still reeling from being so close to one of my possible attackers, but I force myself to plaster a fake smile on my face and say, "I couldn't help but overhear, the gentleman before me mentioned he did your father's taxes?"

"Rich?" she says, grabbing an empty plastic cup and a tea pitcher. "Yeah, he's wonderful. We've known him forever."

My lungs constrict. "I'm actually new in town and looking for someone to help with my taxes."

"That's Rich Smith and he works at Stanford Accounting Services. I'm sure if you give them a call, they'll be more than happy to book an appointment for you. Say Haley sent you," she offers as she finishes someone else's order.

With my heart racing, I clutch the paper cup between my fingers. "Great, thank you so much."

"Of course," she tosses over her shoulder.

I hurry home, immediately returning to my office. I flip my laptop open and start searching the law enforcement databases for anything I can find on Rich Smith. Which, surprisingly, doesn't take me long. It appears that pervert has recently made partner of his accounting firm.

I spend the next few hours reading articles and pouring over the information I find in the county's database, my coffee long forgotten.

I skim through a few minor traffic violations before finding a domestic violence incident from a few years ago. The charges were later dropped by his wife, citing an attempt to mend their marriage. Then I find an address to a house not far from my own. And before I realize it, an intrusive thought is creeping into my mind.

Should I go to his house? Maybe humanize him in some way?

I want to know where he lives. If he is the monster I know him as, because, according to the barista, he's a *wonderful* guy.

Two separate lives. Two completely different personas. A

wife, and possibly kids? Driven by rage and now the answer for why someone who appears like a trustworthy member of society can do those heinous things is perplexing.

The sound of my phone buzzing startles me out of my spiraling thought.

My chest tightens with nerves as I reach for it.

UNKNOWN

Lux.

River. I haven't changed his name in my phone, because he is still unknown to me. Rubbing my lips together, I nervously tap out a response.

ME

Yes?

UNKNOWN

You're not sleeping, again.

ME

Why are you so obsessed with my sleeping habits?

UNKNOWN

Because that's what people do at night. They sleep.

ME

Not all people.

UNKNOWN

And what plagues your nights, Lux?

ME

You already know, River.

UNKNOWN

My team is working as fast as we can.

Rising to my feet, I move the curtain to one side, discreetly peering into the night. I easily find his parked car beneath the tree and wonder what he's doing when a small movement in the bushes across the street alerts me.

UNKNOWN

Hi.

I can't help but chuckle and close the curtains. If River is going to sit outside my house every night until his team takes *care* of those men in whatever way he's implying—which is still a mystery to me at this point—then he can tag along as I conduct my own research.

Instead of responding to his last message, I take a quick picture of Rich's address, grab my coat, and head out the side door that leads into the garage. I start the ignition, and plug Rich's address into my GPS, then pull out onto the street without a sign of River behind me—*yet*.

Less than fifteen minutes later, I'm pulling onto a wide suburban street lined with large bushy trees. With minimal street lights, common for this area, I pull over a few houses down, maintaining distance from Rich's home. After shutting the engine off, I stare at his light blue with white shutters two-story house. It looks perfect and quaint—no one would expect what type of person lives there.

And then, as expected, a black car quietly pulls up directly behind me. And I'm hit with both nerves and a small amount of relief knowing I have protection.

CHAPTER TWELVE

RIVER

Is it possible she's on to him already?

I only recently learned where the accountant's house was after Christian conducted thorough background checks on all the guys, but what is Lux doing here? I need to keep myself level and try to get as much information out of her as I can, before letting her know I know who the owner of this house is.

ME

Why did you come here?

LUX

I could ask you the same thing.

Before I can respond, I catch sight of her car door opening. It's not safe, what is she thinking?

In one swift motion, I exit my car and sprint over to hers and slide into her passenger seat. "What are you doing here?"

She yelps as her hand flies to the handle of the car, ready to escape.

I quickly reach over her, clasping my hand over hers to keep the door shut. "You're not leaving this car."

She whips her head around, the scent of lavender shampoo hitting my nostrils.

Leaning over the center console, my face is only inches from hers. I imagine feeling her breath on my lips, but the fabric on the mask prevents it. I need it, but oh, how I hate it right now.

"I'm protecting you."

"Or scaring me" she bites back.

It's unfortunate she's still intimidated by me since I'd never hurt her. But if she only knew how infatuated I am with her, she'd have every reason to be.

What is she thinking? What was she going to do once she got here?

I shake my head, my facial expression covered by my black mask. "We need to talk about this."

Her lungs take in a sharp rise. "Don't talk to me like you're in charge of me."

"Lux," I warn.

"What?"

"I asked you a question."

She tucks a loose hair behind her ear. "I came to check out the house of one of the men who took me. His name is Rich Smith."

"What makes you believe this is his house?"

Keeping her head down, she picks at her thumbnail. "I ran into him earlier this evening at a coffee shop."

"And he admitted to you he took you?"

Lux whips her head at me, fixing me with an irritated glare. "Of course not."

"Then how do you know, for sure?"

"I was there that night, remember?" she exclaims. "I knew

something was off about him, but he smelled like cherry cigars, the barista called him Rich, and he..." She trails off, a look of determination morphing her features. "He tried to make small talk with me, then when he grabbed his drink, he called the barista *darlin'*. The same thing he called me when I was captive."

I hate that she had to go through this, but I need her to remain safe and out of my way so the team and I can kill each of these men for putting her and the others through hell. I fight the urge to wrap my arms around her and take all of this away, but I still need to know how she found out where he lived.

"How did you find his address?"

"I overheard him and the barista talk about taxes, and when I told her I was new in town and looking for an accountant, she gave me his name. A quick law enforcement database search led me to his place."

Her research methods pique my interest. "Database?"

"My dad works for the police department, remember?" She pulls her lip between her teeth. My guess is he doesn't know she has access. Which surprises me, but also impresses me.

"And what was your plan once you got here?"

"I don't know," she admits.

Her answer irritates me, but how can I expect her to have a plan? She isn't a career criminal so I doubt this was preplanned. Lux is in survival mode and her impulsivity was driven by rage.

I rub my temples, burying feelings of agitation for her, potentially putting her life at risk. "What if he recognized you? You would have essentially delivered yourself to his doorstep."

"What was I supposed to do?" she sneers. "You refused to give me any information, so I had to get it on my own."

"I told you that my team and I are handling it. Nothing

good can come from you being a part of this." I sigh in exasperation, then lower my voice. "You're gonna get yourself killed."

"And why should I believe a man I barely know, who won't even show me his face?"

"It's better this way."

Her eyes flicker to mine, and her expression softens into sorrow. "Have you ever had something so horrendous happen to you that you're unable to move on from it?"

I debate telling her the truth, but seeing the look on her face, I simply say, "Yes."

"Then you understand that I can't return to my normal life, and trust you to take care of it for me."

I stay quiet, unsure how to respond. I want to tell her more of what I have planned to do with the guys who hurt her, but the less she knows the better.

When I don't answer, she faces me with a new determination. "They robbed me of who I was. I want myself back, River."

My eyebrows quickly furrow with confusion. "What are you implying?"

"I need your help."

My help?

"With what?"

Lux takes a deep breath before replying. "I want you to let me take them down with you."

"Absolutely not."

She'd get herself killed. Lux is a regular person, she's not a killer. The anger inside drives her to believe she can do these things, but is grossly mistaken on what type of personality it takes to be able to take a life—or what it does to a person once they do it.

"Why not?"

"Because it's not safe."

"You're already hunting them." Her throat bobs with a hard swallow. "And I deserve to avenge what's happened to me. All I'm asking is to be included."

I groan, running a gloved hand over the top of my cotton balaclava. I wonder if I should have just left her for the police to find. Because now, my curiosity in this woman got the best of me, and I unintentionally created another complication in my life.

"You don't really want any part of this. This isn't who you are."

The moonlight shines through the windows reflecting on the delicate features of her worried face. "You don't know me."

I breathe out, ignoring her question. "It's rage fueling you."

"What if it's not only rage? What if this *is* who I am?"

"Adrenaline," I say evenly, offering another explanation.

"Does that make me fucked up to want to pursue these men instead of hiding from them?"

The urge to comfort her is strong. Reluctantly, I give in and rest a gentle palm on her back, deeply understanding the torment that vibrates through her. "No."

"It's taking over my every thought," she whispers, leaning into my touch.

"Everyone copes with trauma in their own way. It doesn't mean there's anything wrong with you. It means you're not like other people."

"Is that a bad thing?"

"No," I admit softly. A rush of protectiveness floods my system, and the warmth of her skin—even through fabric—is enough to cause a tingling in my palm. My instincts are speaking again and I need to listen. I need to protect her anyway I can.

"What makes you certain?" She lifts her head from her hands to meet my eyes. They're pleading, searching for answers I'm not sure I can give. She doesn't wait for me to respond, but from the narrow slits in her eyes, I know she senses my apprehension. "I don't want to cry or be sad. And I can't move on. I need to be a part of this," she begs, her voice cracking. "Please, River."

The way my name falls from her pink lips again is enough to make me forget about everything, when suddenly a Mercedes drives by us and pulls into Rich's driveway. From across the wide street a few houses down, we watch as who I recognize is Rich steps out, carrying a black briefcase. As he approaches the front, a woman in a long dress wraps her arms around his neck and kisses him.

"That's him?" I state it in more of a question to see if she recognizes him.

"Yes," she whispers before chewing on the inside of her cheek.

The pain in her eyes is something that is familiar to me. The hunger and drive to take matters into your own hands and to bring on your own type of justice. To right the wrongs that have been done to you, feeds into this belief that you—and you alone are the only person responsible for your own outcomes.

Could I help her?

Or let her join Sebastian and me?

That would mean bringing her into my world, and I don't if either of us are ready for it.

"I'll think about it."

"Really?" Lux asks with a slight optimism in her voice. The sudden change in her demeanor and the hopeful sparkle in her eye almost brings me to my knees—a puddle at her feet willing to do anything she asks.

But wouldn't that go against what I'm trying to do by protecting her?

I nod once. "Now, go home. No other stop. I'll be following

you," I order, before slipping out of the passenger seat and heading back to my vehicle.

Once she's safely inside her townhouse, I take out my phone to send Sebastian a brief text.

ME

There's been a change of plans. Meet me in my office in 30 minutes.

Then I head back to the manor.

CHAPTER THIRTEEN

LUX

B y the time the heat from the late summer afternoon slips through the shutters, I wake from a restless sleep —which has become my new normal. After River escorted me home, he remained parked in his usual spot until I eventually crawled under the covers. The anxious energy continues to pulse through my veins, forcing me to spend the entire night staring at the backs of my eyelids.

Slipping out of bed, I make my way toward the window in my bedroom, anticipating he might still be there. But I find myself hit with disappointment when his car is no longer idling.

Sighing, I turn away. I should be terrified about what I asked him but I'm not. It's the only way I know how to move forward.

I'm desperate for revenge and closure, but truthfully, I simply want my life back. The ignorance of not understanding what I've asked to be a part of might be clouding my judgement, as River pointed out, but I don't feel any regret—*yet*.

The sudden vibration from my phone sends a flurry of

butterflies swarming into my stomach, but I quickly tamp it down.

I lean over to my nightstand and grab my phone, only to find that the message isn't from River. Not sure whether my disappointment is from the eagerness to join him or that I want to be in his presence once again.

STEVIE

> Dad's working another late night. Figured we could make him dinner rather than ordering out.

I hesitate for a moment, because I haven't seen either of them since last family dinner and I'd love to see my family, but I hate having to hide what happened to me from him and Stevie. It might be selfish of me since I could help with the investigation, but I know that my dad would never forgive himself if he knew I was one of the women who was taken and my sister would be wrecked with guilt if she knew it happened after she left.

I'm about to tell her I'm too busy, when I remind myself that this could also be the perfect opportunity to gather valuable information about the case that could help River and I.

I'm sure he has his own sources, but maybe it will help me offer him something.

ME

> That's a great idea. I should probably take a break from writing anyway.

STEVIE

> Awesome. I'll stop by the grocery store, then head over to your house.

I toss my phone to the side and fall back onto my bed, my gaze following the rotating fan for an unclear amount of time. I drift in and out of restless sleep before my thoughts no longer let me sit idle.

If I'm to do this with River, I can't be distracted by him. And although I still don't know what his face looks like, his energy and protectiveness is enough to give any woman's stomach that familiar flip. Not to mention how striking the darkness is in his eyes. I almost get lost in them every time they focus on me.

It isn't his usual time, but I can't help but wonder what's next. Am I supposed to wait around until he contacts me or should I reach out and ask what the next steps in our plan are?

I groan and rub a hand over my face. I'm not usually this impatient, but I hate sitting around and waiting.

Fuck it.

Snatching my phone, I immediately open our text thread and send him a message before thinking better of it.

> ME
>
> What's next?

UNKNOWN

Hello to you too, Lux.

I roll my eyes through a light giggle.

> ME
>
> Is this how it's gonna be? Me waiting around for you?

UNKNOWN

Yes. Patience, Raven.

Easy for him to say.

UNKNOWN

I'll be there tonight.

I don't have a chance to reply because there's a loud bang

at my front door. *Stevie.* I almost forgot she was coming over. Sprinting down the stairs, I open the door to find my little sister with a scowl on her face.

"Finally," Stevie snaps, her arms filled with reusable grocery bags. "I only knocked like a thousand times."

"Sorry, I was in the shower." I lie, stepping to the side.

She pushes her way in, making a beeline for the kitchen.

"Your hair isn't wet," she tosses over her shoulder.

"It wasn't hair wash day."

Stevie gives me a skeptical look, before letting it go and dropping the bags on top of the counter. She immediately gets to work, pots and pans clashing together as she preps in a frenzy.

"What are you making?" I ask, climbing onto one of the bar stools lining the other side of the kitchen island. "Dad's favorite. Lemon chicken with a salad on the side."

"Can I help you with anything?"

She gives me a pointed look. "We both know you can't cook. How about you get a glass of wine and unwind? I'm sure you're tired from all the writing you've done over the last week."

"I like the way you think."

While I sip on a glass of chardonnay, I watch Stevie spend the next hour cooking before we pack the food into glass to-go containers and then head to dad's station. I insist we take our own cars since I need to be free to go when I'm ready.

After greeting a few familiar officers, we head toward my dad's corner office that overlooks the bay. As soon as I round the corner, I come face to face with a tall dark-haired man in a navy suit exiting the office.

"Sorry!" I say, moving to the side.

From the corner of my peripheral, I see my dad rise to his feet. "Christian, these are my daughters, Lux and Stevie."

The man nods, his eyes focused on me. "Good to meet you both. Lieutenant Levinson and I were just finishing up."

"Nice to meet you as well." He captures my gaze, and immediately I feel like he can see through me.

Why am I being paranoid of everyone?

"Same," Stevie greets him, slipping through the door behind me.

With a slight quirk of his lip, he turns back to my dad. "We'll touch base again tomorrow. Thank you for your time."

My dad waves him off, then returns to his chair.

Kicking the door with my heel, I close it after he leaves. "He seems a little strange."

Stevie laughs. "Yeah, he was definitely trying to read you."

The tapping of my dad typing on the keyboard is the only response he gives us. I think nothing of it and start unloading the bags of food on his desk. "Brought you dinner, Dad."

A deep sigh fills the room. "He's Agent Sawyer from the FBI. They're working a case with us."

"Should have known," Stevie says. We start unloading the bags on his desk. "Anyway, we brought you dinner."

"Oh gosh, you girls are the best." His face lights at the sight of the food, which means this is most likely his first meal of the day. When my dad is deep into a case, he can go days without thinking about eating. "Thank you. I've been up to my eyeballs with this case. And with the FBI involved..." He trails off.

My movements halt. "The cabin?"

"Yeah," he says, removing the lid off his salad. "We've had many late nights."

"I worked on one of them two days ago," Stevie says with a horrified look on her face, but she quickly gathers herself, taking a bite of chicken. My sister never seems to be affected by her work, but whatever happened to those girls must have been rough for her to react that way. "I have another memorial scheduled later this week."

Sorrow fills the surrounding space, reminding me how grateful I am that River showed up when he did or I might have been one of the women visiting my sister's operating table.

"What always gets to me about these types of cases is how young these girls were. How close in age they were to you girls," my dad says, rubbing a hand across his chin.

Stevie and I exchange a quick look of understanding. It's always harder on our father when the victims remind him of us. The last time it happened when we were younger, he moved Stevie and me into the same room and slept on the floor between our beds for months, scared that we'd meet the same fate as the little girl who was found dead after being taken from her bedroom one night.

"We're safe," Stevie comforts him, placing her hand on top of his.

"I know, but no matter how long I do this, the gut punch of it all will never go away," he says.

Heat pricks the tips of my ears, anxiously waiting for an opening to try to get my dad to give us anything about the case.

"What do you guys have so far?" I ask, being a little blunt. My dad will think I want a few pieces of information as research for another one of my crime fiction stories.

"Always diving straight into business," Stevie quips.

"I'm only asking."

"Sure." She shoves a large piece of lettuce in her mouth.

I roll my eyes and turn back to my dad.

"We've gathered a few leads that indicate these perps are somehow connected to each other. But since the FBI is taking over the case, they're handling most of them."

"Like friends?" I propose, waiting to see if his theories and mine have something in common.

"I'm not sure yet." He pauses before giving me a warning glare. "And remember you can't use any of the specifics for your books. Got it?"

"Of course, Dad," I say. "You know I'd never jeopardize one of your cases."

"Well, after we went public with a few details from the case, we received an anonymous tip from someone who said his employer has been gone a lot over the last few months, going on long weekend camping trips up to the mountains."

"Hmm." I rub my lips together. "What does he do for a living?"

"He owns an insurance brokerage here in the city. The tipster said the behavior was out of the ordinary especially since his boss is typically at the office ten to twelve hours a day."

"Apparently, he was completely dedicated to his career, then a few months ago, something changed."

"And we know when someone's daily habits are drastically altered, it only means one of very few things," I start.

Stevie's eager finger flies into the air. "An affair."

"Drugs," my dad chimes in, twisting in his chair.

"Or murder."

The three of us are silent for a beat, before I ask, "Do you have an ID on the broker?"

I'm hoping he'll experience a lapse in judgement and fill me into the more classified details of the case, but I quickly realize I'm being optimistic since my dad never shares too many details about them unless they're closed or have gone cold.

As suspected, he shakes his head. "You know better, Lux."

I flash him an innocent smile. "I thought I'd try."

"I already tell you two too much." He sighs. "But sometimes it's nice to talk to someone about them."

Stevie and I smile. "Yes, we know, Dad."

We spend the next hour eating and chatting before I notice the time. River didn't tell me when I should be expecting him, but I'd rather be ready whenever that is. Right as I think to excuse myself and call it a night, my phone vibrates with a new message.

I finish stashing away the leftovers inside my dad's personal refrigerator next to his desk but stay crouched down to grab my phone from my back pocket. My eyes dart to my dad and sister to see they're engaged in conversation about the summer thunderstorm we're expected to get, before I open River's message.

> **UNKNOWN**
> You're not home. I'm here.

> **ME**
> I'll be back in twenty.

> **UNKNOWN**
> Say hi to the Lieutenant for me.

How does he know I'm here?

I shouldn't be surprised anymore, but it doesn't stop the unease settling in the pit of my stomach over what I've gotten myself into.

"I have to head out," I announce as I stand. "My book isn't going to write itself."

"Yeah, I should get back to work. This crime isn't going to solve *itself*." A rumble from a full belly laugh has Stevie and I exchanging side glances at his flat humor. He swipes a napkin across the corner of his lips and rises from his chair, his arms wide. "Thank you, girls, for stopping by to bring your old man dinner."

I step into his embrace first still a little uneasy about being touched, but giving him a bear hug before drawing back and hooking an arm around my sister. After a quick embrace, I swiftly exit toward the door. "Bye, Dad. Text you later, Stevie."

I've barely made it to my car when another text comes in.

UNKNOWN

See you soon.

No more hiding behind my keyboard with dark thoughts, or living day-to-day with an unfulfilled longing.

Fleeing from the double doors of the police station, my feet carry me into a night of unpredictability.

CHAPTER FOURTEEN

LUX

It feels like there's a ball of cotton lodged in my throat from nerves during the entire drive home, and it only becomes larger the second my eyes land on River's slick black car.

Once I pull into the garage, I wonder if I should leave the door open for him to come in or if I should meet him at this car. But after a quick debate on whether to text him, his black-cladded figure steps out onto the wet, shimmering street. He makes his way toward me, the heavy droplets of rain pelting down on him while he remains unfazed.

"Hello, Lux." He says my name with a smoothness that rolls down my throat, coating the dryness.

"River," I manage to return. My heart is pounding against the back of my ribcage.

"I brought you something." He lifts the sleek black bag clutched in his hand that I hadn't noticed before.

My pulse quickens, curious about what it could be. "What is it?"

"Let's go inside," he tells me with a steady confidence as he walks past me and toward the door like he's more familiar with my place than I am. With a weighted breath, I close my garage, then slip in front to remind him this is my space. His heavy footfalls are not far behind mine, and with each thud in the concrete floor my heart skips a beat. When we reach the steps leading to the door to the house, I pause for a moment and rethink about letting him into my home.

Am I inviting a monster inside?

I push the thought away, remembering how kind and gentle he's been, although dangerous at the same time—making him incredibly fascinating, but terrifying.

I open the door that leads into the dimly lit kitchen, and with a quick flick of the lock behind me, River and I both stand face-to-face in silence, except for the sound of rain wrapping on the windows. His black hoodie pulled up over his head, while his face is masked once again. Without a word, he walks into my living room and takes a seat on the couch. With one leg bent across the other he leans back and crosses his arms as if waiting for me to speak first.

The pounding from my heart now pulses through my eardrums from fear, or maybe excitement. I can't tell yet.

"I need you to put this on." His arm extends, handing me the black duffle bag.

Taking a step in stride, I walk from the hardwood floor onto the plush carpet.

With a slight shake, I reach out to take the bag from him. His fingers brush against mine, sending electricity shooting down my spine. Our eyes meet for a moment before both dart away.

I clear my throat. "What is this?" I ask, unzipping it.

"Your outfit for tonight. You need to change and we don't have a lot of time."

"Now?" I ask. "It's late."

"You asked if you could help, right?" When I nod, he continues. "Then, for once, stop asking questions and do as I ask. I'll explain after."

My brows furrow at his command. I hate being told what to do and the thought to protest eats at me, but I realize the faster I get changed, the closer I am to getting answers.

"Fine." I quickly step into the guest bathroom and change into the long-sleeved black sweater, matching joggers, and running shoes. I take a look at myself in the mirror, noticing a glow to my skin and feel a flutter in my chest. The exhilaration of it has me almost bouncing on the balls of my feet ready to jump out of my skin.

Running my hands along the fabric hugging my curves, a thought forms. These clothes are in my exact size. How does he know my size?

When I walk back into the living room, River's typing on his phone, lost in whoever he's talking to.

"Better?" I hold my arms out before doing a full turn for him.

"Perfect."

I can feel my cheeks heat at his comment, but I brush it away, trying not to read into it.

"How did you know my size?" I ask curiosity getting the best of me.

A light chuckles escapes from behind his mask. "Lucky guess."

"Lucky guess?" I repeat questioning his answer.

"Yes."

I take him at his word, but know better of it. So, instead get back to what is the purpose of tonight. Taking a seat next to him, but maintaining some space, I ask, "Now, where are we headed?"

River puts his phone away. "We're going to stake out your accountant."

My stomach somersaults, but I act like I have myself under control and can absolutely do this. "All right."

"He's the one we have the most information on at the moment, and he might be our best bet to help find their next location," he says.

"Next location?" I'm unsure about his comment at first, but then remember my dad mentioned he believes this group is trying to repeat the college sex ring from twenty years ago. Which means, they'll be capturing more women.

"I've already told you too much." River rises to his feet.

But on reflex, I grab his arm. Towering over me, his head whips around to capture my eyes. They flare with shock. "No. If we're doing this, I need to know everything you do."

He lets out a groan. "The guys we're tracking are Andrew Hughes, the heir to Hughes Hotels, Nolen Pierce, an insurance broker, Richard Smith, who you already know is an accountant," he continues to name them off. "And Duncan Jones, a security guard."

"How do you know all of this?"

"I have a contact in the FBI." *Of course, he does.* "Any more questions?"

I roll my eyes at him, recalling his frustration with me for showing up at Rich's house that first night. He knew Rich was one of the men the whole time. "I'm good for now."

"We need to leave," he mutters and slides his hand into mine, urging me to stand.

My hand tingles as it's tucked in his while he leads me through my own house, second-guessing every decision I've made in the last two weeks. I forego any previous fears I might have had and follow him to his car.

During the drive to Rich's house, a few stolen glances are exchanged, but we remain silent. My mind is running a million miles a minute, all while being hit with conflicting emotions.

What will happen once we get there? Do we stay in the car?

River's car slows to a stop a few houses down from Rich's, and then he turns to face me.

"What now?" I ask.

"We wait," he simply says.

My palms sweat. "Wait for what?"

"Criminals like to move under the security of the night. It's easier since they can go undetected."

I want to ask how he knows that, but at this point I'm learning River is not one to freely share information. He's more private and reserved, which makes sense with the bits and pieces I've picked up about his nighttime activities.

"I got some information from my dad about the case," I offer, hoping it opens him up.

"It's probably information I already know," he dismisses, his gaze firmly fixated on Rich's house.

"You are stubborn," I mutter under my breath.

"Excuse me?"

"You heard me. You keep shutting me out when we're supposed to be a team."

"You're not on my team, Lux. You asked if you could come along," he reminds me. "That's what I'm letting you—" River's hand flies up to his ear. "We're clear?"

What? Is he talking to himself?

I don't have time to clarify when he turns to me and says, "We're going in. My team told me the family is staying with friends for the night in Bellevue."

"You want us to break in?" My heart rate picks up.

"What do you think we came here for? His alarm system has been disabled, and I have men monitoring his moves."

"Wait, his alarm system? You can do that?"

"Yes, now follow my lead. Stay close and touch nothing without my saying so."

"All right," I reply hesitantly. I've never broken into someone's house before—never even thought about it. This is extremely risky.

"It's time to put your mask on now." He hands over a balaclava, exactly like the one he's wearing.

With a deep inhale, I fill my lungs with air preparing myself for what I'm about to do. I take it from him, open the bottom and quickly slip it over my face. Without checking where the eyeholes are, it slides on crooked.

"Let me help you." River's gentle hands are clasped over mine as he twists the front of the mask to position it into place.

As soon as the black fabric is no longer blocking my vision, my gaze is captured by two deeply mysterious eyes staring at me.

"Thank you."

"Of course." River's warm hand lingers on top of mine for a few moments before he pulls it away, but doesn't break contact. Then, he turns to step out of the driver seat where he proceeds to swiftly walk over to my side. With a soft opening of the door, he extends his hand. "Let's go."

I look at his gloved hand for a moment, before slipping mine into his. For some odd reason, my nerves instantly settle. Almost like I can trust he will take care of me and that he has everything handled.

We make our way across the street, up the short driveway, and through the back fence. I don't have the time to admire the tailored backyard with a swing set, pool, and mini putting green as River drags me beneath the covered patio to prevent us from being drenched even further from the downpour of rain.

River releases my hand to pull out a metal rod from his pocket, and I'm shocked at how disappointing it feels not to be connected with him anymore. With one swift motion, he unlocks the back door and we walk into a giant kitchen that looks like something out of an interior designer catalog.

CHAPTER FIFTEEN

RIVER

"Where should we start?" Lux whispers, standing flush against my back.

I'm not used to having someone tag along during this process and question my every move, but to my dismay her proximity is a comforting nuisance. Besides, the closer she is to me, the better—the safer she is.

At least that's what I keep telling myself.

"His office." I keep my voice low out of habit while scanning the house. It's the same typical coastal-style, like every other house I've seen in the neighborhood.

How mundane.

"You know we're the only ones here, right?" She matches my volume with a hint of sarcasm, but I ignore it, needing to stay focused.

We walk past family photos lining the walls, feeding into this fake reality that men like him hide behind—a facade of the perfect family man with two kids and a dog.

"These look like the stock photos inside the store-bought

picture frames," Lux remarks, her face only inches away from the glass.

"Do you have trouble with your vision?"

She peers at me with a raised brow. "No, what makes you say that?"

"You're like an inch away from the pictures."

"It's how I take in my surroundings. Focus on your own spying."

"Don't touch anything."

"I won't," Lux hisses, clearly unhappy with my constant hovering.

"Good."

She shakes her head in exasperation, but remains close behind me while I inspect each room on the bottom floor. I debate on whether to ask her for space because I can't seem to concentrate when she's rubbing against me like this, but we make it to Rich's home office before I get to think about it too much.

I barely make it inside the musty space when suddenly, a loud thud echoes behind me. I bend to grab my knife strapped to my ankle, but stop short when I see it's still only Lux and me.

"Sorry!" Lux shouts in a whisper, her hands up in surrender. I find a small table lamp at her feet. "I accidentally bumped into it."

"I told you not to touch anything," I snap, releasing my grip on the handle and rising to my feet.

Lux carefully places the object back onto the table. "It's not like I did it on purpose."

"I didn't say you did it *on purpose*, but you have to be more careful." I don't intend for my words to be chastising, but I'm used to working alone. The urge to protect her and my need for control of everything is putting me on edge.

Lux folds her arms across her chest. "How many times have you done this?"

My brow furrows at her question. "I've lost count. Why does it matter?"

"Exactly," she points out. "This is my first time so give me a fucking break."

"Are you two finished yet?" Sebastian's irritated tone chimes into my ear.

"Shut up," I say, blowing out an exasperated breath.

She cocks her head to the side. "Your earpiece friend, I presume?"

"That would be correct."

"Great. Shall we?" Lux asks, gesturing toward the room.

Now she wants to hurry?

I let her comment roll off me and refocus on what we're here to do. "You check that scattered pile of papers on the desk while I look at his computer."

"It's probably password protected."

"I can get into any device," I say.

"Of course you can," she quips, her eyes narrowing, and analyzing me like she did at those pictures earlier. "What do you do for a living, River?"

"I already told you, I work in tech," I say, settling into the leather office chair.

Lux starts sifting through the documents. "But that's not all you do."

"But that's all you're getting."

"Fine, but I'm going to keep asking until you tell me."

I shake my head with a small laugh. The brief glimpse of her attitude are annoyingly addicting. "I'm well aware."

I turn my attention to the laptop in front of me and connect my phone to its server, waiting for the program I designed to determine the password.

"His desk is such a mess which can only mean one of two things," she begins, her fingers combing through each document. "Either he's highly unorganized or he's trying to use this chaos as a disguise for something more important."

She keeps surprising me at every turn. Based on what I've learned, my instincts were correct that night at the cabin and there's more to Lux Levinson than meets the eye. She's highly aware and has a solid understanding of motivations. It only serves to remind me of my favorite poem by Edgar Allan Poe. *The Raven* is a bird who understands the behaviors of other species and uses that skill for its benefit, and Lux's keen profiling skills show she can sense human habits. Perhaps she has something stirring below the surface that is more profound than what she is letting on?

"Good observation," I praise.

"U-uh..." she stutters. "Thank you."

I slip my USB cord into the port at the base of the laptop, then launch the information application on my phone. Pausing before hacking into his computer with the generated password, I glance at Lux. Drinking in her body covered in black, I wonder if there's more driving her than pure rage.

We spend the next ten minutes or so going through Rich's computer and drawers. As to be expected, I find a few hidden files that immediately capture my attention because they're unmarked. With a quick flick of the mouse, I begin downloading each file onto my hard drive.

Lux breaks our rushed silence. "I think I found something."

I finish with the last hidden file before disconnecting my phone from the computer and walking over to the bookshelf she's crouched down next to. "What is it?"

"Look at this." Lux points at the calendar she's holding. It displays the current month of July, where most days are empty except for the first and third weekends of the month—

one of them being the day she was kidnapped. "Andrew's name is written on the weekend I was taken. It's not clear what his role is, but I remember Rich saying he was next when I was..."

She pauses, but doesn't have to say it for me to understand what she means.

Lux shakes her head and continues. "Either Rich was going to come back for me, or"—she points at the weekend where Rich's name is written—"this is supposed to be his weekend."

My brain reels at the idea of what this could mean. Wanting to confirm my theory, I gently grab the calendar from her hand and flip to the next month.

"Are these the other two guys you mentioned?"

"Yeah."

"Are you sure?" Lux asks. I can see the unease dripping out of her.

I wasn't planning on telling her this, but... "I've met them before."

"What do you mean you've met them?" She gasps.

"I met them at a club the night you were taken," I admit.

"Wait...you were at the—"

"Where did you find this?" I interrupt, knowing I've already said too much.

She points to the top of the bookshelf. "Up there."

Lux will figure out sooner or later that we saw each other the night at the club, but right now is not the time for a full explanation. Because once we get into why I was investigating Andrew in the first place, she'll find out who I really am.

Someone I don't ever plan on showing her.

"Why would he be so careless as to keep a paper copy of their schedule?"

"Maybe he thought it would be safer, since things are easier to track electronically nowadays."

"Sebastian?" I say, knowing he's been listening to our entire conversation. "I'm sending you a photo of it."

"On it."

I face Lux again, finding her sitting with her legs crossed on the hardwood floor. "We should get out of here."

"I'll meet you back at the house," Sebastian tells me before disconnecting from the device.

I stand and put everything back in its place before I offer my hand to help her up, which she eagerly accepts. I gently tug her up and our bodies almost touch, but then suddenly a crash of thunder rattles the windows.

Lux startles and buries herself into me. Enjoying her delicate touch, I wrap both arms around her and rest one of my hands on her back.

"It's only the storm outside," I reassure her.

"Oh...sorry." She backs away, apologizing, but I'm eager to hold her again. Her eyes flick upward, holding mine with a fiery gaze.

Intertwining my fingers through hers. "Let's take you home."

We sneak out of the house as easily as we came in—and without knocking over any furniture this time. Rain pours the entire drive to her townhouse. I guide my car to the front of her garage, turning the engine off.

I twist in my seat to face Lux. "Safe and sound."

"Thank you," she whispers, but she's not looking at me.

I'm not sure what happened between the moment she made the discovery and driving her home, but she appears dejected. Cautiously, I reach over, gently slipping two gentle fingers under the fabric of her mask before sliding it off, gliding along her soft skin.

"What's wrong?"

She sighs. "I hate knowing this is going to happen to other women."

"We'll make sure that doesn't happen."

Lux's large brown eyes dart up to mine. "How can you guarantee that?"

I can't tell you.

Letting the backs of my fingers glide along her arm. "Do you trust me?"

"I think I do. I know I want to." Her fingers pick at the loose cotton on her pants. "But I don't even know what you look like."

Despite being a controlled and calculated man, I can be impulsive at times, especially when it comes to her. She's different—unlike anyone I've ever met. Her presence draws me in to want to show her who I really am, even if she might not look at me the same way again. With that, I have agreed to let her be part of this process and at some point, she's going to see me without a mask, so what's the point in waiting?

I straighten back into my seat, breathing in deeply. Then without a word, I grip the bottom of my mask. From my peripheral I catch her unwavering stare, watching me reveal the features hidden underneath the fabric. When my face is free, I turn to her and notice a flush creeping up her neck and cheeks. It brings a lightness to my chest.

The air inside the car is thick with tension. Lux blinks a few times, then looks away.

"Now you know what I look like," I say, trying to break palpable energy.

Lux's head slowly turns back toward me, leaning over the center console. She brings her face only inches from mine. "You're exactly how I thought you'd look."

A light rumble of laughter catches me off guard. "I hope that's a good thing."

My eyes fall to her lips, so close her words dust my lips. "It is."

Fighting the urge to bring my mouth to hers, I back up a little. But to my surprise, she moves with me, maintaining the same distance.

She wants to kiss me. And, fuck, I want to kiss her too.

But I can't. I've already let her in too much, and if I'm not careful this would end badly for both of us.

"We should get you inside," I say, while my insides twist with anticipation of the regret of not kissing her as soon as I get back to the manor.

"Okay," Lux says. Slowly drawing back, I can feel the separation between us. She opens the door, but before stepping onto the street, she turns back facing me fully. "River, I do trust you."

And if I wasn't putty in her hands before, I am now.

After I watch her safety get into her house, I linger outside in my car for a little longer, finding the will to leave her.

CHAPTER SIXTEEN
LUX

In a lucid vision, vibrant with onyx and rose, River's massive body lays on me, pressing me into the frigid cement floor. Intertwined in an ocean of blood dripping from the walls, he thrusts into me. His elbows bent beside my head, while his delicious mouth peppers my lips and chin with soft, sensual kisses.

The ginger rays of dawn settling beyond the horizon set off my internal clock dragging me out of a restless slumber. *I dreamed of River last night.* Like I have over the past week since he dropped me off and we almost kissed.

The feelings still linger from that night we searched Rich's house when I was mesmerized by River's movements as he took off his mask. First, I caught a glimpse of his lips—they were plump and inviting, followed by his nose and finally those endless dusky eyes. If I hadn't been sitting in his car, my knees would have weakened, causing me to fall to the ground. I can still feel the unexpected sharp breath as my eyes traced his perfect bone structure and the light stubble on his chin. He looked no older than early thirties.

He should not have been hiding that face.

River has been outside my townhouse every night, and I've considered texting him multiple times as we get closer to what could be the plan for Rich's weekend, but I figure if he has news to share with me, he will. Not to mention, the last time we saw each other we had that moment, and with the dreams I've been having, I've found myself a little bashful—a feeling I know I will have to push aside now that we're sort of working together.

Sticky with sweat and in need of a shower, I roll off the bed. My toes sink into the cream shag rug at my feet and with a wiggle I enjoy the softness against my skin, but a quick vibration breaks me from the moment.

> **STEVIE**
> Can you pause writing for this evening? I need to come over.

> **ME**
> Sure. Is everything okay?

It's no secret that I'm the organized and levelheaded one between us. Stevie's impetuous and free-spirited nature gets her into some peculiar situations, and I'm certain this time is not any different.

> **STEVIE**
> Yeah, but I broke things off with Nick and feeling a little down.

> **ME**
> No more fuck buddy for little Stevie?

> **STEVIE**
> Nope. He got boring, and I got angsty.

I laugh to myself.

ME

You're growing up. I'm so proud.

STEVIE

Ha. Ha. Like you have any room to judge.
When's the last time you got laid dear sister?

I always hate acknowledging my sex life—or lack thereof, but even more now that I've fantasized about someone I definitely shouldn't be fantasizing about.

ME

What do you want for dinner?

I need to change the subject.

STEVIE

Always deflecting.

ME

Fine. I'm making you fish.

STEVIE

You can't cook and you don't even like fish.

Pizza.

ME

Veggie?

STEVIE

I'd never touch anything else.

ME

Great, see you soon.

After placing our order, I return my phone to my nightstand, then drag my feet to the bathroom. I take a quick shower, letting the hot steam wash away every lewd thought entering my mind—although it does very little to tame them. I throw on some cotton joggers and a light, long sleeved cut off workout shirt before I get a notification that someone is at the front door.

"You have a key," I shout before opening the door.

Stevie's dressed in identical joggers to mine but with a light summer sweater. "I'm aware, but you so lovingly told me you don't like it when I barge in."

"How thoughtful of you," I tease, making room for her to enter. I'm about to close the door behind her, but I can't help but glance outside into the shadowy courtyard, imagining River's dark figure lurking in corners, waiting for our usual meet-up time but I'm sure he isn't out here yet.

Shaking off the daydream, I finally close the door and follow Stevie into my living room. She falls into my couch, tucking her feet beneath her and wrapping herself in a cream colored woven blanket. "I'm full of many emotions."

I grab another throw from the back of the couch and take the spot next to her. "Why did you break things off with him?"

She lets out a heavy sigh. "He got *way* too obsessed, and honestly, twenty was a bit young, even for me."

I laugh at her revelation. "I recall telling you something like that."

"I know. I know." She twists a loose thread around her finger. "I'm worried I'll never find someone who accepts what I do for a living," she confesses, a vulnerability I rarely see in her.

I give her hand a gentle squeeze. "The right person will."

She returns my smile, but it doesn't reach her eyes. "I know. I might play off that I'm happy with being a free spirit..." She pauses." And I am, but sometimes it would be nice to be with someone who understands what it's like to *work* with dead people."

With a loving smirk, I say, "Wow. I'm proud of you for coming to that conclusion all by yourself."

Stevie picks up on my humor and tosses a pillow at me.

I laugh and throw it back.

"Enough about me and my pity party. How's writing going?" she asks, changing subject.

You'd think since I've been lying to her for over two weeks I'd get better at it, but I still struggle with hiding things from my sister. "Um, good." I stand and make my way to the kitchen to occupy myself while we wait for the pizza to get delivered.

"What's the story?"

My stomach clenches at the thought. The justice I plan to give myself—is nothing like what I've ever done before and certainly not something I'll be sharing with Stevie.

"You know I try not to plot too much." I reach for two wine glasses on the top shelf in the cupboard. "Wine?"

"I would never say no to wine."

"Chardonnay okay?" I grab the chilled bottle from the refrigerator.

"Works for me. How's your deadline?"

"Not doing well." I try to sound nonchalant, but I'm feeling anything but. "I'm finding it challenging to write the proper ending on this one."

"Yeah, I bet. You could always write in a detective like Dad. You know he becomes obsessed with a case until it's solved. That could be a quick way to wrap up the story."

"Not every case gets the justice it deserves," I quip. "Even Dad's cases."

She shrugs her shoulders. "Well, you're able to do it through fiction at least."

It's no longer fiction for me.

I make my way back into the living room and hand her a glass of white wine before returning to my seat. "That's true."

Stevie and I spend the rest of the evening finishing the bottle of wine while watching rom-coms and devouring a large veggie pizza before she retires to my bed for the rest of the night. Now that she's fast asleep I find myself downstairs, watching the clock until it reaches midnight.

River has been parked outside my house all week, but he hasn't attempted to communicate with me. It's 11:58 p.m., and my heart is in my throat anticipating his arrival, because tonight has to be the night we discuss next steps for Rich. My legs bounce endlessly because I sense we're running out of time to find out where Rich is going. Frustrated with having to wait for him to show up at my house, I don't like the feeling of not having some level of control in this agreement.

I glance down at my watch—12 a.m.—when a dark figure appears at my sliding door. The movement is steady and fluid behind the curtain, and although I'm aware it's him, that doesn't stop a bolt of fear from shooting up my back.

UNKNOWN
I'm at your back door.

I know.

I wait a brief moment to not seem too eager before heading to the back door.

"Hi," I say when I slide it open, a cool breeze swooping over my cheeks.

My eyes roam over him, remembering the dream I had. Heat creeps up my neck, moving to my cheeks which are on fire. Before he can see my reaction to him, I suck in a deep breath and try to fix my face.

Wait. He's not wearing a mask.

"Lux." My name rolls off his tongue and it doesn't help keep the dirty thoughts at bay. His eyes scan the room, before landing on the two empty wine glasses by the sink.

"Am I interrupting?" he states, slightly accusatory.

Do I sense jealousy in his tone?

"My sister needed some girl time. She's asleep upstairs," I explain. "Do you want to come in?"

"Sure," he says, brushing against me as he steps inside. Leather and ivory scents float into my nostrils and my eyelids fall closed. My body leans into him, craving to bathe in it.

Get it together, Lux.

I shut the door behind him, intently watching him move through my space. River heads over to the living room, casually taking a seat on the same couch with leaving some space between us.

"Any news?" I sit across from him, trying to play it casual, like I didn't melt into myself a second ago.

River leans back, bending one leg on top of the other. "My contact has a lead on where Rich's location might be."

I run my sweaty palms along the tops of my legs. "And where is that?"

"Thunder Ridge."

"Thunder Ridge?" I repeat, wondering if I've heard him right. I'm surprised because tales of the northern forest have circulated among locals for generations. Thunder Ridge is far from civilization. Filled with skyscraper pine trees, the area lends itself to locals which tales claim hikers have gone missing up there since the early nineties.

"He couldn't find anything at first, but when we looked into Rich's immediate and extended family, we found out that there's an estate there that remained in Rich's late great-aunt's name."

"What does that mean for us?"

"My team's working on locating the property since it doesn't show up on any maps."

"But it's already Thursday," I begin, lost in my own

thoughts. "Wait, this means we have to get to that cabin by tomorrow night."

"That's why I'm here."

"So what do we do now? What's the plan?"

A sly grin slowly crawls across River's face. "It's show time." My heart bottoms out at that this is happening. Excitement and anticipation pump through my veins. "I'll pick you up tomorrow evening at nine. My team will be on his tail, watching his every move until we get there."

I nod, my breath becomes labored.

River slides over to where I'm seated and slowly tucks a few loose strands of hair behind my ear. "I'll be there the whole time. You'll be safe, Lux."

I wet my dry lips, looking into his eyes and simply nod.

"It's not too late to back out." His voice softens as his hand comes to cup my cheek.

He wants me to change my mind.

But I can't.

I want justice as any person would, but River's right. I need vengeance. It's being driven by rage—a more powerful emotion.

I flip my head up, locking eyes with the only person who can help me complete this task—the only person who understands what happened to me and the only one willing to help.

With a powerful conviction, as much as the fury of a raging fire, I shake my head. "No, I want to do this. I *can* do this."

"I know," he says with a confidence that settles in my soul.

"Thank you."

River slowly removes his hand from my face, but I wish he'd put it back. "Now, let's go over the plan..." he begins.

While he explains how the night will go, I find myself captivated by his every word. He details most of it, but I can tell there are still aspects he'd prefer to keep me out of. Which I'm fine with at this point.

"There's one more thing."

"What is it?"

"You'll be moving in with me. I think it's the best way to guarantee your safety."

CHAPTER SEVENTEEN

RIVER

"I can't believe you're letting her come along," Sebastian scolds in disbelief, following closely behind as I rush into my office. Ever since he learned Lux will be joining us, there's been a new energy in the air.

"Is everyone in place?" I ask, ignoring his disgruntled attitude. I get that he's upset and I'd normally be weary too, but I still can't explain why I trust her, I just do. My instincts are usually right and they never steer me wrong, so this should be no different.

"You're avoiding the obvious, River," he presses.

I settle behind my computer, checking that all five men assigned for tonight's operation are where they need to be. Each member of the night has specific assignments, including securing the location, standing watch, and providing backup if needed. Sebastian supervises the crew and ensures the logistics of each kill are perfectly coordinated.

"We don't have time for this. Did you check in with your men or do I have to do your job?"

"God, you're such an ass." He lets out an exasperated

breath. "I've already touched base. Hayden is stationed at the bottom of the hill, Apolo and Levi are covering the midpoint up, and Ace and Oliver are guarding the perimeter of the rental house."

"See, wasn't so hard, was it?"

"Fuck you," he replies then starts to march out of my office, but before he leaves, I call out his name.

He flashes me his middle finger, but looks at me over his shoulder. "What do you want?"

"Come on." I stand, readying to apologize. "I'm sorry, okay. You're right. I know she shouldn't be coming, but I can't say no to her."

"That's because you're thinking with your dick," he challenges. "Which is not like you."

He's right and this situation is confusing for me too, but it's either keep her close or risk her endangering herself. And I can't let that happen.

"I should probably tell you...I told her it would be better if she were to stay at the manor."

His eyes widen. "Here? You want to bring her here?"

I nod. "I need to know where she is and what she's doing at all times."

"Unbelievable." Sebastian shakes his head in disbelief.

I'm acting out of character and it's throwing him off, but I can't blame him. Sebastian has never seen me make such risky decisions. "I know what I'm doing."

"What did she say?"

"She was a little apprehensive, but open to it."

"Are you sure?" He glances at the wall of screens, specifically at the one still displaying the inside of Lux's house.

She's sitting at her desk, staring out the window. Waiting for *me*. I peel my focus away from Lux and meet my cousin's gaze head on. "Yes."

"You know I disagree with all of this?" he clips.

I slap a firm hand on his shoulder. "Yes."

"Well then, let's get this fucking show on the road." He shrugs it off.

I slide my phone from my pocket and send her a message.

ME

I'll be there in twenty. Wear what I dropped off last night.

A response comes through immediately.

RAVEN

I'm ready.

It felt appropriate to change her contact name to Raven.

My lungs constrict reading her response, because the time has finally come. After what felt like countless hours of research from the files I stole from Rich's hard drive, Sebastian and I were able to locate an abandoned log cabin which we believe will serve as the next location.

I've briefed Hayden on the plans and let him know what Lux's role will be. She'll stay with him in the vehicle a safe distance away, until we've secured the location and Rich.

AFTER SOME PROTESTS FROM LUX—BECAUSE SHE FELT LEFT OUT OF AN integral part of the project—she's waiting impatiently down the hill in a car with Hayden while the rest of us clear the house. She's eager, which I respect, but doing what we do is not something that develops overnight. It takes time, and she must wait because I will only include her when I feel she can handle it. And if that means going slow, then she'll have to save her push back for something else. Once we've secured Rich and I'm comfortable bringing her into the kill, I'll call for her.

I'm the only one who can keep her safe, and I'm determined to do it while giving her what she needs. But I can't deny the pride I feel at being able to do this for her.

"Keep an eye on Lux," I whisper to Hayden through my earpiece. Sebastian and I have our guns drawn, pointing down a long hallway of the cabin.

Getting into the cabin was a lot easier than I expected. With how much money Andrew has, I'm surprised at how little he's invested in proper security. There was only one guard watching the front—which one of my men took care of—and the rest of the property would seem deserted if it wasn't for the sound of sheets wrestling and metal clanking coming from down below.

"Don't worry, River, I've got her with me in the car," Hayden replies through the earpiece. "She's a little antsy, but waiting safely."

"Of course she is," I respond, keeping my voice low.

He chuckles.

"But I don't want her out of your sight until the house is cleared and Rich is securely in my hands."

Sebastian and I take extra time to clear the house, double-checking every closet and potential hiding area. There is no room for error as the stakes have grown exponentially since Lux is involved.

"Yes, of course," Hayden responds.

The old wooden floor creaks softly as our boots move through each space. With Sebastian at my back, we round the last doorway into one of the bedrooms. I freeze in place.

Sebastian comes up to my side, and from the corner of my

eye I see him cock his head back toward the kitchen. Letting him take the lead, I follow him until he reaches the door beside the refrigerator.

He turns his head back for me to confirm what he's thinking.

I nod and mouth, *The basement.*

We're about to breach the door when suddenly a figure comes right at me. With an aggressive push, I'm slammed into the nearby wall.

"*What the fuck?*" I yell.

Sebastian grabs the guy from behind as I yank the attacker's arm and slam their front against the opposite wall, his face plastered against the wood panel.

"Did he pop out of that pantry behind us?" Sebastian's words come out labored as he's out of breath from the brief scuffle.

"Must have." I keep my forearm pressed into the back of my attacker's neck.

"Who the fuck are you?" he grits out, and I immediately recognize him.

Richard.

"Just the man we're looking for." I rip off my mask so he can see catch a glimpse of my face from where his head is smashed against the wall.

"Thompson?"

His shock quickly transforms into anger, his lips curled into a sneer. "What are you doing here? It's not your weekend."

I smile wide. "Good to see you again, my friend."

Richard doesn't have the chance to respond when Sebastian slams the barrel of his gun into the back of his head. Like a boulder plummeting from a hill, Richard falls to the floor.

Sebastian crouches down, leveling his eyes with our victim's face. "You want me to grab this sack of shit or you?"

"I'll do it, but check the basement first." I want to deliver him to Lux myself.

Jumping to his feet, he descends the steep stairs.

"Holy fuck," He calls out with disgust, then the rapid thud of his boots make their way back up.

"What is it?"

"There's an entire set up." He pulls off his mask and uses his arm to wipe the sweat from his forehead.

"He was prepping?"

"Looks like it. You should take a look."

I sigh. "Let's handcuff him."

Sebastian bounds Rich's hands behind his back. When he's done, I hoist the piece of shit over my shoulder and make my way down to the basement.

The second we clear the low ceilings, I'm face-to-face with a similar scene I saw almost two weeks ago, but this one is still clean. Four wrought iron beds spaced out along the back wall, with a pair of handcuffs lying on each bed prepped with clean sheets.

"Fuck, the bastard's heavy," I grunt, throwing his body onto one of the beds.

My eyes flick to the sink, then to a metal medical table where a number of tools lay ready to use. Something I'm sure will come in handy for us now.

"Make sure he's secure," I tell Sebastian. "I'm going to get Lux."

"Already on it," he says. "But hurry, we don't have much time if we're going to do this and get out of here before daylight."

I ascend the stairs by twos. "We got him. Now the fun begins," I tell the guys through my earpiece.

"Are you heading to grab Lux?" Hayden asks.

"Walking out now."

As I approach the car, I see Lux's large brown eyes wide and hungry. And her excitement fills my chest with pride.

"We got him," I say to her as I open the passenger side door. Lux is covered in black from head to toe, looking incredible but not without a silent fear surrounding her.

Her breath hitches at my admission, but she remains calm. "Okay."

"If you want to do this, you need to come now before he wakes up."

Lux hesitates for a second before climbing out of the car. She seems extremely nervous, understandably. Before I can think too much about it, I grab her hand and give her a tight reassuring squeeze. Her eyes flick up to mine and there's a look there I haven't seen before.

"I'll be with you the whole time," I tell her softly. When she nods, giving me a small smile, I lead her through the house and down to the basement.

I've never brought someone else who is basically an outsider into my world before. I don't plan to have her participate, and my hope is that she will get her satisfaction by witnessing Rich take his last breath.

"How bad is it?" she whispers as we descend the stairs.

"They've only set everything up."

A short gasp escapes her once we reach the bottom, and I give her hand a comforting squeeze to let her know she's not alone.

I'm focused intently on her every movement as she takes in the chains and medical tools, and finally slides across the room to Rich, handcuffed to one of the beds. I've seen my fair share of jarring scenes—as I'm sure she has with growing up her lieutenant father and with writing crime—but nothing can prepare for one you're connected to.

"We have a present for you," Sebastian says, standing next to Richard who's already coming back to consciousness.

Lux stiffens beside me, her grip tightening around my hand.

"What the hell are you doing, Thompson?" Richard spits out when his gaze lands on mine. He eventually notices Lux's presence beside me and he turns his wrath on her. "And who the fuck are you?"

I almost speak first, but hold back giving Lux a chance a respond.

She takes a few steps toward him, slow but with more confidence than a moment ago. "Don't remember me?"

His face contorts in disgust as he brings his attention back on me. "You brought a woman into this?"

I want to punch him, but I keep my calm.

Lux can speak for herself.

Her eyes dart to Sebastian, then to me, before returning to Rich. Knowing she's safe with us around to step in if she needs it, she approaches the side of the bed. I'm taken back when she bends, bringing her face only an inch away from his.

"Remember me now?" she taunts.

I watch in fascination as she slowly reveals her identity to him.

Rich's eyes widen in shock. "You?"

"The woman from the last cabin. The one you left to die with the others."

His face transforms into something more sinister. "You were the one Andrew wanted. He had his eye on you the entire time we were at the club."

I catch the sharp rise and fall of Lux's chest, but she remains in control of her emotions. "Yes."

Rich chuckles. "Andrew was so protective of you. I was

supposed to be learning from him that weekend, but all he let me do was paint your pretty little body."

Her shoulders square as she swallows hard.

How long I will let this go on before I intervene?

But he seems to volunteer useful information. My gaze flies to Sebastian, who raises his hand in the air as if trying to settle me.

"What do you mean Andrew picked me out at the club?" she asks.

His upper lip arches with annoyance. "When he saw you on the dance floor, he about lost his shit. Said his plans were about to get sweeter."

Did he know something about Lux?

Was she not just a random woman they picked up?

"What does that mean?" Her tone becomes rushed. She might be losing her composure.

"I was on my way back to the cabin to finish you off, even if Andrew instructed to leave you alive." Rich licks his bottom lip.

They left her alive on purpose?

Everything goes black around me when my knuckles collide with the side of his face, sending his head whipping in the opposite direction, and blood splatters the wall.

Lux yelps, throwing her hands over her mouth, but doesn't retreat.

"Where is the next location?" I demand.

"Why would I tell you, Thompson?" he snaps.

"Answer the fucking question!"

"Hey." Lux places her hand on my arm, attempting to calm me.

I clamp my eyes shut, then regain my wits again. "Tell us where the next location is."

"You were supposed to be in on it. Did you already forget that no one knows the location until Andrew tells us? He didn't make a move, so I picked my own place. Besides, what is this? What are you trying to do?"

"Making sure you don't hurt any more women," Lux intervenes in a delicate voice.

"Oh yeah?" He clips. "Was this your plan all along, Thompson?"

"Not only his," Lux says. "Mine too."

"Pussy whipped." He chuckles under his breath.

I swing my arm around, clocking him right in his jaw again. A sharp crack fills the room as crimson dots the white sheets. When his head snaps back, I grip his cheeks, bringing my face close to his. "Either you tell us the next location, or you're getting a bullet through your brain."

"So, she's going to kill me?" he mocks, his eyes move in Lux's direction.

"No, I am," I say.

Sebastian steps forward with a smirk. "And I'm going to make sure there are no traces of you left behind."

"I knew from the moment Andrew introduced you to us you were a fucking piece of shit." Rich's nostrils flair. "With all the money and power you have, you could have been running this entire operation."

I turn to Lux, tired of hearing him talk. "Are you ready to witness one of the men who hurt you take his last disgusting breath?"

With her hands now tucked into the front pockets of her hoodie, her eyes bounce between mine and Rich's. "Yes," she says without hesitation.

"You're going to regret this, Thompson," he warns.

I ignore him and say, "Cover your ears, Lux," right before pulling the trigger.

A short yelp escapes from her as soon as the shot fires. I slide the gun back into my waistband, then pull Lux into me. I don't give her time to react, but to my surprise, she melts into my embrace. Relief washes over me.

"One down. Three to go." Sebastian leans against the wall with his arms folded across his chest.

"The rest of the guys will be expecting the cabin to be ready for the girls. Text them from Rich's phone to call it off," I tell Sebastian as I bury my nose into the top of her head. She smells like lavender...*and mine.*

Sebastian grabs the phone from Rich's front pocket and then holds it up to his face to unlock the screen. "You got it."

With a tight hold, I keep Lux tucked into my chest until the night crew comes to clean everything up. Then I put Lux into my car and we leave, on our way to Thompson Manor.

After tonight, I'm more sure than ever the best way to keep Lux safe, is to keep her there.

CHAPTER EIGHTEEN
LUX

I just witnessed a man's murder.

The realization has my head spinning, and I find myself mildly shaking from the adrenaline of it all. River's tight embrace after Rich died was the comfort I needed in that moment, but what I didn't realize, is that as soon as we parted I'd wish to be in his arms again.

It didn't take long for, what River refers to as, the night crew to come in and begin cleaning up the scene at the cabin. Which meant we didn't have to stand in awkward silence for long before he was helping me into his car to leave.

I quietly rest my head against the passenger window while we're on the way to his house. When he first mentioned me staying with him, I immediately declined. Sure, I understood his reasoning, but it was like I needed to prove that those men hadn't taken away even more of my life. But after watching Rich die tonight, I know it's the right choice because of what he's done.

After a short drive down a desolate road, we reach a security gate where River waves at the guard standing watch in a low tower. Then we proceed up a long and windy hill lined with tall trees not too far from the expansive wooded area that makes up Thunder Ridge. His property is extremely large, with one side of the outer perimeter backing up to the forest line.

"You know this is for the best, right?" He turns onto a driveway that leads underground. At first glance, the ample, lit-up space holds more cars than I can count, including models I've never seen before.

"Yes." My eyeballs subtly move from one side to the other. I try squeezing them shut, hoping to alleviate the nausea in my stomach from the rush of adrenaline that's kept me going all night.

River parks in a spot closest to an elevator, and within seconds Sebastian pulls his black four-door SUV next to us. "Until all this is over, you'll need to stay here."

I watched River kill a man tonight, and despite Richard deserving it, River didn't even flinch. I'm not oblivious to the fact that he's done this before—and I'm sure it's been multiple times, based on what he's alluded to.

"I know." I prepare myself to exit the car, but my limbs are so fatigued I don't know if I can even make it past the door.

"Let me help you," River says as he opens the passenger door, and in one swift motion he scoops me from my seat of the car, and I wrap my arms around the back of his neck.

The delicious scent of leather with a hint of spice washes over me, and without thinking too much into it, I tuck my head into his neck.

"Are you taking her to the East Wing?" Sebastian asks him.

"Yeah. She'll have plenty of room there," River replies.

The three of us enter the elevator together. I can't fully make out their hushed conversation, but I can tell Sebastian is wary of my involvement, which causes tension between them. All of a sudden, River's movements slow, prompting me to pull open my eyes to see a vaulted ceiling with ornate wooden walls spread across a dimly lit hall.

"This will be your bedroom," he says, lightly lowering me onto a soft bed. The tip of his nose grazes my cheek as he pulls away, leaving a tingly sensation across my skin. "How are you feeling?"

My heart skips a beat from our closeness. "I'm still a little shaky, but I'll be okay."

"Do you..." He pauses, a piece of his dark hair falls to his forehead, and I get the urge to brush it away, but hold back because I've already been too vulnerable. "Do you want me to stay?"

My stomach fills with butterflies, replacing what had been nausea a short time ago. "Yes."

River draws back and sits on the bed next to me. "Okay, I'll stay with you for a bit."

"Thank you."

"Do you need anything?" His eyes drop to my bottom lip as I pull it between my teeth.

Only one thing comes to mind. "I'd love a shower."

"I can start one." River walks into an attached bathroom that's larger than the entire bottom floor of my townhouse. The light sound of water echoes before River comes back into the room. "There should be everything you need in there, but if anything's missing, just ask."

As I push on the mattress, I extend my arm to prop myself into a seated position. The ringing in my ears has lessened, but my body is still heavy with exhaustion.

River is instantly at my side, sliding his arms underneath me. "I've got you."

Once inside the steamy room, he gently places me on a bench outside of the shower before lowering to his knees. "Can I help you?"

I nod, and the hot steam is thick around us, only relaxing me more.

River unties my shoes first, then removes them. His fingers glide along the arch of my feet, sending chills up my leg. River is a dangerous man, but seeing him on his knees in front of me, with a gentle, commanding presence is jarring.

His demeanor is warm but confusing at the same time.

How can he be two different people at the same time?

There is much more to him than what he shows others.

"Tell me something about yourself, River," I say, hoping to learn more about this mysterious man who has practically tripped and fallen into my life.

"What do you want to know?"

"Anything."

His intense gaze captures my eyes. "My dad used to love building things."

Used. Past tense.

"Is he not around anymore?" I ask carefully. He's clearly not one to share personal details.

"No."

"Was this the home you grew up in?"

"The manor wasn't built until after..." He trails off, a distant look on his face.

"After what?" I softly rest my hand on his.

"After Sebastian and I lost our parents. We were young when it happened."

Sadness moves through me on his behalf, but before I can offer my condolences he changes the subject.

"You handled yourself well today."

"It seems like I've dreamed all of it," I say.

"A *dream*?" He cocks his head to the side. "Or a *nightmare*?"

If I say nightmare, behind it lies the comforting expectations of what is normal. If I tell him it was a dream, that isn't what someone with a moral compass would say. But because it seems my internal morality is in question after tonight, I decide to be honest.

"I haven't fully processed what happened, but at this point it's more of a dream."

With a subtle smirk, River stands. "You're not like anyone I've ever met."

"Is that a good thing?"

"It's an irreplaceable thing," he says then his expression shifts. "After you're cleaned up, get some rest, Lux."

River turns, giving me his back, then without pause, he abruptly leaves the bathroom.

Left with my own thoughts, I sit for a minute with the desire to go after him. I crave to be in his presence. I've only scratched the surface of the darkness in River's eyes and the depth of what's within him. He's been doing what we did last night for some time, and River Thompson is not simply a billionaire tech guy, he is something else entirely. I assume it has something to do with his parents and their tragic death.

How many others have there been? Has he helped other women like me?

I remove the rest of my clothes then step under the stream. Although the water is scorching, the burn feels like heaven. It cascades over me while simultaneously calming every overactive nerve from the adrenaline. Clutching my shoulders, I curl myself into the stone wall in search of more comfort.

After a few minutes, I scrub my entire body from head to toe then get out of the shower right as the sun shines through the thin slit in the heavy black curtains. I walk out of the bathroom in a thick plush robe and realize I don't have any clothes here, but then catch sight of a small bag on the bed that wasn't there when we got to the room.

Zipping it open, I find a few pairs of my own clothes and a piece of folded paper.

I grab the note and immediately read it.

> Lux,
> Here are some of your clothes until I can have a personal shopper visit you. Sleep well.
> River

My heart skips a beat. A thoughtful gesture, one I'll thank him for at another time because I need sleep.

Pulling out a pair of pajamas, I get myself dressed, then crawl under the oversized comforter. The softness of the mattress cradles my sore muscles, sending me into a deep sleep.

CHAPTER NINETEEN

LUX

My eyes open in the late afternoon after the most restful sleep I've had in weeks.

I grab my phone, hoping to have heard from River, and excitement fills my chest when I see a missed message from him, but the feeling quickly dissipates when I read it.

RIVER

Good evening, Lux. I hope you slept well. The personal shopper will be here soon with clothes for your choosing.

It made sense for me to change his name, since I actually know him now. He's not completely *unknown* to me anymore.

Confused with how he abruptly left last night and the formality of his messages, I toss my phone to the other side of the bed. Feeling like I'd like to explore the house because I can't stay locked in this room, I decide to head out.

I walk over to the floor-to-ceiling windows that span the entire far wall in the bedroom. Gripping the corner of the blackout curtains, I push them open, and to my surprise, a romantic garden is revealed. Lush green grass lines a small stone pathway while thriving emerald vines crawl up the side of a far wall. The space looks cozy but expansive. My eyes find a small white bench tucked into the corner under an arbor, before sliding over to a stone fountain surrounded by white rose bushes. *It's beautiful.*

I slip on my shoes and head out the bedroom door into a long hallway. I quietly round the corner into the great room, expecting to see a door to the back somewhere since the gardens looked like they could be entered from a short distance down the hall.

Suddenly, a masculine voice says my name from behind. "Lux."

My hand flies to my chest. "Sebastian, you startled me!"

"River wanted me to give this to you," he says without a greeting and hands me a white box from under his arm.

"A laptop? I already have one."

"River said the one you have is shit." When he sees the look on my face, he adds, "His words, not mine."

Unsure about the gift, I take it, not wanting to turn down a kind gesture. "All right."

Sebastian gives me a curt nod and glances behind me to where my bedroom door hangs ajar. "Going somewhere?"

My ears prick with heat, sensing his suspicious question. "I saw gardens outside my window and was going to check them out. I hope that's not a problem."

"Suit yourself. I'm headed to the kitchen."

At the mention of the kitchen, my stomach growls with hunger. "I should probably grab something to eat as well. Do you mind showing me where it is?"

"Sureee," Sebastian draws out, like my request bothers him.

I shrug it off. I'll only have to be here until we've taken down all the guys.

He gives me his back and walks away without checking to make sure I'm behind him. Taking off at a measured pace to make sure I don't lose him, I do my best to check out in the surroundings as we pass a great room, foyer, and elevator with one entire side of the house comprising floor-to-ceiling windows, lending to a perfect view of the tall evergreen trees of the forest.

We finally approached the large restaurant-style kitchen with top of the line appliances, and there's an older woman with weathered skin and kind eyes sitting at a round wooden table next to a large bay window. There's also a dark haired man in a chef's jacket behind a large island chopping vegetables and placing them into containers.

"Good evening, dear," the woman greets us.

"Good evening," I say, unsure of who she is.

She gives me a bright smile and introduces herself. "I'm Mae. River and Sebastian's aunt."

Their aunt lives with them?

River mentioned last night his parents were no longer around. Maybe she stepped in after they passed.

I return her smile. "I'm Lux. It's nice to meet you."

"River said you'll be staying with us awhile."

Does she know *why* I am here?

"Yes, and thank you for allowing me to stay. This home is beautiful."

"Wish I could take credit. River and Sebastian designed it right after finishing high school." She sips her coffee. "I'm only in charge of their calendars."

"She's being modest. She manages everything around here," the chef chimes in then extends his arm. "Hi, I'm Ben Randell, their personal chef."

"Lux Levinson," I say my name and reach out to shake his hand. "It's great to meet you."

"What can I make you to eat, Miss Lux?" Ben tosses a rag over his shoulder.

Chewing on my bottom lip, I'm unsure what to say. I've never had a personal chef cook for me before. Not wanting to be rude, I settle for the first thing that comes to mind. "How about avocado toast?"

"With eggs?"

"Could they be scrambled, please?"

He smiles. "Breakfast for dinner? You got it."

I respond with a smile before turning my attention outside. My eyes squint to get a better look at the beautiful black bird. It's perched on a branch right outside the window. It's feather shimmer with an evening mist.

"Is that a raven?"

"Yes," Mae replies without looking up from her computer.

"He practically lives here," Sebastian answers despite not glancing over either. "He usually hangs out outside River's office window."

"I've lived in this area my entire life, and I don't think I've ever seen one up close before." I admire how the bird's onyx feathers shimmer under the morning sunlight, and I think of my favorite poet's—Edgar Allan Poe—poem, *The Raven*, and how he's inspired so much of my writing style.

Mae walks over to the marble island where I've been standing. "Take a seat," she says, pulling out a high back leather chair.

I oblige and take a seat right as Ben places a plate of food in front of me.

"Miss Lux," Ben says my name sweetly. "Avocado toast with scrambled eggs."

My mouth waters at the sight. "This looks amazing. Thank you."

"Enjoy." He gives a polite nod then turns to Mae. "Would you let Mr. Thompson know that his *breakfast* is in the refrigerator and remind him that I'll be back around eleven p.m. to go over next week's menu."

Why did the chef refer to River's food as breakfast when it's dinnertime? And why would he come so late?

"Of course," Mae says as the chef bends to give her a quick kiss on the cheek. "If he ever gets up."

It seems River and I have more in common than I thought.

"It was wonderful meeting you, Lux Levinson," Ben tosses over his shoulder while walking out of the kitchen. "I'm sure I'll see you tonight!"

"Thanks again," I call out, but he's already gone.

"So, you're River's aunt?" I ask awkwardly as I start eating. Making small talk for someone who sits behind a desk for a living is not easy, but I do it anyway, wanting to know more about River and his family.

"And Sebastian's," she says, winking at him.

"Yes." Sebastian's tone is clipped, and I can tell he's brushing off a potential conversation with me.

She smiles and lovingly pats him on the shoulder. "Don't mind his grumpiness, he has a hard time trusting people."

I understand what that's like.

A silence settles around us for a beat and I can't help but wonder if she's also involved in their night operations.

I take a bite of my toast. "So, you help run every aspect of their lives?" I try to get more information since River is so reserved.

"I do. The three of us have become close over the years."

The conversation I had with River last night comes back to

me. I turn to Sebastian. "River told me about what happened to your parents. "I'm sorry for your loss, too."

He mutters something under his breath before turning to his aunt. "I'll be in my office if you need me," he tells her before grabbing a premade parfait from the refrigerator and leaving the kitchen.

The old woman lowers her thick-framed glasses from the top of her head before startling herself. "I almost forgot. The personal shopper dropped off some samples for you to try on."

My heart picks up. "Really?"

Her rosy cheeks beam. "Yes! Let's go take a look."

"Wow. Okay." I shove the last bite of avocado toast into my mouth, take a hefty drink of the ice water Ben had given me, and jump off the chair.

"They're in here." Mae grabs my arm, leading me into the main foyer where four large racks of clothes are waiting.

"Are all these for me?" I ask, stunned.

She nods. "Yes. Try on everything and then you can keep what you like. We'll send the rest back to the store."

"Pick the ones I like?" I repeat, confirming I heard her correctly.

A wide smile appears on her face. "Yes, dear. Whatever you want. River will get it for you."

I feel my eyes grow wide as I stare at the beautiful colors and materials.

Mae senses my shock and rests a gentle hand on my back.

"Let's take these to your bedroom." she suggests.

"Okay."

Mae and I each grab two racks and roll them down the hall of the East Wing and into the bedroom. As soon as the clothes are placed to the side of the room, Mae turns to me.

"So, Lux..." Her voice is filled with empathy while her

expression softens. "You're one of the women from the cabin, aren't you?"

My heart falls from my chest, forcing a sharp breath.

"Um, what?" My eyes flutter with shock.

Mae lifts a decorative shopping bag of undergarments from the shelf under the rack and places it on the bed. "Nothing in this house happens without my knowledge," she says. "That includes their nighttime projects."

"You know?" My pulse picks up.

"They were young boys when their parents passed, and yes, it changed them both, but River took it especially hard."

There's a million questions running through my mind, but I know better than to pry. So I settle on saying, "I can't imagine."

"They say time should heal all wounds, dear. I just hope it does for him." She sits on the bed and eyes me. "I also know River has been spending every single night outside your house keeping watch since the moment he took you home."

My stomach flutters at what she's admitted about River.

"Well, I've said too much." She's silent for a beat before her eyes flick to me one more time, then changes the subject. "I guess I'll leave you to it."

"Yeah, I have a lot to go through."

Mae walks toward the door, but then turns to me. "Oh, and Lux?"

"Yes?"

"Each part of the house has its own labeled intercom button, so if you need anything, press the one for the person you want to talk to, and they'll answer if they're in that room."

Rubbing my lips together, I smile once again, continuing to take in all the information. Mae gives me a quick wink, then closes the door behind her, leaving me alone to make sense of everything.

I glance at the many items of clothing in beautiful fabrics, and the buckets of shoes, and undergarments with a dull excitement. Then I begin digging through one of the bags and to my surprise, I find a vibrator. My eyes widen with excitement. I'm definitely saving that for when I need it. I giggle to myself and bury it underneath some clothes.

Suddenly, the low orange glow from the evening hour casts a shadow across my face and catching my sight from the slit in the dark curtains. I set a silk camisole on the bed and walk over to the window. *The garden.*

The cozy space looks beautiful and inviting. I don't think there's any harm in me heading out to see it. I open the bedroom door and wearily turn down a long hallway. Only a few feet down, I spot a white wooden door. I open it and immediately the warmth from the dusk sun is on my face. The small clement pathway winds through tall garden walls, while vines crawl between them from above.

As I walk by the white rose bushes toward a white bench, someone clears their throat behind me.

My heart stills.

"I see you found the gardens."

I whip my head around to see River leaning against a statue of a gargoyle nestled between two bushes. "You scared me."

He smiles. "The gardens off the East Wing are my favorite. I designed them for my mother."

"Were you close to her?"

"I was." His eyes focus on the sun setting over the horizon.

I want him to open up. But I don't know how to ask, so I accept whatever he's willing to give. "I met your Aunt Mae this evening."

"I heard."

I chuckle, thinking of her comments and how kind she was to help me get the clothes settled into the bedroom. "I didn't mind."

He pushes off the stone statue and walks toward me. "She can be bossy, but I don't think Seb and I could do anything if it wasn't for her."

"I can tell."

River takes a few steps closer until his body is flush with mine. The heat radiating off him causes my pulse to pick up. "How did you sleep?"

"Better than I have in a while."

He gives me one of his rare smiles and it sends a zip up my spine. He brings the back of his knuckles to my cheek and gently caresses my skin. His smile is subtle, but with an underlying confidence.

"I thought you'd be at peace here."

A dense silence fills the serene space as I angle my face upward, our lips are only a few inches apart. The sun setting off in the distance casts a shadow across his features. My heart pounds inside my chest. I've dreamed about kissing him since the night we broke into Rich's house. With the urge to taste him growing more powerful with each small piece of information he shares with me. He's letting me in on his terms—and it seems so am I.

"Me too." I lean closer, closing my eyes while his breath feathers across my lips.

I can almost taste him when all of a sudden, he draws his head back. "I have a call with my FBI contact later. Meet me back here at midnight."

Stunned by how his demeanor changed again, all I can do is nod my head in agreement. I'm frustrated with how our interactions play out, because he just closes off and leaves.

There are two sides to him. One side shows kindness, while the other is controlled and cold-hearted—and I'm not sure which one has captivated me more.

CHAPTER TWENTY

RIVER

I slam the door to my office in frustration.

Lux Levinson has my heart in a vise and my self-control is becoming harder to contain.

I became infatuated with Lux the moment I met her, and I've craved to know everything about her since then. And with how familiar she seems with my world, it's making things more confusing. I wasn't expecting her to handle herself so well during Rich's killing and it sent my feelings into a deeper plunge.

I sit on the leather couch, facing the wall of screens with my focus fixating on the one that shows the bedroom she's staying in. She's made it back to the room and is now pacing. Lux's energy reaches into me in ways I haven't experienced before, and I want to open up more to her, but there's something holding me back. Maybe it's because I've never had a woman I've wanted to share my darkness with. Or it could be because I lost my parents when I was young and have difficulty trusting people outside my controlled circle of confidants.

Suddenly, she throws the blankets off the bed and crawls

in. Lying on her back, she leaves the comforter off and slides her pants down, exposing her panties before they're completely off. I lean in to get a better look when I see her drag something over her stomach.

What is she doing?

Unable to peel my focus away, I stare into the screen as she slips a hand over her stomach and a toy into the heat between her legs.

"That's it, Lux," I growl under my breath while my dick twitches at the sight. Pulling out my phone, I swipe up on my house app and set the alarm to my office, locking everyone out.

My eyes snap back to Lux as her head tilts back and a delicious moan escapes from her pretty lips.

Fuck, I wish it was my fingers.

My cock painfully rubs the inside of my pants. I readjust myself to dull the mounting discomfort so I can focus on watching her every movement, but it's difficult.

Mesmerized, I watch Lux slide the toy in and out of her pussy. Each time her back arches and another delicious moan hits my ears. Watching her play with herself, my cock swells, and I can't hold myself back any longer so I unzip my pants and whip it out.

Consumed by her movements, my eyes rake along her hips and curves. The arch of her back draws me in, captivating my entire being, and a soft groan slips from her pursed lips.

With a quick spit in my palm, I run it along the length of my shaft and squeeze tightly at the base. Keeping my eyes locked on Lux, I pump myself slowly, then quickly pick up speed. The sounds of her delicate panting sends me reeling.

"*Oh, River.*"

I freeze. Did she say my name? Holy fuck.

"I'm right here," I grunt.

"Yes, River," she moans, her head tipping back again.

I grip myself harder, stroking in rhythm with the twitching of her legs while my mind imagines what it would feel like if I sank into her, and how her body would invite me into the warmth of it.

"Come for me," I whisper, increasing speed. Then with one more hard tug, I lose it all right as her back lifts off the bed with sweet relief.

Out of breath and shocked at what happened, I chuckle to myself.

She was thinking of me.

I watch her toss and turn in the bed, searching for a comfortable spot while I tuck myself back into my pants.

Thoughts of experiencing that once again flood my mind as I capture a quick glance at the clock and note that in a few brief hours I'll get to be in the same room with her again. But then I'm interrupted by the call I've been expecting from Christian.

The secure landline on my desk rings. While walking over from the leather couch, I take a deep breath then answer the phone.

"Hey." Christian's tone is steady.

Sliding into my office chair, I lean back, eager to hear what he has to say. "What do you have for me?"

"The broker has a trip planned to Portland this weekend. I'll send all the information over to you."

I wonder if this has anything to do with what happened to Rich and they've figured out. Maybe he's weary because of the text Sebastian sent the guys from Rich's phone about calling off his weekend.

"Apparently it's his grandmother's funeral."

"Thanks, man." I tuck the phone between my shoulder and ear while Christian's encrypted message comes through on my burner phone. We use it for any details related to what we do. "Got it."

Turning to my computer, I type the location into one of our TI systems. Out of all my father's early technological advancements, this software is by far the one I use the most. It's able to provide aerial views of locations and property information as well as storing the data for later use.

"Great. When will you head over there?" Christian asks.

"We'll send a few men out tomorrow morning to scope out the location, then Sebastian and I will take the jet by the evening," I say.

"Let me know if you need anything else."

We never do, but I appreciate the sentiment.

"Will do."

"Oh, and River?"

"Yeah?"

"I heard you're working with Lux Levinson," he says.

I'm gonna kill Sebastian when I see him.

"I'm just keeping her safe until we dismantle this group since she was one of their targets," I explain.

He chuckles. "What about you and her?"

"I'm helping her out. That's all."

"Well, whatever she needs, I'm here for her as well."

"We'll talk soon."

I end the call and immediately text Sebastian.

ME

Meet me in my office.

SEBASTIAN

Be right there.

A few minutes later, my cousin lets himself in.

"What's up?" he hurriedly asks.

"You seem in a rush. Am I interrupting something?"

He slumps onto the couch. "I was in the middle of a team meeting with the night crew."

I lean on the edge of my desk, my arms crossed over my chest. "I got off the phone with Christian," I say, and then relay what I learned.

He straightens. "So he's skipping his weekend?"

"It appears so. We'll be flying to Portland tomorrow night."

Sebastian nods, and I can already see him working out the logistics. "We could use a run-down motel?"

"Find a location downtown that rents by the hour and takes cash." I push off the desk and round the corner to the front of my computer.

Sebastian pops up on his feet. "When should I send our men to stake it out?"

"The sooner the better."

"You got it," he says before leaving my office to get to work. I decide not to bring up Sebastian telling Christian about Lux, because I already know he's not fully on board with her.

I've just finished planning with Ben about the menu for next week when I notice it's almost midnight. I head for the East Wing gardens to meet Lux and discuss plans for the next kill.

By the time I get outside, Lux is sitting on the bench under the arch of roses bushes. The moonlight provides enough brightness to highlight each of the features of her face.

Damn, she's beautiful.

"Right on time." She glances at her watch.

The corner of my mouth quirks up. "I'm always on time."

Lux's head tilts as her eyes squint with playfulness. "Oh, really?"

"You seem to be extra happy."

Lux's face flushes. "What's that supposed to mean?"

I sit beside her on the bench and lean back, crossing one leg over the other. "Nothing."

It's hard not to tease her about what I saw on the camera.

"So do you have more information?"

"I got off a call with my FBI contact and he mentioned Nolen, the broker, has this weekend off."

Lux's forehead furrows. "Why? What happened?"

My eyes find hers, wide and concerned. "He's going to be in Portland to attend his grandmother's funeral."

She raises to her feet. "What? So we aren't doing it this weekend?" Pacing back and forth, her nervous energy bleeds into the space between us. "I only watched last time. I need the chance to have a larger role. This is supposed to be his weekend."

A larger role?

I raise, clasping her delicate hands in mine. "Look at me."

"I can't live like this anymore. I don't want to wait."

"Lux." I cup her face with a gentle firmness, forcing eye contact. "Don't worry. We're still going to get him."

The sharp rise and fall of her chest slows. "Are you sure?"

"Yes," I reply with confidence. Her eyes bounce between mine, pleading and desperate.

Her lips rub together, and I can't stop my focus from dropping to them. They're light pink and slightly glassy from an unshed tear.

"What's the plan now?"

My palms are still on her cheeks. and I can't help myself from enjoying the softness of her skin. *How long can I continue touching her before it becomes inappropriate?*

"I promised we'd do this together—and we will. Sebastian and the night crew are finalizing the plan now, but we'll be leaving tomorrow on the jet to head to Portland."

Her eyes widen. "Jet?"

"Yes, my private plane. It will be easier to stay off the radar that way."

Her eyelids flutter. "Okay. And then what?"

"We'll take him to a rented motel and take care of him there."

She lets out a small chuckle. "The ones people rent by the hour?"

I smile. "Yes."

"All right," she whispers.

I should probably let her go, but I can't find it in me to do so. For some reason, I like touching her. It brings me warmth.

Lost in my own thoughts, I don't hear what she says.

"I said, you can let me go now."

"What?"

"You can let me go now."

"Oh, right," I breathe out, dropping my hands to my side as heat creeps up my throat. I rub the back of my neck and take a step back, creating a safe distance between us. "Good night, Lux. Be ready to go tomorrow night by seven."

Before she responds, I leave the garden.

I'm a confident man, but no woman has made me feel shy like she continuously does.

CHAPTER TWENTY-ONE

LUX

After River leaves me in the gardens, I spend the rest of the night writing in my bedroom. River was right, this laptop is better than mine. After countless emails back and forth with my editor over the last week, she's kind enough to grant me an extension on my current work in progress. Diving back into this fictional world, where I can guarantee a happy ending, feels good. I haven't been able to write since the night Andrew abducted me. I'm not sure what has freed my mind now, but I'm feeling more relief.

With my notes and boards at home, I have to spend the time inserting my own rage and violation into my current female main character, which proves to be helpful since the words simply fly out of me. Slipping into the writing zone gives me a glimpse of the old Lux again—and I miss her. It feels good. Refreshing.

Around five in the morning, after writing ten thousand words, I put my laptop aside and fall asleep, waking up several hours later around dusk.

After taking a quick shower, I step onto the heated tile floor in the bathroom and stand in front of the sink. With a quick wipe of the condensation from the mirror, my reflection is revealed. Leaning over the counter, I catch the bags under my eyes. Shocked by my appearance, I draw back. I hope there's some makeup in all those buckets the personal shopper dropped off.

Wrapped in a plush robe, I walk into the bedroom and straight for the items in the corner. It only takes me a second to find a bag filled with high-end beauty products. But then a quick buzz of my phone on the nightstand distracts me. I grab my phone and the bag, then swipe up on my phone while walking into the bathroom.

> RIVER
> I'll be in your room in an hour. Pack an
> overnight bag too.

My palms sweat. *He's coming to my room?*

Dumping the bag onto the counter, I grab for anything I can find to make myself not look like I've been hit by a truck.

> ME
> I'll be ready.

I finish getting myself dressed, then pack a few items off the clothing racks. Unsure of how long we'll be gone, I throw as many things in the bag as I can. With only a few minutes to spare, I sit at the edge of the bed and wait for him—which I'm not the biggest fan of, but him sharing the plans with me last night makes me feel a little more included.

Exactly on time, a soft knock is on the bedroom door. My stomach flips with the anticipation of seeing River.

Climbing to my feet, I let out a heavy sigh from every nerve in my body.

"Hi," River says, leaning against the door frame.

"H-hello," I stammer, feeling all sorts of emotions.

"Ready?"

I nod, turning to grab my stuff, but he stops me, placing his hand over mine. "My assistant will grab that for you."

"Oh, okay."

"The jet is waiting for us outside."

I'm not expecting that. "Like, outside of your house?"

"Yes."

With my hand in his, he leads me down the hall and into the elevator, where we stand in silence until the metal doors slide open, exposing the damp, cool night air. We continue onto the short runway and approach the private plane.

The pilot stands at the base of the steps. "Hello, Mr. Thompson."

"Captain Scott," River greets him with a smile.

He leads us into the cabin. "We'll land in Portland in under an hour," he informs us before heading to his post.

"Wonderful." River's hand is resting on my lower back making the skin underneath my shirt tingle as he leads me further inside.

There are six spacious reclining leather seats, three on each side of the aisle, with a four-seater light blonde wooden table behind the chairs on the left. A door at the back of the plane catches my eye, and I can only assume it's private sleeping quarters. It's overwhelming to think River owns this, but I shouldn't be surprised based on the size of Thompson Manor.

Sebastian's already aboard, sitting in one of the white reclining seat with headphones over his ears. He gives us a curt nod as we walk down the aisle toward the back.

"Have dinner with me?"

"Sure." I smile, trying to act like none of this is out of the ordinary. I've never been on a private plane and have nothing to compare it to, but this is beautiful.

River gets settled across from me. "I ordered for you, I hope you don't mind."

I swallow a chuckle. He has no clue how picky I am about my food. "You did?"

"Yes, and I think you'll be pleasantly surprised."

River glances behind me, lifting his hand up. Before I can ask what he's doing, Ben appears at my side with a rolling a metal cart.

"Miss Lux." He places a plate with a tin lid in front of me. "Lovely to see you again."

"Lovely to see you too."

"I have made a grilled chicken salad, my signature vegetable soup, and a coconut cake for dessert."

"Coconut cake?" I ask, shocked by the choice since it's not as common as chocolate or cheesecake.

"River said it's your favorite," he explains, placing River's meal on the table.

When I glance over at him, River's rubbing the back of his neck, trying to hide a smile.

"How did you know?"

"I have my ways."

I giggle, because I'm not surprised he found a way to learn my favorite dessert.

During dinner, River shares with me details about how the kill is planned to go down. The more we talk about taking Nolen's life, the more I get visions of my blood-soaked dream. And as time goes on, the more I realize it isn't only rage fueling me because this feels natural in some small parts of my mind.

I didn't kill Rich myself, but I was in the room and that makes me part of what happened. Before that night, I could barely eat, I wasn't sleeping, and my thoughts were clouded. I was a shell of the person I was before and only slept for short bursts throughout the day. But now I find myself itching for another man to see his demise.

I need my story to keep moving.

When we're almost done eating, River's eyes meet mine from across the table. It's silent except for the dull echo of Sebastian headphones in the background.

"How are you feeling?" he asks, picking up on my change in demeanor.

"I'm doing all right," I say. I should thank him for opening up to me more. These few little things he's sharing are helping me feel included, but also giving me a glimpse into who he is. "Thank you for sharing things with me."

"What do you mean?"

"In the garden and now during dinner. You're letting me in to the details of what we're doing." I exhale a heavy sigh. "It's difficult to explain what was taken from me that night or how something inside of me changed, but it did. It feels like I've been chasing that old version of myself since then. And thank you for including me."

River rests a comforting palm on my hand from across the table and gives a soft smile. "My parents were murdered when I was young, so I don't know if I would have been the same person I am today if I hadn't witnessed it, but I do know something changed in me too. We all process trauma differently—some healthy, other unhealthy."

Are River and I not as different as I believe us to be?

Did the taste for vengeance unlock something in him too?

A tightness in my chest forms as tears prick the back of my eyelids from both him losing his parents and having someone to relate to. Before they can fall, I rise from my seat. I want to release these emotions, but we're not alone because Sebastian is right behind us.

I clamp my eyes shut. "Is that a private room?"

"Yes, it's all yours." A worried expression sweeps across River's face. "Are you all right, Lux?"

I briskly walk past him, without acknowledging his question.

"Lux." He grabs my hand. "What's wrong?"

"I need a minute." I sprint toward the small room in the back, stopping short of falling onto the bed.

River is hot on my heels, slipping into the room behind me. "What's going on?"

"I think I'm still processing it all."

He locks the door behind us, then bends to cup his hands on my cheeks. "I'm here."

My eyes lock on his as he holds my head in place. Taking in a breath, I try to slow my pulse while tears roll down my cheeks.

"We're going to get all of these men, Lux. I promise."

"It's just hard to see the finish line at this point."

"I know. Because we've only just begun." His thumb glides across my skin and over my bottom lip. "You will hear every one of them take their last breath."

My heart flutters and my mind blurs with how close our bodies are. "Are you sure?"

"Yes."

Squeezing my eyes shut, I let myself feel the emotions. Then a gentle pressure is on my forehead, and before I can open my eyes a light breeze floats across my lips. River's forehead is pressing against mine, and I let a waterfall of tears escape.

"I'm right here with you, Lux. I have been since the moment I brought you home from that cabin. You're not alone."

His raw attempt to comfort me causes me to lean into his touch. "I think I need a distraction," I whisper.

My eyes slowly flutter open afraid of what his reaction will be.

River's eyes bore into mine. "What type of distraction?"

"I brought my laptop. Maybe writing will help," I lie to avoid telling him what I truly want. I suck in my bottom lip, biting until I taste copper nervous and almost regretting what I said.

His finger slides across my bottom lip, pulling it open slightly, before his tongue darts out to lick his lip. "Let me distract you."

"Wh-what do you have in mind?" I stammer, my legs squeezing together, arousal pooling in my panties.

"It's imperative we are both thinking straight when we land." River's hand drops to the waistband of my pants before dipping his finger under the elastic and gliding it across my skin. I let out a small gasp as his delicate but commanding touch causes my skin to break out with goose bumps. "I can't have anything impede our plans. And I gave you my word I'd help you in any way I could."

My heart pounds. "I wouldn't want to ruin this for either of us."

"I hate seeing you upset, Lux." River grips my thigh with his hand and, in one smooth motion, he spreads my legs apart, sliding himself between them. "Let me give you some temporary relief until I can bring you the revenge you crave."

"Okay," I breathe out.

A devilish grin appears on his face, making my legs weak. River removes his hand from my thigh, grabbing both of my arms and swinging them over his shoulders. "Lean on me."

Am I going to let this happen? Yes. Hell yes, I am.

I bend forward, our bodies are flush with one another. The clean, leathery scent of him liquefies my organs.

"Such a greedy girl."

With one arm bracing me, the other slips between us and inside my pants, and then brings his lips to the sensitive skin on my neck.

River glides his other hand across my stomach and into the heat between my legs. "Is this what you need?" he groans.

With two curled fingers, he moves in slow, steady motion. My eyes flutter closed. "Oh, River."

"That's right. I'm the one taking care of you," he growls. "It will be me meeting all of your needs."

With my forehead resting on River's shoulder, he braces my weight. Moving back and forth, he slides his fingers in and out of my pussy, rubbing the arousal over top of my clit, before slipping them back inside. Picking up the pace with his two crooked fingers, he urges me into him commanding my hips to roll forward.

My pussy throbs while my insides clench around his fingers. Bucking against him, my body craves the relief, chasing a precious orgasm before it finally breaks. Tense and locked in place, my breath halts.

"That's right, Lux, you're doing so well coming for me." River's lips are at my collarbone.

I do as he says, sucking in a gulp of air right when my legs tremble and tingles shoot up my spine.

"Oh my god," I moan. My limbs weaken, falling forward into his firm embrace.

Once my orgasm subsides, he gently pulls his hand from out of my panties. Our eyes locked in a deep stare, and then he does something I'm not expecting. He slips his two fingers into his mouth, and with a slow roll of his eyes, he sucks them clean.

My mouth drops, but I close it right away.

"You taste so fucking good."

River's hooded eyes are mesmerizing, and I can't help but think what he looks like when fully turned on.

"Feel a little better?"

"Amazing." I'm feeling groggy from my climax.

"I love seeing that smile on your face." River tucks a loose hair behind my ears, then drags his fingers along my heated cheeks. "And I'm glad I'm the one who was able to bring it back."

Speechless, I lower to the couch with my palms flat on the cushions. "Me too."

River's gaze lands on my unbuttoned pants. "You have no idea how deep my need to give you what you want goes."

He rests his hand on the doorknob. "I'll give you a minute. And when you feel comfortable, come out and join us."

I can't believe I just let that happen.

CHAPTER TWENTY-TWO

RIVER

I can still taste Lux on my tongue for the rest of the flight. It's fucking intoxicating.

We sit on opposite sides of the plane, with her typing away on her laptop while Sebastian and I pour over the details of our plan. Leaning back, I relive how her body felt molding around my fingers. Lux and I exchange subtle smiles here and there, but the energy has shifted.

The night team has been on Nolen's trail the entire day, until he left in an unfamiliar car after his grandma's funeral service. To ensure he's covered, we stationed the crew outside his hotel in anticipation of his return.

As we approach our descent into the private airport, my phone vibrates on the table.

"What's up, Christian?" I answer. Sebastian's eyes flick up at hearing Christian's name.

"Are you guys in Portland yet?" he asks.

Lux turns her head in my direction, resting her chin on her palm.

"We're about to land."

"I made a few calls to my contacts in the area, and one of my informants who manages the Slippery Kitty strip club said she has eyes on him at her place."

"Yeah, that's what my guys are reporting as well, but they haven't gone in yet." I recall the report I received from Hayden not long ago, as some of the guys followed him to the club.

"He's in one of the VIP lounges and has been dropping big money on the ladies. He even bragged about working on a side hustle with a few friends that's been cashing in big time."

"Of course he'd *out* himself."

"Apparently, after he got a few drinks in him he alluded to his weekend activities."

"Men like him always need to brag." I glance at Lux and Sebastian. "We'll head over there now."

"Sounds good." A few rustling papers in the background echo through the call. He must be working late, as usual. "Keep me updated."

"Talk soon." I end the call and toss my phone into my open bag on the floor.

Sebastian clasps his hands together on the table while his leg bounces in place. "Anything new?"

"Nolen's in one of the VIP lounges at the Slippery Kitten."

"A little pregame before the real fun begins," he exclaims.

"Is that a strip club?" Lux drops her arm, her palm facing up with assumption.

"Yes. Nolen's there right now."

"Look up the club's location, we're heading there as soon as we land."

"This will be torture. You're taking me to a strip club, I won't be able to have any fun," he says begrudgingly, burying his head in his laptop.

"You'll be fine." I stand and walk over to Lux. She's sitting with her legs crossed underneath her. The perfect position for me to scoop her up and whisk her away into the private room where I'll throw her on the bed and give her endless hours of pleasure.

"Sebastian and I will go to the club, while you stay with Hayden."

"Why can't I go with you?" she asks.

"Because I'm not going to let you get hurt, and in a situation like that there are a lot of unknowns."

"Will you have to act like customers who are enjoying themselves? You know, to blend in?" Lux pulls her bottom lip between her teeth, avoiding eye contact with me.

Is she jealous?

I lean in, bringing my lips to her ear. "I'm not interested. Especially since I can still taste you on my lips."

She inhales sharply.

"Oh."

I pull my focus away from Lux and turn back to my cousin. "The Slippery Kitten is a little under four miles away from our hotel." I grab the pack of electronics on the floor that Sebastian brought with us. "This is how we'll communicate with you," I tell Lux.

"This little piece goes right in here." I push away a few strands of hair to gain access to her ear.

Once the listening device is in place, she pulls back slowly, her eyes lingering on mine for a beat, and I fight the urge to kiss her. I've been wanting to...I wonder if she'd mind. But if she were to let me, I know there's not enough time for me to simply kiss her and be done because I know I won't be able to stop myself.

"Thank you," she says.

"Got mine in, but thanks for offering," Sebastian says sarcastically.

I roll my eyes, ignoring him. "We'll go in and secure Nolen, then call for you."

"Where will Hayden and I be?" She clips the small radio pack onto the back of her waistband.

I bend over to retrieve the last few items I'll need, then add them to my bag. "You'll be in the van with Hayden outside the club."

Sebastian kneels to the floor, adding the things he needs to his bag as he says, "There are four guys setting up a perimeter around the motel as we speak."

Lux nods, but nervously picks at her nails.

I grab her hands in mine, hoping to provide some comfort. "Are you sure you want to do this?"

She nods with a small smile.

As the three of us deplane, Hayden zips down the tarmac, pulling up in a black SUV. After a quick greeting, we're on our way to the Slippery Kitten. Lux is silent on the ride over while Hayden, Sebastian, and I discuss the plan for the night one last time.

Twenty minutes later, a large flickering neon sign of a black cat comes into view.

"Let's get this party started!" Sebastian jumps out before Hayden has the chance to stop the vehicle completely.

I turn to Lux. "We shouldn't be that long."

"Be careful."

I look down at our intertwined fingers, but I can't recall when we began holding hands.

"Don't worry." A confident grin grows on my face. "I'm the only monster out here."

Lux takes in a shaky breath, and I wink at her before letting go of her hands.

"Don't let her out of your sight, Hayden," I warn.

Sebastian and I are dressed casually in black hoodies and

jeans as we exit the vehicle. Rain drizzles on our backs while we stroll into the strip club.

"Are you sure we don't have a little time to enjoy ourselves?" Sebastian whines.

The drumming of the bass vibrates through the floor, while the clacking of plastic heels in the air drowns out everything but the music.

"Focus." I pull him over to the side and say, "They're just naked women."

"Naked women that look good enough to eat," he points out as I make eye contact with a blonde stripper walking toward us from the end of a long dark hallway.

She walks up to us. "Here for a good time?"

"We are," Sebastian answers for the both of us.

Then she steps closer to me and brings her arms around my neck. "Christian didn't say he was sending a couple of guys who look like you two," she purrs into my ear.

I smile, but I'd rather push her away.

The woman reaches up, pulling down the shoulder of my hoodie and bringing her lips to my collarbone. "I dropped him off in VIP room four, all liquored up. My manager turned off the cameras, but you'll only have nine minutes to get in and out. Give me a moment and I'll bring him out."

"You got it," I say to her.

"Head down the VIP hallway and make a sharp left by the bathrooms. That's where you'll find the back door." Then she gives us both a wink before turning toward the back and gesturing for us to follow.

"Did you get that, Hayden?" I ask into my earpiece.

"Copy that," Hayden answers.

"I have eyes on the room." I remove the syringe from my bag, already prepped with sedation.

Sebastian and I continue with her instructions until we

reach the back door. He has one hand on the doorknob, the other holding a handgun at his side, as he presses his back against the wood to open the door.

When we see the area is clear, Sebastian puts away his gun and we walk outside. "So we wait?"

"She said she'll be right out," I say, scanning the narrow walkway lined with brick walls from the buildings. There's no one around who except the rats scurrying from one dumpster to the other.

The back door swings open, forcing the two of us to back up taking defensive stances in case it isn't Nolen. But it is.

With one arm hooked around our informant, Nolen stumbles into the dark night. "You're going home with me, baby," he slurs.

"I would love to, but I think my friends here want to spend some time with you instead," she says, then dips her head and slips back from underneath his arm in one swift motion.

Sebastian and I stand in front of him.

"Hi, Nolen." I smile.

"What the fuck?" Unstable on his feet, he sways back and forth, his eyes trying to focus on us.

"Always looking to get your dick wet, aren't you?" I taunt, before lunging forward, wrapping an arm around his back, and pricking him with the sedation. "Don't fight it. You're only going to take a little nap."

Nolen's pupils dilate with fear as Sebastian's arms clench his legs keeping them in place.

"Who knows, when you wake you might see that one cabin girl who got away," Sebastian taunts.

My eyes shoot over to Sebastian's at the mention of Lux, not sure how I feel about him bringing her up or what happened to her that weekend, but maybe it means her presence is starting to grow on him.

"Fuck. I wish that worked as quickly as it does in the movies." Sebastian chuckles.

Hayden pulls up then, rolls the window down to hurry us along. "Get your asses in here."

Sebastian and I glance at each other over Nolen's body, exchanging looks, and waiting for the other to be on labor duty. *It'll be me—I'm bigger.*

"Obviously, I'm the muscle in this operation," I say.

Crossing his arms over his chest, his features tighten. "And who's always on clean-up and disposal duty?"

I roll my eyes. "Please. You simply supervise."

"Fuck you," he spits.

"Are you guys done yet?" Lux's sweet voice in my ear is wonderful. "We only have two minutes left."

I bend to lift Nolen's limp body, then throw him over my shoulder.

Sebastian takes one last sweep of the alley as I toss Nolen into the back of the SUV. Then I slide into the back seat next to Sebastian and we head for the motel.

CHAPTER TWENTY-THREE

LUX

Sebastian and I are standing off to the side in the motel room they booked. 1980s flowery wallpaper surrounds us while River handcuffs Nolen's wrists to the wrought iron bed frame.

Buzzing with adrenaline, I suck in a deep breath to calm the nerves, but I'm flooded with the scent of this musty motel room instead so it does nothing to ease me.

On the flight, River briefed me on how the night would go. Similar to Rich's kill, I'm here to face Nolen and show him that the group of tormentors he's part of did not take away my power.

River's slowly letting me in on his plans, and I appreciate it, but as I stare at him securing Nolen, I'm eager for more.

When River's done, he backs away and stands next to Sebastian and I.

"What do we do now?" I ask, unsure what to say or how to let on that I want more of a role in this kill.

River and Sebastian exchange a quick glance before River answers. "We wake him up."

"How?"

"Just like this," Sebastian says as he walks over to the bed and slaps Nolen's face with the back of his gloved hand. "Time to wake up, buddy."

After slapping him a few more times, Nolen startles dazed and confused. "What the fuck?" His eyes flick upward, spotting each one of us standing masked in front of him. "Where am I? Who the fuck are you people?"

Nolen's eyes squint for a brief moment before realization dawns on him. "Wait, you're the guys who grabbed me behind the strip club. River Thompson?"

"You know, Nolen, we need to stop meeting like this. I'm sure there's more to you than the ability to use women as you wish."

"Is that what this is about?" His expression turns smug. "You were going to get your turn, but now that Rich is missing, you're upset that Andrew wants to put a hold on things for a while?"

My eyes fly to River as he steps forward.

On hold? What is he talking about?

I expect River to mirror my confusion, but he doesn't seem surprised.

Instead, his jaw clenches. "You think I took you because I didn't get my turn?"

"Maybe, or like Rich, you didn't even want to do this anyway. This life isn't meant for a timid little accountant like him. And maybe you too?" Nolen baits.

River clicks his tongue. "You're about to find out exactly what type of man I am."

"What the hell is this about?" Nolen asks with impatience.

River looks over his shoulder, giving me the okay to go ahead with what I need to say.

"Do you remember me?" I walk to the side of the bed.

"You do look like a woman I fucked. But you all look the same, don't you?" He laughs devilishly.

River glances over his shoulder at Sebastian with a chuckle, before swinging his arm back and ramming into Nolen's cheek. A loud crack fills the room as River breaks Nolen's jaw. The sound of his crushing cheekbone echos through the room.

"Ah, fuck!" Nolen screams. His head whips to the side.

"You want to know what this is about? Let me tell you." River grabs his face bringing it back toward us. "You and your friends are done hurting women. And you see this beautifully, strong woman standing in front of you?"

Nolen's expression hardens. "Yes."

"She's going to help end your life," River tells him with a quick glance in my direction.

My heart pounds against my ribcage. This part of the plan was never discussed, but I can't say I'm upset about it—more anxious or eager?

Sebastian steps forward, placing a hand on River's. "Quick word, River."

River shoots a threatening look at Nolen before walking to the other side of the room with Sebastian, but not before taking my hand to join them.

"What are you doing?" Sebastian spits out, keeping his voice low.

"We didn't discuss this, but Lux deserves a chance to truly avenge herself." River's words speak for me, verbalizing how I feel brings a warmth.

"How do we even know—" Sebastian begins as if I'm not standing right next to them.

"I can do it," I interrupt.

"I'll show you."

"What the fuck?" Sebastian whispers to himself.

"She can't do it, can she?" Nolen's voice grates my ears like nails on a chalkboard. "I knew you wouldn't."

"Shut up," Sebastian tells him, then turns to River. "Are you sure about this?"

With one more look at me, River nods. "Yeah."

Sebastian clasps his hands behind his head with apprehension and frustration.

I swallow hard. I remember the times my father took me to the shooting range. He told me how important it is to know how to use a firearm, although he hoped I'd never need to. But now I find myself face-to-face with a predator, grateful I learned the basics.

"With a gun, right?" My voice shakes with adrenaline.

Can I really do this?

Am I able to take another human's life?

I have to stop him from hurting someone else.

Sensing my fear, River rubs his thumb on the inside of my palm. "Yes. I'll be right here with you."

I nod, biting my lip.

"You can do it," he tells me, guiding me over the bed where Nolen lies, still secured to the frame.

Drops of blood spill from the inch-long slice in his face while he flushes with panic. "Listen, if you let me go, I will tell you whatever you want to know."

"I already know what I need to know," River says with steady authority.

Nolen grimaces, fighting to keep his mouth shut, accepting he'll have to give in. An attempt to save his own life, but what he doesn't know is that it won't make a difference.

With a heavy inhale, I breath in ready to say what I need to say. "You cannot hurt me anymore," I begin.

"You're still standing, so apparently you didn't meet the same fate as the others. Maybe, be grateful?" Nolen's lips pursed together with anger, the whites of his eye now filling with a deep scarlet.

Anger flows through my veins in combination with adrenaline.

I should be grateful that I'm the one who survived? And how am I using my spared life if not for avenging what happened?

"You have no more power over me. When you're dead, we will move on to the rest of your friends and we won't stop until we've taken care of all of you."

River wraps a hand around my back, placing a handgun into my right palm. The metal shocking my skin, but on reflex, my fingers curl around it.

"Okay, fine, I get it. You're pissed, but this is all Andrew's fault. That's why he had his eyes on you that night. Some stupid vendetta he has against the police because of what they did to his brother." He coughs up phlegm and blood, his words slurring as he drifts in and out of consciousness from the needle I pricked him with. "And Thompson, I knew there was something fucking weird about you."

My chest tightens from his words. "What vendetta against the police?"

"Okay, let's get this show on the road," Sebastian chimes in from behind us, sounding annoyed.

River agrees with Sebastian, because his body is suddenly flush with mine. Standing at my back, he brings both hands over mine as we grab the trigger together. "Okay, Lux."

Bile creeps up my throat, but I swallow it down. "I'm ready."

River brings his face close to mine as we both stand with our arms out pointing the barrel at our target. "This is for everything he and his friends took from you."

"And one step closer to getting my life back."

"Keep your eyes open," he says. "Now, on the count of three."

Sucking in a gulp of air and holding the breath, I let River command my movements.

"One."

My muscles stiffen.

"Two."

A tear rolls down my cheek and my chest burns.

"Three."

One silenced bullet flies directly into Nolen's head. The force sends me backward. Not expecting the kickback from the shot to knock the wind out of me, I lose my balance. But River's arms tighten bracing me as I stumble.

"Wow, Lux," Sebastian comments, suddenly at my side. "Not bad."

My hands come up to my heart as it hammers against my lungs. I struggle to take a full breath. This is happening.

"Are you all right?" River angles his head to capture my eyes.

"I think so."

I finally get a look at Nolen, handcuffed to the bed, with blood, and what looks to be flesh or brain matter, splattered on the dated flowery wallpaper behind him. After only a moment, I have to drag my eyes away from the scene. My head burying itself into River's shoulder. He leans in to press a deep kiss onto my temple.

"Okay, I'm going to call Hayden and the guys to clean up," Sebastian says, sliding off baseball hat to smooth his hair before putting it back on. "I'm sure you're going to want to take Lux back to the plane to rest before we leave."

"Yeah, we should head back."

I listen to their conversation, but my mind is occupied by what just happened. It reels from how River guided me and the lingering effects of the gentlest kiss, that carried so much more with it.

"Let's go," River says as he guides me to the SUV outside. The ride to the airport is blur, and by the time Hayden comes back with Sebastian I'm exhausted.

River and I sit across from each other by the window. Sebastian boards the plane, walks right past us and into the back bedroom and shuts the door. It's the early morning hours by the time we take off.

"How are you doing?" River leans forward on bent knees.

"I'm doing better now that we're headed back." I wish I had more to say, but I don't. Not sure if I'm in shock or relaxed, but my brain is slowly catching up with what my body is feeling.

"You should be proud of yourself."

His kindness makes me break a smile, but the truth is, I helped kill a man. And not like with Rich where I was a bystander. River might have helped me pull the trigger, but *I* did it.

Am I okay with this?

What type of person does it make me that the feelings I get are not remorse, but relief?

"I am, but it doesn't erase the fact that I took a man's life," I confess, looking away from him.

"You shouldn't feel guilty. Not when he deserved it."

I hear his words, and they do resonate, but being conflicted internally is something I'm going to have to carry myself. "I know."

River's hand comes up to cups my cheek. It's comforting and it makes me not feel as alone.

"It will get easier. Just remind yourself that you're taking out the trash in a way that the law would never be able to do. At least, that's what helps me."

I'm struck by how casually he mentions it. This is the first time he's admitted to doing this often, and it does somewhat confirm my suspicions.

A slight change in expression shows he's carrying something.

"There's something I need to tell you."

"Yes?"

"Remember, I mentioned I was at the club that night you were taken?"

"I do."

"I was there to stake out Andrew." My heart stops. Unsure of where this conversation is going, I remain silent to let him finish. "I have been watching him for a while from something he did in the past and unfortunately got away with. He introduced me to Rich, Nolen, and Duncan and asked me to join his group. I was playing along with it once I realized it wasn't only going to be him I was after anymore."

River was after them the whole time?

"Is that what you refused to tell me when I asked you what you meant about you and your guys were taking care of it?"

"Yes. Andrew still thinks I'm interested."

"He thinks you're one of them?" My mind is spinning.

"He thinks I *want* to be one of them."

I knew River was hiding more than what he was telling me, and although I'm grateful for his admission right now, I'm shocked. "Wow. Okay."

"Lux," he whispers my name. "There's something else you should know."

I squeeze my eyes shut making sense of everything he's saying. "Yeah?"

"This is what I do."

"What do you mean?" I ask, but I know what he's alluding to.

"I think you know."

River leans back in his chair, eying me intently. He's searching for more of a reaction to his confession. But what he doesn't know is that I don't care and the darkness in him is something I recognize in myself.

I give him an understanding smile.

He stands. My head tilts upward toward his tall frame, as he moves closer to me. Unexpectedly, he bends to scoop me up. Stifling a stomach of frantic butterflies, I tuck myself into his hard chest.

River sits back in the seat and I melt into him. "That's better."

There will be more time to process and to ask him questions in the days to come, but right now I'm exhausted.

"Are you upset?" he asks.

"No, I get it."

A chuckle vibrates his chest. "I'm infatuated with you, Lux Levinson."

We spend the remainder of the flight in that position.

CHAPTER TWENTY-FOUR

LUX

We arrive back at Thompson Manor a little more than an hour later. The three of us ride in silence up the elevator. Then, with a quick wave from Sebastian, he heads down his wing, leaving River and me alone to walk to my room.

"It's been a rough night." He shoves his hands into the front pockets of his pants as if nervous. We remain standing in the quiet space as a palpable energy passes between us. "I hope you're able to get some sleep."

"Yeah. Th-thanks again for tonight," I stumble over my words as I awkwardly slip by him to stand with my back against the door.

He smiles. "Okay. Well, I'll see you later."

I nod. My heart beats against my ribcage while the words I want to say are on the tip of my tongue. I don't want the night to be over. The desire to be back in his arms again is strong. But not enough for me to say anything.

"Good night."

I watch River's dark frame disappear down the hallway until it's out of view.

My eyes roll with embarrassment. I don't know how to act around him. We've had all these intimate moments so why did *that* moment between us feel like an awkward first date?

Is it because we both want more?

Nothing is stopping us from giving in to whatever it is we both seem to be feeling—because it's simply us alone.

I take a quick shower, to shake off the adrenaline and the feelings toward River. But now I find myself standing in front of my bed, staring down at the red velvet comforter, unable to settle. I can't simply go to sleep and pretend I didn't kill a man or the fact that I have no remorse.

I can't decide what's right and wrong, and the only other person who understands how I feel is on the opposite side of his gigantic home.

Without any more thought, I get myself dressed and walk right out of the door heading for River's bedroom. It doesn't take long before my nerves make me regret coming.

I knock.

"Lux? Is everything okay?" He answers the door with only a towel wrapped around his waist. The light in his dimly lit room casts shadows over him. I can't make out the details of his tattoos, but I can see they expand across his shoulders and back.

My eyes roam over his bare chest, drinking in every divot and curve. "Yes."

"Do you need something?" His focus on me is heated, and I can't help but catch a slight reddening of his cheeks.

"I, uh—"

"Yes?"

I lick my lips, letting my eyes drift downward and imagine where the trail of hair leads. Wetness pools in my panties. "I-I didn't want to be alone. And you're the only person who understands what we just went through."

"I do." Rubbing the back of his neck with one hand, he pushes the door open further with the other. "Do you want to come in?"

"Sure." Ducking under his outstretched arm, I walk into River's bedroom. It's exactly how I picture it with dark colors and an oversized king bed. My eyes scan the room, seeing a large television hanging on the far wall, 360-degree windows covered in thick black curtains, and two leather chairs with a small table in the middle in the corner.

"Couldn't sleep?"

I stand in the middle of the room with my palms sweaty. I'm not sure what to do with myself. "No."

His eyes soften. "I know how you're feeling. It will pass."

"I guess I just don't want to be alone."

River takes a few steps toward me, eating the distance between us. "You're not alone."

"Can I stay here until I fall asleep?" I ask, bypassing the fear of vulnerability.

River slowly closes the distance between us, then a gentle hand comes up to rest on my face. "You can stay here as long as you want."

I lean into his touch immediately feeling a relief, but my eyes fall back to his bare chest. "Thank you."

"I hope you know I'm always here for you, Lux," he whispers and a breeze carrying the scent of Irish Spring hits my nostrils.

Closing my eyes to enjoy the sensation of his warm palm against my skin, I inadvertently let my hands move to his waist. But when I notice what I'm doing, I jerk them away.

"Shit, I'm sorry. I didn't mean to do that."

He's quiet for a moment before saying, "You can touch me if you want to."

I don't respond, and instead hook my fingers under the hem of the towel and give it a quick tug, pulling him into me. I'm too shy to verbalize what I want, and it's easier to show him. Bringing a hesitant hand up to his chest, I let my fingertips run across his warm skin, and he inhales sharply.

"What if I want to do more than just touch you?"

Suddenly, River's mouth is on mine, seizing my breath with his soft and gentle lips. His hands coil around my long hair as he urges me deeper into his kiss. Our tongues tangle in each other. A tight moan escapes from my lips.

River tastes like every depraved thought I've ever had and it's thrilling.

His hands slide up the back of my silk nightshirt, until he lifts it over my head. The cool air from the ceiling fan hits my nipples, making them harden.

River breaks our kiss, drawing his head back to stare at me. His eyes roam across my bare chest taking in every inch as he tugs off my panties. "You're perfect."

A blush creeps up my neck and I smile up at him. "So are you."

Both of his hands are on my cheeks. He runs his thumb across my bottom lip, then leans down to kiss me again.

My arms wrap around his waist.

"Take it off," he gently commands.

My heart skips a beat and eagerly I slip my fingers under the cotton. With a slight tug on the corner, the towel piles at our feet. Then the entire universe goes blurry as I watch him retrieve my panties from the floor, and bring them up to his face and breathe in.

"Mmm," he moans.

Oh my god.

But quickly, my eyes find a row of silver balls that line both sides of his shaft. "Um, you're—"

"Pierced?"

"Yes."

I can't take my eyes off them. It's erotic.

"I've wanted this for so long." His pupils dilate as he smooths over my entire body. With all ambitions pushed aside, I become empowered by how I've caused his length to grow significantly.

I blush.

River's hands move from my hair, sliding down my back, to grip the cheeks of my ass. In one smooth movement, he hoists me up wrapping my legs around his waist.

"Take me to your bed."

"Say no more," he replies. Then a small bite on my bottom lip sends a shockwave through me before River lowers me onto a platform bed.

The black sheets are soft on my skin as my body sinks into them. I scoot myself further, keeping my stare trained on his sculpted body. A light buzz travels up the spine in anticipation of what we're about to do.

"Now"—he palms the bed, bringing his lips to mine—"open up for me."

Thunder pounds inside my chest as my heartbeat quickens. I mirror his movements by lying back and spreading my legs open for him.

With one purposeful thrust, he enters me and forces a grunt from my throat. It steals my breath—in the best way.

"Oh, River." The bottom half of my body trembling on contact. Hitting every spot possible, he rolls in deeper.

"You're so wet."

My back arches, rising me to my elbows, with over-whelming pleasure. I'm allowing the mysterious masked man —who rescued me from the cabin a couple weeks ago—the same one who became my stalker and who I'm now figuring out is a serial killer himself—*to sleep with me.* I'm giving in to him and, every nightmare I've had is turning into a dream.

I squeeze my eyes shut. The intensity is too much for me to form a coherent thought or acknowledge. River continues to roll his hips into me, keeping his movement slow and deep.

"You're doing so good." His voice is kind and smooth and I loosen even more.

"Okay. This feels so intense."

"It's the piercings." He smiles, proud of himself.

With each thrust, my breathing is labored. Struggling to catch a full gulp of air, I focus on the tray ceilings above us. But it does nothing to dull the fierce sensations.

"Look at us." River nuzzles my cheek with his nose, gesturing for me to glance down.

My eyelids fly open, curious to see what our two bodies look like molded into one. He pushes his hard length into me, then withdraws it, as if he belongs there.

"Goddamn, that's hot," I purr.

His mouth meets the sensitive skin on my neck. "You take me so well."

Melting into his praise, I rock into his core, already approaching my climax. A short whimper escapes my lips as River moves his mouth to mine with a deep all-encompassing kiss. It creates spots behind my eyelids.

His movements pick up pace, but remain in rhythm with mine. "Come for me, Lux."

Vibrating as I reach my peak, my chest and face tingle, and I can only respond with a "Mm-hmm."

"Oh fuck." His hands are suddenly at the sides of my face,

cupping my cheeks as his lower body stiffens. An echoing grunt pulls an orgasm from me. Spots fill my vision in the surrounding space. I gasp for breath. My hands claw into the skin on his shoulder blades. And just like that with our mouths connected, we both finish together.

Something I have never experienced before. It's intimate and fucking raw.

"You're all mine," River whispers into my collarbone between soft kisses. He holds himself up on bent elbows on either side of my head. From his rough nature and what I've witnessed with the murder of Richard and Nolen, he is surprisingly tender.

"I think I have been for a while." I glide my fingertips along the grooves of his back. "My life has been turned upside for what feels like forever now. But you've become a bright light in all this darkness."

River lifts his head, his dark eyes lowering as they meet mine. "I wouldn't consider myself any sort of light, but for you I will be anything you want me to be."

"You are unlike anyone I've ever met," I say.

"I'll gladly take that compliment."

"And I'm grateful you opened up to me about your involvement with Andrew."

River rolls off me and onto his side. With his head resting in his hand, I curl into him and bury my face into his hard muscular chest. I breathe in the scent of leather with a subtle sweetness.

"I would never let anything happen to you and that's why I hid so much from you."

"It might be hard for me, but I understand."

River leans in and kisses the tip of my nose. "How about we hop in the shower, then have breakfast together?"

I pull my eyes away to hide my feelings, but fail miserably, because they're written all over my face. "I would love that."

River lifts me off the bed, startling me in the best way.

I laugh. *What did I get myself into?*

CHAPTER TWENTY-FIVE
RIVER

Lux killed Nolen and she did it without a second thought. The way she came down from the high of taking a life, was worse than my first time. It reminded me that she has a darkness within her, but it only seeks revenge.

I may let myself indulge in the fantasy of our likeness, but deep down, I know this is only temporary for her.

I stare at her in a restless sleep from the cameras in my office. The afternoon light spills onto her delicate face. I envision a life where I wasn't born a flawed human or that I won't always carry the tragedy of watching the murder of my parents, but I know it's not reality.

Lux may believe we slept together in a moment of passion —but she's mine and I plan on keeping her forever. Because no woman has come close to the vast obsession I have with her.

I tear my eyes away and walk over to my desk. Picking up the secure landline, I call Christian to update him about what happened with Nolen.

He answers on the first ring. "How'd it go?"

"Everything is done and taken care of," I tell him.

"That's good to hear." He breathes a sigh of relief. "Unfortunately, I have no new information on Duncan Jones. But I'm hoping to have something for you by the end of day tomorrow. The ring only works on the weekends, right?"

"According to the calendar we found at Richard's house, we shouldn't have to worry about them until next weekend. But if we find something sooner, we won't wait until his weekend to get him."

"I spoke with Lieutenant Levinson a few days ago and he didn't mention the missing accountant."

"It's been over a week since I killed him. It won't be long, especially since he has a wife."

"Yeah, I'd expect her to report him any day now," he points out.

"Nolen mentioned that he got cold feet. So Sebastian's text to them from Rich's phone worked."

"Yeah, that's probably why they're moving forward with everything," he adds.

"How is the lieutenant's daughter?"

"Since staying with us, she's doing better. I feel more secure with her here."

A light chuckle from the other end of the phone perks my ears.

"Something funny, Christian?"

"Nothing at all, my friend," he utters a friendly quip at my expense.

"What?"

"Is it for her benefit or yours?"

"I needed to make sure she stays safe. Once Andrew catches on to us, he'll be after blood."

"Fair enough." His voice is tight, like he's biting back a

smile. "You have a thing for that woman and that's okay, River. You are human, after all."

I think about the night I had with her and how good she felt in my arms, but with a sense of protection, I won't discuss it further. "Okay, this conversation is over," I cut him off, refusing to address my affection toward Lux. "We'll keep you updated."

"Talk soon." He ends the call.

I lay the receiver back on the analog phone and lean back with my elbow bent on the armrest. My eyes gaze through the windows and out into the lush forest while dark clouds roll in, preparing for a downpour. With a quick flash of movement from the corner of my eye, I swing around to where a tall tree stands inches from the glass. The raven lands on a branch.

"Hey, buddy." I roll my chair closer. I recognize him immediately, because he's the one who hangs out around the property. Ravens are thought to bring bad luck, but that's never been the case for me.

I quickly turn with a buzz of my daytime cell phone on the desk. The raven flies away, leaving the branch bouncing in its wake.

Before I get the chance to say anything, Andrew's voice is on the other end.

"You're up, fucker."

"Me?" I ask, surprised to hear from him.

"Don't get too excited, you only get to shadow this time."

"Shadow?" I recall the information Lux shared about the other guy in the room who could only watch. And then Rich mentioned his turn was the following weekend—*am I getting trained first?*

"Yeah, like training. I planned for you to shadow Nolen last weekend, but his aunt, grandmother, or whoever the fuck she was, passed away. Now you'll be with Duncan."

"I don't need training to fuck a woman," I grit out.

"If you're going to do this, you're doing it my way," he scolds me in an even tone.

I fight the urge to bite back and instead I swallow my pride. "Fine. But why not Rich?"

He scoffs. "The little chicken shit must have thought he was getting in over his head and disappeared during his weekend. Nolen tried to warn me about Rich, but I didn't listen." He pauses. "So we've had to switch a few things around."

"Do you have an idea where he went?" I ask, gauging whether it has spooked him or not.

"Nah, he was a deadweight, anyway. As long as he shows up before tax season, we're all good," he says. "One of the girls got away a few weeks ago so we need to remain vigilant. The police mentioned only three women, but there were four. And I have an idea of who it was. But for some reason she hasn't gone to them. Maybe skeletons in her closet?" He chuckles.

He's talking about Lux. And I'm glad she's here.

"How do you know who it is?"

"It's a long story, but let's just say she's no stranger to law enforcement."

"That's all I get?" I poke him, hoping to get more information.

"For now," he says. "I'll text you Friday evening exactly an hour before you're supposed to meet Duncan at the club. That's where you'll choose two women, and leave everything else to me."

"Where will we keep them?"

"One of my LLCs purchased an old house down the street from University of Washington. College girls love this club because it's close to campus. Every night, they walk home past our house, drunk and vulnerable, so they won't be much of a struggle."

Fucking monster.

I squeeze the pen, white knuckling the thin plastic until it splinters. "Perfect."

"You'll get the weekend to have fun. Then Duncan will call me and I'll get our crew to come and..." He pauses briefly. "Dispose of everything."

"Sounds good."

"Cool—" Andrew says.

I end the call without letting him finish.

Anger and rage whip at my back. Beyond that, she can't know that Andrew may have targeted her because of her dad. But I have to inform Christian and Sebastian—not now, though. The conversation I had with Andrew rips at my soul, and right now all I want to do is see Lux.

I lift from my chair and thunder toward the door, exiting my office. With a quick set of the alarm, I sprint down the long dark hall of the North Wing, then take a hard left heading down the East Wing. Possession has overwhelmed me. My dick stiffens in desperation to reclaim what is mine.

I walk to the foot of her bed, kick off my shoes and remove my shirt.

"Lux," I say her name as I come closer.

"River?"

"I missed you."

A soft giggle comes from underneath the blankets before she opens them to invite me in. "I'm glad you came to me."

Climbing into bed, I turn to my side as she tucks herself into me. "Andrew contacted me."

Her body stills. "He did?"

I smooth my hands over the top of her head. "We're on for this weekend. He still thinks I'm planning to be a part of it and wants me to shadow Duncan."

The air leaves her lungs. "Oh my god."

"We'll talk more about the plans later. Right now, I want to make you feel good," I say, kissing her temple. With a hand, I glide my fingertips up along the outside of her hip, bringing her silky nightgown with it.

In one motion, I slide myself on top of her as she rolls on to her back.

"You're too good to me."

"You deserve the world, Lux."

She bows her back to get closer, her hard nipples tease my chest, brushing it lightly.

"It was the most amazing fucking feeling in the world to be with you."

Taking one leg, I push it to the side separating them from one another. Lux whimpers, her eyes rolling back as she prepares for me to fill her once again.

"Eyes on me." I gently grip her cheeks with one hand, moving her face to look at me. "There, beautiful."

She smiles through a moan. My dick prodding at her wet core.

"It was amazing for me, too."

I waste no time and push into her. She's as slick and wet as she was earlier this morning.

Lux gasps.

Rolling my hips into her, I groan at her body sucking me in. It's worth dying for, and I would easily take my last breath inside her.

She quickly slides her hand down between us, cupping my balls gently, then massaging them for a minute before tightening her grip.

"That's a good girl. Tell me what you need."

Her head tilts back, her eyes now facing upwards.

Continuing to pump my dick into her, my limbs stiffen, but I want her to use my name. I want her to know who is going to take care of her. I slow my movements, her insides clenching around my hard cock, but I pull out, letting it tap the outside of her pussy. "What's my name?"

"River," she whines, lifting her hips to chase my pulsating length.

"Say it again."

"River, please."

As my climax peaks, I thrust back into her, my frantic movements matching hers as we both release together.

And that's not all I plan to do to show her how a woman like her should be treated. She is perfection—and I'm unapologetically obsessed.

CHAPTER TWENTY-SIX

RIVER

L ux and I spend the entire night together again. Falling asleep with her in my arms is everything. It's safety and protection, something only I can give her.

She mentioned wanting to see her sister since they haven't spoken much, and considering how close they are, Stevie's been asking questions like why Lux hasn't been responsive the last week or so.

I'm comfortable with Lux going over to Stevie's place, but only after I lend her one of my cars with a tracker on it. She parked far enough away from the building so her sister won't be suspicious about the different car. And to be even more cautious, I followed behind her all the way here.

Now I'm parked outside waiting for her to come out of Stevie's condo, when I decide to swipe into one of TI's tracking apps to access the National Missing Persons database. Different from the public website, this one scans all law enforcement databases as well. It's been over a week, and although I can guess Rich and his wife's marriage wasn't perfect, I'm sure she's reported him by now. Not having to scroll far, I spot the accountant—filed yesterday. This means the police will begin looking into his associates, ultimately closing in on Andrew and his friends, which means they'll soon find out Nolen is missing as well.

Readjusting my hat, I glance over at the main entrance of Lux's sister's building as a thought crosses my mind. If Andrew recently figured out Lux is alive, and he's alluding to her being connected to law enforcement, her sister might be in danger as well.

Shit.

I need to speak with Lux about telling her sister what happened—because she will need to stay with us too.

Just then, I catch sight of Lux through the glass windows of the lobby inside the condo building, preparing to leave. I only saw her a couple of hours ago, but my heart pains to be near her again. Tracking each of her movements, I keep a steady eye on her as she climbs into the white Porsche.

The tail lights shine into the windshield of my car as she backs out. Flipping the ignition, I pull out of my spot near the stairs. Following close behind, we both drive out of the back parking lot and onto the city street.

My phone rings through the speakers. "You're behind me, aren't you?" she says the moment I answer her.

"Are you surprised?"

"I should be, but I'm not." She chuckles softly. "Did you wait outside the entire time?"

"Of course I did," I tease her, continuing to tail her as we both merge onto the highway.

"I have some information to tell you when we get home."

Home.

The word falls from her lips and hits my ears like a ton of bricks, causing me to imagine things I don't normally.

I let myself indulge in the possibility of having an average life and someone to share it with. But she's not driven by the same things I am. And the more I live in a world where I let my thoughts entertain a future with her, the more worried I get about the darkness leaving her. Because then I'll have to go back to watching her from afar. The only difference between me and the monsters I kill, is that I take their lives instead of innocents.

"Tell me."

"You have zero self-control."

"Only with you."

"You're incorrigible," she says, and I can hear the smile in her voice before her tone turns serious. "Stevie saw on the news, the accountant's wife reported him missing."

"I know. Which means the police will start looking into his associates."

She says something but my attention halts when a small BMW swerves into my lane, pulling between Lux and me.

What the fuck?

"I think there's someone following you, stay on the line."

"What?"

"Don't panic. I'm right here and I won't let anything happen to you. I'll kill them first. "

I drive into the left lane to get a glimpse of the driver while keeping my eyes on Lux's Porsche. Then I jerk my car past the white line as if to hit the BMW, but it veers away before it's back into the lane behind Lux.

Who the hell is this?

As we get closer to the manor, I call Sebastian.

He barely answers when I rush out, "We're close to the manor, but a white BMW has been tailing Lux since we pulled out of her sister's neighborhood."

"Do you think it's Andrew or one of his guys?"

"I have no fucking idea. Can you meet us at the bottom of the hill?"

"On my way," he says. "I'll tell Wayne in the security tower, too."

I hang up just as I see the car follow Lux onto my property. I speed up and swerve in front of the foreign car, cutting them off from Lux as we all turn off the highway toward the security gate leading to our property.

With my gun drawn, I jump out of my car and rush to the driver's side. "Get the fuck out of the car!"

"River?" Lux's trembling voice is behind me.

"Get back in your car, Lux!"

Suddenly the door cracks open and a small hand with black painted nails sticks up from the top. "Don't shoot. I'm her sister!"

What?

"Stevie?" Lux shouts.

"Get out," I tell her, still alarmed.

"Stevie, what the hell are you doing here?" Lux exclaims.

"What are *you* doing here?"

"It's a long story." Lux's eyes flutter. She steps in front of me, but I reach for her hand. "It's okay," she says. "It's just my sister."

"Your sister?" My eyes bounce between the two of them as recognition forms. *Oh, that* is *her sister, Stevie Levinson.* I remember seeing her photograph in the files Christian sent over when he did background research on Lux. I've also seen her at Lux's house before. But tonight, she's wearing a hoodie with her hair back, and driving what looks to be a different car from her usual.

Maybe that's why I didn't recognize her initially. My shoulders relax a little.

"Yes, her *sister,*" Stevie snaps. "Now can you get your gun out of my face?"

"Tell me why you followed us all the way out here," I press, needing more before I can feel that she's not a threat. "Then I'll lower it."

She directs her answer to Lux. "You've been acting weird lately. You barely said anything to me when you were at my house. And then I see you drive off in this expensive ass car," she says. "What was I supposed to do? You're my sister. I was worried something bad was going on."

Lux sighs, meeting my eyes. Her hand comes to the top of my arm, indicating for me to lower the weapon.

I do as I'm told before calling Sebastian. "False alarm, we'll be up in a minute," I say as soon as he answers the call.

"Are you sure?" he asks.

I tuck my gun into the back of my pants. "I'll explain later," I say, then hang up.

"This isn't even your car either," Lux walks over to her sister.

"I just got it. But none of that matters right now." Stevie frowns before pinning me with a glare. "Can you tell me what's going on? What is this place and who is this guy?"

I wrap an arm around Lux's waist. This might be a good time for Lux to explain to her sister what's going on. "She's staying with me. Why don't we head inside and you guys can talk?"

"I'm not going anywhere with you until my sister gives me an answer," Stevie demands, crossing her arms over her chest.

Great, I can already tell she's going to be a pain.

Lux's expression softens as she reaches for her sister's hand. "We'll talk once we get into the house," Lux tells her sister. "Follow River and me up."

Stevie's eyebrows rise. "Oh, so he has a name?" She looks

unsure but reluctantly agrees, and I lead them up the hill and into the underground garage. Lux takes the spot next to my car while Stevie parks to the left.

Sebastian is walking out of the elevator as we all exit the vehicles. "What the hell happened?"

Stevie leans against the side of her car, her legs crossed at the ankles. "Who the fuck are you?"

Sebastian cocks his head. "Who the fuck are *you*?"

Lux blows out a breath, stepping between them. "Stevie, this is Sebastian, River's cousin." She then turns to Sebastian. "Sebastian, meet my sister, Stevie."

I flip my hat backward. "Now that we all know each other, should we go inside?"

We take the short elevator ride to the main floor of the house and head into the living room, where Stevie casually takes a seat on the couch while Lux leans against the stone fireplace. Sebastian and I remain standing to the side near the window, letting Lux take the lead.

"Okay." Stevie wastes no time. "What is going on?"

Lux bites her lip.

I can't say this is the best time to have this discussion, but she needs to be honest with her sister. And it's not like I want another person to be privy to what we're doing, but I'm worried about Stevie's safety after my call with Andrew.

"River and Sebastian are helping me with something." Lux pauses, weighing whether or not to let her sister in on our plans. With a quick glance over to me, I nod giving her encouragement to continue. She lets out a long breath before speaking again, "You know the cabin case dad's been working on?"

"Yeah?" Stevie's brows furrow.

"I was one of those women," Lux admits. Moisture pooling

in her eyes. I walk over to her and rest a hand on her back. "River was the one who got me out that night."

"Lux..." Stevie's voice trails off as shock drains the blood from her face.

"The night we went to the club—" Lux focuses on the hardwood floor at our feet, her muscles stiffening under my palm.

She's reliving it.

"There is a lot to talk about, Stevie, but the bottom line is, River and I are helping Lux avenge herself," Sebastian adds, still vague.

They need to talk about this privately.

"Stevie, Lux is staying in the East Wing. Why don't you spend the night with her tonight and you two can talk about it?" I offer.

Perplexed, Stevie simply shrugs her shoulders and agrees.

I dip my head, capturing Lux's beautiful eyes in mine. The ones that once were light—and full of life. "Can I speak with you first?"

Lux nods, giving me a weak smile.

The tapping of rain outside the windows has picked up now that nightfall is among us. Hooking an arm around Lux, I lead her into the hallway and out of earshot of her sister and Sebastian.

"Are you okay?" I ask.

"Yeah..." She swallows hard. "I think I need to tell her the whole truth."

Taking two fingers, I pinch her chin, bringing her lips to mine and kiss her lightly. "I think you're right."

"Thanks for the support."

"Of course." I smile, reluctantly. "She'll stay in the room with you tonight. And it's not the best time to tell you this, but

I also think you should speak with her about staying here as well."

Lux's face transforms into confusion. "Why?"

"Remember I told you Andrew called me yesterday?"

"Yeah?"

"I have reason to believe he might know you're connected to law enforcement. Which means, Stevie could be at risk as well," I whisper.

Her eyes grow wide. "Oh god. Okay."

"Don't worry, I'll explain more later." I cup her cheeks, tilting her face up to press soft kiss on her forehead.

She lets out a heavy exhale, wrapping her arms around my waist for a brief embrace. "I'll come by your bedroom later."

"Okay." I drop my hands.

Sebastian and I leave the room, giving the girls time to make their way to the East Wing for the night.

My stomach tightens knowing this conversation will be difficult for Lux and I won't be there to protect her when the emotions of that night return. I hope Stevie understands because it would be hard for Lux if she didn't.

CHAPTER TWENTY-SEVEN
LUX

My sister paces back and forth on the hardwood floors, while I remain seated on the edge of my bed. She tries to make sense of what I'm telling with her. "I can't believe you were taken that night."

"It feels like a bad dream that I keep reliving."

"This is all my fault," she blurts.

"What? How are you to blame for what happened?"

"Because I left you at your front door alone so I could run off and get laid. Who does that?"

I rise to my feet and walk over to her. "Stevie, stop. It's not your fault."

"It doesn't matter, it's like Friend Code 101, and I did it to my sister!" Her voice strains. "What the fuck?"

"Stop." I grab her hands in mine, forcing eye contact. "You walked me to my door. I got home safely. No one could have predicted I'd be abducted as I was walking *into my house.*"

She shakes her head in disagreement as a tear rolls down her cheek. "I should have been there with you."

"And what would you have done?"

"Anything!"

I bite my lip, waiting for her to finish because I know she has to get this out. She's grieving for me and blaming herself.

"I could have done something to stop it."

"They drugged me. I felt a prick in the side of my neck," I admit. The painful memory makes my stomach clench.

"Oh my god," she gasps. Before I realize what's happening, her arms are around me and she's pulling me in for a hug. "I can't believe you've had to deal with this alone."

I haven't been alone.

I think of River and how he sat outside my townhouse every night after he brought me home from the cabin to make sure I was safe. And then he insisted on me moving into the manor—and now, giving me a path for vengeance. River is helping me get my voice back and my heart warms at the thought.

"I'm not alone. I haven't been alone. River has been with me since the night he brought me home from the cabin."

Stevie draws her head back, her hands on my shoulders, her eyes dart away from me implying there's something else on her mind. "What did River's cousin mean when he said they're helping you avenge your attackers?"

This is the part of the conversation I've been dreading the most. How can I explain to Stevie that I watched a man die, and then soon after I took part in another man's death? To only follow it up with the fact there are two more who still need to lose their lives before Sebastian, River, and I are finished?

I let out a weighted sigh, my stomach in knots. "This part you may want to sit down for."

Stevie reluctantly releases me and shuffles over to the bed. Following close behind, I lower to sit next to her. With her eyes widened with fear, she remains silent while waiting for me to begin.

"River and Sebastian are tracking down each one of the men responsible."

Stevie's throat constricts with a hard swallow. "And what does it mean?"

"It means we are killing them."

The blood drains from her face. "I'm sorry, what?"

"We are taking their lives, Stevie."

"Holy shit."

"Yes."

"Like, you're killing them? How?"

My fists ball together in my lap, moist with sweat. "I watched the first one, and River helped me shoot the second one."

"What the actual fuck, Lux!" She jumps to her feet. "Who are these guys?"

I knew she'd have a million questions and unfortunately I'm unable to answer all of them, because some I'm still figuring out myself.

"They have a technology company here in Seattle, so they come from a lot of money. But at night they run this vigilante type organization."

"You know how completely insane this sounds, right? Not to mention dangerous."

River or Sebastian being a danger? No. I match her stance, ready to defend them. River would never hurt me.

"It's not like that, Stevie, they're the good guys."

She runs a hand through her long curly hair. "I don't even know what to say."

"I know. Like I said before, I'm living in a veritable nightmare."

"This is absolutely unhinged. River's this tech billionaire" —she waves a hand around the bedroom—"who's some sort of vigilante who just agreed to help you?"

"Essentially."

"And you're okay with this? Like, you want to kill these men?" A slight inflection in her voice.

"Yes."

"This is not normal, Lux."

"Nothing about this is. Nothing about how I feel or the darkness eating at my insides is. I'm not sleeping at night because I'm either scared or worried, and I'm still trying to figure it all out."

"*Fuck.*"

"But what I do know is those men cannot be allowed to continue doing what they're doing to women."

"Then why not just let Dad and the police handle it?"

"Absolutely not. Andrew has money. He could hire the best lawyers and get away with everything. You and I both know the justice system has its limitations—but River and Sebastian don't."

"Andrew?"

"Yes, one of the men. He's a hotel heir, and River has reason to believe he targeted me because of Dad."

Saying the words aloud is difficult. Not only do they echo inside my skull, but they hit the air with weight. It's overwhelming and leaves me with more questions I hope to be answered in time.

"Oh my god."

"I don't have any more details about it, because he only briefly mentioned it to me tonight. He also said you should consider staying here for your safety."

Her eyelids flutter as her hands fly into the air with palms up. "No way! I want nothing to do with this. I have a job and life."

It's a lot for her to process. Ever since we were kids, my sister gets overwhelmed easily. But she's practical and a realist so after a good night's sleep, she'll be less in shock and more level headed.

"Fine. At least stay tonight?"

"Uh...okay." Her focus is distant, as if she is putting the pieces together. "But I don't have anything here."

I smile to lighten the mood a little and walk over to the closet. "River had his personal shopper drop racks of clothing for me. And since you've always stolen my clothes anyway, they're all yours too."

"Funny." She laughs uncomfortably, then her expression turns. "In a questionably moral way, I think he likes you."

I blush. "Maybe."

Stevie grimaces as she walks into the closet. "Holy shit. I need a fucking glass of wine. Scratch that, I need a whole bottle."

"Maybe later." I smile.

Stevie showers and changes before we both crawl into the enormous bed. I expect more questions from my sister, but she falls into a deep sleep within no time.

But I can't sleep. My mind is unable to settle, so I slip on my shoes and head into the gardens.

I step onto the short pebble lined walkway, as the early morning sun shines through the trees. It casts a beautiful orange glow into the space.

I take a seat on the long white bench, lean back, and breathe in a deep gulp of fresh air. The remaining crickets from the night chirp only a few feet away.

"Couldn't sleep?" a rough, but sultry voice comments from the side.

I don't see at first, but I know it's him.

"Do I ever sleep anymore?" I reply.

River's dark figure steps from behind a tall rose bush and faces me. "Not since I've been watching you."

"I'm sure."

"How's your sister?" The back of his knuckles smooth across my cheek. It's comforting and makes me want to crawl into his arms.

"She took the news better than I thought. After a flurry of emotions, ranging from shock to sadness and disbelief," I say. "Then she passed out. She needs time to process it all."

"I get it." River sits next to me. His leg brushes against mine, sending little tingles up my spine.

"Did you talk to her about staying here until this is all over?"

"I mentioned it, but she wasn't very receptive."

"Give her time." River's arm extends behind me, resting on the back of the bench. I lean into him, tucking myself into his chest. "Like you said, she'll be in a better mindset after some rest."

"I know." Peace washes over me as I cuddle River in the middle of the garden. But something he mentioned earlier in the night is still in the back of my mind. "You said you have reason to believe Andrew targeted me based on my connection with law enforcement..."

"Yes." His chin lowers to the top of my head. "When I spoke with Andrew, he let it slip about you not being a stranger."

"Maybe he's confusing me with someone else?"

"I'm not sure yet, but until we have more information about what Andrew is referring to, Stevie needs to stay here with us. I'll also have someone watching over your dad just to make sure."

I sigh. "I'll talk to her. I need to make her think it's her idea, because Stevie can be a bit of a rebel. If she feels forced, she won't do it."

River's chest rumbles with a chuckle. "You two have that in common."

His playful sarcasm catches me off guard in the best away. I lift my head, pulling my mouth to the side giving him attitude. "Is that so?"

He laughs, pulling me closer to him.

Then I remember what my dad mentioned a couple weeks ago. "My dad said something about this possibly being a copycat from the ring of twenty years ago."

River's brows furrow, but he expression doesn't change as if having background already. "I'll look into that."

We sit together until the sun fully rises, telling us it's time to get some sleep.

CHAPTER TWENTY-EIGHT
RIVER

After taking Lux back to her room from the garden, I got a few hours of sleep. I asked her to stay with me, but she insisted on being with Stevie if she woke up with more questions—which I'm sure she did.

Sebastian and I spend the late afternoon in my office, working through the logistics of this weekend. Relying heavily on my team for most of the setup, we discuss every part to be played out.

"Lux is to be nowhere near the inside of the house until I give the okay," I firmly remind him how vital her safety is. "Everything has to go exactly as planned. I will not risk her getting hurt."

"Yes, River, we know, and I will reiterate once again to the guys." Sebastian still isn't comfortable with Lux's involvement, but I sense he's slowly coming around to her.

With her wanting to be more involved, I'm both proud and nervous. Proud about how brave she's becoming, but nervous for the exact same reason. Her tenacity could become a risk.

"I'm just making sure."

Sebastian's eyes narrow. "You're, like, *into* her, aren't you?"

"I want her safe."

"It's more than that, though. I mean, do you have like *feelings* for her?"

Carrying a weight I'm not expecting, his words fall on me with deep realization of how my view of Lux is changing. I don't want to think too much about it. But nothing could ever come of it even if I did.

"Just make sure to follow my lead."

He senses my apprehension and simply nods.

"Are you going to let her pull the trigger by herself this time?" Sebastian asks, closing his laptop.

I glance over at the screen with the garden. She's buried behind her computer, tucked into the corner of the bench. The same spot where we cuddled together a few hours ago.

"I don't know."

"Maybe talk to her about it beforehand," Sebastian points out. "At least that way, we'll have a plan."

"She should decide in the moment." My eyes flick back to her slight frame and delicate lips.

"I think it's important we know, though." He rests his chin in his palm with his elbow bent on the armrest of the chair, clearly frustrated with this wild card part of our planning. Not typical, Sebastian is pushing back against it.

"I'm not going to pressure her, Sebastian," I spit out. "Lux has been through enough. Whatever she needs in the moment, we'll do for her."

He sighs with a subtle eye roll. "You're the boss."

"That's right." I notice the time on my watch and remember my martial arts training session this evening. Sensei Clark is tough and doesn't like to be left waiting. I push off the desk and rise from the chair, sending the wheels back to hit the window behind me. "I'm late for a session with Sensei Clark."

Sebastian scoops up his computer and slides it under his arm. "I saw him this morning. He kicked my ass."

"It's because you're a little bitch."

He whips his head around as I follow close behind him to the door. "It's been a long time since we've met on the mat," he challenges with a spark in his eyes. "Maybe it's time for us to spar again, like when we were kids."

I pull the door closed behind me. "You seem a little too excited about that."

"Scared?" He shoves my shoulder.

"Of you?" I respond by pushing him into the wall. "I'd beat you like I always have."

Sebastian's eyes bounce around the long hallway.

"Who are you looking for?"

"No one." He swings his arm around, pushing mine down in order to duck under it.

"I think she should stay with us until this is all over."

I briefed Sebastian the other day about my conversation with Andrew, but I left out the idea of Stevie staying with us.

"Who?"

"Lux's sister."

"River, this is our home—not a hotel," he says, cocking a brow. "We can't keep inviting strangers to stay here."

"They're not strangers. She's Lux's family. We can't risk something happening to her."

He may not like the idea, but he knows I'm right. It's a tough situation.

"Fine," he huffs out. "But don't make me keep her company. I can't stand her."

My brows furrow. "Why?"

"She wouldn't shut up about the mortuary during breakfast."

Sebastian and I round the corner to the gym. "And?"

"I don't want to have to listen to her ramble about her mortician job all day." He waves at Sensei Clark who's sitting at his desk in the corner of the gym filling out our tracking sheets.

"And we think our nightly activities are morbid? Their dad's a homicide lieutenant, your not-so-innocent Lux writes about crime and turned into a murderer, while her sister—who looks like she just stepped out of a 2000s Abercrombie & Fitch catalog—is a fucking mortician."

Sebastian keeps talking about Stevie, and I find it interesting but decide not to give him a hard time about it since she'll be staying here.

"They're definitely not an average family, are they?"

"No shit," he says.

While talking about both Lux and her sister staying with us, a sudden bolt of panic shoots up my spine. Lux might want to show her sister around and wander into...*did I remember to lock my office door?*

Fuck. The cameras.

As much as I've told Lux, I haven't told her *everything.*

"I'll be right back, Sensei Clark. I forgot something!"

"You only have a thirty-minute session today, River!" he shouts.

I hurry out of the door, leaving him and Sebastian in the dust. I yell over my shoulder, "You'll still get paid!"

I'm too far away to make out his reply. In a full sprint from one end of the house to the other, I quickly approach the North Wing where my office is. The door is ajar.

I push open the wooden door and take a quick look around the space. Then my eyes land on Lux standing in front of the screen wall with her arms folded at her chest.

Fuck. *Fuck!*

"Lux?" I close the door behind me.

Her head whips to the side, two flared eyes meeting mine. "Is that my townhouse?"

My heart drums against my ribcage. I planned to tell her about the twenty-four-hour surveillance I've had on her since the night we first met, but I haven't found the right time yet.

I swallow hard. "Yes."

She steps closer to the screens, focusing on one in particular. "Is that my *bedroom*?"

"Yeah."

Lux's hand comes to cover her mouth before shrieking, "What the fuck, River!"

My boots thud on the floor, eating the distance between us. "I can explain," I tell her as I reach for her arm.

She jerks away from my touch, and a pang of guilt squeezes at my chest.

"How long have you been watching me? How did you get these into my house?" Her voice cracks with disbelief.

I hate it. But as much as I would rather pretend, I don't want to lie to her. "Since the night I brought you home from the cabin. While you were passed out, Hayden installed them."

"Oh my god!" Her eyebrows snap together. "How could you do that to me?"

"I needed to make sure you were safe."

"You sat outside of my house *every* night," she bites back.

I shake my head. "Yes, but it wasn't enough."

"I can't believe this." Lux's posture straightens.

A beat passes and I let the silence settle between us, aware she'll probably need some time to accept it—and because I'm not sure what else to say or do. I wish I could understand more about human emotions. The ability to read people and properly respond to them, are two entirely different things.

Unsure of how to act, I stand in the middle of my office with my hands at my sides.

"I don't even know what to say."

"Is there something I should say?"

"What do you mean?"

"I mean, what do you need me to say to make you feel better about this?"

Her arms fold across her chest. "I don't know, River. Is there something you'd like to say? Maybe an apology or an acknowledgement that this is really fucked up."

"Sorry you had to find out this way."

"Do you not have remorse?"

I shake my head, then take a couple steps toward her, but she backs away again. "Not really."

"Why not?" The tone of her voice is pleading with me to admit my fault, but I can't. I was infatuated with her and I needed to make sure she was safe no matter *how* I did it.

"From the moment I met you, you became my responsibility. And I was ready to do whatever it took to make sure no one harmed you again."

Lux's nostrils flare as her eyes blink rapidly. "By invading my privacy and putting cameras in my house?"

I reach out to touch her arm, but she doesn't back away this time, giving me hope. She wants to be mad, but there's a part of her that understands my methods—and maybe even finds pleasure in it.

"Yes."

"You should have just told me." Her voice lowers slightly.

"*That*, I am sorry for." I let my thumb caress the skin of her bare skin.

"I don't know what to say."

Lowering my lips to the outside of her ear, I graze my nose along the shallow indentation. "You're mine, Lux. I will continue to do whatever it takes to make sure you're safe. I will go to the ends of the earth for you and gladly walk through fire to do it." A sharp inhale causes a tiny gasp to escape her lips. "And I'm not going to apologize for how I feel."

Her head lowers between us as she grapples with my actions. Fighting between how she feels and what she should believe is morally acceptable.

She starts to walk away from me, but I catch her wrist and pull her into my chest. A tight yelp escapes from her throat. "River!"

Lux needs to accept this is my way of expressing my devotion to her. I grow impatient with the direction this conversation is going, because I know deep down, my obsessive passion doesn't scare her.

"You like that I was watching you, don't you?" I nudge with a low growl. "It excites you, knowing I've seen you come all over your fingers with my name on your lips. Doesn't it?"

"River." Her voice grows deep.

Tightening my hand around her wrist, I bend to meet her fiery gaze. "How would it make you feel if I told you I jacked off watching you pleasure yourself?"

Lux jabs her elbow into my side, but it does nothing for the grip I have on her. "Seriously?"

"Yes." I twist her in my arm, bringing her back to my front. Wrapping myself tightly around her body, rendering her unable to move. "You speak to my soul, Lux, and I know I speak to yours, too," I whisper into her ear.

"So what? It doesn't give you the right to watch me without my knowledge." She fights against my hold. "Have you been protecting or keeping me, River?"

With a free hand, I pinch her cheeks together, angling her head up so her skin runs flush with mine. "Both."

A whimper slips out from her delicious lips before her knees give out. Sensing the shift in weight and preventing her from throwing herself onto the hard, unforgiving floor, I pull her to my desk.

"Bend over." I slip my free hand under her skirt. The silkiness of the black stockings makes my mouth water. If I have learned anything about Lux, is that she is a fucking loose cannon—one that enjoys being controlled.

"River." She slides her leg out and swings it under me, but I catch myself.

"You like to be controlled don't you?" I tease, coiling my hand around a chunk of her hair.

Lux arches her back, inviting me in as she slides her hand under her skirt and yanks her panties down. My cock is pulsating and pokes the inside of my joggers with a painful desperation. "Maybe."

"Open up for me," I command, thrusting my hard length into her ass cheeks, separating her legs.

The last of her fight melts away. I loosen my hold on her and pull my cock out, fisting myself a few times before sliding into her.

"Oh god," she moans.

"There you go." I roll my hips into her.

She lets out another moan, her head falling back onto my shoulder.

Bending to bring my lips to hers, my tongue darts out, licking across the seam of her lips.

"Say it." I enjoy how her body sucks me in. Barely able to slide out, I roll my hips angling upward. "Say that you're mine."

"Yes," she pants. "All yours."

Grabbing the side of her ass, my fingers sink into her soft skin. "That's what I thought."

"Did you really watch me make myself come?" Her eyes roll

back into her head as our bodies move in sync with one another, slapping echoing through the room.

I knew she liked it.

A laugh rumbles inside my chest, while my lip quirks up. "I watched you play with that pretty little pussy of yours," I confess, slamming into her. Lux lets out a guttural groan, arching her back and taking my cock even deeper inside her cunt. "Are you upset about it?"

"Only if you've watched others too."

Pumping myself into her a few more times, I come closer to my climax. "You're the only one."

Lux's body tenses just as she falls flat on top of my desk, sending the pile of documents floating to the floor.

"Show me how well you cum for me." I rest a hand on her lower back.

"Oh, River," she moans.

While her body trembles underneath my grip, I continue to pump a few more times until she pants with a pleasure riding her orgasm. I come shortly after and continue pushing in and out of her until we're both spent.

Throbbing with pleasure, I painfully pull out. Dazed and looking sated, she flips her body around, pushing herself on to my desk. Sweat mists her forehead. Her eyes are dark, feral as ever. Then her legs fly open, flashing me a full look at her swollen pussy, like a tease.

I drop to my knees in front of her. "Look at the mess we've made. Let me clean you up."

"You've been a bad boy, River." Lux shakes her head. "Watching me on those cameras."

"Have I?" I bury my nose into the wetness between her legs, breathing in the scent of us.

But then, before I get a taste of us together, she inches her skirt back down, hops off my desk, and walks toward the door. With a flip of her hair, she turns to me. "This isn't over."

I laugh, shocked and surprised by how much she fucking amazes me. "It's not?"

"No. But for now, I'll let you continue watching me." And with one last glare and a click of her tongue, she says, "I have work to do." Then slams the door behind her, leaving me alone in my office.

For the first time in my life, I am not the one who is in charge.

CHAPTER TWENTY-NINE
LUX

My feelings for River are growing the more time we spend together. And I'm not going to deny the euphoria that pulsed through me when he referred to me as *his*.

River's ability to be two different people should alarm me, but it doesn't. And the coldness that emerges from him when he's carrying out a kill is unsettling, but when it's just the two of us, he's kind and gentle. Both sides are intoxicating.

I still can't let him off the hook too easily because I'm angry he installed cameras in my townhouse and my room here at the manor. But why am I trying to convince myself I don't find it thrilling? To be protected so fiercely by a man who could kill another without a second thought sends every feminine bone in my body plummeting to the floor.

What is wrong with me?

As I sit at the desk in my room at River's house, I can't help my eyes from darting around the room every few minutes, in search of his cameras. But who am I kidding? River's billion-dollar tech company creates devices for the government. Why would he create cameras that could be detectable?

I gave in to him this afternoon in his office by letting him dominate me. I tried to fight back, but he knows me better than I know myself, and it is something I'd never experienced before.

After what happened in his office—both with the cameras and his blatant honesty about his feelings toward me—everything has changed. Because River represents something dark and steady, a power unlike anything I've encountered, and his obsession with me does nothing to steer me away. If anything it's pulling me closer.

A quick vibration on the desk.

STEVIE

Just finishing up at work. Do you want me to come back to River and Sebastian's house?

Stevie has knowledge of almost everything now, and if she's willing to come back maybe she's reconsidering staying here after all. When she said she was going to work this morning, I asked River to assign one of his men to her to make sure she's safe. He chuckled and said he was already on it.

I pick up the phone to call her instead. I'd rather continue to convince her over the phone than through text.

"Hey," she says as soon as she answers. "How are you feeling today?"

Tucking my legs underneath me, I stare at the fully typed chapter in front of me that I spent the first part of the evening working on. The last thing I want to do is ask for an extension from my editor, but it's impossible to devote the time needed to finish this story with everything that's going on.

"I'm okay. Have you made a decision on whether to stay or not?" I ask, hoping she's changed her mind.

"In fact, I have."

"And?"

"I'll stay, Lux. But as long as I can come and go as I please."

I let out a sigh of relief. "I'm glad. It will make me feel much better."

"Me too." She lets out a quiet sigh matching mine.

"River already assigned one of his guys to tail you wherever you go, so you'll be safe."

"Wait, what?"

A flush of heat zips through me as I regret blurting out my comment. I may be slowly accepting River's protectiveness, but Stevie might not be as willing as I am.

"I know it sounds weird, but trust me—it's for your protection."

She's silent for a beat, probably talking herself through whether she wants to protest or not. "Fine," she groans. "I'll see you soon."

I smile to myself. "I'll see you soon."

But before I can end the call, Stevie quickly says my name. "Oh, and Lux?"

"Yeah?"

"I'm not bringing my own clothes because I will be wearing all your new ones," she says. The confidence laced through her voice is in true Stevie fashion.

I laugh. "This is nothing new."

"Love ya!"

When Stevie and I end our call I think about writing some more, but my stomach growls with hunger. With a quick check of the time, I close my laptop and head to the kitchen, knowing Ben usually has dinner ready by now.

The long dark hallway that makes up the East Wing is becoming more familiar. Voices can be heard as I approach the main part of the house, anticipating River already being there.

And with a lightness in my chest and a heart fluttering out of control, I round the corner.

Sebastian, sitting at the counter eating, turns to nod his head in my direction.

Then my eyes land on the man as tall as a tree, donned in all black, leaning against the counter. I'd like to revisit our conversation about the cameras, because I can't let it go that easily.

"Lux," he drawls, flipping his hat backward, making me forget about everything I was just thinking.

Fuck, he's hot.

Letting my fingertips glide across the large island, I sway over to him, stopping with only inches between us. My eyelids flutter up to his. I try to maintain the confidence I had earlier this morning. "River."

Staring down at me, he pops a blueberry into his mouth. "Hungry?"

"Very." I grin.

He brings a blueberry up and glides it across my bottom lip before sliding it in.

My stomach does that flipping thing it does every time I'm around River as I suck the fruit into my mouth. "That tastes good."

River's thumb and index finger pinch my chin, tilting my face up to his. "I have something else that's good for—"

"God, you two," Sebastian interrupts picking up his plate. He walks it over to the sink and drops it. "Get a fucking room."

River and I ignore him. "Ben made you dinner." He wraps his arms tight around the front of my shoulders. "It's in the fridge. Do you want me to heat it up for you?"

Slipping my hands into his back pockets, I give his ass a light squeeze. "I would love that. You have a lot of making up to do for the cameras."

"I know." He walks over to the refrigerator to grab the pre-made food.

"We're getting on a call with Hayden to go over logistics for Duncan," Sebastian tells us, sliding back into the chair at the island. "Is she..." He glances at me then over to River.

With a sigh, River closes the refrigerator, and places the glass dishes on the counter. "Joining the call?"

"Yeah," Sebastian says.

River looks over at me. "Would you like to be included on this call?"

Shocked, but mildly excited, I agree before either of them can change their minds. "Yes, if that's okay with both of you."

River flashes me a wide smile before turning to Sebastian. "Sebastian?"

Sebastian looks over at me, annoyed but not mad which is an improvement from the past. "Yeah, she can be here."

"Cool, let's get him on the phone."

Sebastian opens his laptop and pulls up an app I don't recognize. A camera opens on the screen similar to the programs that are used by companies for virtual calls.

"Hayden," River says as Hayden's face appears on the screen.

"Hello," he greets in an upbeat tone. "Is that Lux I see?"

I move my head into view. "Hi, Hayden."

Hayden is around our age and loves to joke around. We've been able to get to know each other since we've spent a lot of time together waiting outside while the boys got things ready.

"Look at you," he says. "You're really becoming part of our operation, aren't you?"

"She is," River chimes in.

"I knew I'd eventually wear River down." My eyes bounce between the guys and they exchange a quick glance humoring me.

"Finally, someone to keep you two in line on the job," he replies, chuckling.

River rests his hands on the counter, leaning in. "Sebastian sent the game plan to you earlier this morning," he says with authority, and I inappropriately find it sexy as hell. "Do you have questions?"

"Nope. It looks pretty standard." His expression shows unease. "The only thing I'm concerned about is they'll know who you are."

"Duncan knows who I am and will be expecting me," he says. "Unfortunately, it's the only way. Which means, you'll take all directions from Sebastian to ensure I'm not compromised."

Sebastian steps in. "Lux will remain in the surveillance van with you, until we get the clear from River for her to come out."

"Yeah, River won't let me go near anyone until they're completely secured."

"Exactly." River shoots me a firm glance. "I'm meeting Duncan at the target house at eleven p.m. From there, we'll have to take it one step at a time since Andrew wasn't too forthcoming about the details."

River removes his hat, smooths out his hair, then slides it on backward again. My eyes trace the features of his face before sliding down his arms. Unapologetically, I let my gaze linger for a moment, appreciating how tightly his T-shirt hugs his biceps. I swallow hard, forcing myself to refocus on what they're saying.

"Hughes won't be there?" Hayden asks.

River rests a steadying hand on my lower back and shakes his head. "No. I didn't get the feeling he'd show up, but we need to be prepared just in case."

"We'll be ready."

"I will let you and Sebastian work through the remaining details while I take Lux to get her things ready."

River grabs my dinner, loops his arm around my back, and guides me out of the kitchen.

"Let's eat in the garden tonight," he says.

I go along, letting him lead me down the hall. I have a feeling he let me sit in on the call not only because he wants me to be more a part of the team, but he's also trying to make up for me finding out about the cameras in my townhouse and room.

"How are you feeling about tonight?" River asks once we're seated at the small white table next to the white roses bushes.

"We need to talk about the cameras, River." I brush off his question.

He leans back, bending his leg over the other. "I thought we discussed it already."

"No," I say. "We fucked."

River's eyes lower. "What else would you like to talk about?"

"You put cameras in my house without my knowledge." I pick my thumbnail, avoiding eye contact with him. "That's an invasion of my privacy."

"I needed to keep you safe. And I told you I was sorry for not telling you sooner."

"It's a bit controlling, don't you think?"

"You think I wanted this?" He bends forward. "I never expected to fall for you, Lux. But I did. And if you think I was obsessive about your safety before, you have no idea how much more I am now."

I draw in a sharp breath at his confession. My heart sinks. It falls from my chest with force. River just admitted to having feelings for me, and I'm speechless. "I don't know what to say."

His thumb runs across my lip. "Say you don't mind my flaws."

My pulse thrums for him. Every moral bone in my body tells me not to accept what he did, but I can't bring myself *not* to. "I don't mind your flaws, River. I have feelings for you, too."

"You do?"

Tears prick the back of my eyelids. "Yes. You are the reason my heart continues to beat and the reason I'm healing."

River's eyebrows knit like he can't believe what I'm telling him. "I'm *healing* you?"

I nod through a smile, while a tear rolls down my cheek.

River's lungs fall as a breath escapes and he leans in to bring his mouth to hover over mine. Chills span my body every time his breath dusts my skin. "Can I kiss you?"

"Yes."

His warm lips are on mine, peppering my mouth with light kisses, I savor every moment of our contact.

Then he slowly pulls back "You should eat before your food gets cold."

River watches me with a slight smile as I finish my dinner. Every time our eyes lock, the corner of his upper lip slightly curves like he's appreciating this sweet moment.

I never thought the man in the mask who helped me escape that dreadful night would be on this journey with me, or that we'd develop deep feelings for one another, but I'm so grateful we have.

River is the light in the endless darkness I've lived in.

CHAPTER THIRTY
RIVER

A brief, unexpected call from Andrew this morning left me with more information than I had yesterday, but he's still being evasive about what he's sharing. It was difficult to keep my frustration under wraps, but I had to push it aside in order to get access to Duncan.

I turn down a dark narrow street just a few miles away from the college campus. A well-populated city would not be my first choice for a kill, but here we are. Built some distance from the walkway, the driveway leads to a faded yellow 1970s-style bungalow. Then I make my way around to the back of the home, like Andrew mentioned when giving me directions. I park my car under a dark, covered structure.

"You guys there?" I ask, confirming my team is in place.

Sebastian is the first to respond. "We're here."

"We got you covered, River," Hayden adds.

"Lux?" I prompt when she doesn't reply.

"I'm here," she says sweetly. "Be safe."

"It's *go* time."

I climb out of the car and throw my kill bag over my shoulder, then take out my phone to follow the directions step-by-step. Heading up the shallow stairs on the back stoop, I rest my gloved hand on the doorknob. With a light twist, it opens just as Andrew said it would. Sliding my gun from the waistband of my pants, I keep it down to my side with a finger hovering over the trigger. There's a musty, stale odor which overpowers my senses, making me gag.

"This place smells like shit," I mutter under my breath.

"You murder people, but you're bothered by a little dust?" Sebastian teases.

I ignore him and continue scanning the house, searching for any sign of Duncan.

"River Thompson."

I swing around, my gun pointed at a tattered fabric chair in the corner of the room. "Fuck, dude. You scared the shit out of me."

Duncan chuckles. "I'm sorry. You should have seen your face."

"Fuck you."

"I've been expecting you. There's something waiting for us in the basement." He continues laughing like we're a couple of friends casually hanging out on a Friday night.

His body language shows no signs of fear or unrest—a cockier man than our last two targets. I hide the smile pulling at the corner of my mouth. *I'm going to enjoy ending this prick.*

"A woman, I presume?" I slip my gun into the back of my pants.

"Better." He grins, nudging me to follow him. "A college student. Young and ripe."

Motherfucker. He already grabbed one.

Andrew never directly said we'd pick one up together, but I assumed—and was hopeful—we'd take care of Duncan before another woman got hurt.

I slap him on the shoulder, taking every bit of self-control not to wrap each one of my fingers around his neck and squeeze. "My favorite. Especially when it's one of those sorority girls."

"I knew you were one of us, Thompson."

He leads me into a cement-walled basement, similar to the one I found Lux in that first night.

A low, painful whimper echoes throughout the place as we round the corner to find a naked woman chained to a wrought iron bed. Not sure if she's completely coherent or not. Her eyes are blindfolded and hands are bound behind her back. She already has bruises spanning the inside of her legs and I wonder how long she's been in here. Duncan must have had her here prior to only earlier this evening.

Anger creeps up my neck just as Hayden confirms they've cleared the perimeter.

Duncan walks over to the woman, a shit-eating grin on his face with his arm extended proud of what he's showing me. "Usually we don't share on our weekends, but Andrew wanted me to test you out first to make sure you're legit."

"What do you mean?"

"I hope you don't mind sloppy seconds."

My eyes move over to the girl, and all I can think of is Lux being in the same position—the pain she felt and the fear and terror when I showed up.

All I see is red. I slip my gun from my back and lunge at Duncan, hitting him on the side of the head with the handle of the gun. He stumbles back, the wind knocked out of him. He tries to brace himself by grabbing at the shower curtain.

"You sick fuck. It's your turn to die now!" I grit.

Sebastian screams in my ear, but my rage drowns out everything else as I continue beating the shit out of the man.

Duncan falls to the floor. I'm reminded of my promise to Lux. This is supposed to be for her and I can't take that away.

"We're on our way in!" Sebastian's hurried voice yells in my ear.

"We need to secure Duncan. He's lost consciousness temporarily from when I hit him. Make sure to bring Lux."

"Okay," he agrees, probably going through all the ways of pushing back. "You sure she should head in now?"

"Yes, she needs to be here."

I grab Duncan's limp body and throw him over my shoulder. Walking him over to the mattress on the floor in the corner of the room, I toss him on top of it. And with a quick removal of handcuffs from my bag, I restrain him to a pipe that runs from the ceiling to the floor.

The sharp creak of the stairs alerts me. I'm expecting Sebastian and Lux, but I can't be too sure. I draw my gun, point it at the base of the steps, and wait.

Sebastian appears first. "Get that thing out of my face."

I lower it as soon as I see Lux. Her eyes fly to the woman lying in the bed. Fear transforms face for only a moment, before it turns to anger. "Is she dead?"

"No, she was moving a few minutes ago," I reply. "Probably drugged."

"Oh god," she gasps, ambling toward the girl.

"Careful," Sebastian warns. "Even though you have gloves on, we can never be too safe."

"Okay." Her bottom lip shakes, but I don't think it's from fear. It's anger.

"And that reminds me." Sebastian lifts a finger into the air. "Hayden brought us something on account of how messy the last kill got."

My eyebrows snap together, unsure of what he is referring to. "What?"

"Send in the plastic wrap," he tells Hayden through the SEs.

"Plastic wrap?" I question.

"He said too much blood got onto the wall behind Nolen."

"Good call." I flash him an upside down smile, a little shocked, but impressed with his preparation skills.

Lux pays no mind to the conversation or the team covering the room with plastic as she gazes at the young woman. "These men are disgusting."

Resting a gentle hand on her back, I remind her of the time. "Duncan will wake up soon and we don't have a lot of time before we need to leave."

Lux's head whips around, her eyebrows furrowed. "What about her?"

"She's out of it right now. Let's talk about it more when we've secured the job we're here to do."

She nods, turning her focus to the man lying only a few feet away. Squaring her shoulders, I'm mesmerized at how she evolves from being a compassionate woman to a killer determined to dish out her form of justice.

Fuck, she's amazing—and she's all mine right now.

"How long until he wakes up?"

"Here," Sebastian tosses her the smelling salt inhaler. "This will speed up the process."

Lux glances at me for approval. I give her a nod, then she turns to Duncan.

He stirs awake a short time later, confused. "Wh-what happened?"

"Hi, Duncan." I smile.

His head tilts up, noticing he's handcuffed to the pole. "What the fuck is this?" I'm sure he's still dizzy from the knockout, so I give him a few seconds to get his bearings. "What are you doing, Thompson?"

"Looks like you're stuck, Duncan," I say.

"Let me out," he snarls before glaring at me. "What the hell is going on?"

I shrug. "Ask her, she's the one in charge."

"Who are you?" He glares at Lux.

Lux smiles. She kneels on the mattress, leaning in. I step forward, not liking how close she is to danger, but maintain my distance. Grabbing his face, she pinches his cheeks between her thumb and index finger. "I'm your worst nightmare."

"What are *you* going to do?" This must be his attempt at baiting her. "You look like a girl we'd probably pick up. A tight little pussy."

I take another step forward, ready to intervene, but Lux keeps her composure.

With a quick lick of her lips, she grins once again, trying to muster up the courage from her darker side. A side of her I not only relate to, but am addicted to.

"You abducted me, you piece of shit." Duncan's skin chaps from her leather gloves squeezing tighter. "But I got away and now I'm out for revenge."

"A little thing like you? You can't kill me," he spits, his eyes challenging her.

Lux clears her throat. "When was the last time you heard from Rich?"

"What's that supposed to mean?"

"What about your buddy Nolen?" she taunts.

His gaze searches Sebastian and I standing at the food of the mattress, flanking either side of Lux. A wave of fear slowly washes over his face. He's figuring out that he's not going anywhere. "What happened to them?"

Cocking her head to the side, she watches him like a bird

would play with its prey. "What do *you* think happened to them?"

Panic captures a hold of his limbs. His legs flail and his arms jerk at the metal locked around his wrists. "Let me go!"

Lux releases her fingers from his chin, leaving red dots from broken blood vessels. She bends, reaching for her ankle, and to my surprise, she removes a large knife.

My arms fly up, worried about how personal a stabbing can be. I'd prefer her to kill cleaner, with a single gunshot wound to the head.

"I gave it to her," Sebastian defends with a subtle firmness, stopping my hand before I can grab the knife from Lux.

Although reluctant, I step back not sure how to react because my perfectly planned kill is taking a different turn. I don't care that Lux is taking charge or doing what feels right, but it irks me I wasn't the one to give her...

"What the fuck?" Duncan screams. His eyes bore into the sharp blade as Lux holds it to her side. "Help! Help!" He jerks his arms, attempting to break free.

Unfortunately for him, he's not going anywhere.

If this is how Lux is going to carry out this kill, I will support her. I'm not in agreement with what is happening, but I push my concern aside.

"I'm going to help you, Raven." The nickname slips out as I lower behind her and wrap my hand around hers which is clutching the leather-bound handle of the knife.

Duncan's fear-ridden screams fill the room.

Before I can direct any further, Lux sucks in a deep breath and quickly slams the blade down, slicing right through his chest. A guttural groan is all we hear before Duncan's head falls to the side.

White-knuckling the leather binding, Lux holds the knife

in place while blood spills around it. A slow clap starts from Sebastian behind us, as Lux is staring down at her target.

Sebastian's boots appear from the side. He points his gun at Duncan's head and shoots a single shot. "Making sure. In case she didn't go directly into the heart."

My eyes glance up at him in approval, then I turn back to Lux.

"Lux?" I uncoil her fingers. "You can let go now."

Her gaze slides from Duncan to me. Wide and dilated, her pupils eclipse the darkness of her irises. A light tremble rumbles through her limbs while the corner of her mouth curls up into a smile I'm not sure she was expecting.

"I can't believe I did that."

Something unexpected happens—Lux comes into her self-realization. And my job of protecting her only intensifies with how she will be in more risky situations.

I glide my hand over Lux's cheek, threading it through her hair. "You did."

A tear rolls down her face as she nods. "I don't know what to say."

"You don't have to do or say anything right now."

"Can you and Hayden drop the girl off at the hospital and keep the guys positioned around the perimeter?" I ask Sebastian. My thumb caresses Lux's cheek as she leans in. "Give us some time alone, then come back to clean up."

Drunk on what a regular person would label *love*, I can't find the courage to peel my eyes away from her.

My Lux is beautiful, strong, and incredibly brave, and I don't know how I'll be able to let her go after all of this is over.

CHAPTER THIRTY-ONE
LUX

Once Sebastian and the team have left the room with the woman who remains passed out but breathing, I exhale with relief.

The exhilaration about it all is nothing short of unique and nothing like I've ever experienced. To be a part of something bigger than myself—this world with River is dangerously addicting, and I find myself entrapped by the thrill.

I stare at River while he faces me. His forehead knits and his expression is difficult to read. I'm not sure if he's proud or upset by the change in direction the night went.

"How are you feeling?"

I struggle to find an accurate word to describe how I feel so I settle on the only words I can think of. "Good, I think."

"You're bleeding." His fingers wrap around my wrist, lifting my hand to eye level.

My eyes glance down at blood dripping from a cut inside the black gloves. The injury looks deep, but oddly, I can't feel any pain. "I didn't even notice."

"Let's get you cleaned up," he says, helping me stand.

I nod and follow him into the bathroom also covered in plastic wrap which brings out a laugh from both of us. River's soft but commanding hands grip my waist as he lifts me onto the counter. He nestles himself between my spread legs and pulls my hand up to his face. With a gentle tug, he removes the black leather glove, exposing a slice in my palm from the corner of my wrist to between my thumb and index finger.

"I don't think it's deep enough to need stitches, but we can have our on-call doctor take a look at it when we get back to the manor." He moves my hand under the water to rinse it off. "Hold it here, I need to grab some bandages from my bag."

River twists to walk away, but my legs lock him in place.

"Don't leave," I say. Deep red blood drips from my palm and down my arm. I need a Band-Aid, but I also need something else more. Adrenaline pulses through my veins making me more alive than ever.

He meets my gaze. "Are you all right? Do you need something else?" he asks me in a low whisper. Then he brings my palm up to his lips and presses a long kiss on top of the wound. My throat runs dry.

"I killed a man with that hand. And I'm not sure how to feel about it," I say, thinking he's going to be repulsed.

"And you think that bothers me?"

My eyes remain locked on his as he kisses around the flicker of my pulse at the base of my wrist. "It doesn't?"

"Not one bit."

Carefully, I pull my hand away from his hold and cup the front of his pants. "I want you, River."

River's jaw flexes. "Now?"

I pull my lip between my teeth and tug down his zipper just enough for his pulsating dick to spring out. With my palm wet with blood, I slide it along his shaft.

"Fuck," he groans.

Squeezing tighter around the base, I let my hand coat every inch of his ribbed skin.

River's body falls into me, the sound of crinkling plastic in my ears. Pushed against the chilly bathroom mirror, I free my other hand to continue rolling up and back down his length. As his dick stiffens in my grasp, River's shoulders tense.

"Come for me." I stroke him.

"You are wild and beautiful, you know that?" he says into the sensitive skin behind my ear.

I move my head to the side, capturing his darkened eyes. "It's because of you. You bring it out of me"

"You do it all on your own." With one hand, he grips both of my wrists pinning them above my head against the mirror. Then, he uses his free hand to shove it down the front of my pants and gives them a quick tug. My hips shimmy both articles of clothing down, but without warning, River thrusts his red-coated dick into me.

My head falls back. "Oh god."

His movements are fast and erratic right off the bat, like he's craving me just as much as I am craving him. With every roll of his hips, my pussy clenches around him, not wanting to let him go.

"River," I moan.

Thrust.

"My blood is everywhere."

Thrust.

"I know," he responds with a distant smoothness in his tone. "And it's fucking beautiful."

His words cause a deep groan from somewhere in my body —I'm not sure where, but it's raw. The lower half of my body hums as tingles inch their way up my spine and a climax builds.

Thrust.

Suddenly, he lets go of my wrists and snakes one arm through my hair, gripping the back of my head.

"Look at us, Raven." He tilts my head, giving me a full view of the scarlet mess covering where we're joined.

My eyes roll with pleasure but I snap them back as I feel his stomach muscles tighten from underneath his bunched-up hoodie. He's about to finish, and so am I.

With one last powerful dip of his hips, my most sensitive spot gets sent over the edge. Panting, he releases my hair and collapses into me afterwards. With my limbs trembling, I thread my fingers through his longer on top strands and hold him tighter into my chest.

"This place is going to be a bitch to clean up," he comments, which make us both laugh.

River's hard body slides down mine until his lips are back on the sensitive area between my legs. "We *just* had sex for the second time."

A short time after River and I had sex in the bathroom of the house we killed Duncan in, the guys returned to clean up. We made the drive back to Thompson Manor together, where River bandaged up my hand and then we spent all day in his bed.

Stevie was just leaving for work as we returned. I wasn't in the mood to give her a complete rundown of the night, so I sent her a quick text saying I'd be in River's room and I'd see her later after she was done with work.

"What can I say, I can't get enough of you," he mumbles into the soft skin beside my pussy. His warm tongue slides over, lapping up everything when he made me come minutes ago.

I giggle, enjoying every minute of euphoria. Killing and fucking is a high unlike any other. His cock makes me feral, desperate—and I don't recognize myself.

"God, you taste good," he mutters. He darts his tongue inside me, then takes a generous lick from back to front. My stomach drops, and my eyelids flutter closed. "Feed me again, Lux. I'm craving everything that comes out of you."

Letting my legs fall to each side, I give him exactly what he wants—full access to all of me. A tight moan escapes, as I drift back into oblivion. But a beep from the intercom rips me back to reality.

River flips the blankets up, his mouth wet and shiny. "Ignore it."

"You should get that."

He groans with a playful frustration. "It can't be as important as this."

I thread my hands through his tousled hair and reluctantly pull his head away from me. "We've been in your bedroom since we got home. Besides, I'm getting hungry." River lets out a resigned groan. "Fine. I can't have you starving."

"We could have dinner together," I suggest.

"I wasn't planning it any other way. But after, we come right back in here."

"You got it." I pull the blanket up over his head, then I swing my legs off the bed and onto the floor, skipping over to the intercom, and pressing the talk button. "Hi," I greet whoever's on the other line.

"Ms. Lux." Ben's voice sounds surprised. "I was just calling to ask if you had any dinner plans."

"River and I will be having dinner in the dining room this evening."

"Of course, I'll prepare the table for four."

River props himself up on one arm. "Four?"

Sharing the same thought, I ask, "Who else will be joining us?"

"Ms. Lux's sister is here with Sebastian."

"Stevie is here," I say under my breath, then grab my phone on the nightstand to find missed text messages from Stevie.

> STEVIE
>
> I'm back. Do they know I'm staying here?

Another text came through ten minutes after.

> STEVIE
>
> No worries. Security called River's cousin. I told him to let me in.

River lifts off the bed and heads to the closet naked. My eyes follow his tight glutes as they shift when he walks, giving me a fully delicious view. "I'm glad she decided to stay. It's safer."

"Me too." I swiftly grab my joggers and sports bra from the floor. "I was getting a little worried she'd change her mind. My sister is hardheaded."

"I know. Like I said before, it runs in your family."

I slide on my pants and chuckle at his comment.

River's head pops out from behind the wall. "I love strong women."

"I'm glad."

River emerges a few moments later wearing a tight black T-shirt and gray sweatpants. "I guess we're all having dinner together then."

It's a shame we don't have time for round three.

"I guess so."

He grabs a hat from one of the many hooks on the wall.

"Ready?"

"Let's go." He gives the wound on my hand a soft kiss, then reaches around to clutch the other. I fall in step behind him as we leave his bedroom, and walk to the large dining room where Sebastian's already seated.

"Are you two done fucking yet?" Sebastian quips, grabbing a roll from the bowl in the middle of the table. "I had to let your sister in since neither of you were answering your phones."

"Yeah, sorry about that," I apologize as River pulls out the chair for me. I smile at him, a light flush on my face. But then I scan the room and don't see my sister. "Where's Stevie?"

Sebastian opens his mouth to speak. "In your bed—"

"No. Stevie's right here." She walks into the dining room and gives me a quick hug, then rounds the corner of the table and sits across from Sebastian. "I had to find my way around this insanely large house all by myself."

"Glad you were able to find your way around. I'll ask Aunt Mae to give you a tour," River offers.

Stevie sips from the wine glass in front of her. "That would be helpful. Thanks, Batman."

Sebastian spits his water out, spraying droplets across the table. "River? A superhero?"

"What? I could be a superhero," River says, like he's offended by his cousin's response.

"I mean, he's a tech billionaire"—Stevie's eyes dart to Sebastian—"and you're the assistant. The shoe fits."

"I'm not Robin."

The door to the kitchen swings open before Stevie has a chance to rebuttal. Mae comes barreling into the dining room. "A family dinner and I wasn't invited."

"This isn't a family dinner," Sebastian corrects his aunt, before shooting a glare at Stevie.

River lifts from his chair to pull one out for her. "Join us."

Mae shuffles excitedly and takes a seat. "This is great."

Then he returns to my side.

"Okay, who's thirsty?" Ben calls out, emerging from the kitchen with a bottle of red wine in hand. When he finds Aunt Mae seated with us, he adds, "It's a full table tonight at the Thompson Manor."

Mae's rosy cheeks beam with happiness. "It is."

Ben adds a place setting for Mae, then pours each of us a glass of red wine before he goes over what's on the menu tonight.

"So, how did the project go last night?" Mae's focus bounces between River and Sebastian. They must have mentioned to her about my sister knowing. That's why she feels comfortable bringing it up.

River brings his napkin to place on his lap. "Well, it didn't go *exactly* according to plan, but we were effective and finished in record time."

"That's great to hear." She raises her glass in the air, proposing a cheer.

We all raise our drinks for a quick toast. It should be unnatural to toast about a man we murdered, but this is becoming my new normal and I'm ready to embrace it.

Sebastian clears his throat and leans back with a smirk on his face. "Oh, and Aunt Mae, guess who ended up surprising us at the last minute and pulling out the knife I gave her?"

Her fork suspended midair while her eyebrows raise with curiosity. "And who would that be?"

River turns his head toward me, a prideful expression on his face, while I watch the color drains from Stevie's face.

"Lux?" Her pupils dilate.

And suddenly the tips of my ears burn with being put on the spot. I push the food around on my plate, avoiding the stares from everyone at the table. *Should I be proud of this?* "Yeah, it was me."

"Oh, Lux," Mae gasps. "How are you feeling? Are you all right?"

"I feel better now." I shrug. "He deserved what he got, and I'm glad I was the one to do it."

"Well, all right," Mae replies with slight disbelief. "River must have been shocked," she adds, glancing over at River.

"I didn't know he gave her a weapon," River says, shooting Sebastian a glare.

"*Mr. Controlling*," Mae teases. "I bet that was difficult for you."

I finally get another glance at my sister, and I hate that I'm responsible for the look on her face.

Maybe we should change the subject.

"How was *your day*, Stevie?"

Her eyes rapidly blink as if trying to collect herself. "Um, yeah, fine."

"Stevie owns a mortuary," I tell everyone, full of pride for my sister.

"She mentioned that," Sebastian says.

Mae turns to my sister with a smile. "Yeah, she was telling us about it the other day at breakfast. And you will be staying with us too, right, Stevie?"

"It looks like I will."

"Good. I can't wait to hear all your stories from the mortuary." Mae brings her wine glass to her lips and sips it.

I catch a subtle but genuine smile on my sister's face at Mae's comment, and it makes me grateful to have included her. I'm sure after tonight's dinner conversation she'll have a lot of questions and will need to process things all over again —especially in light of the new events.

We spend the rest of the evening talking about Stevie's

business, my writing, and small bits about how we grew up. After dinner, Stevie and I walk back to my room hand in hand like when we were kids.

"I'm really glad you're here."

"I know. Me too," she says with a light hearted eye roll not wanting to admit she's intrigued by this family too.

"I'm sure you want to talk about the conversation we had at dinner..." I trail off, not sure if I should breach the subject again.

"Yeah, what the hell was that? What did they mean about you *stabbing a guy?*"

I take a deep breath as we approach my bedroom door. It's going to be another long night of questions.

"I'll answer any questions you have. And I'll also do my best at explaining everything and how I'm feeling."

I don't want to keep things from her anymore, and I really want her to accept what we're doing. There's a difference between hearing about it and actually experiencing it. This is the new me and it's important my sister accepts who I am.

CHAPTER THIRTY-TWO

LUX

It's mid-morning when an uneasy feeling wakes me from my sleep. I open my eyes to find an empty space on River's side of the bed, and it saddens me.

After spending the most of the night with Stevie, I came to River's room once she fell asleep. I can tell she's still working through it all, but compared to a typical person, my sister is handling everything much better than I expected. Perhaps we're more alike than I thought.

I climb out of River's bed and throw on a black silk robe. After a quick peek in the bathroom and closet, I assume he's in his office working. I tiptoe across the hallway of the North Wing and see his office door ajar. Recalling what happened last time I went in there and found the cameras, I think there isn't much more he can hide at this point. Before barging in, I peek my head through the cracked door to see him sitting at his desk, talking at his computer screen.

Pushing the door slightly more open, I wait for only a moment for him to glance up from the screen. With how private River is, I'm not sure he'll be all right with me here.

Maybe I should go back to his room?

As soon as the thought crosses my mind, he sees me and his face lights up. Butterflies fill my stomach. I give him a smile back. Then a quick wave, motioning for me to come in.

I tiptoe to the leather couch below the windowpane. It sounds like he's in a virtual meeting with some people from his company, Thompson Innovations.

"The lip gloss Taser is performing well in the field?" River assumes, his gaze unwavering as they stay locked on me from across the room.

"Yes," a male voice from the call exclaims. "We're pleased with the preliminary results."

River casually leans back in his chair with his chin in his hand. "That's what I like to hear."

My eyes glance over the wall of cameras. Eliciting mixed feelings, I search for the screens that display my townhouse and the bedroom I'm staying in, but I can't find them. Did he remove the surveillance? Is this a small gesture from him to admit wrongdoing?

When I look over at him, I find him already watching me, and it puts a smile on my face. He returns his attention back to the meeting and they spend another few minutes discussing logistics and new proposals.

"And how is the request for the proposal for new FBI recording equipment doing?"

"The marketing team is building the proposal as we speak. It should be on my desk for approval by the end of the week," the same man states.

"Wonderful. I trust everything will go smoothly, but can you send me a copy before you submit for final check?" Rivers asks. "Also, the TI smart glasses prototype as well."

"As always with the RFP copy," another person answers. "And the smart glasses will be sent to you this evening."

"But we believe this RFP is a shoo-in. We've worked with this division of the FBI before, so I'm sure we'll get picked up," a feminine voice adds.

"All right, everyone. Unless there is anything else to check in with, I've already taken up an hour of your time. I'll let you all get back to work," River says, wrapping up the meeting. "Thank you for everything you do."

A collective round of "goodbyes" can be heard before River ends the call and closes his laptop top.

"You're up earlier than you typically are, Raven."

"Once I woke up and noticed you weren't there I couldn't fall back asleep."

River rounds his desk and struts over to the couch. He lowers, extending his arm for me to cuddle into his lap. "Sorry about that. I forgot I had a board meeting this morning. Most of the time they're in person, but thankfully this one we decided to hold it virtually."

I rest my head on his shoulder. "I heard you talking about the lip gloss Taser."

He chuckles. "Yes, the same one I brought you. Do you still have it?"

"Of course."

Suddenly, he straightens and turns his body to face me fully. "I want to take you somewhere today."

I can't help the smile that breaks, although I don't know where he's thinking of taking me. "Really? Where?"

He rubs a hand along my bare thigh, peeking out from the slit in the robe. "My COO's daughter's birthday party is this afternoon."

"And you want me to go with you?"

"Yeah." He smiles.

My heart flutters with excitement. The thought of being a typical couple with River for an afternoon is extremely tempting and sounds like an absolute dream. But Andrew is still out there and now we're aware he knows who I am, it changes everything.

"What about Andrew?"

"You're always safe with me." River tucks a loose hair behind my ear.

"Yeah, I know."

"So you'll go with me?"

I hook an arm around his neck, bringing my forehead to his. "Of course, I'll go with you."

He presses a soft, lingering kiss on my skin. "Awesome."

I pull away and hop off his lap. "Thank goodness I have a closet full of brand new clothes."

He slaps my ass as I walk out, looking forward to an afternoon of pretending to be a typical couple.

"This is where your COO lives?" I ask in awe when we pass the giant security gates, each side of the driveway lined with full evergreen trees. "You must be paying him really well for him to afford a place like this."

River chuckles at my comment as he drives the narrow road until a historic house comes into view. "Felix has worked for my company for as long as I can remember, and I like to make sure my employees are taken care of."

I catch sight of a light pink sign with *Happy Birthday* written on it and a bundle of matching balloons tied to the top of a tree in the middle of the circular driveway.

"And Nancy, his wife, makes me the most awful fruit cake every year on my birthday."

I laugh. "Who eats fruit cake anymore?"

"Apparently, Nancy." He pulls around to the front of the house and a young valet walks up to us.

"Good afternoon, sir," the blond in a white and blue suit greets River, opening his door, while another valet comes to open mine.

A crisp, but warm summer afternoon wind whips through my yellow sundress as I step onto the paved driveway.

"We'll be back in exactly two hours. Make sure my car is ready," River states, handing them each a hundred-dollar bill, before sliding his hand into mine.

"Thank you," I toss over my shoulder as we ascend the steps to the front door of the home.

"Welcome," a woman in a matching blue suit greets us as we walk in with glasses of lemonade with freshly crushed strawberries inside. River politely refuses, but I take one, savoring the sweet, cool taste. "Could I get your names?" she asks.

"River Thompson and—," he says.

Her eyes widened. "Yes, Mr. Thompson. Right this way."

The woman leads us through a grand living area with vaulted ceilings and pink party decor everywhere. Guests are scattered throughout, and River introduces me to each one as we pass them.

I smile, repeating each name back to them, trying to remember everyone. This feels more like a whirlwind of people rather than a child's casual birthday party. I am aware about the amount of money and power he holds, seeing the effects in person is another level of intrigue.

River dips his head toward me to whisper in my ear. "I care little for any of these people. They're part of the elitists who think they have all the money and power to do whatever they like."

I stifle a chuckle at his two lives. But it is clear he enjoys one more than the other.

"Good to see you." River's voice rises as he greets another group of people waving him down.

We finally reach the beautiful backyard. The bright green, manicured lawn goes on for more than just a few acres. There's a cotton candy station, women dressed up like animated princesses under a flower laced gazebo, and other kid themed activities, which I have no clue what they are.

"I think I might pay him too much," River jokes about the lavish birthday party. He slows, giving my hand a gentle squeeze. "There's Felix and his wife."

I suck in deep breath ready to play the part of a regular couple who didn't just kill a man in cold blood less than twenty-four hours ago.

"River!" Felix calls out as we walk beside a slip and slide.

"Looks like the perfect party." River extends his arm for a hand shake as we approach them.

"You came." Felix's wife Nancy leans in to hug River, but lingers a bit too long.

I don't like it.

River pulls away, then rests a hand on the small of my back. "This is Lux."

"Hi." I smile, making a point of sliding my arm around the River. "You have a beautiful home."

"Thank you, Lux, It's great to—" Felix starts but is interrupted by a little girl in a princess dress running full speed toward River.

"Wiverr!" A high-pitched voice attached to a pink flash is suddenly at our side.

"Sophia!" He says her name with excitement, bending to lift her into his arms. "Happy birthday!"

Oh my god. My ovaries burst for the first time in my life.

"Thank you." She twists her arms together.

"And how old is Princess Sophia today?" River asks her with a wide grin. *He likes her.*

"I'm four." She giggles, holding up four fingers.

"Yes, you are." River lowers her into the grass and she straightens her ball grown dress. "This is my friend, Lux." River looks up at me.

I lower to meet Sophia at eye level, smiling warmly at her. "You look like a beautiful birthday girl."

"You're pwetty." She twirls her corkscrew blonde hair.

"Why don't you go see Grandma," Felix says.

Nancy grabs her daughter's hand, leading her away from our group. "Come on, baby."

"See you later, River." Her tone takes on a sensual nature, and I see red.

Glaring at her until she's a comfortable distance away, my eyes drag back to River only to find a slight smirk on his face. Slightly embarrassed about being caught, my cheeks flush. He turns his attention back to Felix, but not before sending me with a sly wink.

Felix sips his pink lemonade. "So where did you guys meet?"

My stomach drops at his question. With how carefully curated River's double life is, we failed to prepare an explanation for us if anyone asked.

"Lux reached out to the office to do research for a novel she was working on," River adds casually.

Stunned by his quick response, I have no choice but to go along with it.

I swallow cotton. "Yeah, River has been very helpful."

Felix's eyebrows rise. "A writer, sounds intriguing."

River changes the subject before Felix asks me more questions, and I breathe a sigh of relief. I'm not that great of a liar, and if he continued, I might accidentally say something I shouldn't.

"I bet Sophia's going to get some fun gifts today. I saw the present table on the way in." The expression on Felix's face suddenly changes. "I'm afraid to ask what you got her."

River pats his shoulder and flashes him a mischievous smile. "A pony is being delivered in less than an hour."

Felix's eyes grow wide. "Fuck you. Really?"

I chuckle at the rapport they have and that River really bought Felix's daughter a pony. Of course, the way she interacts with him, and how gentle and caring he is toward her gives me a glimpse into what type of family man he could be.

As River continues to charm everyone at the event for the rest of the afternoon, I stand by his side watching how well he can control both parts of his world. But underneath the friendly good-guy facade and passionate lover in the bedroom, is a natural killer—a hunter prowling the city streets of Seattle in search of the next *bad guy* to take down.

By the time we're in the car heading back up the hill to Thompson Manor, my adoration for him has grown even more.

CHAPTER THIRTY-THREE

RIVER

A large red banner rolling across the bottom of the TV screen catches my eye as I walk out of the bathroom.

**PRESS CONFERENCE SOON, UPDATE ON CABIN
WOMEN'S CASE**

Wrapped in a white towel around my waist, I stand in front of the TV with the local news playing. The police will never find the bodies of the men because they're all swimming with fish in their underwater graveyards. But they will discover the connection between them once Nolen and Duncan are officially reported missing.

Which reminds me that I haven't heard from Andrew. I assumed he'd touch base after my night with Duncan, but he's been silent. Which leads me to believe he may have caught on to everything we're doing and is backing off. Or maybe the police reached out for questioning?

"Whatcha doin'?" Lux emerges from the bathroom, her delicious body hidden behind a fluffy cotton robe.

Keeping my eyes on the screen, I open my arm for her to come to my side. "The police are about to give a press conference on the case."

"I spoke with my dad last week and he said that they dissolved most of the local resources due to a lack of leads," she says, leaving my side to walk into the closet.

The news suddenly cuts to the press conference, and standing at the podium is a familiar man. "Lux, isn't that your dad?"

"My dad?" Lux comes out wearing one of my white button up shirts, her eyes boring into the screen with confusion. "I thought the case was handed over to the FBI since the cut in resources?"

Seems like he's still involved.

I grab the remote from the top of the dresser and turn up the volume.

"As you all know, Richard Smith, a local accountant, was reported missing by his wife over three weeks ago. Due to recent information that has come to light, we suspect that him and a few other accomplices are connected to this case. One of those individuals is Andrew Hughes..."

They've discovered Richard's link to Andrew. It's only a matter of time before they interview others in his circle.

Lux's eye flick toward me with panic.

"If they're going public with this—" I begin.

"Then they've already tried arresting him and he's nowhere to be found."

I nod. "Exactly."

She pinches the bridge of her nose and squeezes her eyes shut. "If we hadn't killed the accountant, his wife wouldn't have reported him missing." She paces. "And then we would have had a little longer to get to Andrew," she rushes out. "Now they've probably scared him off—or worse, they'll get to him before we do and all of this will be for nothing."

I step closer, grabbing her arms to steady her. "This isn't all for nothing."

She rubs her lips together, unsure if she believes me. "How can you be sure?"

"I have been doing this a long time," I say. "Trust me. We'll get him."

"We are not as different as you think we are." Lux's hand coming up to my face.

The similarity between us is there, but I will always carry a darkness more dangerous than hers. Despite my growing feelings for her, she can never see the real me.

A life with kids and a house like every regular person on this earth isn't meant for monsters like me. My hunger for the hunt will always remain unsatisfied. And once Lux finds out my desire to kill is not just based on the need to stop predators from hurting innocent people, will she still want me?

"Maybe," I say with a forced smile before I make my way into my closet to get some clothes on. "I should touch base with Sebastian."

Flipping through my shirts, I mentally recap the last few weeks. Everything has fallen into place with each of the kills. But my instincts never steer me wrong, and I foresee getting our hands on Andrew might be more difficult than expected. Something I don't want to share with Lux because all she needs to worry about is healing and getting her vengeance.

"I think I should go see my dad," Lux says.

Pulling the shirt over my head, I step out. "What for?"

"He might be able to give me some useful information like last time."

"You already knew the information last time," I remind her.

A smirk plays at her lips.

I have my own sources, but if Lux is trying to help, I'll let her. "All right," I tell her. "Once I meet with Sebastian, I'll follow you out there. How about later this evening?"

She shoots me a side eye. "Always following me around."

"You love it." I pull her toward me, pressing a kiss to her lips. "And I love—" I stop myself from continuing.

She draws back quickly, her eyes the size of saucers. "Did you just almost say *love?*"

I clear my throat, ready to play it off. "Uh, I don't think so."

Replaying what I was about to say, my heart pounds. The words escaped without a second thought, as if my subconscious was telling me something.

It can't be true.

"Okay, well"—she runs a hand through her hair—"I have some writing to do, and you're meeting with Sebastian."

This situation turned awkward quickly. "So, I'll go meet with Sebastian. I'll text you in a bit, okay?"

She follows me to the door. "Yeah."

"Okay." I smile. Standing with my arms at my sides in the doorway.

"Okay," she repeats, her cheeks blushing.

We both walk down the hall of the North Wing in silence, before parting ways. After the exchange with Lux, my mind is spinning with questions.

Do I love her?

Am I capable of loving anyone?

I shake off the thought and refocus on the important thing at hand. If the police outed Andrew's name to the world and he gets wind of it, he'll try to leave the country as soon as possible, if he hasn't already.

I open my laptop and pull up a flight tracker app my team uses to monitor personal planes. It was one of the first systems

I was able to hack into years ago. Then I take out my phone and send Sebastian a quick text.

ME

Are you at the manor?

SEBASTIAN

Yeah, I'm in my office.

ME

Can you meet me in mine right now?

SEBASTIAN

You know you could come to the west wing
once in a while.

ME

Be here in 5 mins.

I slump into my leather chair, waiting for Sebastian to come down. Within a few minutes, he's walking through my office door.

"Ah, you left it unlocked for me," he comments as he walks in. "How thoughtful of you."

"Did you see the press conference the police held?" I ask, getting down to business.

"I did."

"I figured Andrew would be trying to make a run for it, so I've been tracking his personal plane."

Sebastian slumps onto the couch. "Awesome. That's exactly what I've been doing."

"He's definitely trying to flee."

"And I'm sure the police are right behind us with tracking him."

"But they don't have him in custody yet, so that means we still have time." I sigh, resting my chin in the palm of my hand, I glance at the real time flight plan on the computer screen.

"Can you find a list of properties owned by the Hughes family?"

"Like commercial or personal?"

"Both."

"Personal might be more difficult. I'd need some time looking into each member of his immediate family."

"You know what hacker-extraordinaire would help this move quicker?"

Sebastian nods. "I'll touch base with Christian."

My eyes focus on the screen. "Make sure to check Spain."

"Spain?"

"Yeah, the projected destination just popped up."

Sebastian rises to his feet. "I'm going to work on this. We'll touch base soon."

I rub my temples, frustrated with having to get him on foreign territory. "If he's in Spain, that's where we're going to have to go."

"Looks like it," he returns. "It's only a matter of time before the police find the same information."

After Sebastian leaves my office, I lean back in my chair, taking a minute to think through the resources and tools we have at our disposal. But then my eyes find the window and the lush green forest. Gray clouds roll in casting a dark shadow into the office. A flutter from the side catches my eye. Wings spread wide, the raven flies right up to the glass.

"Hey, buddy." I roll closer to him.

His eyes dart around the environment, on the lookout for both predators and prey. Perched comfortably on his favorite branch, we both enjoy the silence and solitude of the dense forest surrounding us.

"I saw him in the kitchen the first night I stayed here." Lux's quiet voice sounds from behind me.

I open one arm, gesturing for her to come to me. She walks

around the desk, a lightness in her steps I haven't seen before. She's more comfortable in my house and with me. And my heart warms at the thought.

Lux crawls onto my lap, wrapping her arms around my neck and resting her head against mine.

"He's beautiful, isn't he?" she whispers. Our eyes locked on the mysterious bird inches away from us, only separated by a layer of glass.

Clasping my hands behind her back, I pull her tight. "Yes."

"I love ravens," she tells me. "I haven't really seen them much before, except here on your property."

"This one hangs around often."

She draws her head back, her eyes flickering to me. "He reminds me of my favorite Edgar Allan Poe poem, *The Raven*," she says.

I smile, already aware she's a Poe fan.

"It's mine too. Which makes it even more fitting to call you Raven."

"Yeah." She blushes. "I'd like to say his writing is what inspired my own."

"I'm glad you found comfort in his words." I lean in close, letting my breath dust her lips.

She smiles and kisses me lightly. "I am a crime writer, remember?"

"Of course. His work shows our shared human experience." The bond growing between Lux and I intensifies with each passing day. "Sometimes it can be the most effective way to communicate."

"Through writing?" Her eyelids close as we both pepper each other's mouth with kisses.

"Yes," I say.

"The poem's beginning verses have remained with me

since I was a child. I might even remember the final ones if I tried hard." She tucks her head under my chin.

"*Once upon a midnight dreary, while I pondered, weak and weary...*" she recites the first line in a whisper.

The two of us, alongside the raven, watch as the rains come in and not until the flashes of a few distant lightning bolts does the raven leave us in search of shelter from the storm.

She lifts her head to make eye contact. Her once light brown-green eyes have changed to a darker shade, reflecting the transformation occurring within her.

CHAPTER THIRTY-FOUR

LUX

When my phone buzzes with a text message, River and I have been cuddled together in his office for some time. It's not until it goes off again that I catch the time and realize it's been almost an hour. I lean to the side and pull my phone out of my pocket to check the notifications.

STEVIE

Just getting off work.

Coming back to River and Sebastian's manor.

"My sister is on her way back," I tell River. "I'm glad you have one of your guys tailing her."

"I'm glad you feel better about it," he says.

"And as long as I'm here, I feel like she'll want to be here anyway."

"You two are close, aren't you?" He slides a hand along my face, threading his fingers through my hair.

"We are. She lived with me for a while after she graduated

until she made enough to get her own place," I tell him. "I was sad to see her go, because growing up it was just the two of us. We always had each other's back no matter what."

He smiles. "Like me and Sebastian. We may be cousins, but we grew up like brothers. We've always been there for each other."

"That's probably why they're both supportive of—" I pause. "What we do."

"*We?*"

"Yes. We." I lean in, bringing my lips to his for a soft kiss.

His hand cups the back of my head, holding me steady, and his tone takes a serious note. "Stevie should officially move into your bedroom in the East Wing. I want you to stay with me."

"You have quite the possessive side, don't you?" I smirk playfully.

"And that surprises you?"

"Not anymore."

"Just got off the phone with—" Sebastian halts his words when he spots River and me. "Sorry, I didn't know. Wait, Lux is in here," he says, quickly glancing over his shoulders where the wall of monitors is.

"I know about the cameras, Sebastian," I say, melting into River's embrace. "It's all good."

His brows furrow, as if he's perplexed by how I'm okay with it. "Okay?"

"How'd it go with Christian?" River asks, changing subjects.

"We're all set to head to Spain," Sebastian explains.

My posture straightens with surprise. "Wait, what?"

"Andrew fled the country once he got wind the police were looking for him."

"So he went to Spain?"

"We believe someone tipped him off before the police intervened."

"Andrew's family has an estate in the country." Sebastian leans his arms against the desk.

"And we're going after him?" I stand, feeling a little lost, which is how I feel mostly when River and his team handle the details behind the scenes. But I try my best to pay attention, and to my surprise I am starting to understand more.

"Looks like it." River looks at Sebastian.

"We need to discuss the details," Sebastian says.

"Okay." River leans back in the chair, bending one leg over the other. "Go on."

Sebastian shoots me a brief glance before opening his laptop, maybe unsure about showing me more detailed notes about their operation. But the feeling must pass, because he flips it around to River and me. The screen shows a beautiful Spanish colonial-style home with a vibrant white exterior and red roof.

Him and River continue discussing their plans, while my mind cycles through the fear of us not being able to get to him.

"Are you still going to see your dad?" River asks me, breaking me from my thoughts.

"Yeah, we should go before we leave for Spain."

"We? Looks like someone's on a tight leash," Sebastian quips.

"She's not going anywhere without me." River walks by and slugs him in the arm.

Remembering my sister is on her way back, I turn to Sebastian. "My sister is coming back. Would you mind letting her in?"

"Sure."

River and I walk out of his office with Sebastian right behind us. Then River and I turn into his bedroom.

I need to tell Stevie about what's going on. So I pull out my phone to send her a text.

ME

River is going with me to see dad.

STEVIE

Who's going to let me in?

ME

Sebastian.

STEVIE

Okay.

ME

We'll be back shortly.

STEVIE

Is everything alright?

ME

Yeah, just want to see if he knows anything about the case he can share.

STEVIE

You know he won't tell you much.

I begin to text Stevie back, but my thoughts return to traveling to Spain and the possibility of not getting to Andrew. The weight of the last month and a half is suppressive on my chest and I can't imagine doing all of this for nothing.

Someone's suddenly at my side and when I drag my eyes up, they land on the only person representing comfort and strength.

River bends, scooping me up. "Sebastian, would you mind leaving a bottle of red and two glasses outside my bedroom door?"

"What? I'm not your—"

"Thank you!" River cuts him off.

"What are you doing?" I ask.

"Giving you what you need." His head tilts down toward mine, his eyes flare with passion.

"I was going to see my dad."

"We can go in the morning," he says. "Tonight, you need another distraction because I know you're worried about what's about to happen." My stomach flutters, knowing exactly what type of distraction he has in mind. "We will get him, Lux. I promised you we would, and I'm not one to break promises."

"It's hard not to be worried."

River walks over to the side of the bed, lowering me into the cushioned comforter. "Take off your clothes."

Eagerly, I rip my shirt off and claw at my pants. Inching them down, I'm completely naked before River has the chance to remove any of his clothes. Wasting no time, he crawls on to the bed on his side and faces the opposite direction as me. Then he lowers his pants and kicks them onto the floor. "Come here."

I scoot over to him, my eyes boring onto his red, swollen dick. A small bead of precum appears on the head and it gets my heart pumping. Filled with confidence in what he has in mind, I know River is about to give me the distraction I need.

"Eager, aren't you?" he baits me with a smirk.

"Yes," I say, licking my lips.

"Go on, then," he says, fisting the base of his dick. "Use me."

Hungry and desperate, I lower my head and wrap my mouth around his hard length. The taste of him brings chills down my spine and I moan around his cock.

River whimpers, and I gently bite down his head, nipping at his sensitive skin.

"Yes, just like that, Raven," he groans. Lying on his side, his head slides between my legs at my core and forces them to part. "I need some too."

"Is that what you need?" I mumble and open my legs for him.

His tongue slides from the inside of my thigh, licking to the top of my clit, not quite entering me yet. "Fuck, you taste good."

He continues to lap me up, my pussy pulsating with pleasure, causing me to pain for more of him. Taking him deeper into my throat, I suck harder while little whimpers slip out of my mouth.

"I need more," I beg.

River's tongue darts inside me, his head twisting in every direction, trying to gain deeper access. My legs tremble as my orgasm already builds. His lips takes turns with his tongue, licking and kissing. Ravaging me, he clutches my thighs, holding me in place. His mouth is all over, his tongue tasting everything.

"I'm going to give you everything you're ever going to need," he growls, sliding lower and wrapping his lips around my puckered hole. A tingling sensation moves up my lower back, forcing it to arch into him. "Mmm, and you smell good. Now let go for me."

Sucking harder, I wrap a hand around his base, feverishly trying to coax out what I need.

River's tongue glides from front to back, licking and sucking at everything he can. Wet and throbbing, my climax breaks.

"Oh fuck, Raven, I taste it. Keep going."

Bucking into his face, my movements around his cock become frantic. He moans as his licking slows, savoring everything. His legs stiffen and he spurts warm ribbons of sweet cum into my throat. My body relaxes, sucking everything out of him, and like a starved person, I lap up every single drop.

"Is that what you wanted?" he grits out, leaving wet kisses along my thighs.

"Mm-hmm." Relaxed and lying on my side, I continue to let him spill into my mouth, sucking only when I sense the flow is ending.

"Better?" He flips onto his back.

I do the same, satisfied and feeling fulfilled. "Yes."

We lie side by side on the bed for a few minutes before he sits up. With a smirk on his face and drunk with lust, he flips around. "That should tide us over until after our next kill."

"And then what?" I purr, curling into his chest.

"Then I'll fill every hole in your body to make sure you're always satisfied," he tells me, wiping a finger across his bottom lip and then sliding into his mouth.

I smile and coil my tongue around his finger. Then he rises from the bed and walks over to the bedroom door.

"Good ol' Sebastian coming through for me," he says, bending to retrieve a bottle of wine and two glasses from the floor.

Bending my arm, I lift my head to rest in the palm of my hand. "I didn't think he'd actually bring it."

River sets the items on the small settee table by the window and then pops the cork. "I didn't either." Then he turns to me with a smile on his face while filling up one of the glasses. "This is for you."

"Thank you." I extend my arm right as he walks over to me.

"Enjoy the wine. Then we'll get some sleep."

Breathing in the fruity tannins, I close my eyes to savor the moment, then take a sip. Because as soon as we get to Spain, I'll finally get the revenge I crave.

CHAPTER THIRTY-FIVE

RIVER

S tanding outside a coffee shop in downtown Seattle, I wait for Lux to grab an iced latte. Ben could have made her any type of coffee beverage she wanted, but she insisted on coming to one of the local Overcast Cafe locations.

I lean against the wall, while my eyes scan the surroundings watching for anything that might look out of the ordinary. Trying to maintain a low profile, but my gaze lands on a man standing under a tree in a dark corner of a high school parking lot. He is watching what looks to be a girls' soccer team practicing on the grass.

I quickly dismiss my paranoia, assuming he's a parent. But then I find a group of adults scattered on metal bleachers across the field. *Is he hiding?*

I focus on the man again, and this time more of his face comes into view. He looks familiar, but I can't place him yet.

An unsettling feeling settles inside my chest, so I step over to my car to pull out a pair of the TI smart glasses prototype to get a better look at him.

I slide them on and return to the same spot against the

wall. With a light tap to the frame, the glasses allow me to zoom in to get a clearer view.

Still struggling to place him, I slide my phone out and quickly swipe to the list Sebastian and I keep for future targets of our nightly projects. With a quick search, I find a copy of his mugshot.

"Fester Harrow," I mumble.

Authorities charged him with raping his girlfriend's teenage daughter, but he got off two years ago on a technicality. Assuming he left the state since we had lost track of him for some time, we moved on to other predators still in the area.

But in my experience, it's not common for them to change their behaviors. Which would explain why he is lurking under a tree close to a high school campus.

"Feeling a little bold, Fester?" I mutter.

Glancing down the street, I make a note of how close we are to the police station. Over the last month, I've mainly focused on Lux and bringing down Andrew and his crew, and I've neglected my own needs.

My focus on Lux and her kills has caused me to suppress the monster in me. Since I haven't had any kills of my own, it stirs violently inside its cage and will not allow me to push it aside anymore.

Before I can act on it, Lux is at my side with two coffees in hand and a smile on her face. "Okay, I'm ready."

I'll get him next time.

Pushing any thoughts of Fester aside, I bend down to kiss her forehead.

"Perfect, I'll be right behind you."

Lux flips her head up to slide her sunglasses down with no hands. "I know you will."

God, she is so fucking adorable.

For a moment I forget about the predator across the street,

and it is not until Lux is safely in her car and we're driving past the high school, that my desire to kill intensifies again. It's pricking at my back and getting harder to ignore.

Lux turns onto a side road leading to the back of the police station, where the entrance to most of the offices are located. I asked her to park in the lot's corner to not draw too much attention to it for anyone around. And that is what she does, pulling into a secluded area. With a coffee in each hand, she cocks a hip to close the car door, then turns back to glance at me one more time before ascending the steps into the rear of the building.

Flicking off the engine, I am determined to push killing Fester from my head. I need a distraction, but my usual distraction is currently *unavailable*.

I twist my neck, cracking it a few times to get comfortable in my seat. And for what feels like hours—has only been thirty minutes—my eyes bore into the old brick building.

Between the intrusive thoughts of darkness and my skin crawling with an anxiousness, I am on the verge of losing the fight.

He shouldn't be anywhere near a school.

What if that's where the ex-girlfriend's daughter attends?

The incessant inch propelling up my back while flashes of Fester standing outside of the high school, searching for a victim, overcome my vision.

Oh, fuck it.

I am a controlled man, but also an impetuous one. I give in, jerking on the ignition to start the car. It would take me no time to grab him and give him a little strangle and be on my way back to the police station—with time to spare.

My fingers tense with anticipation as I turn the steering wheel onto the side road, leading back toward the downtown high school. Before long, I'm pulling up to the side of a home with a For Sale sign on the opposite side of the high school back lot. I immediately spot Fester, still lurking in the shadows beneath a large tree, his disguise is anything but appropriate as he's dressed oddly in tan colored clothes.

Of course he's still there. He's on the prowl, stalking his next victim.

Sliding a baseball cap onto my head and flipping up my black hoodie, I reach into the back seat to grab a syringe from my bag, preparing to give him a quick injection. I get everything ready, then leave the car. I tuck both hands in the front pockets of my sweater while scanning the perimeter of the forest and parking lot.

As I get closer to Fester, there's no one else around, so I break out into a slow jog with my feet barely hitting the ground. Reaching for what I need, I take the syringe from my hoodie pocket and pop off the cap, then approach him from behind.

"Hey," I say in a low voice, getting his attention.

As he turns, I jam the needle into the side of his neck. Dazed, he stumbles back unstable on his feet, and I hook an arm around his neck, bracing his fall to the ground. Then I flip him against the side of the car. Only a few seconds later, his limbs go limp.

"You're just going to take a little nap." With hesitation, I slightly release my hold and deadlift him into the back seat of his car.

After a quick search of his pockets, I find his keys. Sliding into the driver's seat, I head to an older part of the high school. Growing up around here, I've gotten used to many areas downtown. Built in the 1980s, many of the buildings are no longer used or abandoned, making it the perfect place to carry out this solo project.

I drive the car into a shaded area full of overgrown bushes, and a quick glance confirms the area is hidden enough for us to remain unseen for a while. I slide Fester's limp body from the backseat and wearily carry him to the door. With a swift kick, the rotted wood swings open. I walk past a devotion of love carved into the wooden wall, which will only last until the school finally tears this building down.

I spot an open area in the corner of the room. Dropping Fester onto the concrete, the sound of bones hitting the floor fills the air. The impact to his back wakes him earlier than I'm expecting.

I reach for the handcuffs in my bag, then kneel to bind him to a long pipe protruding from the ceiling. Once secure, his eyes peel open.

"Hello." I smile. While crouching down beside him, my body buzzes with excitement. "Sorry you had to wake up like this."

"What is going on?" he slurs, his eyes darting around the rundown shack. When he realizes that he's chained and I'm holding a gun, he shouts, "Who the fuck are you? Let me go!"

"Oh, sorry about that, Fester. Where are my manners?" I extend my arm for him to shake it. "I'm River."

He jerks at the metal cuffs. "How the hell do you know my name?"

"I followed your case two years ago." I rise. "Quite the situation you got yourself in. She was only a kid."

"The little bitch who said I took advantage of her?" he spits. "She came onto me."

"She was fifteen, you sick fuck."

"Not when she looked like that."

"I rub my chin then squat next to him. "Wasn't she drugged too?"

He clicks his tongue, possibly getting agitated. "What do you want?"

"For you not to hurt anyone else."

"So how would you make that happen? Are you some type of rogue cop or something?"

"Oh god, no." I shake my head. "I'm far from being a cop."

"Then what the fuck do you want?" He's growing angry. "Why am I here?"

I rub the back of my neck. "Well, you see Fester..." I lower myself to face him once again. "I haven't been able to take part in my extracurricular activities lately, which is making me a little restless. And lucky for you, my friend, you have the honor of fulfilling that need today."

"What's that supposed to mean?"

"I make sure guys like you never hurt anyone again," I tell him.

"And how the hell do you do that?'

I let a devilish smile transform my face, enjoying the feeling of it. "How do you think? I know you saw the gun."

"You're going to shoot me?" Panic laces his tone.

"Yep."

"Help!" he screams as he bangs the metal cuffs onto the pipe.

In one swift motion, I slip behind him, both arms wrap around his neck with my hands pressed into the top of his head and chin. Preparing to break his neck, I lean into his body thrashing underneath me.

My arm tightens around his neck. I take the barrel of my gun and bring it to his temple. "Say good night, Fester."

And after one last muffled scream, I pull the trigger. The silencer mutes the shot and then Fester's body is deadweight in my arms.

Relief washes over me. Like a runner's high, my body tingles with adrenaline. And with a heavy inhale, I sit on the dirty ground and bask in a moment of pure release.

Then my phone vibrates in my front pocket.

"Stevie can't get a hold of Lux," Sebastian tells me before I have the chance to say hello.

I clear my throat. "What?"

"Lux's not answering her phone."

I step over Fester's lifeless body. "What do you mean?"

"Are you with her?" An urgency in his voice has my hair standing on end.

"She's at the police station with her dad."

"Their dad told Stevie she left a half hour ago," he rushes out.

"What do you mean a half hour ago?" I look down at my watch and realized it's been just under two hours since I dropped her off.

My insides twist as panic seizes hold of my body. It takes every ounce of self-control not to run out of the building because I don't want to make a scene. So I walk with purpose back toward Fester's car, then take it back to park in the original spot. Then, finally I'm sliding into mine.

What the fuck did I do? I told her I'd always protect her and I let my impulsiveness get in the way of her safety.

"I need you to send a cleaning crew to the location I'm about to send you." Immediately I flip the engine on.

"Why?"

"I took care of our old friend Fester Harrow." I don't say anything more and end the call.

While peeling out of the parking lot, I swipe into the tracker app. My heart sinks when I see Lux's car is still in the back parking lot of the police station.

"Fuck!" I scream. I white knuckle my steering wheel, pain and fear coursing through my veins.

How could I have left her alone?

In a frenzy, I call Sebastian again. "Are you sure her dad doesn't know she's missing?"

"No. As far as he knows, everything is fine."

"Okay good." I hang up again and call Hayden.

"River," he answers right away like always. "What's up?"

"Hayden, I need you to find Lux. I dropped her off at the police station downtown to visit with her dad, around nine a.m. this morning. It's eleven now, and her sister said she left a half hour ago, but my tracker shows her car and phone still there. Get into the surveillance system and see what you can find."

"Lux is missing? What happened?" His panicked tone does nothing for my growing anger.

"I'll call you back." I drive into the parking lot and skid to a halt. Jumping out of my car, I run over to Lux's car faster than my feet can carry me. Her door is ajar and her purse is lying on the passenger seat which means she made it back, but never got in.

Fuck!

I asked her to park in the back of the lot, the one shared with another government building so I could hang out in my car without being noticed, but I never thought it could work in someone else's favor.

I fucking left her. This is all my fault.

My hands come up to my head, twisting at all angles as my eyes dart around the area with fear as I search for something—anything that might give me a clue to what the hell happened.

A call from an unknown number comes through, causing my stomach to drop.

"Hello?" I answer, flatly.

"River, River," Andrew bitterly chides me.

My back straightens at the sound of his voice. Anger turns

into rage, and I instantly know he has something to do with this. "Where is she?" I demand.

"Oh, the lieutenant's daughter?" He plays darkly. "I have her. Put up a bit of a fight, but she eventually gave in."

Rage.

"If you fucking touch—"

"Shut the hell up!" he shouts.

My jaw clenches as I climb back into my car, then circle the parking lot, searching every tree, van, and car for any sign of where they could be.

"She's mine! I found her first. You can imagine how pissed I was when I saw you sitting outside her house every night. I thought you wanted her for yourself, and was just trying to do something with her beyond me and the guys, but boy, was I wrong. You were doing something completely different, weren't you?"

If he saw me outside of her house, that means he was trailing her after I rescued her from the cabin.

"I will find you, and I will crush your fucking windpipe before I kill you, making you suffer for ever putting your hands on her."

"Maybe." He enjoys this sick game.

"Where the hell did you take her!?" I scream inside the confines of my car. The volume of my voice vibrates the windows.

"I'm at one of my properties," he says.

My eyes blur, as the world around turns red. "Is this some sort of clue? You think this is a game?"

"I quite like games. Don't you?"

"I'm going to fucking kill you if you touch her," I threaten, ignoring his question.

"That's a shame. But River, when you find where I am, I

suggest you come alone or I'm blowing her pretty face off." He ends the call before I get a chance to say anything.

"FUCK!" I yell. But quickly pull myself together to call Sebastian.

I need to find Lux now and every minute I'm not level-headed is one more that she's stuck with Andrew.

"Andrew took Lux. I need that list of Andrew's properties," I demand, the wheels screeching over the street as I haul out of the parking lot and rush home.

CHAPTER THIRTY-SIX

LUX

A hot, sticky breeze floats across my face, forcing my eyelids to peel open. Fresh paint fills one nostril while the other is clogged and sore. My limbs are heavy and my thoughts are clouded. In a panic, I realize my white sundress is ripped at the collar, exposing the top of my chest.

What happened?

Where am I?

Dragging my eyes to one side of the room, I spot a window covered with a black tarp.

"Ahh," I gasp, jerking against the tight resistance holding down my arms. Fear grows inside my chest when I attempt to slip my arms free but can't do it. I blink a few times to gain my bearings, and manage to make out a blurry figure hunched over a table in the room's corner.

"Hello?" I say, although my mouth is dry.

The figure, which I can now tell is a man, slowly straightens. With a calculated turn, he faces me. My blood run cold the second our eyes lock.

Andrew. Oh my god!

"Good evening, beautiful," he greets me with a sinister smile. He casually walks to the bed and sits on the edge.

Sheer panic has me in a chokehold.

He kidnapped me.

Again.

Where the hell is River?

My heart pounds in my ribcage as I try to remember how I got here.

"Let me go, Andrew," I demand with an unstable confidence.

His chubby fingers come up to my cheek, then run down my face and onto my bare chest.

I shiver in disgust under his touch and recoil from it.

"What? I thought serial killers got you going, Lux?"

"Don't fucking touch me!" I spit.

"I'm going to do whatever the fuck I want to you," he sneers, resting his cheek against my breast. His tongue slides out, dragging a long wet trail until he nudges his nose to push the fabric farther down, exposing my nipples. "I can still remember how good you tasted."

A desperate whimper escapes from my throat. I try to hold it in for fear I'll show him my weakness, but it doesn't work. Sucking in as much as I can, I muster the courage to stay level headed.

"Stop!" I grit out.

His movements pause, his eyes flicker to mine. "This will be so much sweeter to take you in front of River, but I'm not going to wait for very much longer."

"He's going to kill you, you sick bastard." I clench my jaw. "It's only a matter of time before he gets his hands on you."

"Maybe." Andrew draws back. "Or he's going to watch me fuck his girl."

"I won't let you fucking touch me," I bite back.

"You don't have much of a choice, you're at my mercy," he says in an eerie tone, pointing at my restraints.

"What do you want?"

His eyebrows raise. "What do *I* want?"

"Is this all because women won't willingly sleep with you?" I ask, needing to distract him anyway I can so he keeps his hands off me. "Are you so pathetic that not even your money is enough to convince them?"

"You better shut that pretty mouth of yours before I shove my cock into it."

"Why are you doing this to women? To me?" I manage to ask despite the bile creeping up my throat.

A sly smile rolls across his face. "You were just a fun little bonus. Fate has a funny way of having people's paths cross."

My eyebrows snap together. "What are you talking about?"

He walks over to a table filled with objects I can't make out from here. "Did Daddy never tell you about me, Lux Levinson?"

"My dad?" I swallow hard. "What does my dad have to do with this?"

"He needs to pay for what he did." Andrew's teeth clench together. "And you'll be perfect for that."

"You're making no sense."

"It will."

"What are you talking about?" I press, still confused.

"So you really don't know what your daddy did to me?" he snarls, obviously losing his patience with me because he believes I should know what he's referring to. But I'm clueless and wish he'd tell me already. "Let me enlighten you then. Twenty years ago, my stepbrother was running one of the most prolific sex rings on the West Coast. Until your father put him away." Andrew frantically paces back and forth as he recounts the story, a knife in hand. "I was a young kid when it happened, and he was the only person who cared about me. So when he died in prison two years ago, I knew I had to resurrect it in his honor."

"What do I have to do with this?"

"Your dad is responsible for my stepbrother's death!" he yells. "If he had just left it alone, none of this would have happened. He took my only brother from me!"

"So you're going to kill me?" I push away the fear from his threat.

He shakes his head. "Now, where would the fun be in that?"

"I don't understand."

What does he want then?

He cocks his head to the side and glides the sharp end of the knife up my bare leg, dragging it across the top of my panties.

I inhale sharply.

"You were supposed to be at the cabin when the lieutenant showed up at the crime scene, so he could find his daughter beaten, raped, and left for dead. Poetic justice, don't you think?" He pauses. "That's why I didn't let the other guys fuck you. I wanted to be the only one who got to you, and boy, was it nice. That sweet pussy of yours was..." He trails off, smiling into the empty room as if reminiscing on that night.

Another repulsive shiver travels up my spine, watching him relive the moments he raped me, and there is nothing I can do about it. "I survived, you prick," I say with more confidence this time, chasing away my terror.

Andrew's head swings in my direction, his eyes darkening. "Yes, all thanks to River fucking Thompson."

"He is going to kill you, just like we killed the others," I threaten.

He rolls his eyes, as if not in shock. "You think I didn't

know it was you?" He stalks around the bed, kneeling next to me.

Pursing my lips together, I try to pull back. "Get away from me."

Andrew ignores my plea and leans in, bringing his lips to my cheek. I squeeze my eyes shut as his tongue darts out, sliding down my cheek and along the seam of my lips.

"You're fucking disgusting." I gag on my own words in response to him.

Andrew pulls away and lets out a dark chuckle. "With how much time he spent outside your house, I'm surprised River let you out of his sight this long."

"You were watching me?"

"Of course I was," he says. "When I saw him at your house so often, I knew he'd taken a special interest in you. Which only made this whole situation that much sweeter." His tone drips with distaste.

"You really are a sick bastard."

"You know I tried to recruit him into our group because of how powerful he is with his technology and all the money and power he fucking has. But of course, he had to fuck with my plans and get in the way of what I want." He pauses, suddenly changes his expression with his face now softening. "And then to find out he's not only a killer, but a *stalker*?" His high pitched chuckle sends chills up my spine. "Then, of all the people he could be stalking, he chooses the lieutenant's daughter. You became the whole package, sweet cheeks. I could get back at your dad *and* River."

Andrew slides his phone from his pocket. "River Thompson."

"River!" I scream, hoping to show him I'm still alive.

"Shut up, you bitch," Andrew warns before putting the phone on speaker. "Don't make me gag you."

"I will hunt you down and make you pay with your life."
River's voice is dark on the other end.

"Then you better get here," Andrew retorts. "My dick can't
wait any longer."

"If you touch a single h—"

Andrew hangs up before River can finish.

"Noo!' I cry out, tears stinging the backs of my eyes. "Let
me go!"

Andrew stalks over to me and straddles my hips. "God,
you're so annoying." He slaps me across the face and my vision
blurs. "I don't know how River can stand you."

"Fuck you!"

Then he hits the side of my face, and this time everything
goes black.

CHAPTER THIRTY-SEVEN

RIVER

Racing down the highway, I approach a hundred miles an hour. Rage has taken over. Lux is the most amazing woman I have ever met and I will not let anything happen to her.

All those nights sitting outside her townhouse, watching her from the cameras on my phone, hoping one day I'd get to touch her—until I finally did. To say being with her is like heaven, will never be close enough to how it feels. The softness of her skin, the intensity in her eyes, and the way she looks at me like I'm not the monster that I am.

I grip the steering wheel, staring down the narrow, windy highway with my thoughts clouded. The impulsivity of my darkness is what fucked it up. Andrew got to her, because of me. I vowed to protect her, and I didn't.

I feel nothing but everything all at once.

Andrew doesn't know who the fuck he is messing with.

My phone rings through the car. "Did you check into the planning and zoning databases?" I ask before Sebastian has a chance to speak.

"Yes." Sebastian clears his throat, then in a rushed tone he names off a long list of local Hughes' family properties. "We could start one by one. Or simply check his primary residence?"

I nod, pulling into the underground garage at the manor and skidding to the spot closest to the elevator. "He wouldn't keep her at his house. He might be a twisted fuck, but he isn't stupid."

"You're right." Sebastian pauses. "Seems like a dumb move, even for him."

I grab my phone, step out of the car and head straight to my office. "I'm here. Meet me in my office," I tell him before hanging up.

By the time I make it down the hall, Sebastian is right behind me, furiously typing on his computer that's held in one hand.

"What about new construction?' I continue our conversation.

"Or a building they've just closed escrow on? Can we check the MLS for any property updates?"

He takes a seat on the leather couch. "Already on it."

I sit next to him and bring my hands up to my face. "Fuck!" I yell in frustration spiked with raw fear.

"We'll find her," he reassures me without looking up from the screen.

Suddenly I remember Fester and leaving him in the building. "Did you send the crew to take care of—"

"It's already done," Sebastian interjects. Then he leans in with a worried expression. "What the hell happened today?"

I rise to my feet, unable to remain still and walk over to my desk. "I don't want to talk about it," I tell him as I grab my laptop to look into any CTV footage that could help us while Sebastian works on the properties.

"I think we should."

"Not now."

"Fine," he says. "I just sent you the list of local properties."

I open his encrypted email and scroll through the properties on the planning and zoning databases. "We should also check lien holders and proposed structures, not only titles."

Sebastian comes to stand next to me, his finger pointing at one of the properties. "Check out this one. It's in escrow with the Hughes Enterprises."

My eyes narrow. "That's The Henderson downtown."

"Weird," Sebastian mumbles. "I didn't know his family owned that piece of shit."

I highlight the date of purchase. "They recently acquired it."

"It's worth a shot," Sebastian says. "I can hack into the commercial security system to see if there was any movement."

I shake my head. "You think Andrew would go through a regular door?"

"They probably have cameras all over that place."

"He would not walk by a spot where there are cameras. Especially if he took her there, he would have to feel comfortable with the security."

"You could be right."

As we're planning to check out the first location, I recall the conversation I had with Andrew. My eyes dart up to my cousin's. "Andrew called and he wants me to come alone."

His eyebrows snap together. "Not happening."

"Yes. I can't risk Lux's safety any more than I already have."

He slams his hand on the wooden desk. "Absolutely not. I'm not letting you walk into a suicide mission."

My eyes bore into his. "That's not your decision to make."

"River, that is insane," he argues. "You don't know what he has planned or what you're going into."

"I can take care of myself." My arm muscles flex, knowing full well I'd burn this fucking world down for her.

"You're such an egotistical asshole," he spits. "Let me and the team take the perimeter."

I rub my lips together, contemplating what I know would be the safe move, but I cannot risk Andrew getting word of it. "I'll keep you updated."

Sebastian squares his shoulders. His expression hardens. "When we first put this operation together, we agreed we'd be a team. But you slowly took the lead. And I was fine with it because you're like my older brother—by only three years, but it's something."

"Your point?"

"My point is, I stepped back from being CFO at TI in order to run this," he continues, his fingers gripping the edge of the desk. "I am in charge of what goes on with the night team, which means I'm going with you. And if you have a problem with that, then you can fuck off."

I blow out a breath of frustration. Sebastian is my brother and partner, which leaves me little room to protest. "Fine, but be careful and maintain a good distance."

"This isn't my first rodeo," he retorts smugly.

Knowing we're running out of time, I stand from my chair and say, "Download the PDF and send it to Stevie. Tell her to look for any more locations. If he has one in escrow, he might have more."

"Okay?" he says, confused by me involving Lux's sister. "Should I tell her about Lux?"

I nod. "Yeah, but reassure her everything is going to be okay." Then I turn and race out of the office and back down the hall, before tossing over my shoulder, "Oh, and keep her here."

"River, wait!" Sebastian chases me out the door. "We need to come up with a plan first."

"The plan is I get back my woman and kill Andrew in the process."

Sebastian's boots hit the tiled floor behind me, mirroring the weight of my steps. "This isn't like you." His voice is sour and frustrated the farther away from him I get.

"Do you guys know where Lux is?" Stevie asks softly in the background.

Lux's sister's concern stops me in my tracks. I take in a painful breath, slowly turning to face her. As my posture straightens, my eyes burn with revenge. "I'm going to get her right now."

Sebastian is suddenly at my side, and his expression is firm as tensions run high between us. "River will handle it, Stevie."

"What does that mean?" Her voice shakes with fear. "Does someone have her?"

Sebastian steps forward, cupping her elbow. "Andrew took her. He's the guy whose group we've been hunting."

I need to set her mind at ease. Searching for the more human side of me, I lock eyes with her. "There is no place on this fucking earth Lux can go that I will not find her."

Stevie's eyes are misty with worry as she nods. "Okay, River."

"Sebastian has a job for you. It'll help us find her," I say in a tender tone. "Do you think you can handle it?"

She cocks her hip to the side, irritation flashes across her face. "Of course I can handle it."

Sebastian chuckles at Stevie's response, but his focus is on me. "I'll be right behind you."

"I figured you would." I turn away from them, head into the elevator and down to the garage.

In no time, I'm speeding back down the hill. My breath becomes shallow and steady as I pull onto the highway. A light drizzle and clouds rolling in at dusk, makes for a dreary evening not unlike the many summer rains that have come before it. I am the most collected, controlled on days like these, and with nightfall creeping in I'm coming alive.

A threat hangs over a life more precious than any other, changing the energy this time, and I will never forgive myself if I cannot get her back. Lux represents the closest thing to love I've ever experienced. She pulses through my veins and I don't know how I'd survive this world without her.

The highway opens for me, clearing a path into the bright lights of the city and directly to the dated hotel downtown.

A quick glance in the mirror proves Sebastian has already caught up with me. Despite believing that I can handle this on my own, I need him more than I'd like to admit.

I reach The Henderson in record time and look up at the deserted hotel. As I drive closer, my eyes dart to each floor, examining the dark windows until I find one with a dull yellow glow.

I doubt Andrew would be this obvious, but maybe there's a hidden room somewhere. A basement, perhaps?

My head falls in frustration with how this doesn't fit and lacks sense to be the correct location. I pull my car to the curb, parking in front of the desolate entrance, because I need to clear the hotel anyway, just in case.

I yank the door open and climb out. With a brisk walk into the lobby, I am met with a view of fabric couches littered with holes and covered in stains.

"Hello." An older man with a beard stands behind a check-in desk.

"I'm looking to have some company tonight." I say, with a subtle gesture at the women standing on the corner outside the entrance with ripped fishnets stockings that have seen some action in recent days. They must still be able to operate from the previous owners.

He grins mischievously, showing yellowed teeth with one missing on the top left. "Say no more," he says. "The Henderson is the perfect location for your nighttime activities as we pride ourselves on being a discreet hotel."

"Wonderful." I lean in and rest my elbows on top of the counter. "I also want to make sure we're able to be loud, if you know what I mean. Are there a lot of guests booked here for tonight?"

The man smiles once again, understanding *exactly* what I mean. "There's only one other guest checked in for the night," he whispers. "And let's just say, you both are here for a little nightcap before heading home to the misses."

"Great," I tell him with a smile.

"I can put you on the fourth" His fingers tap the information onto the keyboard. "He's on the third, so you two shouldn't hear each other."

"Do you have a restroom?" I ask, needing to get to the third floor.

"Yep." His finger comes up to point down the back hall.

I nod. "Be right back."

I walk past the first set of elevators in the lobby, and then turn a sharp corner to find another next to the bathrooms. With a quick look behind me, I approach the doors and hit the arrow going up. It comes in handy that these old hotels don't need room keys to roam the property. Once I'm on the third floor, I scan the area before stepping out of the elevator. Red wallpaper lines the hallway and the air is musty and humid, like water damage has done a number on the structure.

Keeping my movements slow and calculated, I listen for any movement or noise I can detect. Turning the corner to head down one side of the hallway, I hold my ear up to each tan colored door. My breath halts, moving from one room to another until I reach the end and switch sides. Before long, I am down the opposite side, with only five doors left. Anger bubbling inside, I'm about to punch a hole in the wall when the faint sound of a man panting fills me with rage.

"That motherfucker." Panic and rage seizes hold of limbs as everything turns to deep red. I will burn this fucking place down if he touched her.

I rush the door, lifting my boot to kick it down. The wood snaps but keeps the deadbolt in place.

"I'm going to fucking kill you!" I climb through, pushing wood beams aside.

A scream comes from behind a wall, and before long I am face-to-face with a naked man on top of a woman with her skirt hiked high.

"What do you want?" he cries out with fear while his dick is still inside of her.

Blinking a few times, I gather my thoughts, adrenaline coursing heavily through my veins.

It's not them.

I'm relieved, but still on the hunt.

My hand goes up into the air in surrender. "Sorry, wrong room!"

The woman scurries to the back of the bed.

"Get the fuck out of here!" the man yells as I rush out through the broken door.

Once I'm back in the hallway, facing the sickening wallpaper once again, my anger takes on a new fold. "Fuck!" I scream, my hands brushing through my hair.

I have to find Lux. There is no me without her.

I push open the door to the fire escape, taking the stairs two at a time, as it leads me into an alleyway behind the hotel. And with one deep breath of cool night air, I refill my lungs before thundering around the building back to my car.

CHAPTER THIRTY-EIGHT
RIVER

I slam the back screen door on a small new build home in an up-and-coming neighborhood south of the city. The third location Sebastian has followed me to in the past couple of hours, and still no Lux. My patience is running thin and panic continues to build.

Stevie found an LLC which the Hughes family uses to purchase properties. They buy them with cash, then resell them to the highest bidder. That's based on what she's been able to research at this point.

"Fuck!" I grind my teeth.

Sebastian steps out of the woods with his arms crossed over his chest and judgment written on his face.

"What?" I yell, shoving past him.

"Can you be any louder?" he snaps in a hushed tone.

Giving him my back, I make a beeline for my car. "Fuck off."

"There are people around. It's night, but we're in a very populated part of town." He kicks up dirt, trudging through the landscape behind me.

"I don't fucking care," I bite back, then yank open the car door. "You disabled the cameras in the surrounding homes, anyway," I point out. "And the house to the left is still under construction. The workers would have gone home by now."

Sebastian lays a friendly hand on my shoulder. "River."

"What?" I jerk it off and turn around to face him, circling my temples with my fingertips.

"I've never seen you like this."

I roll up my sleeves, flexing my arms. "I can't let anything happen to her."

Sebastian's face softens and suddenly he understands what's going on inside my head—something I refuse to admit to myself. "You love her, don't you?"

"I'm incapable of love," I state with unwavering conviction. "I failed to protect Lux, Sebastian. She trusted me, and I let her down."

The first opportunity to experience being with someone and I fucked it up. Instead of watching over her, I let my impulses get the best of me and endangered the first person I've ever cared about this way.

"We will find her," he reassures me, but his words fall flat.

"I'll believe it when we do." I go to shut the door when I get a call from Christian.

My heart gets trapped in my throat as I answer the phone. "What'd you find out?"

"There is a property about thirty minutes from your location that Hughes purchased to turn into a small bed-and-breakfast."

"And?"

"For some reason, construction halted last fall, which means it's vacant and located in a secluded part of the woods," Christian continues.

My ribs constrict my lungs, adrenaline pumping through me. "That's got to be it."

"Put him on speaker," Sebastian tells me.

I roll my eyes, but oblige.

A few papers wrestle in the background. "It's the only one that makes sense. It's within thirty minutes from where he took her, and taking the highway directly over, he wouldn't have to wait for the ferry downtown—."

"Bingo," Sebastian blurts out.

"Send us the address," I cut him off.

"Wow, he really did pick somewhere close to home, didn't he?" Sebastian quips.

Christian laughs sarcastically. "Maybe he's dumber than we thought."

"Or he's more comfortable hiding in plain sight," I mutter. Something I'm not proud we have in common. "Thanks, Christian."

"Oh, and River?" he says.

"Yeah?"

"Lux is one of us now. Do whatever you can to get her back," Christian says without knowing the extent of what I would do for that woman.

A calm heat moves through me and I'm a predator on the hunt once again. "Andrew will take his last breath today," I reply, then end the call.

Christian sends me the address, and I'm on my way to another location in search of Lux.

I will not sleep.

I will not stop.

Racing down the highway toward the woods with only my headlights and Sebastian's distant beams from behind to guide the way through the dense and cloudy night sky. I grip the steering wheel, hoping I'm getting close to finding her while the pain inside me squeezes every fiber of my being.

This has to be it.

The GPS leads me where Christian had said we'd be going —into a secluded part of the small town west of the city. When I'm within about a mile of the location I pop in my SEs.

"We need to turn our lights off. I don't want to tip anyone off about our presence," I tell Sebastian, assuming he's already mic'd up.

"Yeah." He holds close to my tail. "Right behind you."

Swiping up on my phone screen with one hand still on the steering wheel, I hit the TI location app, allowing me to get a visual of the area. After a quick check, I proceed to the guided route toward the building.

Sliding out of my car, I pull on the hood of my sweater, then slip on the smart glasses and a double tap to the side to switch to night vision. Jogging at a measured pace, I head up the steep incline toward the log structure. A few trees snap in the distance, but it doesn't shake me until my boots crunch on crisp leaves. The sound alerts what looks to be a man with a shotgun at the back entrance.

Of course, Andrew wouldn't be alone. *Pussy.*

Ducking under the wood beam lying next to where he's keeping watch, I run my back flush with the outside wall. The wet panels lay a damp layer of newly fallen rainwater on my sweater, awakening every nerve in my body.

With the guard's back in my sights, I leap over the step and wrap my arms tightly around his neck. Stunned, he swings his gun into the air but before he can pull the trigger and send bullets flying into the sky, I constrict my grip on his neck and crush his windpipe. The man struggles for a few moments before his body goes limp. Only then do I loosen my hold and let him fall through my arms, his lifeless body meeting the earth with a thud.

"Got him," I tell Sebastian through my earbud.

"Good. Do you think he'd only bring one man with him?" he asks.

"I'm not sure." I wipe the heavy drops of water from my eyes. "From your vantage point, can you see if there's a cellar or a basement entrance?" I scan the perimeter. The downpour makes it more difficult to see. A gray hue blankets the forest, similar to my property. Spending nights training among the trees makes it easier for me to navigate through the overgrown bush, but still presents a challenge.

Sebastian is silent for a beat. "I can make out what might be cellar doors on the south side of the building."

"Okay." I turn and jump off the porch into a mud pit below. The increasing rainfall drowns the water, splashing by the sound out hitting the roof above.

"About five, maybe six yards in front of you," Sebastian instructs.

"Got it." Walking over, I spot light shining through a pile of leaves pushed against the cement foundation. With a low squat, I take a gloved hand and slowly clear them away to peer into the window. Then I spot Lux. "Holy fuck."

"What?" Sebastian belts out. "What is it?"

"Lux," I murmur. Hit with rage *and* relief, I gasp as I see Andrew has handcuffed her to a bed in an unfinished room. With her skirt pushed up, exposing her thighs, I have a clear view of fresh bruises. "Motherfucker." I snap to a stand.

"She's there?"

Fueled by darkness, I ball my fists and crack my neck. "I'm going to fucking kill him."

"Wait for me. I've got your back," Sebastian demands. But all I hear is a ringing in my ears.

Sliding my gun from my waist, my slippery fingers grasp at the handle. I turn around and stalk straight for the back door.

"River, no," he scolds but I ignore him.

Andrew's fucked up game is over. I didn't know how I would find Lux, and my imagination went to many horrific places, but the moment I saw her—*my Lux* lying on that bed helpless, like she was before—something in me snapped.

I swing the door open.

"River! Get yourself together!" Sebastian screams into my ear.

I hear him, but can't respond, and his words do nothing for the violence brewing inside. Holding my gun pointed in front of me, I clear a small lobby area, then continue heading down each hallway.

"I'm coming in, you asshole," Sebastian hisses. "Just head to wherever you saw her."

I acknowledge him mentally, moving through the dark house. Against my better judgment, I turn off my earpiece to immerse myself in the surroundings. I have to get her back unharmed and I must focus to do so.

I pass a large commercial-sized kitchen and send a silenced bullet between the eyes of a man playing solitaire with himself on a folding card table. Taking a step over him as his body falls into a rolled up carpet on the floor, and continue on my way.

Searching for something that would indicate a basement or cellar, I start opening doors. The first two are closets—then finally the creaky one on the side opens to a steep wooden staircase. Flexing my shoulders, I blow out a breath to gather every ounce of self-control in me in order not to kill Andrew on the spot.

I descend into the cellar two stairs at a time before rounding the corner and coming face-to-face with him. My heart drops when I see he has Lux in a headlock with his forearm pressing against her neck. The other hand wields a gun with his finger hovering over the trigger as it grazes her temple.

I try to maintain my composure, but I feel like shattering into a million pieces on the floor. Lux's eyebrows crease when she sees me, her body weakening against Andrew's grasp. Pleading sounds escape from under the duct tape across her mouth.

"River!" Andrew greets me with a menacing grin. "Just in time."

"Let her go." I grip my gun, my finger hovering over the trigger as I aim it at him. Andrew ducks his head halfway behind Lux's, using her as a shield from my impending bullet. "Or I'm going to drown you in your own blood."

"I want you to know this wasn't supposed to go this way," he offers like I care what he thinks or feels. "You got in my way."

"What's that supposed to mean?" I clench my jaw.

He shakes his head. "I knew you weren't as smart as everyone believes you are."

I raise the gun higher in response.

"Touchy, are we?" he attempts to bait me.

"Let her go," I demand. "Let's settle this between us."

"But I'm not finished yet," he warns. The barrel of the gun rubs across her forehead. Lux whimpers and it's fucking eating me alive. "I wanted to make my brother proud by recreating his sex ring to get back at Levinson. He would have loved it," he says. "And then I had Levinson's daughter to help me do it. But you and your fucking questionable morals had to ruin it by setting her free."

"This is about you getting back at her dad?" I try to remain calm, but I'm about four seconds away from blowing his brains out and that is making things more difficult.

"Then you had to go and make it worse by helping her kill off *my* team!" he screams angrily. "How about I kill *your* team?"

"You could never touch my team," I spit.

"Agree to disagree." He cocks a brow. "But you know what makes it even better?"

I stay silent, formulating a plan. The longer I keep him talking, the more time it gives for Sebastian to figure out we need back up. With my earpiece off now, I hope he figures it out quickly.

"You know what makes all of this even better?" His voice escalates. Andrew senses my indifference and it makes him more agitated, but I remain calm. "Listen to me or she's getting it, you fucking prick! What makes it better is because she's *yours*."

Tears fall from Lux's eyes, her mascara smears across her cheeks. All I want to do is carry her home, and never let her go again. My eyes squeeze with a hard blink. I'm hanging on by a thread, as if any moment I will lose control.

"I said, let her go." My finger grazes the trigger.

He chuckles, darkly. "Perfect River Thompson, tech genius, most eligible bachelor on the West Coast," he mocks. "But never taking advantage of all the women who trip over themselves to be with you." His eye darts to the side, his head cranes to the back, making eye contact with Lux. "Except for this one."

"I won't repeat myself," I threaten.

"Never would've pegged you for a hopeless romantic." He flashes his expensive white teeth behind his sinister intentions.

Suddenly, from the corner of my eye, I catch Sebastian inching his way down the stairs with his gun drawn. And I know this will be all over soon.

CHAPTER THIRTY-NINE

LUX

The barrel of Andrew's gun pushes against my temple with every erratic movement he makes, causing my shoulder to rise with tension.

The moment I see River come down the stairs and our eyes meet, he's filled with anger and fear. My knees give out with relief, and tears spill from my eyes as my insides experience every emotion all at once.

He found me.

My body pains for him, being so close but unable to touch him sends an ache through my limbs, and splits with my heart yearning for his embrace.

River's gun points at Andrew. But this weak bastard is hiding behind me, knowing River won't take a chance and shoot him as long as he has me as a shield.

"You're going to die," I grit out through the tape, but he can't hear me. My voice trembles with terror.

"Shut the fuck up," Andrew warns, shouting into my ear.

I flinch.

"Do not speak to her that way," River threatens.

"Drop the gun, Andrew." Sebastian's tone is hard as he comes into view, stepping down from the cellar stairs.

My shoulders fall, but Andrew's stiffens behind me. "I told you to come alone. We could have run this entire thing together, River," he chides, clicking his tongue. "Now, say goodbye to—"

River lunges at us. A bullet zips through the air. In defense, Andrew releases me and the bullet ricochets off the stone ceiling.

I cower. My arms flying up to cover my head, not sure which gun the shot came from. Then I'm thrown to the side. My chest falls to the mattress as my stomach hits the side metal frame of the bed. Like being punched in the gut, the breath is knocked out of me and a cramp cripples my core, forcing me to gasp.

Frightened, I whip my head around to see River's massive frame towering over Andrew. He has him pinned against the wall. His hand is wrapped around Andrew's neck pressing into his windpipe as gurgling sounds escape his throat, searching for precious air.

My body hums with adrenaline from what's happening. It pumps through my veins like a drug. Gathering courage and strength, I straighten to a stand, my eyes bounce between Sebastian's and River, unsure what to do.

Sebastian stands wide, his gun pointed toward Andrew. "Get him on the bed, River."

River doesn't move, his grip tightening around Andrew's neck.

"We could have shared everything," Andrew says through strained breaths. "We could still share the lieutenant's daughter."

"Enough, River!" Sebastian shouts.

"I don't share what's *mine*," River growls.

Andrew chuckles, his face red from the pressure, his blood pocketing around his cheeks. "You and I are no different. Power hungry, murderous billionaires incapable of love."

River applies more pressure and Andrew's eyes roll back.

He's killing him.

"River!" Sebastian steps forward.

I don't know what comes over me, but my arm shoots out, stopping Sebastian in his tracks.

I muster any strength I have left, and with a purposeful stride I approach River and place a hand on his tense arm.

He immediately releases Andrew, sending his body plummeting to the cement floor from lack of oxygen. But he's still alive.

Sebastian rushes over to secure Andrew's arm to a pipe coming down from the ceiling.

River backs away, panting with his arms hanging at his sides. I step in front of him and squat next to Andrew, making eye contact with his weak, bloodshot eyes.

River stands silently behind me, but maintains a close distance.

"I told you he'd find me," I say.

"You fucking bitch," Andrew spits. He is helpless, unable to raise his arms. From the corner of my eye, I catch River moving quickly forward, but my arm comes out once again to block him.

"I've got this," I say, as my anger overtakes my earlier fear.

Andrew organized the entire operation. He not only helped his friends capture and torture women, he drugged, raped, and killed them. With no plans on slowing, he attempted to rope another billionaire into his ring of terror—River. But to his surprise, River had been hunting him all along. He targeted my dad and raped me—all in the name of revenge.

A light sigh from River who's standing at my side, is

quickly followed by a pair of heavy boots coming up, and a shiny, sharp knife appears in my peripheral vision.

Turning, my eyes fall to Sebastian holding a knife in his hand with the blade facing downward. A smile tugs at the corners of my mouth.

"He's all yours, Lux." Sebastian's soft smile is accepting and filled with pride.

I return with a grateful expression, which I feel inside my bones. With my eyes wide, I carefully grab the leather-bound handle from his gloved hand.

"Thank you," I whisper.

Sebastian's eyelids slowly blink, while he subtly nods and backs away, giving me the space to complete the project I've been waiting weeks for. I have the power and it is now woven into the rubric of who I am.

I turn back to Andrew, and River steps forward, picking Andrew up by his neck. Then he shoves him against the wall as Sebastian slides in to assist River in keeping Andrew upright.

I tremble, buzzing anxiously. Staring at these two men who have given me my voice back while they both flank the man who raped me, is justice.

"He's all yours, Raven," River says.

River's approval is all I need to unleash everything that's brewed inside me for all this time, because Andrew was the big prize all along. I pull in a long, heavy breath, then clamp my eyelids closed. Tightening my right hand, I pull it back with a force manifested from every corner of my body.

"This is for my *dad.*" I drive the knife into his chest.

Andrew cries out in pain as blood spills from the wound dotting his white colored shirt.

"This is for *River.*"

Andrew winces, but it's weaker this time. A burgundy liquid sprays on my face, blocking my view. But I continue.

"This is for every single fucking *woman* you've hurt." I stab him again.

I yank the knife out, my sore arm tenses. And with one powerful last thrust, I drive the knife back into Andrew's chest. "And this one's for *me*."

After a few blood curdling screams, a deafening silence transforms the room when Andrew takes his last breath.

He's gone.

I fall to my knees—the knife hits the cement ground at my feet. River releases Andrew, and in a flash he's crouching in front of me, his thick arms extend to embrace me fully. My face hits his shoulder as I release everything.

"You did so good, Lux," he praises and presses a soft kiss on my head. "I'm proud of you."

I did this.

I took his life.

Andrew's ring of terror is over.

"You found me." Relief floods every bone in my body as I bury myself into his damp clothes.

River's arms tighten around me and I can barely take in a breath, but I don't care, I sink into it. "I will always find you, Raven."

Blinking a few times, I take in my surroundings with fresh eyes—sharper, vibrant eyes. Scanning the room from the safety of River's arms, I catch Sebastian standing proudly beside Andrew's bloody body with a devilish grin on his face.

"Now this is what law enforcement calls a *crime of passion*," he smirks.

River releases me slightly, but keeps a comfortable arm around my shoulders and looks back at Sebastian with a laugh. "Definitely. There will be no doubt they'll theorize Andrew knew his attacker."

I lift my head, forming an idea. "Let's burn this fucking place down."

"Burn it down?" Sebastian repeats with uncertainty, his mood changing.

River's silent for a beat. He rubs his chin, contemplating my proposal. "We could."

"It's been a long time since we've burned down a crime scene with the body in it." Sebastian shoves his hands inside the front pockets of his pants. "It was tricky not to prove arson, and we had to pull out the guy's teeth..." He trails off, thinking out loud.

River and I rise to our feet. "You have pliers in your bag, right?" he asks, Sebastian.

Sebastian shrugs, like it's obvious he'd have those packed and prepared. "Always."

"Grab them," River instructs. "So I can start plucking Andrew's teeth."

Sebastian's palms hit the air between us with shock. "We're doing this? We're actually doing this like old times?"

River and Sebastian's interaction reminds me of Stevie. "Wait, where's my sister? Does she know I'm okay?" My hands run over my head while my legs tremble from the chill in the room. "Oh my god. She must be incredibly worried."

River threads a calm hand through my hair, his face soft. "Stevie helped us find you."

"She did?" My brows shot up in disbelief. It's hard for me to imagine Stevie could keep a level head through something like this. "I'm surprised."

"Your sister is more capable than you think." Sebastian smiles, tossing River the pliers. "Let's get on burning this shit-hole down, because I'm starving."

River cranes his neck as a tooth falls into a small Ziploc bag to his side. "Looks like Andrew has quite a few cavities."

My chest rumbles from a belly laugh, given the setting we're in—next to a dead body of the man I stabbed to death, while my murderous boyfriend plucks out each one of the man's teeth—and I let myself feel the humor.

"I could go for a slice of Ben's amazing avocado toast right now," I say, trying to think of something comforting in the moment.

"Here." River slips his hoodie off and slips it over my head

I slide both arms through the sleeves. "Thank you."

"You're doing better after this kill," he observes with a prideful grin.

"He deserved every bit of what he got and then some," I say. "I feel empowered, vindicated."

But why do I still feel the foul wetness of Andrew's saliva and the sensation of fingertips rubbing against my skin? The churning in my stomach isn't from taking a human life or seeing a mutilated dead body covered in blood—it's from being touched when I didn't want to be. He may not have raped me this time, but being violated once again by him feels even more defeating.

"Sebastian?" River suddenly says.

"Yeah?" Sebastian is on the phone with Hayden.

"Leave us."

"Are you kidding?" Sebastian's eyes lowered, annoyance written on his face. "Hayden and the guys are on their way with gasoline for the fire."

"Get out," River snaps at Sebastian. "Lux and I need a minute."

"Fine." Sebastian huffs, heading upstairs.

Once Sebastian is out of ear shot, River walks over to me and says, "Talk to me."

CHAPTER FORTY
RIVER

I walk over to her, my heart breaking for what she's been through. "Talk to me," I say softly.

I let Sebastian think I wanted this time for sex, but I can tell Lux isn't okay and I want her to have the space to share privately whatever she's feeling.

Her teeth are chattering as she slowly blinks. Her head angles upward. "I'm fine, it's just adrenaline."

I wrap my arms around her, and pull her closer. "Probably, but I know you better than that."

Lux gives me a weak smile and steps deeper into my embrace.

"You don't have to talk about it, but I'm here if you need me."

"I just hate that he got to me again." Her voice cracks.

Then a realization forms in my head. Lux has never shared with me what happened the night I found her, but I always had my suspicions that Andrew had been the one to hurt her.

"Did he..." I trail off, refusing to verbalize it. Lux's clothes are back in place, but the marks of the battle are still visible.

Scarlet stains litter her once beautiful white sundress, which my sweater attempts to cover.

"Not this time," she whispers as tears spill down her red, swollen cheeks. "I didn't want to tell you at first because I knew you'd kill him the moment you got your hands on him. But I wanted it to be me. I didn't want someone else to carry out my justice." Lux's hand comes up to swipe a hair that's fallen on my forehead. She cups my cheek lovingly. "I want to go home."

Home.

That simple word which now carries so much meaning. The manor was just the manor before, but now it's become a *home.* And with it, I'd like to believe is the hope and possibility of a future for Lux and me.

"Let's go." I wrap my arm around her waist just as the guys come down the stairs with containers of gasoline.

"Was that enough time?" Sebastian clips sarcastically.

I straighten to a stand. "Light this place up," I tell the guys, ignoring my cousin's comment.

"Yeah, River!" Hayden gleams. "We're gonna burn it to the ground like the good ol' days," he says with excitement, but when his eyes land on Lux, his face falls. "Are you all right, Lux?"

"I am." She smiles at him, masking exhaustion.

I grab her hand and give it a gentle squeeze. "We're heading home. Make sure you take care of this place and leave no traces behind."

They all give me a quick nod.

Sebastian steps forward, his eyes scanning the room. "Well, shall we leave them to their work?"

"Is there anything you want to do before we leave?"

Lux's large almond-shaped eyes flick toward mine. I've

watched the color change dramatically over time and it's been one of the greatest gifts.

"No." Her voice sounds softer than a low whisper. "Let's get the hell out of here."

I look back at Andrew's body, slumped over against the wall, blood pooling around him. "Well, my friend, it's been fun."

Sebastian laughs, slinging his bag over his shoulder. I do the same with mine, then grab Lux's hand to help keep her steady.

Her eyes squint in disgust as she gives the man who tormented her one last glare. To my surprise, she lets go of my hand and stalks toward his body.

Lowering, she crouches in front of him. "You're going to rot in hell," she threatens with a subtle smirk playing on her lips. She angles her head to the side as an animal would after it's captured their prey. "And I'm going to sleep like a baby every night knowing I'm the one who sent you there."

The room is quiet. Ten men in total, including myself and Sebastian, all who have taken many lives without thinking twice. But this tiny brunette, who has been to hell and back herself, even hiding monsters of her own, renders us speechless.

Watching Lux is almost like staring at different versions of myself.

She is one woman by day, another by night.

Lux flips her back to Andrew, her shoulders squared with confidence. "Let's go, River," she beckons me, and I'm right on her heels.

When we reach the top, my protective instincts kick in. All known threats have been eliminated, but I slip in front and grab her hand in mine anyway. Then I lead us through the obscure, grim building. Lux is silent until we get outside into the cool night air.

The crisp coastal breeze dances across my skin with a sting, and with a desperate breath in, I refill my lungs with power. A dense silence settles around us in the heavily wooded area. I turn to Lux, with a fire in my soul and relief flowing in my veins, I twist her in my arms. She moves with me positioning her front against mine.

"It's almost midnight." Although she smiles, she's hiding additional trauma that will need to be unpacked in the hours, or days, to come.

"Yes."

"Thank you for saving me," she whispers into my thin, cotton shirt.

She never should have been taken to begin with.

Keeping my tight hold steady, I lock my arms in place imagining the sheer agony I'd experience if I was to lose her again. "I told you I'd always keep you safe." A low rumble of thunder vibrates through the forest from miles away. "I'm sorry Andrew got to you."

"It's not your fault." Lux's head shakes.

I gently pull her away, bringing my index finger and thumb to her chin tilting her head skyward. "It is."

"What do you mean?"

"I saw a man who's been on the team's radar for a while and I went after him," I tell her, ashamed at my admission.

"And what does this have to do with Andrew taking me?"

I swallow a cotton sensation in my throat. My thumb glides across the slickness of her chin searching for the proper words to explain my darkness in a way she'd understand. "I left you at the police station and went after him. I failed you."

Lux's eyes flick to mine, laced with a strong conviction. "It's not your fault."

"I put my own impulses before your safety."

"You were doing what you thought was right," Lux retorts, defending my actions.

Lux knows I'm what most might call a vigilante, but what she'll never know is my darkness craves the kill. And every day, I have to choose to use the darkness for good instead of bad. But this woman is a part of me and I can't let my urges get in the way again. My life is not about myself anymore, it's about her. And I've caught glimpses of a similar darkness in her, but she's different. She was driven by rage, revenge. I am, but not in how I get my fill. The more I kill, the greater the hunger to do it again grows—it's a never ending perpetual cycle.

"That doesn't matter if it means you get hurt," I say.

"Then what is all this about then?" she rushes out. "I know you don't do this simply because you want to bring justice to people, River."

"Lux," I say to her in shock.

Has she always known this?

Her eyebrows knit together as her voice lowers. "There has to be a level of pleasure you get out of it."

"You think I take *pleasure* in it?"

Lux's hand comes up to cup the side of my face. "Yes. Why else would you do it?"

"Fuck, it's getting cold out here," Sebastian shouts, jumping from the top step of the wooden deck. "It's supposed to be summer."

My head snaps over at the interruption, and I see the team laughing amongst themselves while jogging out of the house.

"This baby's gonna blow!" Hayden excitedly yells.

Lux has seen the darkness in me with what we've been through together, but I need to say the words to her. She needs to fully understand this is not only about justice, it's about me too. We'll talk again once we're back at the manor.

"Ready?" I ask Lux.

"More than ready. Let that fucker burn."

A smile breaks over my lips. An authentic, truthful, and borderline loving smile. "Anything you want."

The guys finish dumping the rest of the gasoline around the exterior of the building before gathering a short distance away. With their heads angled upward, they look on with prideful expressions. These men love the violence almost as much as I do.

I give Sebastian the final nod, and he steps forward. Within seconds, fire races up the walls, engulfing the structure.

I pull Lux with me as we all slowly back away, creating a distance between us and the flames. The powerful heat radiating off the fire pierces through my pricked, cool skin.

As the team's eyes bore into the fire, mine are on Lux. The blaze reflects in her retinas as a subtle sparkle flashes across them. Although hurt and shaken up, she settles into peace. That visceral feeling I get when I claim someone's life.

Lux's hand comes up to my chest. Her wild, fierce eyes shift to me—and for half a second, I believe we might be the same.

Am I capable of loving another human?

Lux accepts all the sides of River Thompson: tech mogul, vigilante, and a hero who helped get her life back. Something I'd never thought possible. But where do we go from here?

CHAPTER FORTY-ONE
LUX

I barely make it out of the elevator when my sister jumps into my arms.

"Lux!" she shouts, burying her face in my shoulder.

Tears immediately spill from my eyes. "Stevie." I tighten, forcing a deep hug.

It feels so good to be in my sister's arms. What also feels good is that I don't have to hide what happened to me from her. The first time was difficult because I wanted to cry on her shoulder as we held each other like we were kids, but couldn't. This time, I don't have to hide it. She's here and she knows everything.

River rests a gentle hand on my back, and I know I'm truly not alone.

"Lux, why don't you and Stevie go get you cleaned up," River suggests before pressing a soft kiss on the top of my head. "I'll call Ben, and send over some food."

"This late at night?" Stevie asks with a cheeky undertone.

River pays her no mind and heads toward the North Wing. "I'll let you know when he arrives."

I break from our embrace, keeping my arms locked with hers. "I'm glad to be home."

Stevie lifts a brow. "Home?"

This is my home now. *River* is my home. "I've been here for so long, I guess I'm getting confused."

Stevie's body twists to the side, and finally takes a look at my state. "Are you hurt?"

"Not really." I usher her toward my bedroom.

"But you're covered in blood?"

A smirk plays on my lips. "That seems to be the norm for me lately."

With her free hand, she twirls a corkscrew curl then flips it to the side. "Yeah, you're definitely changing, big sister."

I swing open the bedroom door and my eyes fall directly on the bed. A sudden memory of being secured to the mattress by Andrew a few hours prior flashes through my mind. My stomach is in knots and my thoughts are in a spin.

"U-uh," I stutter, backing away.

"Are you all right?"

I blink a few times to push the memory aside, but I can't because my skin still crawls with the sensation of his touch. "Yeah. I will be."

Stevie's worried pupils bore into me as she watches my every move heading toward the bathroom.

I take each step in stride, but the closer I get to the shower, the more desperate I become to rid my skin of any trace of Andrew.

"I need to get him off me." With a low mumble, my trembling hands claw at the faucet in the long shower.

"Hey, Lux." Stevie's compassionate voice is behind me. "Let me do it." Her fingers curl around mine, gently pushing them to the side.

I give in and start undressing. Sliding off my ripped white

dress, dotted with burgundy blood stains when Stevie's worried eyes land on me from across the room.

"Are you okay?"

The shower water cascading from the rain faucet in the ceiling is the only sound as my bare feet shuffle across the heated tile floors. I step under the flow and rest my shoulder against the wall.

"Hotter."

"Okay." Stevie leans into the shower and turns the knob closer to hot.

"Hotter," I demand.

Steam fills the room. "Are you sure? It's already pretty—"

"Hotter." I know I'm being irrational but I still don't feel clean.

Without answering, she nods moving the knob further to the left. She settles onto the bench that wraps around to the outside of the walk-in shower with her legs crossed underneath her. The scolding water stings my skin and it's painful, but I am desperate to remove any traces of him.

I reach for the loofah hanging on the wall, then frantically snatch the body wash from the shelf.

"Hey, Lux," my sister whispers, her hand back on top of mine.

"I need him off of me." My stomach is churning with disgust.

"Here. "Stevie stands and squeezes the bottle on top of the loofah before handing it back to me. "Did he..."

I quickly grab it from her, shaking my head. "No, but he touched me, licked me—" I rub my legs up and down, then repeat the action on both sides, then reach for my back, but I can't reach it and panic. "I need to get my back. I have to clean my back!"

"Okay, okay." Stevie's voice is soft. "I can do it."

She's not cleaning my skin hard enough.

"Harder."

She increases her pressure.

"Harder.'

With a sigh, she rubs deeper.

"Harder."

"Lux."

"Stevie," I snap, then suddenly my sister's arms swing around my shoulders once again forcing the breath from my lungs.

"You're safe, Lux." She soothes my wet hair. "Andrew's dead. He can't hurt you anymore. None of them can."

I let my head fall to her shoulder, and everything I've been holding onto over the last two months pours out of me. A waterfall of tears flows from my eyes. Then my body takes over. My stomach contracts as I bow forward and dry heave.

"Let it out," Stevie comforts me, rubbing my back. "You've been holding on to so much, for so long."

Panting and screaming, I grip the side of the shower letting it all come out. "Goddammit!"

"I know," she reassures again in a soft voice.

"I feel like the weight of the world is on my shoulders."

She cocks her head to the side. "I bet."

"I can't believe all of this happened. It's all so overwhelming."

My sister remains silent for an unclear amount of time, letting me cry on her shoulder, before she speaks. "Lux, you're a strong badass woman who saved herself. You took your power back, and that's something unworldly. "

I've gained my power back over the last couple months and I'm not the woman I was before. But am I finished? Why do I feel like there's still more work to be done? There will always be a predator who slips through the system, and I'm confident

River and his team will be hot on his trail making sure he doesn't hurt anyone again.

Can I be a part of this world, too?

Because I'm not the woman hiding from her inner darkness any longer.

Andrew and his men are dead, but I can't fully say I'm done. I have unleashed a monster so powerful and intense, that nothing can suppress it again.

I turn my back to Stevie, and she squirts shampoo into my hair.

"What if I'm like River and want to continue doing this?" I confess.

"Do what?"

"Like hunt people down and kill them."

Stevie's scrubbing on my head slows. "You want to be a part of what they do?" she asks as if confirming more for herself than me. "Like how he and Sebastian have a full on operation hiding behind Thompson Innovations. You want to do this with them?"

"I think I do." I glance up at my sister.

Her expression is filled with disbelief. "Maybe think about," she suggests. "I mean, you might think you know what you're getting into, and obviously you *know*, but do you *really* know?"

I rest my head against the wall, facing my sister who is standing right outside the large walk in shower. "Stevie, I know everything. Including how much I care for River."

She sighs. "That man does have it bad for you, doesn't he?"

"Should I be scared?"

"Um..." Stevie sighs. "I don't think so. You seem more confident with this than I've seen you with anything."

I pop a bubble floating nearby. "But shouldn't I be? It's

weird that I'm not, right? And if anything, I want to continue what we're doing. I can't imagine going back to my old life. "

"You have a gift. An ability to read people." With a soft hand, she moves my face, forcing my eyes to fall in sight with hers. "And you can choose whatever life you want with whomever you want."

When she finally gestures for me to leave, my fingers and toes are wrinkled from the water.

"Stevie," I say as my sister stands to grab the white robe hanging by the bathtub.

"Hmm?" she answers, handing it to me.

"I have so deeply fallen for him."

"I know," she says, as if not surprised.

Stevie helps me onto the bed, because my limbs are weak and craving a minute of rest. Then she grabs some comfy clothes for me to put on. "Is it that obvious?"

She aches a brow in my direction.

"I guess that's a yes." I smile. "He's been there through all of this. Holding my hand, comforting me, giving me the tools to get my voice back..." I trail off.

"Helping you is not charity to him. He is all in with you, Lux."

In a moment of raw joy, I let myself feel the flutter in my chest, but it's quickly interrupted by the rumble of hunger in my stomach.

"I'm starving," I say.

She rolls her eyes. "Your personal chef is probably here already preparing our food."

"He's not mine, he's River and Sebastian's," I correct, pulling on the sweater she grabbed for me.

Stevie falls to the bed, her head resting in her palm. "But you two are out of your minds for each other," she gushes. "It's only a matter of time before this manor becomes yours, too."

My eyebrows snap together. "What do you mean?"

Does she think I'm moving in here permanently? River and I discussed only having me stay here until it was safe for me to return home. It's safe now.

Do River and I continue seeing each other after I move back into my townhouse?

"I just assumed you'd stay here. Your eyes literally sparkle when you talk about him."

"We haven't talked about any of that yet," I say.

"That's why you have me."

There's a light knock on the door.

"Speak of the devil," she jokes, popping off the bed.

I cross my arms over my chest, blushing. "You don't know it's him."

"He barely lets you get ten feet from him," she says, placing her hand on the knob and giving it a twist.

When it opens, my eyes meet River's with a rush of energy. "Ben said the food is almost ready."

River and I exchange charged looks.

"We're coming," I say.

Stevie grins, giving his arm friendly pat. "She's all yours."

River humors my sister with a half-smile, before she slips past him and skips down the hall, leaving him standing in the door frame.

"How are you feeling?"

I saunter over to him, eating the distance between us. "Much better."

"Good to hear." The back of his knuckles feather my cheek. "Shall we? I'm sure you're hungry."

I nod, tucking myself under River's arm, but after my conversations with Stevie, there's only one thought at the forefront of my mind.

What happens next?

CHAPTER FORTY-TWO

RIVER

"Have I told you how proud I am of you?" I tighten my arm around Lux's shoulder.

Dipping her head into my chest, she rumbles softly with a delicate chuckle. "That means a lot to me."

I'm grateful to see she's looking better. She took an emotional beating for this last kill, and all I want is for her to experience some peace. Anger still boils under the surface about putting her in danger, but I try not to dwell on it. I bite back my heartache while we are together, but questions of the future are lingering.

Does she return to her life, while I watch her from afar and dispose of every man who shows an interest in her?

Echoes of familiar voices from the dining room drift into the dimly lit hall and pull me out of my thoughts. Sebastian and Stevie must already be at the table, and depending on how much time they've spent waiting for Lux and me, they're probably deep in the thick of irritating each other.

"If you're not up to being around everyone and would

rather eat in bed, I can bring everything to your bedroom." I rub my thumb across her skin. "Or mine."

Lux flashes me a coy grin. "I appreciate the offer, but I'm all right. Being around everyone will ground me again."

"You got it," I say. "Tell me if you need a break and we'll dip out."

She nods, smiling through the bruise on her face which is more swollen than earlier. It pisses me off every time my eyes land on it. The only thing appeasing me is knowing Andrew has been reduced to ashes.

"I'm starving," Sebastian whines as Lux and I round the corner.

Stevie is sitting on the far left side of our long dining table, sipping water while Sebastian has taken the seat across the table—with a breadth of distance between them. His head is down staring at the phone in his hands. After leading Lux to the first spot on the left, I take a chair at the end.

"It smells incredible in here." Lux scoots her chair in.

I lean over to get Sebastian's attention. "Do you know where Aunt Mae is? Will she be joining us?"

"I think so." He puts his phone on the table, glancing up at me. "She was worried about Lux, I'm sure she'll be down soon."

"Your aunt?" Stevie asks. "She's up at this hour again?"

Suddenly, Mae walks into the room, awake and alert for it being two a.m. She races over to Lux with a worried expression and pulls her in for a hug. The scent of Mae's soft linens and hint of Elizabeth Taylor perfume float past me. It's a comfort, reminding me of how my mother smelled when I was a kid.

"Lux, honey, I was so worried about you." She tightens her hold around Lux's shoulders. "Thank goodness for Sebastian keeping me updated. How are you feeling?"

Lux pulls back slowly. "I'm doing okay, actually."

"I bet you were scared." Her face hardens and she places her hands firmly on her hips. "That bastard. I hope River and Sebastian gave him what he deserves."

"You could say that." Lux's eyes shoot over to me. I try to hide a silent smirk, letting her handle the response. "I knew they'd find me."

"Of course they did." Aunt Mae smiles confidently. "I'm beyond grateful you're here, and those men can no longer hurt you or anyone else."

"Me too." Lux slides her hand under the table to my leg.

I place my palm on top, giving it a subtle squeeze of reassurance.

"Nice to see my nephews." She switches her tone, walking over to Sebastian. She gives him a quick peck on the cheek, then heads around to me to do the same. "Stevie." She smiles at Lux's sister, before taking the spot on the opposite side of the table.

"Does this family ever sleep?" Stevie fires off a friendly quip.

Sebastian glances at Mae and then me. "Sometimes."

"Clearly not at night," Lux adds, finding her humor again after the last twelve hours she's had.

The door to the kitchen swings open and Ben enters, holding two serving dishes. "No, to answer your question, Ms. Stevie, this family does not sleep," he jokes placing the food in the middle of the table.

I laugh. "Ben is a professional with our late-night work schedules."

"That's true," he chimes in, adding two more dishes in the center. "I'm like a doctor getting called out of bed in the middle of the night."

I raise a finger into the air. "But paid better."

Mae laughs. "I handle the finances and that is accurate."

Sebastian lifts the stainless steel lid to the scrambled eggs, then adds a scoop to his plate. "Food is very important in our line of work."

I laugh, glancing at the plate Ben made for Lux with her favorite avocado toast. "How is it?"

"Perfect." She beams before taking a bite of her food.

Ben winks at her. "I agree."

We all serve ourselves from the breakfast spread Ben cooked for us. It feels good to eat after the night we've had and then I hope to follow it up with bringing her into my bed.

Lux will never have to worry about him again—and neither will I. This project is closed and I have never felt so satisfied with using justice to feed my primal urges.

"So, how did it go tonight?" Mae casually asks with slight excitement in her voice.

"We burned the place down," I say.

Sebastian pops a piece of fruit into his mouth, pushing it to his cheek and smiles. "Yep. And it was exceptional."

Mae's eyebrows raise with surprise while her eyes dart to me. "Like old times?"

She's shocked because I control every crime scene down to a single bullet in the head as the main event. It's cleaner, and with the disposal of the bodies into the water, they naturally get swept into the open ocean. But since Lux has joined us, the crime scenes have become more interesting, and now with the recent burning like the old ways, things are slightly more chaotic. And I'm okay with that right now.

I click my tongue slowly. "Yes."

"It's unlike you to deviate from your system," Mae comments.

Sebastian chuckles. "Right?"

"And who closed this time?" Mae takes a bite of her food.

Stevie and Lux exchange a brief look. But I remain quiet for a moment to give Lux the chance to share her news.

I squeeze her hand, flashing an encouraging smile.

With a quick clear of her throat, Lux straightens her posture. "I closed."

"Again!" Mae shrieks. "You got the big finale, didn't you?"

Lux's cheeks redden. I can tell she's still uncomfortable talking with the topic of conversation. "Thank you."

"Another project down," Sebastian gloats, smugly. "What's next?"

My eyes find Lux's. Those once light brown eyes have darkened in the most intoxicating way. Drowning out Mae and Sebastian's conversation only inches away, my thoughts are elsewhere. How can I possibly say goodbye to this woman? Will I be able to accept the end of us when the shades of darkness within her dissipate? I've witnessed that fire grow from inside her, even fanning the flames myself. But is she like me?

I want her to help find new projects.

Research with me.

Accompany me on stake outs.

Help plan the kills.

I need her presence in my world, but would she want to walk into the night with me?

Letting my arm rest on the back of her chair, our gaze remains connected. The slight pull of her upper lip moves into a grin, which could easily bring me to my knees if not for the company of our family.

"River?" Mae sounds distant.

Lux's eyelashes flutter as a flush creeps up her neck, turning her skin into a deep shade of pink.

Will you stay with me tonight? I mouth to Lux, keeping my voice silent to others.

"River?" Sebastian hisses, vexed by the lack of response.

She pushes her loose hair aside, rubbing her soft pink lips together bashfully. "Of course."

"Lux." Stevie reaches across the table to steal a bite of Lux's toast.

Lux catches her, breaking eye contact. "Hey. That's mine."

"Sorry." Stevie leans back in her chair, arms crossed at her chest with a satisfied look that she's the one who captured her sister's attention.

My focus returns to the rest of the people at the table with a smile impossible to hide. "Yeah?"

Aunt Mae's tattooed eyebrows form high arches. "What's next? Have we identified our next project?"

An awkward silence blankets the table as Lux pushes around the food on her plate, possibly contemplating if she wants to be included in our operation, or if she has the bravery to tell me she won't.

Not sure yet which one, though.

Sebastian and Stevie most likely think the same, while Aunt Mae with her sweet soul is oblivious to the awkwardness of it all. She is simply happy to have women in the house for once.

"I have a couple in the pipeline but no decisions have been made," I tell Mae, admitting I haven't planned past Andrew and his buddies yet. Which is unlike me. I always have more than one predator in my pipeline, but I find myself holding out to hopefully get Lux's input.

If she's inclined to give it.

Sebastian senses my apprehension in discussing this and speaks up. "I think we'll take a few days to breathe from this last one."

I appreciate him for answering, because I'd like to speak with Lux before any plans are made.

CHAPTER FORTY-THREE

LUX

Stevie and I glance down at the primrose and white casket as I shove the check River gave me back into my clutch.

Although I didn't know this woman personally, I do feel connected to her since we both had a shared experience. I almost didn't come when Stevie mentioned she was holding the memorial services for one of the women from the cabin. But she ended up convincing me, saying it could be a good way to continue healing and to pay my respects.

When River found out, he offered to pay for the funeral costs, but I told him no. I thought it would be weird since they don't know him or my connection with her, so instead, he gave me an anonymous check for a million dollars. Obviously, I choked on my spit when I saw that many zeros, but I couldn't turn down his generosity on behalf of the family. It wasn't my place.

Since breakfast in the early morning hours yesterday, we haven't had much time to speak. Stevie wanted my help at the mortuary, so I came here after a few hours of sleep I got instead of going to River's bedroom. I had every intention to, but the weight of how to move forward feels intentional.

Without a doubt, he has feelings for me, but what does life look like for us now that this is over? Will he let me join his world full time? If not, I don't know how I'll move forward. And do I want to?

River followed behind me as I drove into the city today, but gave me the space to assist my sister with the services.

I look around the crowd of grieving people, when my eyes find a woman in a wrinkled dress hanging over the side of the casket. Her hair is tousled, her shoulder bounces through silent sobs and I can't imagine how her heart has shattered into a million pieces.

I'm about to ask my sister who she is when Stevie angles her head into the air and says, "That's her mother."

"I can't imagine the heartbreak she's feeling," I say.

"She held off on having the services for a few weeks, because she was still in denial her daughter was gone."

I rub my lips together, sadness filling my chest. "Oh gosh."

We're silent for a beat before Stevie speaks. "How does it smell here? I'm trying hard to get rid of the heavy embalming fluid scent from the previous owners."

She worked as a mortician for six years until the previous owners finally retired and sold the mortuary to her.

My brows furrow at her and I stifle a huffed laugh at the absurdity of her question. Leave it to my sister to care about how it smells in a funeral home.

Breathing in heavily, I'm surprised when I am only hit with a light floral scent. "Flowers, with a hint of an old building? Why does it matter?"

"It matters to my clients."

"The dead people or their relatives?"

She rolls her eyes, lashes long and curled. "The deceased

are my clients. They are my priority. I don't want it to smell bad for them. The families are just here for support."

I shake my head.

My sister's respect for the dead has never ceased to amaze me. She's devoted her life to making sure everything about their services are completed with honor and beauty. And it clearly explains why it was difficult for her to accept what River and I were doing at first, but that she understood.

Stevie grabs my hand bringing it up between us. "Who writes checks anymore? Actually, what *billionaire* writes checks?"

I yank my hand back. "River does what River wants."

With a sly smile, she pulls her bottom lip between her teeth. "I know what River wants."

"Stop it." I quickly jerk my hand away and tap her in the stomach. My cheeks flush at her comment. "Not here."

"I'm going back to the entrance to see if the rest of the family needs help greeting the guests." She pats me on the shoulder before pivoting, her high heels clicking the hardwood floors as she walks away.

"Okay, send Dad to find me when you see him arrive," I tell her, although there's distance between us now.

Now, standing alone, my heart aches for the person who saved me—who helped me vindicate myself and these women.

Wearing my new expensive dress, which was delivered to my bedroom just hours before I had to meet Stevie here at Nevermore Mortuary and Funeral Home, I glide across the floor to the window.

Pinching the white satin curtains, I pull them open to a dark and dreary morning. My eyes fall to the black car with tinted windows across the street, parked beneath the shadows of an old cottonwood tree. *River*—watching me like always. Monitoring my every movement, more now than ever before. It bothered me at first—an unsettling, creepy sort of way but I found it erotic. But now, after the almost two months we've had together, I'm comforted by it.

My eyes bore into the dark tint on the driver's side door, and when it unexpectedly opens a sharp inhale forces from my lungs. First, I see his black boots hit the pavement, then his large stature, dressed entirely in black, slides from behind the door. His sunglasses mask the delicious darkness in his eyes on this typically cloudy day. With a quick flick of his hand, the door shuts. Facing me, his energy sears into my chest, tethering me to him. River leans back against the car with his arms folded and his ankles crossed. With a quick nod, he acknowledges my peering out of the window.

My focus slides back to the woman's mother, still hunched over. I bet she never imagined having to bury her child—especially under these circumstances.

Mustering up the courage, I make my way toward her.

"Ma'am?" I whisper, and with a tender hand I rest my palm on her shoulder.

She lifts, her makeup smudged and eyes bloodshot. "Yes?"

"I'm Lux, Lieutenant Levinson's daughter," I say. "His team worked on your daughter's case."

Her lips pursed together, forming a small smile. "Thank you for coming, Lux."

I smile while clutching her hands in mine. "I'm sorry for your loss."

A tear rolls down her raw cheek. "Thank you, dear."

"I know nothing can bring her back, but I would like to give this to you." I slide the check from my purse and tuck it into her palm. "It's from a very important person."

Confused, she unfolds the paper, but her expression quickly turns into shock. "What is this?"

"It's something to make life a little easier."

Flustered, her arm shoots out, trying to hand the check back to me. "I can't accept this."

"I insist, please."

"How can I?" The grieving mother's eyebrows knit together. The amount is nothing to River, but it is life changing for most people and is why I understand her apprehension to accept such a gift.

"There are no strings attached."

"Are you sure?" she asks again. "Who is it from?"

"Yes, I'm sure," I say firmly. "The donor would like to remain anonymous, but I can tell you he would be heartbroken if you did not take it."

Her eyes dart down to the sum in her hands, then flicker back to mine. "Did you know Crystal?"

I swallow hard, searching for the words to explain to this woman's mother what her daughter meant to me. "We worked on a project together once." I come up with it on the fly. "She left a lasting impression."

The woman's face scrunches as she tries to mask the pain she is experiencing. "That was my Crystal."

The backs of my eyes sting with tears. I let them fall. "Thank you for allowing me to give you this gift."

"Thank *you*." A grateful smile cracking through her sorrow. "I just wish we had more information about the case."

"I hope one day they'll find who did this."

Another guest approaches her, so I excuse myself and go find my family. Stevie and Dad are chatting in the corner of the foyer. I hurry over to them, my heart still aching from the conversation with Crystal's mother.

"How are you doing?" My dad pulls me in for a hug.

"I'm good."

"It was nice of you to come," he says.

"Of course." I cross my arms at my chest from a slight chill in the air. "This case has touched us all."

"It has." He glances off into the distance, his eyes scanning the room before coming back to mine. "So, how's writing?"

I nod. "This story is taking a little longer and has kept me busy."

"You're so driven, Lux." My dad smiles, cupping my cheek with his palm. "I'm proud of you both, I hope you know that."

"Thanks, Dad," Stevie and I respond in unison.

My dad clicks his tongue. "Well, since the leads have dried up and the FBI has fully taken over the cabin women case, I'll have more time again to spend with my two best girls." My dad tries to play if off like this is just part of the job, but I know he's bothered about not being able to close it himself.

"Great," Stevie deadpans. "More family dinners."

I laugh, but still curious about the next steps. "So, everything has been handed over?"

"Yeah." He shrugs. "It's for the best. It's been almost two months without another incident, so the working theory is whoever was involved either got scared away or, as we suspect Andrew Hughes has, maybe they've left the country. But as I mentioned before, the FBI has taken over, so my involvement is being phased out," he repeats, almost like he's still trying to convince himself he's accepted this outcome.

"Hmm." I rub my lips together, acting like this is brand new information.

"We had a team respond to a commercial fire up north yesterday morning." My stomach flies into my throat. *Andrew.* "It was purchased with an LLC matching a few other new builds in the county. So we're working on that now."

I guess he doesn't know it's Andrew's property yet.

"Interesting." Stevie taps her chin. *She's horrible at this.* My sister has the worst poker face.

"Do you think it's related to the cabin case?" I rush out, diverting focus away from Stevie. "Like, will the FBI take over this one, too?"

"We did at first, but forensics found no bodies or human remains." He's perplexed by this revelation. "And yeah, they'll be taking it over."

No remains?

We burned Andrew, and from what River and Sebastian said, the police would mostly likely to find something. I wonder if Hayden and the guys went back and removed everything?

Silence.

Picking up an increase in tension from Stevie's energy, I can tell she has the same questions as I do. We exchanged another brief look. I'll talk to River about it when we leave later.

"Lux has a new boyfriend," Stevie blurts out with a smile, changing the subject.

Not expecting those words to hit the air, I turn to my sister, eyes bulging and with my mouth agape. "Not the time or place."

Stevie innocently shrugs her shoulders at her own impulsivity. "What?"

"Luxy?" my dad calls me by the nickname he's used since I was a kid. "You do? That's wonderful."

A little annoyed, but also wanting to gush about River, I blow out an exasperated breath. "Yeah, uh, I am seeing someone."

Stevie leans in, resting her head on my dad's shoulder. "And he's a billionaire."

"Unbelievable." I shake my head, bothered by her remarks.

My dad's eyes widened. "He's a *billionaire?*"

Scratching the back of my head, I tap my heel on the floors. "Yeah. He is."

"He owns Thompson Innovations." Stevie's on a roll and she won't stop.

"Thank you, my lovely little sister, for revealing this piece of important information."

She lifts her head to even our gaze, with an imperious smirk. "You're welcome."

"Wow." My dad's face beams. "That's great. I'd love to meet him, do a background check and—"

I extend my arm, palming my dad's chest. "Okay, enough. Let's talk more about this later."

CHAPTER FORTY-FOUR

LUX

After the funeral, Stevie, my dad, and I went out to dinner. And like a shadow, River mirrored my every move following close behind.

As expected, my dad asked many questions about River, his company, and when he could meet him. It was sweet.

He took my unwillingness as a hint that he was prying too much, which I let him believe so he'd backed off a bit. I know he's excited, but I don't know what River and I look like outside of hunting Andrew and his men.

I'm also torn about how I'm supposed to move on with my old life. River and I haven't expressed love for each other, but I'm certain in my deep feelings for him.

Now, I find myself sitting in the bathtub of my townhouse —which is small compared to the one I've become accustomed to at River's—with a bottle of red wine in my hands.

I came back here after dinner, to the place I once called my home—*my sanctuary*. I'm not completely sure why I didn't head back to the manor, but something inside was craving to be in my space again.

Andrew and the other guys are now eliminated, so I'm free to come and go as I wish. *Right?*

Then why does my own home not feel like *home* anymore?

Not only am I returning to my townhouse, but I'm revisiting the life and *freedom* I once took for granted. Many things changed me that Friday night in the cabin—a piece of my soul was stolen, my security and my trust—and I also gained a stalker that night. A stalker who is a violent serial killer, but also a man of justice and a moral compass which doesn't always point true north.

While I still don't completely understand how I've changed, whatever's simmering below the surface leaves me at its mercy once again. It's become part of who I am and the part which most desires to walk hand in hand at River's side as he continues to deliver justice on his terms.

I attempt to drink away the short period in my life which rewired the chemistry of my brain. Hitting like terrible whiplash, I search for a way to move forward, but get captured by my benevolence.

If I travel with River into the night, I will never return to my old life again—I will seal my fate, surrendering to him my newly found darkness.

Is that what I want?

Since the moment he entered that basement I felt his energy, and since then I've painstakingly tried to push the thoughts of my devotion to him aside, but as I sit here, skin stinging from the hot bathwater, I can't. Because assuming I can simply fall back into my old life would be naïve of me. Even now, my body aches to be with him, close to him. I do not wish to discover where he begins and I end, because I can't fathom any point that could ever exist.

I'm in love with River and I can't live my life without him.

The realization is thrilling, yet terrifying. Which brings me to...*I need to tell him how I feel.*

Rising to stand, I grab my towel from the holder behind the door and wrap it around my wet body. Swiping my phone from the counter by the sink, I bring up my text messages.

ME

Come inside. I know you're out there.

RIVER

Who said I'm not in your house already?

My heart stills. I drop my phone, sprint from the bathroom, and with only a towel covering me I race down the stairs. Out of breath, I come face-to-face with a masked shadowy figure leaning against the wall with his arms crossed at his chest.

"I missed you today." I grip the towel tightly.

"I miss you too, Raven."

My pulse pumps like a thick gel through my veins with a desire to shout as loud as I can how much I'm in love with him. "River, I—"

He peels off his mask, showing me those vastly dark eyes I've come to know. "Why did you come back to your place?"

"I needed to."

"Did you miss being here?"

"I did." Angling my head upward, water droplets fall from my hair into my eyes. I blink a few times to clear them. "But this place doesn't feel like my home anymore."

A steep raise in his chest, followed by a slow release. "What do you mean?"

"Because you're my home, River Thompson."

His boots thump as he gets closer to me. "Do you not want to return to your old life?"

Without a second thought, I shake my head. "No. The only life that exists now is with you."

"I won't ever stop killing," he says. "My darkness only grows stronger after every person. You need to understand that."

I clear my throat, trying to find the voice where I accept all of this, because to me there is no other alternative either. "I understand more than you know. This whole thing has forever changed my life."

River's eyes blaze with fire, boring into mine. "Lux, my darkness follows me wherever I go. It weighs me down and relentlessly pulls me in. It controls my thoughts and mind. And as soon as I feel like I've satisfied it, it returns." He closes the remaining distance between us. "It nudges me, sending reminders that it's lurking beneath the shadows in the deepest part of my soul, waiting for a moment of vulnerability to let me know what it needs and reminding me I can never escape it. That is what you need to realize."

No truer words have ever been spoken to describe what I've experienced. "I know how it feels."

His eyelids lower with a few slow blinks. "A life with me will forever involve the nighttime operations."

My mind races as my thoughts blur and an entire life with him between dusk and dawn flashes before me.

"I know. I hoped I'd wake up the morning after finally killing Andrew to be somehow cured—but nothing changed. Only the small high of completing what I set out to do lingers. The hunger is still there."

River's eyes soften through what I recognize as relief. "You think it's the same?"

"We are more alike than you realize." My hand finds his face, then I thread my fingers through his dark hair. "I'm in love with you," I admit, tears fill my eyes.

Two fingers come to pinch my chin, and with a gentle urge

he lifts my face to his. "I think I love you too, but I'm not sure I'm capable of such an emotion."

A cotton ball forms in my throat. "You think you love me?"

"I'd burn this fucking world down if you asked."

"That is more than anyone else could ever give," I mutter.

River draws back and runs a hand down his face. "Is it?"

"Yes." I take in a weighted breath to refill my lungs. "I refuse to live without you. River, you helped me save myself. You've supported me as I've healed. You make me feel so good and encourage me to be my true self. You give me everything."

"Because you're perfect the way you are, Lux." His eyes rake up and down my exposed body, but he takes a few steps back, as if trying to convince himself I'd be better without him.

"I was made for this life and I want to walk beside you as we live it together."

River's jaw clenches. He bites his bottom lip as if processing my words, but continues toward the door giving me a way out. "I could easily just stalk you for the rest of your life," he says, a slight curve of his upper lip. "However, I cannot promise you I will not kill every single man you try to bring home."

He thinks he's scaring me, but he is failing miserably. I step back and extend my arm to find the dining chair behind me, then slide my bare bottom onto it, getting comfortable while I wait for him to realize there is no future for me without him.

"I'm sure you'd quickly find out that I'd bring them around you only so I could see you again."

A smirk shows his satisfaction of my response. "Is that right?"

"Yes."

"Are you sure you want to choose a life with me?"

"There is no choice. My fate was sealed the night you

brought me home from the cabin. You're mine, River and there's no way I'm letting you leave me."

Before I can register what he's doing, River lowers himself to his knees. "Is this what you want, Raven? Me devoted to you?"

My heart skips a beat. "Yes."

With a quick lick of his lips, he moves to all fours, then on his hands and knees he crawls across the hardwood floor back toward me.

My breath halts.

"I belong to you." Dipping his head down to press a long kiss on the tops of each of my feet, he then moves his arms upward to wrap around my waist. In one smooth motion, his lips travel along one leg until they lightly dust my core. He draws back to stare up at me. "What do you need?"

Licking my lips, I rub them together for a moment before I give in to what I'm yearning for—*control*. I slide my palms over the tops of my knees and with a gentle grip, I pull my legs apart further exposing myself to him. "Eat."

A low chuckle rumbles through his chest, forcing a wide smile. "Anything for you."

River leans in, hooks both arms around my legs, and then presses a lingering kiss on the inside of both my thighs. Chills span my body as my head falls back, my limbs melting from his warmth.

"Oh god," I moan. Relaxing into the chair, I let him take whatever he wants from me, but suddenly without warning, my legs lock in place. My heart pounds and a buzz of panic rolls over me. I'm vulnerable all over again. "Stop."

River stills, just enough for me to calm again, regaining my comfort.

I'm in control.

"Okay, continue."

River peppers my core with soft, wet kisses before slipping his tongue in once, then back out just as quick. "Raven," he purrs. His nose glides along my pussy like he's enjoying being close to it.

"Y-yeah?"

"Eyes on me," he gently commands.

As my focus returns, I pull my eyes open, dragging them over to him. They capture me in an unflinching gaze. With my heart pounding behind my ribcage, energy ties us together and forces me to watch as he devours me, sucking every part.

"Mmm," he groans. With a tilt of his head to each side, he gains a deeper angle. My hands find the back of his hair, threading through the soft strands as I move his head in the direction I want. Riding his face, my thighs pull open even more, craving him to crawl inside.

"You taste so fucking good," he hums against my pussy. "Thank you for letting me get my fill of you."

"I have to take care of your needs just like you take care of mine."

My stomach clenches, preparing for an orgasm. It starts small, then increases as River picks up speed until I reach my climax.

Then he draws his head back, locking eyes with mine. "Will you move into the manor with me?"

Panting and dripping with sweat, my heart is in a death grip. "I already live there."

"I mean, for real. No more townhouse."

My mind bounces through what our life will look like together. Whether it's choosing and researching our next target to stakeouts—we will be a team. River and I will head into the night to feed our darkness—*together*.

I smile cupping his face. "I want that more than anything."

"Can I make love to you?"

I barely recall uttering the word "yes" before River carries me to my bedroom to do just that.

EPILOGUE

RIVER

Two Weeks Later

It has been two weeks since we killed Andrew, and the local news has only covered the story a few times, which surprises me, since Nolen, Duncan, Rich, and Andrew were all from the area.

My assumption is, if the police aren't talking about it, maybe their disappearances are not much of a headline. I guess the public can make of that what they wish.

Leaning back in my office chair, I gaze out at the mountains. The clouds hang low between the trees, and when I think the raven won't stop by today, a pair of black wings flutter past the window.

"Hey, buddy," I greet him and wheel my chair closer.

The raven, now more meaningful than ever, has been a symbol of the bond between Lux and me. She's *my raven*—fiercely smart, agile, and observant. It's only been half an hour since I've seen her and I already miss her presence. She's in the middle of a self-defense class with Sensei Clark which she started taking five days a week, and I promised not to interrupt this time like I have the last few. I take interest in what she's learning, so when we spar together, I can keep her on her toes.

Because she's the most precious thing in my life.

Now, finally completely moved in, her and I spend most of our time together. She's decided to take on a less aggressive publishing schedule which will let her be more involved in our nighttime projects. We've spent late afternoons hiking along the property, evenings having dinner in the main dining room or in the garden. The nights are my favorite when we both come alive and I get to make love to her over and over until we both fall asleep by the time dawn breaks.

I stand from my chair, nod at the majestic animal outside the window, and then head out of my office. It doesn't take me long before I'm rounding the corner into the gym.

Wearing workout clothes that hug each one of her delicious curves, Lux is gloved up and punching the focus pad repeatedly. She puts up a good fight with Sensei Clark as his body jerks back with each of her blows.

"Looks like she's kicking your ass," I say.

Lux stops jabbing, but her feet continue to bounce in place. "Couldn't stay away long, could you?"

I lean against the door frame with my arms crossed over my chest. "Of course not."

"You're up next, River." Sensei Clark wipes the sweat from his chin with the back of his hand.

"Ben has fresh green smoothies in the kitchen—" I begin.

"Say no more." Sensei Clark whips past me before I can complete the sentence, leaving me and Lux alone in the gym. He can never resist them.

Her eyes narrow. "Since I live here now, I assumed you wouldn't have to follow me around all day anymore."

"Your assumption was incorrect." I push off the wall and walk toward her.

She does the same, her hands firmly on her hips. "Clearly."

"You like it," I bite back.

Stepping onto the mat, I close the distance between us. Her large, dark eyes focus upward, meeting mine with a fire I'm obsessed with. "The joys of having a serial killer and stalker as a boyfriend?"

I lean in, bringing my lips to graze hers. "Exactly."

Lux's eyelids close as she breathes in heavily. "And can't forget the obscene amount of orgasms you tease out of me on the daily."

"What can I say? I can't get enough of you." My mouth captures hers as her arms swing around my neck. The sweetness of her lips mixed with the subtle salt from the sweat on her skin sends me to heaven. Remaining connected, I bend to bring my arm around her ass and lift her up. With a smooth movement, her legs wrap around my waist and deepen our kiss.

"Break it up, you two," Sebastian calls out as he enters the gym.

Both Lux and I turn his direction.

"What is it?" I spit in response to his interruption.

"Hayden was going through the last of the things we collected from the night we set Andrew's bed and breakfast on fire," he begins. With a squaring of his shoulders, I can tell he has important information to tell us.

"Is this about there being no remains at the scene?"

Hayden rounds the corner into the gym. "Hey, River. Lux."

"Hey, man," I return.

Sebastian flips his hat on backward as if to focus, then removes a card from his front pocket. "One of the guys found this card at the scene."

Lux jumps down from my arms.

"It was Jacobi who found it. He thought little of it at first, but brought it to my attention since the word is out that the police weren't able to recover human remains from the burn site. Which we all know is suspicious."

Sebastian pinches a small rectangular card between his fingers as he extends his arm to hand it to me. "Here."

I remove it from his grasp, holding it close to get a good look at what it is.

Embossed with a shiny cream-colored font are the words: *The Black Veil Society*. I flip the white card around to see a ten-digit number on the back.

Lux approaches my side. "A phone number?"

I glance at Sebastian and Hayden. "Do you know what this is?"

Seeming perplexed, Hayden shakes his head.

"A simple preliminary search of the TI database only pulls up a mid-century secret organization that well-known murderers belonged to."

"Shut up," Lux gasps. "Do you think that's what this is?"

My mind spins. "It might just be a coincidence." Then I turn to Hayden. "We'll look for more information and keep you updated."

"Of course," Hayden replies. After a quick goodbye, he leaves the gym.

"What the fuck?" I exclaim as soon as it's only Sebastian and Lux. "Let's go to my office and get Christian on the phone. He might have some insight."

The three of us sprint down the hall and back toward the North Wing. Barreling through the office door, I head straight for my desk. With Lux and Sebastian on my heels, I pick up the secure rotary line and dial Christian.

As expected, he answers on the first ring. "River. How are you liking some downtime with the missus?"

My eyes shoot to Lux, and I catch a blush forming on her cheeks.

"That's not why we're calling," Sebastian speaks up from where he's standing by the window.

"I have Lux and Sebastian on the line as well," I tell him as Lux leans on her elbows over my desk.

"Oh, the entire gang's here." His response is upbeat. "Hey, guys."

I clear my throat. "We're calling because something interesting turned up regarding Andrew and the night of his murder."

"Oh?"

"Do you know anything about The Black Veil Society?" I ask.

Silence.

"Where did you hear that name?" he asks, which means he knows something.

"One of our guys found it on Andrew before we burned the place. They thought little of it until news got out about no human remains being found at the site. Which is difficult to imagine, since we were all watching it burn," I say.

"Interesting," Christian drawls.

Sebastian and I exchange a glance with each other, suddenly understanding there is more to this business card.

"What is it, Christian?" Lux asks.

He sighs before responding. "This suspected society of serial killers has been around for at least fifty years."

How did I not know about this?

"What?" Sebastian is in disbelief, as I am sure Lux is as well.

Christian continues. "It was an urban legend which started

in the 1970s, since that's when the FBI encountered many well-known serial killers. We believe the crackdown on crime in the 1990s and advancements in forensics forced the group to dissolve. That being said, in recent years, there has been talk of a resurgence."

"Holy shit." Sebastian paces behind my desk.

His nervous energy is clouding my thoughts. "Do you think this group is still active and Andrew may have been a part of it?"

"It's difficult to tell unless we take it on as a new project," Christian says.

I turn my head toward Lux. The tormented expression on her face tells me everything I need to know. She wants nothing to do with this group or to head back into a world where she has finally found closure. Then my eyes fall on Sebastian.

"We'll call you right back, Christian," I say and quickly hang up the phone. Leaning back in my chair, I face both my cousin and the love of my life. "Sebastian."

Under other circumstances, I would dive into this, but my priorities have shifted to taking care of my darkness and Lux's as well. She and I have spoken about working on another project, but this is not the right one.

"Yeah?" He runs a hand through his hair.

"Do you got this?" I ask.

"Me?"

I nod. "Yes."

Sebastian has done well with the night crew and if anyone is as fucked up as I am, it's him. I trust my cousin and have faith he'll be able to take the lead on this project.

He pauses, then swallows hard. "Fuck yeah."

It's time for Sebastian to do things his way.

A WILD DARKNESS

Check out the next book in the ***Into the Night*** trilogy below:
"Pretending to be monsters is easy. Pretending they don't feel anything is harder."

<u>Sebastian</u>

I hunt monsters in the dark. A billionaire vigilante, my next project has me obsessed with taking down a secret society of serial killers. There's just one problem. The society will only let me join if I have a girlfriend. Unfortunately, the only woman I trust enough to ask to go undercover is the one who can't stand me.

<u>Stevie</u>

Being cold and disconnected feels like a part of my job. As a mortician, I spend my days honoring the dead, treating each body with dignity and respect. But when bodies arrive in ways that haunt me, I can't look away. So when Sebastian

Thompson proposes a deal—to pretend to be his girlfriend so he can destroy the killers responsible—I should say no. Instead, I agree. But when the hatred between us ignites into a dangerous obsession, it puts our lives and the success of the entire operation in jeopardy. Because when you hunt monsters ... you risk falling in love with one.

Read it Here: https://a.co/d/03P3Z7lw

Scan me

ABOUT THE AUTHOR

M.J. Huxley is originally from Los Angeles, California, but resides in the Southwest. When she isn't jamming to 80s music, eating tacos, or hanging out with her family, she's writing about the characters she loves.

She strives to tell authentic stories of imperfect love. She writes darkly delicious romance with banter & spice. M.J.'s books will always have a happily ever after, but that doesn't mean her characters won't have to work hard to get there.

- **Newsletter:** bit.ly/3U6EXxW
- **Facebook Readers Group:**
- https://www.facebook.com/share/g/1B9iSqUyNt/
- **Instagram:** https://instagram.com/author mjhuxley
- **Tiktok:** https://tiktok.com/@authormjhuxley
- **Goodreads:** https://bit.ly/4aouWSG
- **Pinterest:** https://www.pinterest.com/author mjhuxley/
- **Website**: https://www.authormjhuxley.com

ALSO BY M.J. HUXLEY

INTO THE NIGHT

<u>Dark & Spicy Vigilante Romantic Thrillers</u>

A Midnight Romance

Dexter meets Promising Young Woman in this twisted and spicy dark romantic thriller. When a crime writer seeks revenge with the help of the serial killer who saved her life, it leads to a dangerous obsession between them.

A Wild Darkness

Cruel Intentions meets You in this dark romantic thriller within a dangerous secret society. When a billionaire vigilante needs a girlfriend to infiltrate a secret society of serial killers, he recruits the one woman who hates him. But their fake relationship spirals into obsession, blurring the line between hunter and monster.

TANGERINE SKY

<u>Character Driven Contemporary Romance</u>

Light Behind the Lies

Check out Bailey and Mason's steamy brother's best friend, enemies-to-lovers, and single-parent romance.

Love Beyond the Illusion

Check out Piper and Jack's steamy accidental Vegas marriage, forced proximity, and fake relationship romance.

Beauty Beneath the Sorrow

Check out Lina and Carter's age gap, dad's best friend, and pilot/flight attendant steamy romance.

Memories by the Shore

Check out Avery and Jasper's story in this second-chance, small coastal town, first-love steamy romance.

GET THEM HERE!

<u>**Scan for books here:**</u>

ACKNOWLEDGMENTS

First, I want to thank the readers who have taken a chance on this dark romance. I have wanted to write this story for so long, but never had the guts to do it. And now that A Midnight Romance is complete, I can't wait to continue creating in these dark romantic thriller novels.

To my husband, thank you for putting up with my endless conversations about plots, character ideas, and scenes that seemed to jump into my head at the most inconvenient times. Thank you for putting up with my inability to stay stationary, as I'm consistently running at full speed through life. I love you and all of the ways you show up for me every day.

To Salma, Nicki, Melissa, and Caroline, thank you for helping to bring this story into the incredible book it is today.

Thank you to the beautiful indie authors who have become a network of resources, knowledge, and support. Lauren, Jay, and Jenna. I'm so grateful to call you my friends. Thank you to my PA Paige, you are amazing and I don't know what I'd do without you.

To all the romance authors who have shared their love and creativity with the world, thank you. Your stories inspire me and provide an escape from reality. Please don't ever stop writing. We need those happily ever afters.